BELGRAVE DYNASTY

KING
OF THE
SOUTH

CALIA READ

Cover Design: Clarise Tan of CT Creations
Editor: Jenny Sims of Editing 4 Indies
Interior Design: Juliana Cabrera of Jersey Girl Design

OTHER TITLES BY CALIA READ

Series

Sloan Brothers
Every Which Way • Breaking the Wrong • Ruin You Completely

Fairfax
Unravel • Unhinge

Surviving Time
The Surviving Trace • The Reigning and the Rule • Echoes of Time

Belgrave Dynasty
King of the South

Standalones
Figure Eight

To Kim

Belgrave's designated genealogist and Livingston's first true love.

"The two most important days of your life are the day you are born and the day you find out why."
- Mark Twain

PROLOGUE

RAINEY

I was born on June fifth, 1891, during the heat of the summer.

The days were so hot you could barely breathe. When the sun set, the humidity stubbornly held its place. People slept with their windows open, braving the risk of mosquito bites. A sheen of sweat would cling to your forehead and neck through the night.

However, the night I was born, a storm swept through Charleston. It rattled the shutters and caused the wind to whistle through the cracks of the front doors along The Battery.

"The thunder swallowed your momma's screams and your cries," my daddy would tell me when I was a little girl.

"The devil knew you were comin', and he got scared," my momma would say.

To me, it's fascinating what they each remembered from that night.

My older brother, Miles, was supposed to be removed from the home, but due to the storm, he was sent to the third floor. Once I was born, Miles came pounding down the stairs with his best friend hot on his heels.

They burst into the doors just as the midwife placed me, swaddled and content, in my momma's arms.

"This is your little sister, Raina Leonore."

According to my momma, Miles patted my head and said hello. His friend came up to me and stared at me intently. "Why is her face so red?" Livingston Lacroix asked bluntly.

Seconds later, I began to wail, and it became a joke between our families that it was a precursor to the relationship I'd have with Livingston.

When he poked, I protested.

However, as the years passed and I grew older, I would be the one to do the poking. My chagrin for Livingston grew exponentially. The high jinks became grand and artful. When I knew our families would see each other, I would preoccupy myself with the best ways to torture him. And in turn, he would do the same.

At the mere age of seven, I took our antics one step further when I shot him in the leg with Miles's bow and arrow. Livingston was eighteen. My temper always got the best of me, and when he told me to leave them—him, Étienne, and Miles—be, I made up my mind then and there it was war. I ran into the house and up the stairs. I searched Miles's room until I found his bow and arrows and ran back outside where I climbed a tree and waited quietly for Livingston.

Livingston had a charm that no one could deny. He could smile himself out of trouble and laugh away your tears. But no smile or words he said could escape the sleek precision of my aim.

In 1899, when my daddy died, the agony I felt seized every breath I took, and I freely waved a white flag between the two of us. Livingston chased away the pain with his grand stories. Each one better and brighter than the last. So vivid and real, they transported me to a different world, and my pain faded. It was temporary, but for a moment, I felt as though everything was all right.

Like most men, he wasn't fond of tears. He saw them quite frequently the first year after my daddy passed, but that couldn't be helped. My eyes felt as though they were fountains that couldn't be turned off. Late one night, when he was visiting my brother, he found me in the garden crying. Underneath a Spanish moss tree, he sat beside me and patted my hand. I'll never forget what he said next. "Rainey, you have more strength in your pinky finger than most grown men will ever possess. Soon, you'll conquer this pain. You were born to survive this."

In 1901, at the age of twenty-one, Livingston would be the one to wave the white flag when he lost his parents and younger brother in a train accident. I returned the kindness he gave to me by telling him stories. It was a dark period for the Lacroix family and especially for Livingston. I knew better than anyone that even though he would become better at coping with the pain, it would never leave. He would merely adapt to living without his loved ones. During that period, Livingston became a frequent visitor at the Pleasonton household.

By 1902, Livingston Lacroix became the king of the South with his gorgeous looks that bordered on being dangerous. He drank and charmed away his pain while I felt abandoned and left in the dust. Stories and comfort were no longer needed. To the utter horror of our relatives, I was the first one to pick up the proverbial weapon and end our treaty of peace.

While he finished college with his twin brother, Étienne, and my brother Miles, the times I saw him were few and far in between.

"God be with the woman who marries him." Momma would sigh whenever Livingston visited.

"God be with the world with which we live in," I would mutter whenever he left because wherever he walked, there was potential for a trail of broken hearts.

Very swiftly, he was growing into a man. Though he never grew tired of our antics as the years passed, he still saw me as just his best friend's baby sister. As I grew older, I wanted to do things to make him see I was not a child, so I would wear dresses that flattered my figure, or leave my hair down, or even go as far as using rouge. Momma was appalled by my desires. She said a true Southern lady would never do such things, but I vowed the moment I was old enough, I would do all three to simply prove a point. Not for Livingston's affections.

I did not care for Livingston in that way. I would never be one of the many ladies who fell for his charm. Of that I was certain.

Throughout the years, we would find ourselves at war with one another. If I took aim at him with my words, he returned the favor every time with a consistency that I more than relied on. Women came and went from his life, and I was there to remind him that he was an impossible reprobate. And he would grin with his devastating smirk that made most women blush, and say, "*Le savauge*, you sound upset that I'm not *your* reprobate."

He had his life before him, and I believed the same for myself.

But then everything changed when the Great War struck. He left. My brother left. In 1919, Livingston came back. My brother did not.

We both lost pieces of ourselves.

The problem was, neither of us knew how to ask for help. And we were all out of white flags to wave.

CHAPTER ONE

LIVINGSTON

Blood seeps between my fingers, coating my skin and covering the dirt lining my fingernails. With both hands pressing on his leg wound, I use as much pressure as possible, but it doesn't seem to help. Sweat drips down my forehead and into my line of vision.

Artillery shells impacting No Man's Land cause smoke to billow around us. The metallic scent of blood saturates the air. The trench my unit's been in has become my home for the past eight days. I sleep here, eat here, and protect myself with my Chauchat.

Others aren't so lucky. Others die here.

The sergeant beneath me is losing too much blood, so I press harder on the wound. *Stop the bleeding. Stop the bleeding. You'll save him!* Those words loop in my mind.

The blood is never-ending. I scream for a medic until my voice cracks, and then I look around. The rickety walkway, spanning the width of the trench, is overhead.

Strands of barbed wire are looped near it.

A fellow soldier is tending to a wounded soldier. The entire time my pressure on the wound never lessens. The sergeant, though, I'm losing him. I repeatedly call out for the medic. Even when the sergeant's eyes close for good, I don't remove my hands from the wound because maybe, just maybe, there's a chance he can be saved on this hell on Earth...

When I wake up, sweat coats my entire body. I'm not

tending to a wound and hearing the sound of men dying around me, calling out for their mothers. I'm not hearing the sound of gunfire. No, instead my eyes blink slowly, adjusting to a white ceiling. A few seconds pass before it truly sinks in that I'm home. In Charleston. In my room, lying on the floor.

But I'm safe.

Then a pretty redhead blocks my view of the ceiling.

"Shit," I say, jolting at her sudden appearance.

"Oh, good. You're up," Serene says dryly.

Rolling onto my side, I prop myself onto my elbow and peer up at my sister-in-law through half-lidded eyes. "What are you doin' here?"

Standing up straight, she looks down at me. "The better question is why have Étienne and I been banging on the front door for the past ten minutes?"

"I'm not receivin' guests at the moment," I grumble.

"Well, it's a good thing your brother and I are family and not mere guests then, right?" Serene says as she walks across the room and jerks open the curtains.

Bright light seeps into the room, making my headache grow exponentially. "Are you tryin' to kill me? Close the curtains," I groan as I lie on my back and place a forearm over my eyes.

The rapid movement makes my stomach feel queasy, and even though my eyes are closed, the room around me begins to spin as though I'm on a boat.

Serene's heels click against the floor as she approaches. Thankfully, she's not wearing a strong perfume like some women wear. That would probably send me over the edge.

Sighing, she nudges my thigh with her foot. I open one eye in time to see her point at her very large stomach. "Obviously, I can't bend down to your level. But I can try to help you up."

I'm not entirely muddled from last night where assistance from an expectant woman is needed. I do have some pride left. Very slowly and carefully, I sit up, resting my back against the bed frame. Curling my arms around my knees, I let my hands dangle between my legs and stare at the wood floor that has felt the brunt of many Lacroix ancestors' footsteps.

They've achieved so much...*Unlike you*, I think to myself.

I lift my head. "What can I do for you, Serene?"

Serene begins to walk around the room. I expected her to see the state it was in and have a look of disgust on her face, but she doesn't. Her hand curls around the bedpost as she picks up a dirty shirt off the floor. She searches for a place to put it and chooses a chair in the corner. With her hands on her hips, she looks down at me with no judgment or disdain. It's almost as though this setting is one she's not surprised to see.

"Neither Étienne nor I have heard from you, and we were getting worried."

"I'm not a child."

Serene scoops up a pair of pants with the toe of her shoe. She snatches the material and lets it dangle between her fingers before she gives me a pointed look. "You were saying?"

I tilt my head to the side as a lazy grin comes across my face. "Want to do my laundry, darlin'?"

"Get one of the many ladies in love with you to do it, Lacroix," she replies and throws my pants in my face.

I nearly gag at the smell and toss the pants away from me when Étienne walks into the room. Unlike Serene, he appears less than pleased at the state of my room. His permanent scowl grows deeper until his brows are nearly touching.

Groaning, I rest my head against the bed. "Does anyone in this family knock?"

"Yes," my twin replies. "We did. For quite some time. And when you didn't answer, we let ourselves in." Étienne crosses his arms over his chest and levels a contemplative look my way. "You missed the memorial."

Of course, I did. No one knows I missed the memorial more than I do. When I cannot get the dark thoughts to leave my head, I drink and drink and drink until there's nothing left to think about. Until what my close friend's final moments could've been cannot find a way into my mind.

"Étienne choked on Miles."

Slowly, I lift my head. "Excuse me?"

Étienne narrows his eyes at his wife. "You promised me

you wouldn't say a word."

"Yes, but some things are too good not to share." Serene gives her attention to me. "When Rainey and her mom began to spread some of Miles's ashes along The Battery, the wind picked up, and the ashes went with it. Étienne here chose that moment to yawn and then choked on Miles."

"Are they allowed to do that?" I regard the two of them. "Spread ashes?"

Étienne sternly regards his wife, but a reluctant grin tugs at his lips. "No, but only Miles's closest friends were there, and you know how he enjoyed the water."

It's such a preposterous story and happened to the most aloof man I know. In spite of my blinding headache and overall ill health, I can still find the humor from the picture Serene paints, and I grin.

She smiles back. "Thought you would get a kick out of the story."

Étienne arches a brow. "Serene, can you please focus on Livingston and not me. Please?"

She shakes her head as though to clear her mind and claps her hands. The sound vibrates through my head. "Right. Back to Livingston." She points a finger at me. "Why did you not go?"

"I had a date with…" I see the empty bottle on the floor and pick it up. Focusing on words hurts my eyes. "An-go-stur-a," I pronounce slowly. I spin the bottle around, and when I see the profile of a man at the bottom, I squint. "My, that woman has masculine features."

Étienne snatches the bottle from my hands and shakes his head. "That's Franz Joseph I of Austria."

"My God, that explains the mustache."

Étienne swears and drops the empty bottle. Instead of breaking, it clanks loudly onto the hardwood floor and slowly rolls beneath the bed.

I'm far too slow-moving to reach for the bottle, and my head won't stop aching. Groaning, I close my eyes. "Now why did you go and do that?" I drawl. "There could've been one last drink in the bottle."

Upon opening my eyes, I find my brother staring at me with barely contained indignation. I grin.

"Serene," Étienne says, his voice tight. "Can you leave my brother and me for a moment?"

"Of course," she says. Before my sister-in-law leaves the room, she glances at me. She doesn't try to mask the sadness in her eyes. In recent times, that's an expression Serene gives me frequently.

Once she's gone, Étienne sighs and sits in the chair in the corner of the room. He sits back, crossing one leg on top of the other.

"As pleasant as this strained silence is, what is on your mind, Étienne? I have a bed to sleep in."

Suddenly, Étienne leans forward, resting his elbows on his knees. He steeples his fingers together and stares thoughtfully at the floor. "Precisely how long shall this go on?"

"Shall what go on?"

Étienne kicks the toe of his boot toward the direction of my bed where the empty liquor bottle rolled underneath. "That."

"That has been goin' on for quite some time," I say with a grin.

Étienne curses under his breath. "You are thirty-nine."

"I am aware. We share the same birthday."

"Doesn't this routine become tiresome?"

When you've seen what I've seen? Never.

We all have specific positions in life, and when we detour from those positions, the people closest to us notice. Hence, why my brother is here. Étienne recognizes I'm no longer the jovial Livingston at all times. He wants things to go back to normal, but it's less for me and more for himself. And if it was that easy, I would be the Livingston I once was. God, would I ever.

"I am perfectly fine. You can go, Étienne."

My brother takes his time to scrutinize me. To get him to leave, I stare back even though my body is begging to lie down on the nearest flat surface. "Very well. I'll go. We'll speak soon." Étienne walks toward the door, and I give his retreating form a weak wave.

At the last second, he turns and looks at me. "You need to find somethin' that gets you out of this house. You're goin' to drive yourself mad livin' in the past."

"I will get on that first thing tomorrow mornin'. Right after I bathe and eat." Although, just the thought of eating makes my stomach churn.

Étienne's eyes harden. Just when I think he can't respect me less, I set the bar even lower for myself. "Denial builds a prison stronger than iron bars," he replies.

I open my mouth, but the sound of the slamming bedroom door stops the retort from sliding from my tongue. Closing my eyes, I rub my temples. Moments later, the house rattles from the force of the front door slamming. Étienne may be displeased with me now, but he'll compose himself soon enough.

I cannot say the same for myself. I realize my brother is right. I need to find something in this world that sparks my interest or keeps me busy. But I don't have the energy or the will. There seems to be no fight left in me. And that's why I drink. So all my todays can fade into tomorrows…and the days after that.

I haven't lived long enough to drink the way I do, but I can say I have seen enough to make a man go mad. My headache shows no signs of abating, and for me, the best cure for pain is to drink more alcohol.

My stomach chooses that moment to churn. I can't decide if I'm going to be sick or just belch. Quickly, I roll to my side, closing my eyes tightly, waiting for my body to decide what it needs to do. Loudly, I belch. My chest sags, and for several seconds, I remain unmovable. I've had many low moments in my life, but this might be the lowest.

Dragging all ten fingers through my hair, I sigh. I need a miracle. I don't care what form it comes in or in what way God saves me.

I just need something to hold onto.

CHAPTER TWO

RAINEY

A funeral is only for the living, never the dead. It forces loved ones to say good-bye even when they don't feel prepared.

Since I was child, I've never been adequately equipped to face death or entirely comfortable with funerals. I've seen far too many for one person.

However, my brother's memorial was beautiful, with every close friend he's had through the years in attendance. All except for one person. I could have sworn I saw Livingston at the beginning, but when I blinked, the image of him was gone. Maybe it was the trick of my imagination. Perhaps I wanted to believe Livingston would try his hardest to be there. Maybe I got him confused with his brother, Étienne. There are times the two of them make very similar expressions.

Of course, Étienne attended with his wife. Momma didn't care much for Serene. Said she was uncouth. Many people in the circle Momma surrounded herself with thought as much. I enjoyed Serene's presence and considered her a close confidant. Her straightforward opinion was refreshing to me. Serene Lacroix was no wilting wallflower, and she made no apologies for it. It seemed to me as though the mommas trying to marry off their daughters and any single woman above the age of eighteen resented Serene because she did something no woman had ever done before: she tamed a Lacroix man.

There was also the matter of her background. No one

had ever laid eyes on her family. In passing, I'd heard Serene mention her brother Ian. And Nathalie confirmed Serene had two brothers. Serene said her family lived in the Midwest, but there was no deeper explanation. I didn't care to pry because we all had a past.

I was simply overjoyed we got along so well. And as of now, I needed all the support I could get. Because now there was the matter of the will.

I couldn't sleep last night thinking about today. Even though I was a child when Daddy passed, I still remember his funeral and flashes of the days following. It was incredibly difficult to accept he was gone. Perhaps that's why I dug my heels in this morning at the prospect of going to Miles's memorial. I didn't want to begin the process of my mourning.

The methodical ticking of the grandfather clock in the hall is the only sound that can be heard.

Across from me sits Momma with an embroidered handkerchief clutched between her hands. Momma has been beside herself all day. Miles's body was found in May, but they believed he died in March. Once they found him, it took months for his next of kin, Momma, to be notified. The entire time he remained missing, Momma never gave up hope that he would come home. It was nothing short of inspiring. In my heart, I knew he wasn't coming back to us. It felt as though a candle had been snuffed out, and I was blindly trying to find my way around. Momma's faith, no matter how fruitless, was far easier than facing the truth. Once we received the news, she started crying and hasn't stopped. Lips that once readily moved upward to smile now curve downward and resemble two upside-down commas. She's in a perpetual state of sadness and cannot be bothered. The light has been extinguished out of her eyes.

She lost a husband many years ago, but there was faith and promise. And that lay within Miles and me. I would be the sweet, Southern lady, and Miles would be a smart, handsome fella every woman set her eyes on.

Then Miles passed, and her promises were gone. But

there's still hope for me. One out of two isn't bad, if you ask me.

Sitting at the head of the table is our family's attorney, Mr. Parson. He's indifferent to the strained silence and continues to methodically flip each page upside down, creating a neat stack beside him.

Beneath the table, my leg nervously bounces up and down. I'm desperate to leave the room. I need air. The sweltering July heat is making this black dress unbearable, and the walls feel as though they're closing in on me. I focus on my laced fingers on my lap and breathe through my nose. When my vision started to blur, I would focus on Mr. Parson's jowls. It gives him a grandfatherly appearance, but he can't be but a few years older than my daddy. If he had lived long enough, would he have jowls, too? My nails dig into my skin as I fight to maintain my composure. The very last thing I need to think of right now is Daddy.

After several agonizing minutes, Mr. Parson clears his throat. I lift my head as he straightens the stack of papers against the table. I'm not as rigid with Southern traditions as other residents in Charleston are, but it does feel awfully tasteless to read the will less than twenty-four hours after my brother's memorial. I express my thoughts to Momma before Mr. Parson's arrival, and while she dried her tears, she said, "I don't care when it's done, just as long as it's done."

And that was the end of that.

"Before we start, I must give my condolences. Mr. Pleasonton was truly a wonderful man, and he will be deeply missed."

In unison, Momma and I dip our heads, and murmur our thanks. We have become adept at accepting condolences with a numb sense of detachment. The quicker you accept them; the faster people shift the topic of conversation. It was one of the few things Momma and I saw eye to eye on.

"I'm sure the two of you are ready to begin," he says with a weak smile.

When neither one of us says a word, he shifts in his seat

uncomfortably and takes a deep breath.

"I, Miles Thomas Pleasonton, in the city of Charleston in Charleston County and State of South Carolina, of the age of thirty-five years, and being of sound mind and memory, do make this writing, as and for my last will and testament.

"First, after my death, I bequeath to my mother, Leonore Mae Pleasonton, all real estate in my name. She may accept monies owed to me at the time of my death. Equal parts of my personal belongings shall go between my sister and mother.

"Secondly, I request for all my debts and—"

For the second time today, I stare down at my hands and swallow the bile in my throat. When someone creates their will, do they feel death upon them or do they entrust their belongings, money, and estate in good faith? This seems incredibly macabre to me.

I know it'd be rude and disrespectful, but I'm tempted to feign exhaustion or the flu. Mr. Parson has Momma here, so why do I need to be in the room? Sounds as though everything will go to her anyway. I'm preparing to clear my throat—in the most ladylike fashion, of course—when Mr. Parson directs his attention to me.

"I have established a dowry for my sister, Ms. Raina Leonore Pleasonton, with a future sum of 60,000 dollars. The stipulation being she finds a suitable husband within sixty days of said will being read."

Immediately, I sit upright in my chair. My heart is pounding so rapidly, I can barely hear the words pouring from Mr. Parson's mouth. All my mind can focus on is one thing: sixty thousand dollars.

Sixty. Thousand. Dollars.

"Your dowry has been placed in a trust, and a Mr. Livingston Adrien Lacroix has been appointed as the executor."

My mouth drops upon his words, and I can't help but interject. "I apologize, but I don't believe I heard you correctly. Who did you say?"

Mr. Parson glances at his papers. "Mr. Livingston Lacroix." He continues speaking. "It's also stipulated you have sixty days to find a suitable husband or your dowry will be dissolved and the money will be donated to a charity of Mrs. Leonore Pleasonton's choosin'."

This will be the second time I hear the words dowry and Livingston Lacroix in the same sentence. The words still don't entirely make sense. What is happening?

Momma wears the same expression of horror on her face, but it's for an entirely different reason. "Charity?" The single word flows from her mouth like poison. "The money will go to charity?"

We glance at one another, our confusion written across our faces.

Mr. Parson pushes his glasses up his nose only to have them glide down. He clears his throat. "That is Mr. Pleasonton's request."

"What is the matter with him?" Momma huffs.

At the same time, I say, "I don't need a dowry!"

Mr. Parson stares back and forth between the two of us, uncertain of who to respond to first.

I glimpse at Momma to make sure we don't talk at the same time again. She's back to staring at her handkerchief. "When was this will drawn?" I ask.

Once again, Mr. Parson thumbs through the papers. Momma had a small outburst, but now she's become reticent. I have no qualms in voicing my thoughts. This simply doesn't make sense, and I need answers.

"Mr. Pleasonton visited my office on October thirteenth, 1917."

His reply brings a heavy silence into the dining room. Miles had this will drawn more than a year and a half before his death. I stare at my interlocked fingers and swallow the lump gathering at the back of my throat.

In October, was I romantically involved with any gentleman? Probably not. The fact Miles placed this dowry in the will while I was unattached to anyone is more than humiliating. My brother knew me so well that he predicted my own companionless life.

If my brother were here, I'd shake him by the shoulders and demand an answer. Why? Why would he do this? I thought we had a close relationship, and if he was concerned about my lack of suitors, he should've come to me and voiced his concerns. This didn't seem like something he would do.

After a moment of strained silence, Momma stops rubbing her fingertips over her handkerchief and patiently regards the older man. "Is that all, Mr. Parson?"

Mr. Parson readily nods and begins to gather most of his paperwork. He leaves the will with us. This is by far the most lively I've seen the man since he stepped through the door. Who can blame him for wanting to leave our home? The sadness is palpable, causing the air to be so thick that everyone who steps through the front door has the potential of being choked by the grief.

Momma stands to walk Mr. Parson to the front door. My body is numb although my mind runs in circles as I follow them toward the foyer.

Mr. Parson gives his condolences one last time before he leaves. The second the door closes behind him, I begin to pace in the foyer, unbothered that our butler, Stanley, is standing beside the door. "This will not do. This will not do," I announce.

"Rainey —"

Abruptly, I turn, allowing my panic to reveal itself in my eyes. "Momma, Livingston can't be allotted this...this power! It will go straight to his head, and he'll probably lose the money."

"The money is in a trust," Momma points out.

"It's Livingston. Don't discredit him," I remark dryly before I resume my pacing. Why was this happening?

Momma attempts to intercede me, but the walls are closing in on me again. I need to keep walking.

"Calm yourself, sweetheart. Livingston is a responsible, stand-up man, and when we explain the situation, I'm positive he'll be supportive."

One thing Livingston's never been toward me is supportive. And vice versa.

"Momma, the only thing he'll support is marryin' me off

to one of his bachelor friends who has a worse reputation than him!" I suck in a deep breath before I continue. "For the life of me, I cannot understand why Miles gave me a dowry." I shake my head. "A dowry!"

Momma gives up the fight of trying to calm me and walks toward the stairs. "Unfortunately, we will never know."

For Momma, this conversation is effectively over. As for me, it's just begun. It's time for her afternoon "respite." That's what she called it after Daddy died. Now that Miles is gone, I know she goes to her room to have a cup of tea with a hearty splash of old grand-dad whiskey. I can only surmise what occurs behind the closed doors by her red eyes when she appears hours later for dinner. But she never makes a scene, and she never, ever discusses her pain. That would be ungenteel for a Southern lady.

I take a deep breath. "Did you tell Miles to do this?"

Momma stops walking. Looking over her shoulder at me, she raises both brows.

It should come as no surprise that I asked this question. Momma never misses an opportunity to remind me how I've spent my youth gallivanting around Charleston like a hellion instead of a proper Southern lady trying to find a husband.

"Pardon me?"

"Did you tell Miles to give me a dowry with outlandish stipulations? He would never think of somethin' like this on his own."

"I did no such thing, and you'll do well to remember that. What your brother decided to place in his will was done of his own volition. I couldn't control his actions any more than I can control that mouth of yours," she replies and continues to the second floor.

Ignoring Momma's retort, I follow her up the stairs. "If you're in charge of Miles's estate, then surely you can have this rescinded."

"No," she replies at the top of the landing.

I rear back. "No?"

"No," she repeats. "I will respect your brother's wishes

and support this decision no matter how unexpected it may be. Perhaps you should try to do the same."

"You want me to marry for money?"

"I married your father for money, and he was the great love of my life."

At the mention of Daddy, a small bit of anger goes out of me. "Be that as it may, not everyone is that lucky."

"You could be lucky if you gave someone a chance."

"Perhaps. But we'll never know because I refuse this dowry."

Momma closes her eyes and rubs her temples before she replies. "Raina, I have more concernin' matters at hand. I will not fight this decision, or with you. This entire day has been very tryin' on my spirit. Please send for someone to bring a restorative beverage to my private quarters immediately."

Momma doesn't wait for my reply. She allows her cryptic words to hang above me. Today was tiresome for us all. I should step back from this twisted situation and take a deep breath because, at the end of the day, all Momma and I have now are each other. I hear her door shut and close my eyes.

I don't need the dowry. The money is of no importance to me, and I don't need a husband. What I need is a miracle. Or for my brother to come back and explain this all to me, and since that isn't going to happen, I need to think of a practical alternative. There's someone out there who is very much alive.

Someone who I didn't see today but who owes me answers.

That person is none other than Livingston Lacroix.

Immediately, I act and turn toward the front door. Stanley opens the door for me, but then I remember I don't have the will, so I quickly turn on my heels and rush back to the dining room. I snatch it from the table, and when I do, my eyes snag on the words Livingston and dowry and husband.

I snort and say very quietly, "The day you become my executor is the day I become your wife."

CHAPTER THREE

LIVINGSTON

In the midst of the raucous laughter and crude wisecracks, a persistent pounding on the front door gives me a sense of déjà vu from yesterday. Are Étienne and Serene back? No, they can't be. Since they've had Alex, the two of them have retreated to Belgrave. Once the sun falls, they're in for the night.

Whoever it may be will either stop or find their way inside.

The entire first floor of my home is filled with bodies. Many faces I'm just seeing for the first time, but I've never met a person I didn't like. Especially with liquor coursing through my veins. The more, the merrier!

I ignore the knocking, mainly because I'm being a lazy bastard, and eventually, it subsides. I become convinced whoever is there has given up and take another drink from the bottle in my hands.

And then, the infuriating pounding renews once again. Muttering every curse word I know in my mind, I give my apologies to my guests. They're so foxed they don't notice my absence.

My body feels warm, my muscles relaxed as I saunter toward the front door. Now this, this is why I drink. I could face my demons right now without armor and a battle plan, and win the fight.

I could. If my demons would come out and face me.

"Open this door, Livingston Lacroix. I know you're

inside!"

I recognize that voice. I'm beginning to regret letting go of my butler, Charles. If he was here, I'd have him politely rebuff Rainey Pleasonton.

With a half-empty bottle of whiskey in one hand, I open the door while Rainey's fist is midair, ready to land against the hard grain of the oak door. When she sees me, I have the pleasure of watching her momentarily lurch forward. She gains her balance and straightens her spine. Crossing my arms, I dip my head in acknowledgment. The bottle of alcohol dangles from one hand. "*Le savauge.*"

I've called Rainey *le savauge* since she was a little girl simply because she's ferocious and untamed. Her tongue was as sharp as her mind. Her confidence as big as her opinions.

The world was a small, simple place against her strong will.

Within seconds, a red flush stains her cheeks. "Rainey. My name is Rainey."

"When you've had the number of nicknames you've had, is your name Rainey?" I counter with a half-smirk.

She doesn't return the smile. A guest laughs, grabbing Rainey's attention. Standing on her tiptoes, she tries to peer inside the house. I know she's furiously counting the many people spilling into the foyer in her head. I step in front of her, blocking her view.

Growing up, that was an easier feat but not any longer. As a child, she was skinny and far shorter with large, almond-shaped eyes that were disproportionate to her small features.

But now, at twenty-eight, Rainey Pleasonton has grown into her features. For a woman, she's tall and lithe. Her eyes, the color of cognac, now perfectly complement her.

She appears so delicate. Perhaps some men would find her pleasing on the eyes. But then she opens her mouth, and the pleasing feeling fades.

"My apologies for bein' so sensitive, Limp Lacroix." She gives my leg she once used for target practice a pointed look.

"Did you come here tonight to trade nicknames?"

"No. I need to speak to you regardin' a matter of utmost

importance." Abruptly, she stops speaking. Her eyes become shuttered, and it's plain to see why. The woman who was kissing my neck and whispering all the indecent things she wanted to do to me moments ago has interrupted us. I blink at her rapidly. When she entered my home, she told me her name. I'm sure of it. I can't remember what it was. I'm almost certain it starts with an L.

Lydia? Or was it Lillian?

Rainey arches a dark brow and inspects Lydia/Lillian with a regal stare. One that dares her to utter a word in her presence.

Rainey's confidence fiercely clings to her, and when it's not being directed toward me, it can be highly entertaining to watch. For Lydia/Lillian, she's too busy clinging to me to notice.

"Well, I am so sorry, Livingston. I can see you're terribly busy." Disdain drips from Rainey's words.

Lydia/Lillian tugs on my hand. She's ready to retreat to the party, but I'm more curious about what *le savauge* wants. Grinning at her, I discreetly step away from Lydia/Lillian. She'll stay, but Rainey won't. Rainey never does. And so as baffling as I find Rainey Pleasonton, it's important to remember every interaction with her. There's always a hidden message with her.

"Who are you?" Lydia/Lillian asks at the same time as she wraps an arm around my waist.

Rainey's chin juts out. Rather than dignifying Lydia/Lillian with a reply, she remains silent, staring Lydia/Lillian into submission. I'm surprised Lydia/Lillian doesn't apologize and beg for Rainey's forgiveness.

I clear my throat. "To what do I owe this unexpected pleasure?"

Rainey gives Lydia/Lillian an irksome expression before she pulls out a folded letter from her reticule and all but slams the paper against my chest. "I received some interestin' news today."

I recognize Miles's signature at the bottom of the page,

and my heart sinks. My smile fades as I slowly lower the letter. As the seconds tick by, Lydia/Lillian takes the alcohol from me, and takes a drink. She laughs at something someone says behind us and begins to have a conversation with them. My ears have become muffled, and my vision dims. And I swear the longer I hold my dead best friend's will, the more my fingers grow numb. It becomes too much. I shove the papers between Rainey and me. "And this pertains to me how?"

"I think you know how," she says through gritted teeth. She doesn't take the blasted paper.

The paper feels like fire in my hands. Once more, I review the contents of Miles's will. There's very little that pertains to or interests me. But when I see my name linked with Rainey's, I raise my brows. I see the word executor, a substantial dowry, and the heavy stipulations attached to the dowry. It's so outlandish I force myself to read over it five more times.

My hands are shaking when I finish. Regrettably, the words haven't changed. This time, I wave the will in front of Rainey until she has no choice but to take it. Breathing deep, I place my hands on my hips and stare at the floor. I can feel Rainey's eyes burning holes into the crown of my head.

What does she want me to say? The idea is preposterous, but that Pleas would entrust me to be the executor of Rainey's dowry cuts like a knife. It was indicative of the type of man Pleas was, and the friendship we had, and I was too much of a recreant to attend his funeral. If it were me who died, he would have paid his respects.

As the time ticks by, I can feel the whir of buoyancy from the liquor fading. This was far too soon for Pleas's will to be read. I understand it came with death, but I still wasn't exactly comfortable with that to begin with.

Suddenly, I look at Rainey. Right now is not the time to have this conversation. She needs to go. I have a house filled with guests who see me as fun and jovial. Their eyes aren't all-knowing. They don't see the cloak of death that's clung to me ever since the war. And there's a woman, whose name I cannot remember, waiting for me. And perhaps, maybe later, she might warm my bed. Doubtful. But it's a possibility.

"I don't care," I say coldly. "Leave me, Rainey."

Her head jerks back as though I've slapped her. "What?"

"Leave," I command like the king people expect me to be.

When she makes no effort to move, I curl my hands around her shoulders and spin her until she's facing the gardens. Rainey, who's in a complete state of shock, lets me. Soon enough, though, she gathers her composure and whirls around with her mouth open to undoubtedly tell me her thoughts.

"Go to hell," Rainey says through gritted teeth.

I place a palm against my heart. "*Le savauge*, you wound me. You know damn well I'm goin' to stop by Vincent's Chicco's and drink until I can't drink no more. Perhaps I'll journey to New Orleans. I hear it's quite enjoyable there. Then I will go to hell." I wickedly grin at her. "Anythin' else?"

A crowd has gathered behind us. Lydia/Lillian is back by my side. Reaching back, someone hands me my half-empty bottle of whiskey. Eyes on Rainey, I take a drink and arch a brow.

Everybody has heard my last words to her, and unlike her, they found it highly amusing. Their laughter gathers and echoes throughout the foyer. Rainey remains utterly still, her cheeks staining from her fury. Her hand reaches out, and I brace for her palm to meet my cheek. Instead, her brother's will makes direct contact with my chest. I don't make any effort to grab it, and the paper flutters to my feet.

Before she has any more opportunities to touch me, I slam the door in her face, proving Southern manners are born and bred, but the war will bleed everything out of a man.

CHAPTER FOUR

RAINEY

There is a reason I was dubbed "The Deplorable Debutante" at my first cotillion.

My etiquette was subpar, social grace contrived, and my patience? It was nonexistent. I don't take kindly to being dismissed. Corsets itch. And I believe opinions shouldn't be contained when they hold wisdom.

Slamming the door in my face was a big mistake on Livingston's part. Worse, it was done in front of that woman who clung to him as though he was a life vest. The satisfaction in her eyes as Livingston closed the door on me still causes my hands to curl into fists.

I tried to sleep my anger away, but when I woke up this morning, vengeance coursed through my veins. As Momma prattled on during breakfast, I plotted how to bring Livingston Lacroix down. In a way, this felt...normal. Even though I felt the heavy sting of his rejection last night. First, he didn't show up for Miles's funeral, and then he barely batted an eye when he read the will. I expected him to say it was ridiculous, and he would have no part in the dowry deadline my brother has placed over my head. Instead, he put on a façade for his guests and snubbed me as though I was nothing.

There will be no truce between us. I'm quite familiar with plotting and games when it comes to Livingston. He took his first shot, and his aim was impressive. But now I need to retaliate. However, the longer I sit across from Momma, the more I can feel a noose around my neck. It becomes tighter with each second. I cannot remain idle. I have to do something.

"I'm goin' out," I announce as I push back from the table.

Momma appears shocked by the sudden change of subject. "Where to? Rainey, dear, it's too early for any shop to be open."

"I need to clear my head." I keep my gaze focused on the table. "I'm still thinkin' about yesterday."

Momma's eyes fill with sympathy. "Of course. Do what you must, but don't be too long, all right? It's unbecomin' for a woman to be seen in public without a chaperone."

Chaperones weren't a worry when I volunteered my services to help with the Red Cross last October when influenza swept through Charleston. But now a chaperone is a must? When I have a large dowry over my head?

"Of course," I say. I will agree to anything so I can leave.

The moment I turn my back, though, I grin and make one last stop in my room.

The only thing that's unbecoming is what I'm about to do…

As I stroll toward the Lacroix house, I inhale the crisp, clean scent of the morning air. I encounter very few people on the sidewalks. Just a nursemaid pushing an ornate wicker pram. When she sees me, she takes one look and quickens her steps. At first, I wonder what's the reason for her worry, and then I look down at my hand and realize I'm carrying my weapon.

It's not a gun, though.

Oh, no.

A gun is too loud. Guns smoke, and I believe it would bring Livingston back to his days at war. Make him jumpy. And we can't have that.

First and foremost, I am a lady. Comfort your target with silence before you go in for the kill.

No, I prefer a bow and arrow. Miles taught me how to use it when I was a little girl, and I instantly took to it. I enjoyed how tense my muscles became as I pulled back my arm. The concentration required as you squint with one eye and focus on your mark.

I am a perfectionist and prefer one shot to land my kill. Today, I have no intention of killing Livingston, but I do plan to capture his attention. The first time I used this on him seemed to do the trick, so why not try it again?

The tips of my shoes point toward the cobblestone road as I look both ways, and my heels click against the brick as I hustle across the road. When I lightly hop onto the opposite street, the hem of my skirt brushes against my calves. Up ahead, I see the Lacroix house hidden behind brick walls draped with ivy. With the birds happily chirping, you'd never know a debauched gathering occurred the night before.

Shaking my head, I grab the knob on the door and step into the narrow pathway. To my left is the Lacroix's lush backyard. It remains one of Charleston's most coveted gardens. With my head held high, I walk toward the door and stop short when I spot a man sleeping face down in Livingston's nounou's prized collection of azaleas.

My God, if she were alive, she would be speaking French at a rapid-fire pace, all the while beating this drunken man with a rolled-up newspaper all the way to The Battery.

As I walk by him, the man continues to snore. I shake my head and sigh. Luckily, I don't come across any more drunken guests. But can the same be said for inside the house?

There's only one way to find out. Holding my weapon behind my back, I give three sound knocks and wait. I strain to hear for any sounds coming from inside when the snoring man sounds like a blowhorn.

Impatiently, I turn and narrow my eyes. "Will you stop?" I hiss.

Of course, he continues to sleep. I knock four more times before I make the decision to try the door. I turn the knob, and the door opens.

"Oh, Livingston..." My voice fades away as I step into the foyer. Partially because I was getting ready to tsk him on his lack of safety, but the words slipped from my mouth the moment I saw the disarray before me. All I saw last night was a home filled with people. Now that they're gone, the damage is unveiled, and it's worse than I imagined. Curtains are torn and dangling from the wall. A vase is shattered on the floor. And this is only in the foyer.

I scrunch my nose from the rancid smell of liquor and vomit and begin to roam throughout the first floor. It will take several days to air this smell out and clean up everything. As I walk through the rooms, I spot no guests, and there's no trace of Livingston. I stop in the middle of the ravaged sitting room and slowly tilt my head back to stare at the ceiling.

But I don't hear any noises. I'm quite familiar with Livingston's extracurricular activities, but if his inebriated state last night is any clue, then there's no possible way he would be busy right now. He's probably facedown in a pile of his own drool like the man sleeping outside. Or he might not even be here, but out with that strumpet. I tighten my grip on my bow at the very thought of her. From the smug expression, it was clear she enjoyed my humiliation. I can stand here, and guess where he is or simply find out. It will only take a few minutes.

Before I can change my mind, I hurry up the stairs. When Livingston moved into the Lacroix's home in Charleston, he took over the entire third floor. He probably turned it into a harem den. I can only imagine how many women he's entertained in that space.

I hurry up the second flight of stairs, gripping the banister with my left hand. Once I reach the third floor, I stop and turn my head to the right. Heart racing, I stare at the closed door and take a deep breath. The door is open a crack. There's some rustling in his room. Good. He must be up.

With the toe of my shoe, I open it farther. My anger and humiliation from last night become my strength, encouraging me to pull back the string, and nock my arrow. I expect to see him blurry-eyed as he slowly sits up. Instead, I find a very naked Livingston on top of the woman from last night. At least, he's naked to me. His shirt is off, and his pants are down to his knees. For some reason, my gaze settles on his ass. I'm not a connoisseur on behinds, and this is the first male one I've ever seen, but I'm certain it will be the best I'll see. I feel my cheeks turn red. Squinting my eyes, I focus on the area where the woman's leg is wrapped around his waist. I let the arrow go.

And then everything goes wrong.

As if he can sense me standing there, Livingston twists around, eyes wide with a sheen of sweat on his forehead. The woman, who finally realizes Livingston's no longer moving, follows his gaze. When she sees me, she scrambles to cover herself. My beautiful aim now becomes a miserable miss. The arrow grazes his hip and becomes embedded in his nightstand.

"Christ!" he shouts and jumps out of bed.

With my heart pounding, I regard the once moaning cow for a second and saunter into the bedroom while Livingston scrambles to pull his pants up. Funny, I thought his only skill was removing his clothes with speed, not putting them back on.

He's so enraged he forgets to button his pants, causing them to hang around his narrow hips. Shirtless, he stalks toward me. All's well for me. The man drives me mad, but he has never hurt my eyes.

"What. Was. That?" he says between clenched teeth.

Happily, I go toe-to-toe with him. "What. Was. Last. Night?"

Rubbing his hands down his face, he gestures to the bow, and shouts, "You just tried to kill me!"

Sighing, I stare down at my bow and lovingly pet it. "Livingston, if I wanted to kill you, I would've done it years ago."

He snatches my beloved weapon of choice out of my hands, causing me to cry out. I lunge for it. "Give that back!"

"Like hell!" he snarls. "You've become unhinged, stalkin' into my room while I'm...I'm—"

"Entertainin' a guest?" I provide with a cheeky smile.

He does not smile back. My gaze drifts to the woman who he was lavishing all his affection on minutes ago. In the midst of all our wordplay, she had managed to slip out of bed and get dressed. We stop our war of words just in time to see her inch toward the door. She freezes and stares at us guiltily.

Livingston gives her his signature grin. "Don't leave, darlin'." His accent grows heavier as he turns on the charm. He gestures toward me. "This one is leavin'."

"This one is not," I chime in. "I am not goin' anywhere."

The woman looks at the two of us. When I first set my eyes on her as I burst into the room, a red haze briefly covered my gaze. It was unexplained and unnecessary but disappeared within seconds. Now, I feel pity. If someone is not prepared for Livingston and me, you can feel as though you've been swept into a hurricane. By the time we're done snarling at one another, all the poor, unsuspecting people around us are a bit lost, scratching their heads, and saying, "What just occurred?"

"Livingston, I need to go." The woman gives me a furtive glance before she shoots Livingston a sultry smile that even a blind kitten could read. I barely suppress the urge to gag.

I lean in toward her and lower my voice. "In case you're wonderin', the man who you were moonin' over used to call his underwear wiener wear when he was a boy."

I have the satisfaction of watching the female's eyes widen and Livingston's mouth dropping open. "How do you know that?" he says.

I wickedly grin. "You are forgettin' your sister is my closest confidant."

He arches a single brow, and my grin fades. "By that logic, your closest confidant is my only sister, and I know you captured a tadpole in the pond while you went fishin' with your brother, named it Milton, and then cried when it died."

"Milton lived a short but wonderful life," I defend as I continue to try to grab my bow back.

"Milton also needed water to live," Livingston points out, continuing to hold the bow above his head.

"I was eight!"

The sound of the door slamming in the distance causes us to look toward his open bedroom door. Slowly, I turn back to him. "I think your *darlin'* just left."

Livingston narrows his eyes. "Are you pleased with yourself? Your antics scared her off."

Honestly, I do feel a bit better. I'm still upset about Miles's will and how Livingston reacted, but I don't have the burning desire to kill him over it. "So, who was she?" I ask.

"Why?"

"She doesn't appear familiar to me."

"Because she isn't from Charleston." He scowls. "Care to tell me why you're smilin' so?"

Shrugging, I lace my fingers behind my back, and try to ignore how unclothed he is. The first few minutes were okay, but I can't seem to stop taking peeks at him. "I just find it interestin' that you've been intimate with every woman in Charleston and now have to set your sights on the ladies in surroundin' towns."

"Clearly, not every woman." Livingston's expression cuts right through me. It's as if he sees a shapeless woman dressed in a burlap bag. To him, I will forever remain his sister's childhood friend and best friend's sister.

"I must say, thank you for gettin' dolled up for me, *le savauge*." He waggles his brows as he reaches the tip of the bow around me and taps the ends of my unbound hair hanging down to my waist.

I swat him away, trying my best to shove down the peculiar feelings that rise to the surface when Livingston gets too close. He simply has a way about him that is so very...male. Even half- clothed and bedraggled from the night before, he still looks charming.

He just had a woman in his bed not two minutes ago!

That does the trick. Instantly, I come to my senses and take a step back. For Livingston's part, he does the same, and much to my relief, he grabs his shirt, sliding his hands through the sleeves. Livingston knows me too well and keeps the bow behind him. He can have it his way for now, but I will leave with what I came with.

"What is it you must speak with me about?" He begins the

process of buttoning his shirt.

This almost feels more distracting than having his shirt off. Clothing yourself is an intimate act that should be done in private. Livingston is so at ease with his body and surroundings. I find myself surveying his room as though this is my first time visiting.

"My brother's will." I jab a finger in his direction. "Shall I recite to you what it entails?"

Livingston frowns momentarily, and then his eyes widen before he smirks. "It's comin' back to me now. You're my ward, correct?"

The word ward is like nails on a chalkboard, and I grind my teeth. "No. Not quite."

"Ah, but I think you're mistaken. I've read my fair share of documents. The will was quite clear: you are under my care."

"I'm not an orphan child left on the streets!" I burst out.

Grinning, Livingston finishes buttoning his shirt. "That all hinges upon your conduct. If you keep on behavin' this way to me and bargin' into my home with weapons, I might have to rethink your future."

Feeling more at ease now that he's dressed, I advance on him. "Oh, Livingston, we both know that will is ridiculous, and you control nothin'."

Grabbing my bow, Livingston jabs it in my direction and winks at me. "Ah, but it seems as though your money is."

"You can barely place both feet into a fresh pair of pants in the mornin', so why would I believe you could handle sixty thousand dollars?"

"That is harsh, Red Rainey. I don't dress in the mornin'. I dress in the afternoon."

With that said, I rub my temples and suppress a groan. I should've known there would be no meeting of the minds, but I have to make one last-ditch attempt. "Livingston. Listen to me. Please. This is utterly insane If I'm gonna marry, it shall be for love."

Livingston's brow furrow so tightly they almost connect.

"What word do you not understand? Love or marry?"

"Both." He shudders as though he's averse to the very idea of love.

"So you're not an admirer of love?" I rush out. "That means you don't think I should be forced to marry someone?"

There's a pause before he patiently replies, "I did not say that."

I groan in frustration. "I will marry who I decide to marry not because a dowry is danglin' above my head. It's positively barbaric!"

"If any man will have you," Livingston points out. "Are you forgettin' that your reputation precedes you, *le savauge*?"

Crossing my arms over my chest, I cock my head to the side. "We don't need to dwell on reputations. Must I remind you of yours? We need to dwell on this absurd will."

"Agreed."

My hands slowly drop to my sides as I stare openly at Livingston with shock. "Truly?"

"No." My upper lip curls up as I lunge for him. Livingston chuckles, places my bow behind his back, and holds me at arm's length. "Rainey, that's what you get for almost shootin' me in the ass."

As much as I want to pummel Livingston with my fists, it will get me nowhere. I will not win this battle today. I turn to the door, defeated and angry with myself. All I did was encourage Livingston to be an active participant in this will.

Frustrated at my lack of progress, I shake my head. "What possessed my brother to change his will?"

"Why are you askin' me?"

I cross my arms. "Why do you suppose I am?"

Livingston's face remains emotionless. "Rainey, are you suggestin' I wanted to be in charge of your trust?"

I'm so incredibly desperate for answers that I'm willing to consider anything as a possibility. "It's a substantial sum."

"Indeed." He grabs his boots next to his bed. "But it comes at a price. Dealin' with you." Sitting down in the chair in the corner, he begins to put his boots on. He keeps a grip on the bow, but it's not firm enough. While his head is bent, I make my move and snatch the bow out of his grasp. As he jumps from the chair toward me, I toss the bow to my other hand. Livingston stops within an inch of me, our noses nearly touching. I lift both brows and tsk slowly. "Look what I have."

"I was doin' you a favor, *le savauge*. Women don't behave like you."

"Why not? I can shoot and tie a knot better than most men I know. And pants are far more comfortable than skirts."

"If you keep speakin' in such a manner, you'll never find a husband," Livingston says from behind me.

Turning around before I can take a deep breath, I find myself in the same position I was in not ten minutes ago. Livingston has his back to me as he walks toward his armoire. I've already been dismissed. The arrow moves through the air with a sleek precision that leaves me satisfied. Livingston turns right as the tip of the arrow cuts through the back of his sleeve, grazing his bicep, and settling into the solid oak of the armoire.

With his arm essentially pinned, Livingston stares at me. Mouth open, and eyes wide.

Slowly, I lower my bow. I don't bother to retrieve my arrow. "If you keep turnin' your back on me, you won't live to see the end of these sixty days."

Feeling pleased with my shot, I give him the curtsy that would make queens throughout the decades weep and my past governesses nod with approval. "Have a good day, Mr. Lacroix," I say sweetly.

CHAPTER FIVE

RAINEY

My frustration is a veritable storm, beginning in my stomach and spreading throughout me. Not a single thing will lift my spirits. Well, there is one thing, but I couldn't even shoot an arrow properly.

Oh, do I want to turn around and stomp back to Livingston's home. I want to pound on the front door and demand he listen. Truly listen. This isn't a time for tomfoolery because my future is at stake. When I walked to his house this morning, I was out for revenge, yet I hoped he would realize the severity of the situation with a sober mind. In my haste to seek vengeance, I had shown Livingston my cards. He saw just how much this upset me, and now, he's maintaining that there's nothing wrong with this ludicrous dowry.

He's trying to get underneath my skin, and it's working. I walk into my home and slam the door behind me. A servant in the foyer jolts at the noise, takes one look at me, and rushes toward the kitchen.

I need to be alone and think of a better strategy to approach Livingston because anger is getting me nowhere. My feet are heavy on the stairs, and my shoulders are slumped. I feel pulled down by the weight of my worries.

"Rainey? Is that you, dear?"

I stop in the middle of the stairs and look over my shoulder. "Momma." I sigh. "Who else would it be?"

"To clear your head, you were certainly gone for quite a

while."

I take my time walking back down the steps. "That's because I had a lot on my mind."

Momma gives me a thorough inspection. She knows I'm being evasive. "Where did you go?"

"If you must know, I went to speak with Livingston."

My mom's eyes widen with understanding. "Oh, Raina Leonore. You didn't."

"I did."

Closing her eyes, she shakes her head. "Whatever did you do?"

Like a trophy, I hold my bow above my head before I place it on the foyer table. Immediately, my momma rushes to my side. "Is he dead? Severely injured? My God, Raina, will officers be knockin' on our door? My poor heart cannot take much more."

Sighing, I place my hands on my hips. "He's not injured. And no, officers will not be comin' around."

The sad part is my own momma doesn't seem convinced. "What possessed you to go over there?"

"Because…" I take a deep breath. "He…he dismissed me last night!"

Momma blinks. "He dismissed you," she repeats.

"I went to speak to him regardin' Miles's will, and he kicked me out of his home!"

Momma arches a brow, a gesture that says, "And?"

"Raina, you must apologize," she says.

My upper lip curls in disgust. I'd rather drink curdled milk. "Why?"

"Because you cannot let your anger get the best of you. To begin with, ladies do—"

"Yes, yes, I know," I cut in. "It's not somethin' a lady would do. But I wanted to reason with him. I wanted him to realize how nonsensical it is for him to oversee a dowry, as if I'm an orphan child with no family."

"Livingston is a reasonable man. Perhaps he merely wants the best for you."

My brows scrunch together. "The last two times we've discussed him, you've described him as responsible and reasonable. Do you have him confused with his twin brother? This is Liv-ing-ston," I pronounce distinctly.

"I am aware of who he is. If the two of you stopped your bickerin', you'd see he is a pleasant gentleman. Is pleasant a better word for you, dear?"

"My Lord. I've heard it all," I mutter underneath my breath. Momma wouldn't be calling him pleasant or a gentleman if she saw what I saw this morning. An image of his body above that woman runs through my mind. I shake my head to rid myself of Livingston's naked form. I didn't anticipate seeing him in such a way. That's why my heart is pounding so fiercely. It's nothing to concern myself with.

"Why are you so opposed to findin' a husband?" Momma asks.

"Because to want a husband is one thing. Bein' told is another. I refuse to let a piece of paper dictate the rest of my life!"

Momma becomes silent for a moment. She stares at her hands before she lifts her head and looks at me solemnly. "You have no other choice."

With those words, my blood chills. I look at her from the corner of my eye. "What do you mean?"

"If you want to have a chance at marryin' well, this is it. We have no money."

The words roll so freely from her tongue. It's almost as if we're speaking about the weather. I watch Momma's face for any sign of emotion, but she stares back at me, nonplussed. As for me, I'm stunned speechless.

I shake my head. "Momma—"

"It's true," she cuts in. "And it's been this way for quite some time."

"How long is quite some time?"

Momma looks me in the eye. "Since the war started. Your brother was instrumental in keepin' us floatin' along, but..." Her words fade as she looks away.

But he's gone, I think to myself. My outrage over the will and Livingston's dismissal did one thing: it was a momentary distraction from losing Miles. Grief is incredibly complex. There's no right or wrong way to navigate your pain. You can only hang on as tightly as possible and remember that each day you wake up you are far braver than you know. Much stronger than you think.

Of course, I'm still in the early stages of Miles death, and his absence still cuts like a knife. There's an extra silence in the house, a sense of finality that was never there before. Sometimes, I tell myself he's still at war, but then the truth inevitably sinks in.

Right now, I curl my hands into fists, so my fingernails dig into my flesh. I cannot cry right now. I need to remain focused.

"When were you goin' to tell me?" I ask, keeping my gaze focused on the floor.

"I didn't believe I should burden you with such information."

I gaze up at her. "But you thought when the house and all our belongin's were bein' taken from us would be better?"

Momma sighs. "It will never come to that."

A sudden thought occurs to me. "If we are penniless, where is the money comin' from for my dowry and what happened to all the land Daddy's family gave him?"

"Your brother sold the land throughout the years to keep the creditors away. When your daddy died, he left a generous portion of money to your brother," Momma patiently explains. "Naturally, Miles set the money aside."

I don't know whether to laugh or scream because the irony is Miles received the money, and in my daddy's will, I was to receive the home on my thirtieth birthday. A home that we were now perilously close to losing.

"And please do not use the word penniless." Momma pauses to shudder. "It's so…crude."

"Crude is livin' on the streets because you lost your house because you have no money!"

Momma shakes her head. "You worry far too much."

"And you worry far too little! Listen to what you're tellin' me." Just like yesterday, I begin to pace. I'm not an admirer of liquor, but if there was any offered to me right now, I would gladly take it.

"I am. I'm attemptin' to give voice to reason so you'll see the best course of action is to go ahead and accept this dowry. Take Livingston's help. We need it."

"He's not offerin' his help," I say through gritted teeth. "The only thing he's offerin' is his vast expertise in tormentin' me!"

Momma says nothing; she just merely watches me. I continue to rant; my irritation is mounting. "I'm positive Livingston has no desire to be the executor. Believe me on this, Momma!"

"You cannot be certain of what his intentions are."

Whirling around, I face Momma. My eyes are ablaze. "Oh, I've never been certain of anythin' more in my entire life! If last night was any indication, I don't know what is."

"Since you have no faith in Livingston, then I will. Everything will work out the way it's meant to."

Momma can cling to her faith. What she doesn't understand is that only people with money are afforded the luxury of faith because they've never been told no. As for me, I'll continue to cling to rationale.

But the whys of everything going wrong in my life become too great of a burden. Very slowly, I feel myself begin to crack. All I see in my mind are images of my brother, and I need to get away from everybody right now.

"I certainly hope so," I mutter to Momma before I rush out of the room. My lips quiver as I race up the stairs. I'm terrified. I don't know what the future holds. That's why I snarled at Momma like a feral animal with its foot caught in a steel trap. It seemed just as I was let free from one trap, I fell into another.

Once I make it to my room, I slam the door behind me and collapse onto my bed. Curling into a ball, I let the tears fall freely, hoping to release the pressure I feel in my chest.

CHAPTER SIX

LIVINGSTON

There were many titles and names Rainey Pleasonton wore well throughout her life. *Le savauge*, Red Rainey, Stilts, and Wild Rainey were just a few.

Wife was one title I can't imagine she would carry with aplomb. She might walk down the aisle, but she'll be kicking and screaming the entire time.

She's far too disorderly and bold for one man to contain. Just mere hours ago, she had burst into my bedroom and tried to shoot me in the buttocks with her favorite weapon of choice. She couldn't have interrupted at a more inopportune time. Since I came back from the war, I haven't been intimate with a woman. There have been times when I was close, but there was no desire. After Rainey pounded on my door last night, the brief conversation we had gave me an extra pep in my step. The woman who was hanging on my arm all night was the very one I took to my room in the early hours of the morning, but it was useless. She was naked beneath me, and I was…flaccid. It was useless. Something in me was broken.

And then Rainey burst into the room with her bow and arrow. My ass throbs from thinking of her near perfect aim. If I wasn't moving, I know she would've struck me and I'd be lying in my bed right now, on my stomach, with ice on my ass instead of walking into Belgrave.

All in all, I consider it a victory.

The plantation I grew up in as a child, where my twin

brother and his family now live in, is relatively quiet. I look around the foyer. The doors to the sitting room are open, revealing servants quietly cleaning, but they pay me no mind.

Ben, the head butler, who's standing beside the front door, clears his throat. Turning around, I find him pointing toward the hall. "I believe your brother is in his office, Mr. Lacroix."

"Thank you."

Whistling, I stroll down the hall. I'm the very picture of nonchalance. Internally, I'm thinking of how to broach this subject with Étienne.

I knew Rainey well enough to know that if you forced her to do something, she would do the very opposite. It didn't mean I was inclined to be part of this dowry business. In front of Rainey, though, I will profess nothing of the sort because I can't help myself. Any opportunity I can get to watch steam come out of her ears, I'll take. Since I had the pleasure of seeing that and then some, it's time to get to business. And who better than to speak to the expert on business?

I knock on Étienne's office door before I enter. "Mornin'."

My older brother by seven minutes, who's poring over a document, lifts his head. He looks unsurprised to see me. "It's the afternoon, but considerin' you wake up at eleven, this is your mornin'."

I sit in one of the seats across from him and cross one leg over the other. "Étienne, I need to speak with you at once."

"About?"

"I have a problem we need to discuss."

"So do I. You see, I keep tryin' to work, but this man child continues to interrupt my day, makin' it virtually impossible to run a business and provide for my family."

I arch a brow. "I'm bein' serious."

"So am I." Sighing, Étienne slips his glasses off and tosses them onto this desk. "What is the matter?"

Pulling Pleas's will from my back pocket, I place it on Étienne's desk and slam my palm on top of it. "This is the matter."

I didn't have Étienne's attention when I sat down. But

I do now because he cannot help himself when it comes to documents. Finding the fine print is a game to him, and he enjoys negotiating what he wants changed, the contract length, and the terms or money. Almost immediately, Étienne snatches the papers and begins reading. I watch as his brows slowly furrow, then nearly connect. My stomach drops. When is that ever a good sign? Moments later, Étienne lowers the will onto the desk and whistles. "I presumed you were jestin' when you walked in, but I stand corrected." Étienne grins. "You truly do have a problem."

"Thank you for statin' the obvious." I drag my hands down my face and gesture to the core of my problem. "What do I do?"

Étienne leans back in his chair and laces his hands behind his head. "I think the answer is obvious. You do the right thing and help Pleas's sister. This would be a perfect project."

My blood runs cold at the very thought. "No, no, no. Absolutely not," I immediately reply.

"And why not?"

"I think we both know why not. Rainey isn't a project. She's a livin', breathin' nightmare. I prefer all body parts to remain intact. And if the first two reasons will not suffice, I'm not a governess."

Étienne gestures to the will and arches a brow. "Oh, but it seems as if you are."

"Rainey is an adult. She's free to do as she pleases."

"Did you tell her that?"

I surge out of the chair and begin to pace. "No. Naturally, I allowed her to believe the will is set in stone."

"Naturally," Étienne repeats.

"I can't help myself. She was furious." I fling my hand in the air. "It's entirely too easy to get beneath her skin when she gets that way."

Étienne gives me a hard look. "Some might say the same for yourself."

Ignoring the last bit, I walk back to his desk and sit back down. A powerful headache pounds against the base of my skull, and I rub my temples. We are not making the progress I thought we would.

"What's the real reason you don't want to do this?" Étienne asks.

I take a deep breath and contemplate whether I should tell my brother the truth. The very last thing I need right now is to have a ward. Especially if that ward is Rainey Pleasonton. She is the very opposite of pleasant.

If someone were to cut me open, they would see how black and unsalvageable my soul is. It has seen too much. It is beginning to rot, and it's only a matter of time before nothing's left. When that happens, I'll celebrate the occasion with some Old Fitzgerald.

"Livingston?" Étienne prods, pulling me out of my thoughts.

I think of a reply on the spot but am saved by a loud knock on the door. Étienne and I turn in time to see my sister-in-law open the door and then slam it loudly. She shoots it an annoyed look and waddles over to us.

"Question, Étienne. How big of a baby were you?" she asks.

He eyes her warily. "I'm not certain. Why do you ask?"

"Because I'm convinced this child is going to be a beast master."

Serene places a hand on her lower back as she slowly sits down. She closes her eyes and sighs with relief once she makes herself comfortable. She looks at me from the corner of her eye. "What's the matter, Livingston? Never seen a person sit in a chair?"

I shake my head. "No. I've simply never heard that much noise come out of one person while they're sittin'."

"Well, imagine carrying a baby who thinks your internal organs can be made into balloon animals."

"I don't know what balloon animals are, but since you said it, it probably isn't an appropriate conversation to have in public."

"Is it appropriate to have a human being use your ribs as a

jungle gym?" Serene retorts.

When I look at my brother, he subtly shakes his head. I've heard of women becoming…uncomfortable during their pregnancy and especially during the end. However, Serene appears as if she wants to tear my head off, then place it on the tip of a stake so she can roast it over a burning fire and feast on it for dinner.

After a few seconds, Serene takes another deep breath and lifts her head, staring at Étienne and me. She smiles, and it's as though she didn't snarl at me like a rabid dog seconds ago.

"What are you two talking about?" Serene asks.

"This." Étienne holds the paper out for Serene. She scans the document, and a frown causes her brows to crease.

She glances back and forth between Étienne and me. "What's this mumbo jumbo bullshit?"

"This is Pleas's will. Rainey has a dowry and sixty days to find a husband. Oh, did I also mention I was the executor of her dowry?"

Her brows nearly lift to her hairline. "You are? Oh, poor Rainey."

"Poor Rainey? Poor Rainey? Where's your loyalty?"

Serene scoffs and hands the will back to Étienne before she begins rubbing her belly. "You know I'm loyal, but it's fascinating to me how you can charm everyone in Charleston. Hell, you can sell ice to an Eskimo. The only person you can't charm is Miss Rainey. Speakin' of my favorite Southern belle, I heard she shot you in the ass."

"She told you?" I say.

At the same time, Étienne says, "What?"

Serene looks at her husband. "Rainey walked in on Livingston doing it with some chick and shot him in the ass with a bow and arrow because she was pissed at him. She didn't elaborate on why. I just assumed Livingston did something to tick her off because he's, well…Livingston."

"This was recent?" Étienne asks.

She nods.

Étienne rises from his chair and gives me a quick once-over before he sits back down. "For bein' shot in the buttocks, he's sittin' remarkably well."

The two of them converse about me as though I'm not there. Finally, I lift my hand, and they look over at me impatiently. "She did not shoot me in the ass, as Serene so eloquently put it." I pause. "She almost did."

Étienne arches a brow. "How many times must you learn to never turn your back on Rainey Pleasonton?"

"Obviously more than once," Serene quips.

"I do not care for the two of you very much right now."

Étienne stops chuckling long enough to focus on the will and slip on his glasses. "Ah, Livingston. You know we're jestin'. Where is your sense of humor?"

Somewhere in France. Lost in a trench with my soul.

Instead, I smile tersely. "Forgive me. I have more pressin' matters that need tendin' to."

"Very well. Let us have a thorough look, shall we?"

Étienne scarcely has his eyes on the first page before shrieking coming from the hallway drifts into the room.

"Miss Alex! Miss Alex, no!" someone cries.

The three of us turn in time to see the door fly open and a five-year-old come running into the room. Curly, dark red hair drawn back by a pink ribbon is all I see at first. Then a flash of more pink with white-capped sleeves. My niece finally stops running and stands in front of me, holding her arms out. Her hands are always sticky, she has a slight lisp, and for such a small thing, she has an unbelievably loud wail. But she has captivating almond-shaped green eyes heavily fringed with black lashes.

It was one thing Alex inherited from Étienne. Everything else was thanks to Serene.

I pick her up and place her on my lap. She laughs, and it's a soothing moment when I forget that Rainey Pleasonton is now my responsibility.

"Okay. Let me down," Alex says.

I follow her request, holding her out in front of me. But as I lower her to the floor, I misjudge the distance, and Alex kicks her feet, promptly hitting me between the legs.

Shit. Oh *fucking* shit.

I think I see stars. If it wasn't for her governess grabbing her at the last second, I would have almost dropped her. At once, I cradle my groin, forgetting ladies are in the room for a second.

"Like mother, like daughter," Étienne says dryly.

"Serene," I croak, "you better be prayin' that baby is a boy because I don't know if I can carry on the Lacroix name."

While stars continue to form behind my eyes, Alex cries. It isn't the first time she's heard me say expletives. But it is the first time I've shouted them in French and English in front of her. It's then that one of the strongest men I know scoops up the little life crusher and becomes putty in her hands. "Alexandra, *excuse-toi. Vous ne pouvez pas le faire.*"

Alex turns and gives me a bashful smile. At least I think she does. It's hard to tell. My vision is still quite blurry. "*Désolé, Oncle* Livingston."

Once I manage the strength to nod in her direction, Étienne puts her down. Alex rushes to Serene and buries her head in her skirts. Étienne looks my way and winces. He isn't laughing at my predicament, so I feel a small sense of solidarity on this matter.

"Chan-Chan is lost," Alex whines at Serene.

"I do apologize, Mrs. Lacroix. I tried to stop Alex from coming in here, but she's so distraught. We can't seem to find Chandler. She believes he's lost," her governess says.

"He's not lost. He's right here." As best as she can, Serene bends down, and dangles her hand till her fingertips graze the carpet. A calico moves out from under Étienne's desk, causing me to nearly have a heart attack.

The cat slinks up to Serene's hand and rubs against her. Serene picks the animal up and places it on her lap. I watch in astonishment; neither Étienne nor Serene are cat lovers. I once heard Serene say she'd rather own twenty snakes than have a cat. I sit up straighter in my chair as feeling returns to my lower region. "When did you two get a cat?"

"When I took Alex for a walk and she discovered this fur ball hiding behind the carriage house. She insisted on caring for him. Turns out, Étienne and I created a little human who prefers cats over dogs."

Serene shrugs. It only seems natural to shrug back.

"What's his name?" I ask.

"This is Chandler Bing," Serene says proudly.

"What kind of name is Chandler Bing?"

"It's a long story, but Chandler Bing is one of my favorite characters from one of my favorite shows ..." Her voice fades as she strokes the cat's back, and a faraway look appears in her eyes.

It's a rarity for her to speak of her era. At times, I forget she's not from here. And then she will speak an unfamiliar phase or say, "one of my favorite shows."

"I better leave before Alex causes any more damage to Livingston's most prized possession." It takes Serene three tries to get up from the chair. Étienne and I watch her. We don't attempt to help because we know if we do, she'll, well... then my brother's head will be joining mine on the fire. When Serene does make it to her feet, Chandler Bing's nails are digging into her shoulder, and Alex is running circles around her.

The governess wrangles Alex, ushering her out of the office. Serene walks behind them. "Good-bye, Livingston," she calls and looks over her shoulder. "Don't think we won't be talking about your little problem later."

There was no question in my mind that Serene would make good on her word. Once they're gone, I whistle. "I would ask how Serene is farin', but that seems pretty evident."

Étienne gives a grunt in reply.

"I have spare bedrooms if you would like a place to stay," I tease.

"I would laugh, but it could be several weeks until the baby arrives." Étienne drags both hands down his face. "My God, I'm convinced when she gets out of bed in the mornin' and places her feet on the floor, the devil cowers in fear."

I can't help but laugh at his description. "Well, my door is always open. But before you come over, read through this again." I emphasize the last of my words by slapping my palm against the surface of the desk.

He holds his hands before him, palms up. "I'm not a lawyer, Livingston."

"You're smart."

"In this regard, you're givin' me far too much credit. Besides, from what I read, there's nothin' that Pleas has severely imposed on you. It's not as though you're the one with the dowry."

"You're correct," I concede. "I don't have a dowry. I have somethin' much worse. I have Rainey. This dowry means we have to stay in contact for the next sixty days. Sixty days."

"I can count," Étienne says drolly. "And it does not specify the two of you have to speak every single day."

"I presume we have to stay in contact."

Étienne takes off his glasses and rubs the bridge of his nose. "I truly believe you're overthinkin' this. I've known Rainey the same length of time you have. I know how headstrong she can be. You might not even have to worry about this will."

Sighing, I drag my hands through my hair and pull until the ends stand up. "Did you not hear your wife? The crazed woman shot me in the ass."

My brother smirks. "Enlighten me on why she did that again?"

I make a noise of frustration. "The details are inconsequential to this matter."

"Oh, but I think they are."

The memory of Rainey walking in on me with Lydia/Lillian makes me shiver. Only Rainey can ruin sex and nearly incapacitate me at the same time.

"If my somber brother could return for the moment, I would deeply appreciate that."

Étienne holds his hands up. "My apologies." Clearing his throat, he leans back and stares thoughtfully at the desk.

We're granted the silence I'd hoped for since I walked

through the front door. But it only highlights the lack of progress neither one of us are making in this dowry situation. After a few minutes of staring out the window, I look toward Étienne and find him staring at me with raised brows.

He lifts both shoulders, a gesture that says, *I still don't have a resolution for you.*

Groaning, I drag both hands down my face. This was quickly moving from bad to terrible.

"Everythin' will be fine."

Dropping my hands, I look at him. "Are you certain?"

Étienne leans back in his chair and links his fingers behind his head. "Absolutely. Trust me, she won't do it. But a word of advice? It might be best if you wore some extra paddin' around Rainey." He gestures to my lower half. "Best not to take any chances."

CHAPTER SEVEN

RAINEY

Y ou have to do this. There's no other option," I tell my reflection.

It's been two days since Momma told me of our financial peril, and my mind has thought of nothing else. When I look around our home and what Momma has filled it with — our staff, belongings, the food that's placed in front of me during each meal — I tally the total cost, and it doesn't seem improbable that we've found ourselves in this predicament.

Many families in the South come from old money. But what most forget is that at some point, the well runs dry. I suppose it was bound to happen to the Pleasonton family. My great-great-granddaddy Arthur Pleasonton was a suggested colonist (although it was never historically proven) who amassed thousands of acres across South Carolina. He would try his hand at anything if it guaranteed money, but what truly interested him were numbers and what led to the money. His sensible ways with money didn't pass down the line, though. And that would be the root of the problem. Some relatives would squander their inheritance before one could blink. I never imagined the money my ancestors had worked so hard for would suddenly be gone, and so would the land. I think that hurts the most because it shows how vulnerable our finances have been, and I've been none the wiser.

Perhaps Miles and Momma attempted to give hints and I wasn't paying close enough attention. But this deserved more than a hint. This warranted caution so I could prepare, and I wouldn't find myself in the very situation I'm in now.

I can think of no other way to save our family home and debts than to go through this ridiculous façade. Is marriage the worst possible thing to happen to me? No. But I don't particularly care for being strong-armed in any situation. Any choice I make, I want it to be mine. Especially when it comes to my future husband.

Momma seems oblivious to my anguish. She typically spends her mornings dedicated to her needlepoint in the sunroom. Later, she'll "retire" to her living quarters and change into a tea dress (black, of course).

She's not meddlesome and carries on polite conversation, but I know better. It's almost as if she knows I need a bit of time and silence to process the news and come to a decision.

I adjust the high waistband of my navy blue skirt and the round neckline of my embroidered, ivory silk blouse. I purchased the pleated blouse for the orient design with no thought of the cost. Now, I'm lamenting over all the careless spending I've done. But there's no use crying over spilled milk. I've done enough crying to last a lifetime even though my face doesn't show the signs. My eyes aren't bloodshot, and my nose isn't red from running. If I was accidentally locked inside my room for the next week, I don't think I'd object.

Tucking my hands into the pockets of my skirt, I reluctantly walk out of my room and downstairs. I find Momma just where I expect her to be, sitting at the table, demurely picking at her breakfast. It's all a ruse, though; she's waiting to speak with me.

When I enter the room, Momma lifts her head and smiles at me. There are wrinkles around her eyes, and dark circles beneath her brown eyes. For months now, I've told myself it's because of Miles's death, and it more than likely is, but she's also had to bear the financial burden all on her own.

I'm not good with math. My skill with an arrow and words, doesn't extend to numbers. But I love my family, and when you love someone or something fiercely enough, you learn to be good at what you're not great at.

I could peruse the books. Perhaps things aren't as dire as Momma believes, and if I confuse myself, I can call on Livingston. Although he doesn't appear it, he's quite intelligent, and I know I have his confidence.

He is many things, but a rumormonger he's not.

Yet I'm not naïve enough to believe that will happen overnight. Poring through the finances is a tedious task and will take time. Until I get a clear answer for myself, I need to continue with this farce of finding a husband.

The light clanging pulls me out of my thoughts. Momma's scooping sugar into the teacup with light blue daisies painted around edge. Years ago, she insisted on buying the Wileman set because her previous collection became "outdated."

I can only imagine the exorbitant price of this set. Perhaps, if we sold the tea set, it could help with our money troubles and then...

No, I can't think about that right now.

What I need to focus on is talking with Momma about my decision. Taking a deep breath, I walk to my seat across from her. "Good mornin'."

She lifts her gaze, continuing to scoop sugar into her coffee. "Mornin', sweetie. How did you sleep?"

"Very well."

Lie. I slept horribly.

"And yourself?"

Momma blows into her coffee and takes a sip. Her nose scrunches, and she gives one of the servants standing in the room a displeased look as though they were the one to pour all the sugar into her coffee. Momma's blood type is sugar, sweet tea, and some more sugar. "I slept quite peacefully."

Quite peacefully has been Momma's answer for as long as I can remember. She could sleep through a hurricane quite peacefully, love you quite peacefully, and mourn quite peacefully.

We settle into our comfortable morning routine of silence while a servant places a plate of food in front of me. Forks scraping against the expensive china plates, and birds chirping directly outside are the only noises to be heard. My stomach is in such knots I can only eat my toast. I poke at my eggs with the blunt tips of the fork and watch the yolk seep onto the plate. I can't help but envision it as my hopes and dreams slowly fade from me. It's a bleak thought, but nothing about what I'm about to do makes me happy.

I clear my throat. "I wanted to talk to you."

"What is it, dear?"

I take a deep breath. My stomach continues to churn. "After much thought, I think it's best I follow Miles's will and attempt to find a husband."

Momma's reaction is tepid at best. You'd think from the way she slowly nods I'd just announced I wanted to update my entire wardrobe, instead of changing my entire life by marrying.

She finishes chewing, gingerly places her fork next to her plate, and dabs at the corners of her mouth with her napkin. "That's lovely to hear. I knew you'd come around, so I took the liberty of invitin' someone over tonight."

Dread trickles down my spine. I stare at Momma, my mouth slowly parting. "Who? You haven't invited a man over, have you? Momma, I just came to this decision."

Momma waves away my words. "Oh, it's nothin' of that nature. Although it is a man." She beams at me. "It's Livingston."

I swear, that's even worse. "Oh, Momma, no."

Momma goes back to eating her breakfast, delicately cutting the pieces of her sausage as though she's a child. "I presume from your reaction you haven't spoken to him yet?"

I shake my head.

"Then tonight is the perfect opportunity for you." She suddenly looks away. "Perhaps you can apologize."

I toss my napkin on the table. I've suddenly lost my appetite. "You want me to apologize?"

"Yes." Momma stabs her fork in my direction. "You are as stubborn as your daddy, and I know you'd rather swallow glass than make amends."

"Correction. When I've done somethin' wrong I will make amends. As long as that person is not Livingston Lacroix."

"Well, you're gonna have to figure out what to say."

"Not if he doesn't come to dinner," I point out.

"I will not rescind an invite. That's highly improper. Not to mention, uncivil. A lady only rescinds an invite if she has a logical reason."

Lifting my hand, I point a finger downward at my head. "Me. I'm your reason. I'm your flesh and blood, and this flesh and blood does not want said guest to come."

Momma leans in, her eyes remaining determined. "Rainey, you have nothin' to be worried about. I'll be at the dinner and will tell you what to say beforehand."

"I'm not a marionette. There is no reason to pull my strings and feed me lines."

"When it comes to Livingston, I'm afraid I may have to. He's in charge of your dowry, and it's important that you be on your best behavior."

I know she's right, but I thought I had more time to think over my course of action. I never thought I had mere hours before I had to see the man who I used my bow and arrow on days ago. But, then again, I never thought I would have to use it on him for a second time.

"Please cancel this dinner. Please," I beg, making one last attempt to change her mind.

Momma averts her gaze and moves her food around her plate. "Raina, I'm afraid that cannot be done. Livingston will be here tonight. Consider this matter put to bed." Briefly, she lifts her gaze back to mine. "Oh, and, sugar? Try to wear a blue dress. It's such a flatterin' color on you."

CHAPTER EIGHT

RAINEY

I do not heed Momma's advice and change into the blue dress. I wear my favorite black dress because this is a day of mourning.

I've lost many people I loved dearly, and tonight, I will be parting with one emotion that has never left me or let me down: my pride.

Oh pride, we've had quite the relationship. It's remained strong in me without becoming hubristic. But desperate times call for desperate measures. I'm still not for certain what I'll say to Livingston, or how I'll gently broach the subject. If I'm kind to him, he will undoubtedly notice something is amiss.

Not only am I mourning my pride, but also my sheer ignorance to my family's plight.

In 1917, while the war raged on in Europe, I saw an article in *Harper's Bazaar* about the House of Chanel. It was on "the list of every buyer." Nat had garments from House of Chanel she coveted. But then the war broke out, and it was virtually impossible to order a dress from any fashion house in Europe. I didn't receive this beautiful creation until two weeks ago.

From afar, my ankle-length dress appears simple. The material skims over my curves. It's sleeveless with a square neckline. Upon closer inspection, you can see the heavily beaded design with a layer of black silk faille draped to my waistline. It goes up and over my shoulders and down my back. Around my waist, in the same shade, is a belt loosely tied to the side. Heavy tassels hang from the belt, grazing the hem of the dress.

If I knew then what I know now, I wouldn't have been so liberal with what I purchased.

Adjusting my hair clip in my chignon, I slowly lower my hands and stare at my reflection. I know I'm not an ogre. I'm somewhat attractive, but can I pull off an engagement in sixty days? I don't know. It might take an act of God.

Minutes before six o'clock, I leave my room. I'm getting ready to walk down the stairs when the front door opens and in walks the devil himself, Livingston Lacroix.

While the butler tells him to wait in the sitting parlor before dinner, I move down the steps. Straight away, Livingston's eyes meet mine. His bright green eyes start at my ankles and travel up my body before settling on my face. I'd rather endure years of torture than admit that being the focus of Livingston's attention can be intoxicating.

Two steps away from the landing, I stop and grip the railing. Livingston tips his hat in my direction before he hands it over to the butler. Compared to the last time we saw one another, he looks very put together. That's one thing that's never been a problem for him. He fills out his tailored, gray worsted suit well.

"Good evenin', Rainey."

"Livingston," I say, tilting my head in his direction.

Livingston saunters closer with his loose-hip gait. Livingston and his brother have a similar walk, but for the two tall men, their stride is for very different reasons. Étienne quickly assess his surroundings to find what he's come for. Livingston casually surveys life around him in a manner that is only befitting for a king. The world halts until he finds whatever is pleasing to him at the moment.

Livingston's life has always centered around pleasure. At that moment, he gives me his undivided attention and his well-practiced half-smirk. It appears I'm his amusement for the night. "I must say, receivin' an invitation to have dinner at the Pleasonton house was a shock."

"Why were you shocked? You're like family."

"I didn't feel the warm embrace of family when you barged into my room days ago."

I bite down on my tongue and force my lips to curl into a polite smile. "That was an unfortunate misunderstandin'."

Livingston tucks his hands into his pockets. From my vantage point, I'm taller and able to turn my nose down on Livingston. I could become quite comfortable in this spot.

"And the scar on my leg? Was that a misunderstandin' too?"

Crossing my arms, I lean against the wall. "I was a child and didn't know how to properly hold a bow or nock an arrow. A mere slip of my hand. I do apologize."

"My God, you have an answer for everythin' tonight, don't you?" His eyes rove over my body. "Rare form, *le savauge*. Rare form."

I feel anger, of course I do, but it's breaking apart and giving way to something else that I can't properly describe. The feeling makes my skin tingle, almost as though thousands of needles are underneath my skin, and it travels directly to my fingertips, causing me to flex them.

Standing straight, I walk down the rest of the steps. My reign of power is over. Livingston and I are back on equal footing. I step closer until our faces are inches apart, just to prove to myself that I'm nothing like the trail of women fawning over Livingston.

His eyes look exceptionally light tonight. It's because of the chandelier. It basks him in a glow that makes his skin tone golden.

Men shouldn't be beautiful, but Livingston is. Michelangelo would want to sculpt him. I'll never admit that. The last thing Livingston needs is more admiration for his already massive ego.

Averting my gaze from his symmetrical face, I sigh. *Rainey, you need to remember what tonight is about.*

Looking both ways, I make sure nobody is watching. I always try to avoid using the dreaded H word at all costs. The word that can diminish your confidence with the first letter. We all know the word.

Help.

"Can I speak with you for a moment?" I ask, keeping my voice quiet.

Livingston's brows furrow. "I suppose so."

Exhaling, I look down at the ground to gather my courage and then move my eyes back up to Livingston. Before I can say a word, I'm interrupted.

"Livingston!" Momma says. "When did you arrive?"

Livingston holds my gaze for a second longer before he looks over my shoulder at Momma and gives her the award-winning smile he's best known for.

"Only minutes ago, and may I say, Mrs. Pleasonton, it is a pleasure to see you again. I swear, you are agin' in reverse."

Momma beams under his praise. My mourning has an expiration date. As for Momma, she's been mourning since I was a child. She has every mourning gown available. It was her status symbol. When you thought of Leonore Pleasonton, you immediately thought of her dedication to her deceased husband and now, her fallen son. She was on par with Queen Victoria.

Momma adjusts the black piping around her shirt cuff before she pats Livingston's arm. "Bless your heart, dear boy. You're too good to me."

Depending on who you ask, "bless your heart" can either be said as an insult or with earnestness. Momma has always used it sincerely and detests when it's used with derision.

"Dinner is ready to be served," a servant announces from the doorway.

Livingston holds both arms out to escort Momma and me to the dining room. I take his arm and stare straight ahead.

"What is it you needed to speak with me about?" Livingston asks.

I look at him from the corner of my eye, trying not to show my shock. I'm not having this discussion in front of Momma. For her part, she remains silent, but I know she's hanging onto every word. "Oh, I...um, I can't remember."

"It seemed urgent."

"It must have slipped my mind. If I think of it, I'll let you know."

That earns a sharp look from Momma. To her, I had the perfect chance, and I didn't take it.

"Please do," Livingston replies as we approach the dining room.

Momma strategically places Livingston across from me, and herself beside him. I have empty seats next to me and can't help but feel I'm on trial.

It would've been better if Momma had invited more people over. Then I could distract myself. With only Livingston here, I'm forced to see his face and engage in conversation the minute I look up.

Dinner is served, starting with okra soup, a Lowcountry staple. Afterward, there's Charleston red rice with crushed bacon and bell peppers as the seasoning. Livingston compliments the food profusely. He assumes our cook of sixteen years, Tandey, made this meal. Little does he know she left this morning with her daughter for North Carolina. Her reason? "To be with family."

I could unravel the true meaning of her words and so could Momma. Tandey wanted a job that paid. It didn't matter how long she's been with our family. Money is the driving force of this world.

In the end, Momma pulled one of the servants from her daily chores and had her work in the kitchen.

While the two of them politely converse, I listen closely, looking for any way I can sneak my way into the discussion so I can continue my talk with Livingston. I'd rather not have this conversation around Momma, but I can't continue dinner like this anymore. I am an utter catastrophe right now. I can't eat, I'm breaking out in a cold sweat, and my heart is beating so rapidly I'm convinced it's going to break free from my chest.

I place my fork on my plate, and not for the first time does Livingston look in my direction. He knows I'm being almost reticent tonight. He knows I'm hiding something.

Once again, Momma interrupts me before I have a chance to speak. Does she time these moments? "Well, I do believe it's time for me to relax in the sittin' parlor."

Instinctively, Livingston begins to stand at the same time she does.

Momma smiles. "No, no. You stay where you are. Escort Rainey and take your time. I'll see the both of you soon." With her hands linked in front of her, Momma strides out of the room.

My gaze narrows as I watch her walk away. Her abrupt departure from dinner was not a coincidence. She's giving me another chance to speak with Livingston, and this time, I won't let it go to waste. As her footsteps echo down the hall, Livingston slowly turns his gaze toward me. I shrug as though I'm also bewildered by Momma's actions and take a bite of my food.

Livingston wads up his linen napkin, places it next to his empty plate, and leans back in his chair. "Your momma is in an interestin' mood."

"Is interestin' the correct word?"

"How would you describe her mood?"

I mull over his question. "Unpredictable. She has her good days and her bad. Today is good."

A corner of his mouth lifts. "And yesterday when your momma invited me over for dinner?"

"Must have been another good day." I give him another shrug and smile serenely. "Lucky you."

Livingston doesn't reply. He watches me carefully. My hands are practically shaking from the weight of his gaze. It's because I'm skittish about our impending conversation. That's all.

I take another bite of my food and aggressively chew. I've barely swallowed before I'm pushing away from the table. "Lovely dinner and a stimulatin' conversation, but we should keep Momma company, don't you think?" I ask too brightly.

Livingston arches a dark brow but doesn't challenge me.

As we stroll through the doorway, I clear my throat and make sure to keep my tone light. "I've always felt we've had a...close bond."

Livingston looks at me, and the corner of his mouth lifts. "Is that so?"

"Well, perhaps close is the wrong word. Unique?"

Livingston looks ahead, the smirk spreading into a devastating, all-knowing grin. "Rainey, I'm gonna make an educated guess that you want somethin' from me?"

The snort that slips from me is instinctive and can't be helped. If you're bitten by a mosquito, do you not swat at it? For me, the same can be said for pompous males. It's ingrained in me to turn my cheek to them. "I don't want somethin' from you."

"No?" Livingston counters.

"I merely..." I look down at the floor, ignoring Livingston's stare. "I need a favor from you."

"That requires somethin' from me."

Swallowing my pride, I look at Livingston and find his eyes gleaming with unshed laughter. "Very well, I need somethin' from you."

"Very well, I'm listenin'."

I stop in the middle of the hallway and pull away from him. I wait a few seconds. Is Momma going to take this opportunity to burst from the sitting parlor and interrupt us again? Thankfully, that doesn't happen, so I blurt the words out that I've been meaning to say all night. "I've decided not to fight Miles's will."

Interesting enough, Livingston only appears mildly shocked by my admission. "Is that so?"

I nod. "I was upset when I first found out the news. I've processed the information, and perhaps it wouldn't be... terrible if I had a husband."

My Lord, just saying the word husband makes me cringe.

Livingston makes himself comfortable and leans against the wall, crossing one leg over the other. "And where do I come into this equation?"

"You come in because I know you want to be rid of this entire executor situation. The quicker I find a husband, the better."

There it is. My false explanation in its entirety. I know Livingston is having a difficult time accepting my explanation because even I am. What I just said goes against my personality.

With my shoulders held back, I solemnly look Livingston in the eye while he watches me sharply.

"So in the span of days, you've decided you need a husband?"

"Don't say it in such a manner. It's perfectly normal for a woman to want to get married."

Livingston nods. "No, you're right. But you came to my home and tried to shoot me with your bow and arrow for a second time because you were so outraged by Pleas's will, so forgive me if I'm skeptical. And while we're on the topic of your arrow. Would you like it back?"

My blood begins to boil. "If we're on the subject of my bow and arrow, I shot you because you humiliated me in front of virtual strangers. And no, you can keep the arrow as a reminder never to anger me again."

"You are not helpin' your argument." With a mock sigh, Livingston stands up straight, turns around, and begins to walk in the direction of the foyer.

"Wait, wait, wait!" I rush out. Livingston stops walking. I close my eyes and take a deep breath before I speak. "Don't go."

Slowly, Livingston pivots and arches his brows. Interest lights his gaze. It's been a long time since I've said those two words to Livingston. "Continue," he says.

"As I was sayin'…before I lost my…temper." Livingston smirks. "I think it's time for me to find myself a husband."

I must say, in those next few minutes, I almost convinced myself I could've been an actress because Livingston eyes were sharp. He's searching for any clue that would indicate I was lying. But I don't break. No, not once. Too much was at stake.

"All right," Livingston drawls out. I nearly sigh with relief.

"Do you have an arrangement prepared to help you find a husband?"

At those words, I frown. "I didn't think of that. Does Charleston have a shortage of men who I haven't been made aware of?"

"As charmin' as I may find you," Livingston says dryly, "other men might not feel the same."

"Thank you for the encouragement," I retort. "Like I said, the quicker I find a husband, the faster you get out of bein' the executor of my dowry. But now you're causin' me to think that I never will find a husband, and if I don't find a husband, then what do I have? Nothin'! I will have nothin' and…" My words fade as I take a deep breath. In truth, it's not a husband I'm worried about losing; it's me and my momma losing everything Daddy and Miles had worked so hard for.

Livingston becomes every man when he senses a woman on the verge of hysteria. His eyes widen, and he holds his hands up in front of him as if to ward off a wild animal. "It's all right. It's all right. You do not need to worry. I have a plan. Everythin' will be all right."

And like every man who's encountered a hysterical female, Livingston stiffly comforts me. I could receive a more soothing embrace from my family driver than this. Nonetheless, I lean into him because I need this hug. More than I realize.

I can count on one hand the number of times Livingston Lacroix has hugged me. The day of my daddy's funeral. When I was twelve and the boy I proclaimed to love and would spend the rest of my days with let it be known he'd never be sweet for a bony amazon like me. And there was the time after his brutal attack when we spent a lot of time together. As his lack of memories for the things and people around him continued to grow each day, I suddenly felt helpless and hugged him, hoping that for one moment I could silence the discord in his mind and give him peace.

Similar to what he's giving me now. My eyes remain open the entire time, and as the seconds pass, my pulse grows louder and my heart beats faster. I'm the first to disentangle from the hug and take an inelegant step back. I keep myself distracted by staring at the floor. I don't know what I just experienced. Today has been incredibly peculiar, filled with many firsts.

When I look back at Livingston, I find him staring at me with a faint furrow between his brows. He clears his throat and subtly shakes his head. "Meet me tomorrow at my home so we can discuss this in greater depth, all right?"

Eagerly, I nod. I don't know what he has planned, but I'm more than willing to listen.

I've said what I've needed to say tonight. I can't tell whether I feel relief or if I'm going to become sick. Either way, my energy is drained. I want to crawl upstairs, directly to my bed. My exhaustion must show because Livingston pulls out his pocket watch. "I need to be on my way. Tell your momma dinner was lovely."

"I will do that."

Livingston dips his head. He gives me his signature smirk that he uses on every woman. The one that makes a dimple in one cheek become prominent. The one that causes his eyes to become hooded as though he's thinking secretive thoughts about you and counting down the moments to have you to himself so he can tell you every little detail.

"Good night, *le savauge*." Livingston says, knowing I hate the nickname with a fiery passion.

Oh, we were doing so good. For a moment, I thought we were going to end tonight on a good note, and then he deliberately ruined it.

Livingston brushes past me before I can reply. Breathing deep through my nose, I watch the butler open the front door for him, reminding myself that I can plot my revenge later. As of now, Livingston has agreed to help. He has a plan. That's all I need.

Out of nowhere, Momma pokes her head out of the sitting parlor. I nearly jump out of my skin. "Dear Lord!" I say, clutching a hand to my chest. "Don't do that."

"Did you speak with him?" she presses.

"You didn't listen?"

Momma appears appalled that I would ever ask such a question. "Of course not."

"I'm surprised you didn't have your ear pressed against the door."

Finally, she steps away from her hiding spot and walks toward me. "A lady never eavesdrops, sugar. Now tell me what you said."

"I told him I decided I needed a husband."

Momma's face lights up, and a satisfied smile lights up her face. "What did he say?"

"He said he had a plan."

Momma's shoulders sag at the same time as her eyes widen. "How wonderful! I knew he would be of help. Did I not tell you Livingston is a gentleman?"

"Yes, Momma. You told me," I say, my tone flat.

Stopping in front of me, Momma grabs my arms. "What's the matter? He said he would help."

I muster my brightest smile. "Nothin' is wrong, Momma. I'm simply relieved the conversation has taken place."

"You must collect yourself. Everythin' will be all right." Momma steps back, telling one of the servants she'll have a cup of tea in her bedroom. Twisting around, I watch Momma. I'm surprised she doesn't float up the stairs. She's nearly buoyant from her happiness. And why shouldn't she be? She saw no flaws in the dowry and finding a husband.

Slowly, I walk up the stairs. Nothing has been solved, not even close. But for the first time in days, I take a deep breath and don't feel the weight of my family's burden pressing down on me.

CHAPTER NINE

LIVINGSTON

When I told Rainey I had a plan, I may have embellished a bit. All right, I embellished a lot. I had no plan.

I wasn't Étienne. The only times I brainstorm fast and effectively is when I have to get myself out of a bad situation.

Well, here was a bad situation. Being stuck with Rainey Pleasonton for sixty days. I couldn't think of a worse situation. I'm also becoming more and more convinced that every time I'm around her, I put my life at risk. My God, experiencing the war was almost easier than being near that hellion of a woman.

The minute I arrived home last night, I flipped to a fresh page in my notepad and began to deliberate over Rainey's sudden desire for a husband with a renewed vigor that took me by surprise. My dedication had more to do than with having Rainey as a ward. Maybe it was because for once in my life, someone was coming to me first for help rather than my brother or someone far more responsible, and I didn't want to disappoint Rainey. However, there was no denying sixty days was a short length of time to find a suitable spouse. It's been done before in shorter amount of time, though.

But this morning, as the sun slowly began to rise, I could no longer keep my eyes open and woke up to the sound of the car horn outside my window. Drool ran down my mouth, and the paper stuck to one side of my face.

The predicament I faced was the men I associated with

were good-for-nothing bastards at times. I wouldn't approve of their unions to a newborn kitten, much less to Rainey. And the rest of the men who are respectable have more than likely heard of or felt the wrath of Rainey. They won't be lining up in front of her door anytime soon unless they're strong-armed.

As I grew more and more frantic, I sent for the one person in Charleston who not only has one idea, but many. And they're probably insane enough to work. I never received a reply to my message or call. Now I was left to wait and wonder what I'd say to Rainey if I had to face her without a solution.

Right then, I hear three brisk knocks on the door. Springing into action, I hurry to open the front door.

"I got out of bed for you. This shit better be good," Serene says as she nearly waddles into my home.

"Well, nice to see you, too," I say and shut the door behind her.

"Two hours of sleep, Livingston. Two hours." Serene holds two fingers up as though I'm hard of hearing. "And that's being generous."

"I don't understand. Why two hours?"

Serene walks down the hall toward the sitting room as though this house is her own. "The human inside me decided it would be fun to use my ribs as a jungle gym so I couldn't breathe, and Alex thought it would be super adorable to wake up at the butt-crack of dawn."

"Well, I'm deeply grateful you're here."

At that, Serene turns and arches a graceful brow. "Livingston Lacroix is grateful. Dear God, this really is serious." She takes a seat on the settee, and with a dramatic sigh, she makes herself comfortable. You would think she walked into town instead having her driver drop her off by how out of breath she is.

She claps her hands and points them at me. "First thing's first. Do you have any shrimp?"

"Pardon?"

Serene closes her eyes and rests her head against the back of the settee. "You clearly need my help for something, but I'm working for two. I need brainpower, and I woke up craving shrimp. Shrimp with lemon juice. Wait, no. I'm gonna go with Worcestershire sauce. No. Lemon juice would be perfect."

I hold up a hand before Serene has the chance to change her mind. "I'm sorry, did you confuse my home with a restaurant?"

"I'm sorry, do you want my help?"

"What makes you think I need your help?"

"Because you never ask to speak with me alone, so I'm assuming this has to be something serious. But not too serious or otherwise you'd reach out to Étienne. So what is it? Do you have ten baby mamas banging down your door demanding you step up and be the father?"

I wince at her words. "Absolutely not. Even I have a small shred of honor."

"Gambling debt?"

"Sorry to disappoint you, but no."

Understanding lights her eyes, and she claps her hands. "Ah…this has to do with Rainey!"

I see trying to formulate the best way to ease into this conversation is futile. "You don't know that."

"Of course, I know that. Rainey is the only woman who does not give you the time of day. Rainey drives you mad. Also, you're forgetting that I was there when you told Étienne about the will and her shooting you with the bow and arrow."

"For your information, Rainey does not 'drive me mad' as you put it. But you are right on one account. This does pertain to Rainey."

Serene grins. I continue before she has a chance to say a word. "I've asked for your assistance because we need to find Rainey a husband."

Serene furrows her brows. "Why?"

"Why?" I repeat. "How sleep-deprived are you? She needs a husband to inherit the money."

Serene impatiently waves her hands in the air. "I know that. But why are you suddenly so gung ho on helping her?"

At her question, I look away. Is this a bad situation for me? Yes. But there are more layers to my motives. When I had dinner with her and Leonore, I watched her from across the table. I saw the furtive looks she gave the hallway. Rainey was trapped in her own purgatory and managing the death of her brother. Perhaps this could serve as a nice distraction for her.

"Because I want to be rid of her, that's why," I lie.

Serene's gaze is unflinching. Without breaking a sweat, I stare back, but after a few seconds, I'm the first to look away. "Whatever you say. Are you so determined to find her a husband because you're the executor?"

"Yes, and I called on you because I know you're diabolical at times but very inventive at findin' solutions."

"Oh, I am loving the compliments. Keep them coming."

"I will as long as you begin thinkin' of solutions."

"All right, all right," Serene says with a smile.

She heavily sighs and focuses on the pattern of the chair beside mine. I rest one ankle over my knee and carefully watch my sister-in-law. She remains quiet and repeatedly drums her fingers on the armrests.

"Do you have anything?" I probe.

Her eyes widen. "I just started thinking!"

"Rainey will be here soon."

"She's coming over today? Why didn't you tell me?" Serene hisses.

"Because I didn't want you to feel unnecessary pressure while your mind thought of somethin'."

"Well, too late now!"

In the midst of our bickering, there's a knock on the front door. The two of us immediately stop talking and stare at the hall as though we're on the run from the law. We're still for so long there's another knock, this time louder.

Serene makes a shooing motion with her hands. "It's your home. Go answer the door!"

Holding my hands out in front of me, I stand and take a few steps backward before I turn. "I'm goin'. I'm goin'," I grumble.

I wasn't concerned that I didn't have a solution. With Serene made aware of Rainey's intentions, I felt confident my sister-in-law would think of something while Rainey's here.

I open the door, and I can't stop myself. My eyes examine Rainey to make sure there's no possible way she's hiding her bow. I don't have the desire to be shot today.

Much to my relief, she appears to be weapon free, so I pull the door wider for her. Upon entering, Rainey takes one look at me, and her eyes instinctively narrow. She's appraising me the same way I assessed her. My lips kick up into a grin as I wonder what's going to come out of that wicked little mouth.

She's unpredictable in every way.

It doesn't appear that way, though. Even now, she's wearing a yellow dress in a style Nat would fawn over. Her hair's in an updo that I see many women wear. She's as fresh as a daisy, and I bet my life she hates every second of it and will pull the barrettes out of her dark hair as soon as she gets home. When she was a little girl, she would run barefoot with her hair flying behind her, and her momma would chastise her and demand she come back to put some shoes on right that second.

As she walks past me, I catch the scent of lavender. Rainey has a sharp tongue, but the floral scent is a reminder she has a feminine air about her.

"Good mornin'," she greets.

"Mornin'." I'm relieved to see she's no longer emotional. It feels reprehensible to see her in such a state. Doubtlessly, it's because I can count on one hand the number of times I've seen her at her most vulnerable.

"Let's go in the sittin' room and talk," I say before she has a chance to ask me about the plan that doesn't exist.

Rainey's silence as we walk down the hall is unsettling. When I look at her from the corner of my eye, she appears perfectly normal, but something isn't quite right.

I stop before we enter the sitting room and reach out to keep her from walking. My hand gently curls around her arm, near her elbow. Rainey jumps as though she forgot I was beside her and stares at her arm where my hand is. At once, I let go. "Do you no longer wish to seek a husband?"

She blinks at me rapidly. A few seconds go by before she

answers. "Yes, I do. And there's no changin' my mind." A determined glint fills her eyes.

I watch her carefully. "I'm not tryin' to change your mind. I'm merely reiteratin' what you said yesterday."

The fight slowly deflates from her. What is wrong with her today? Where are her thoughts? "Oh. Very well, then. Let's carry on with why I'm here." She gives me a meaningful look.

"Yes, let's do that, shall we?" Serene says drolly from the sitting room. "While the two of you have been having the most riveting conversation, I think I've passed out twice from exhaustion and hunger."

On the spot, Rainey's head snaps in Serene's direction. In the span of a second, her face transforms. When she truly smiles, Rainey has dimples, and her eyes crinkle at the corners.

What would it take to get Rainey to smile at me in such a way?

"My word," Rainey drawls. "I didn't know you were here."

"I know you didn't. Otherwise, you would've offered me a beverage or food." Serene winks at me, but Rainey doesn't notice. She's too preoccupied staring at me as though I'm the devil reincarnated.

"Livingston, where are your manners? Get Serene a beverage."

"God forbid Serene go one hour without eatin'. And she's family. It's never prevented her from forcin' her way in here and makin' herself cozy."

Rainey waves a hand in the air as though my words are neither here nor there. Without giving me a second look, she rushes to Serene's side. As I watch the two of them talk, it occurs to me that having my very pregnant sister-in-law here might be brilliant. She and Rainey will talk for hours, and Rainey will forget the very reason she came here.

"What brought you to Livingston's today?"

"I'm here because Livingston made me aware of your intentions to find a husband."

Serene could see me wildly gesticulating behind Rainey for her not to go any further, but she was simply ignoring me. Rainey looks over her shoulder, her eyes blazing. "You told her already? Lord, it's been less than twenty-four hours since we've seen one another. Did you also notify *The Post and Courier*?"

Crossing my arms over my chest, I observe her. "Of course and also *The New York Times*. They said it will be front page tomorrow."

Rainey is not amused by my words.

I roll my eyes. "Serene will not tell a soul."

"He's right. I won't," my sister-in-law cuts in and places a hand over Rainey's.

"In fact, you'll find that she'll be of great assistance when she's not yammerin' about food."

"He's right again. Just not about the food part."

Rainey looks at Serene with something close to hope. "Do you have an idea?"

At that, Serene hesitates. "Not yet, but I will. And if I don't...hell, you can marry Étienne if you want."

Rainey laughs and shakes her head. "If only it was that easy to have a man like yours for the choosin'."

My brows furrow. "It's your future husband, not a car from a production line."

"I know that. That's why I said 'if only.'"

Something about her words doesn't settle well with me, and I simply can't let it go. "I'm baffled. I presumed you truly wanted to find love, not pluck the first man you saw from the street, wipe the dust from his jacket, and call him your fiancé."

The irritated glance Rainey gives me would send most people scurrying in the opposite direction. For myself, my blood pumps faster through my veins. If you want to feel more alive, have a disagreement with this woman.

"You can remain baffled somewhere else, Livingston. I'll stay here and have a lovely conversation with Serene. I'm positive that when Serene has an idea, it will be outstandin'."

I snort. "That's fine, but let it be noted the only reason Serene knows you want a husband and is here is because I informed her."

"I would've told her!"

"When you were an elderly woman?" I challenge.

By now, Rainey's turned in my direction. "You know what, Livingston? You can go take a—"

"Oh, my gosh. Oh, my gosh. Both of you shut up! I just thought of something." In unison, we look at Serene. She stares at the opposite wall with a faraway look in her eye and a cockamamy grin. Slowly, she turns to us. Rainey leans forward. Even I inch closer to hear what she's about to say.

"We should have a bachelor ball."

While Rainey frowns and stares at Serene as though she's grown three heads, I lift a brow. "A bachelor ball?" I repeat.

Serene nods anxiously and smiles. "Absolutely. We— Étienne, me, and you—will select about thirty or so men who we think will be good choices for Rainey. And from there, we allow Rainey to meet the men. Perhaps she'll have dinner with some of the bachelors to better get to know them."

It sounds ludicrous and barbaric. Rainey will never agree to this arrangement.

Crossing my arms, I wait for the outrage, but it never comes. Slowly, I turn my head in Rainey's direction and see her thoughtfully considering Serene's proposition.

"Rainey?"

She remains silent for a moment before she lifts a shoulder. "There are no other suggestions."

While Serene squeals and nearly throws herself into Rainey's arms, I throw my hands in the air. "This cannot be the only idea!"

"Yes, it can because it's just that good." Serene gestures to Rainey. "Look at our girl. She's not bad to look at."

"I'm standin' right here," Rainey interjects.

Serene continues. "Men will be lining up for a chance to win her hand."

"Yes, but for Rainey or for her dowry?" I challenge.

"The amount of her dowry will not be made public. Besides, the Pleasonton name is as well-known as the Lacroix name."

"Serene," I say somberly. "The amount of the dowry will

be made known. There will be fortune hunters."

Serene smiles. "It's up to us to weed out those little fuckers then, isn't it?"

My sister-in-law's crass language makes Rainey's brow lift nearly to her hairline. "I'm startin' to regret invitin' you over," I mutter, rubbing my temples.

"Oh, there's no reason to clutch your pearls, Livingston. It's the truth."

"You truly think you can find her a husband by September?" I challenge.

"I'm confident I can."

"Why can't she?" Rainey chimes in.

I face her. "For starters, you're an uncivilized hellion."

"I am not!"

Crossing my arms, I smirk at her. "Okay. Define civilized then."

Mimicking my actions, Serene steps forward. "Civilized is the opposite of how I feel when I'm around you." Rainey finishes her words with a bright smile.

I look her up and down. "Should we all expect to see this charm that will lure in the man of your dreams?"

"Oh, this charm is only for you."

"Okay, okay. You guys can feed each other compliments later. Right now, we need to focus." Serene steps up to Rainey and holds her arm. "We'll take care of you and make sure you only have the best. No idiot is going to slide past us. You trust me, right?"

Rainey's eyes are wary, but that's not what fills me with apprehension. It's that Rainey isn't promptly rejecting Serene's plan. This is Serene's first idea. Her second is bound to be better.

"Are you positive you want an arranged marriage?" I prod.

"It's not an arranged marriage!" Serene interjects.

"Sounds that way to me."

"An arranged marriage is where the groom or bride is picked out by the parents. That's not the case here," Serene argues as she sits back down.

"Absolutely. This situation is considerably different because her guardian will be the one to have final approval," I say mockingly.

Serene crosses her arms and gives me a murderous expression. "Rainey will obviously have the final say."

"Of course, as long as we all agree this is a thinly veiled arranged marriage."

"Call it an arranged marriage again, and I'm going to re-arrange your face."

"Enough!" Rainey hollers, pulling Serene and me out of what was about to be a long argument. She takes a deep breath. "I agree to Serene's proposal."

Serene claps her hands together in victory and squeals, while my mouth falls open. "You cannot be serious."

"As long as all the bachelors have a significant fortune of their own, I don't see why not."

Not once did I ever picture Rainey agreeing to this preposterous idea.

Sheepishly, Rainey shrugs. "It's just that I would appreciate the bachelors all havin' money of their own."

"How is Serene's bachelor scheme any different than Miles's dowry?" I ask.

"It's different because she'll be the one to make the choice," Serene answers. She looks at Rainey, her gaze imploring. "Rainey, I understand none of this is ideal. But I think, deep down, the reason you said yes to my idea is because you truly want to settle down, marry, and start a family of your own. Am I right, or have the hormones gone straight to my head?"

"Your hormones have gone straight to your head," I reply

"Can it, Lacroix," Serene says, without looking my way.

Biting down on her lower lip, Rainey looks back and forth between Serene and me before she nods. "Havin' a family wouldn't be terrible."

My eyes widen at the same time Serene says, "I knew it! I knew you wanted to settle down!" Serene is beaming from ear to ear, but I watch Rainey carefully and I know she's hiding something.

"I need to pee for the fiftieth time today," my sister-in-law announces.

"And for the fiftieth time, you don't need to tell us," I say as I help Serene up. She waddles out of the room, but not before she hugs Rainey. She steps back and directs her attention to me.

"I will acquiesce to calling this a marriage of convenience. Deal?" Serene holds her hand out for me to shake. Reluctantly, I take it. "Fine. The two of you can do what you want. But this is never going to work. Serene, you can't tame this." I gesture to Rainey.

By this point, Rainey is seething with annoyance. "Once again, I'm standin' right here."

Turning to her, I grin. "I am quite aware of that."

Serene isn't listening, though. She's too thrilled that both Rainey and I have agreed to her bachelor idea. "I will speak to Étienne tonight, and we'll get started on finding your eligible bachelors immediately!" she calls out happily and leaves the room. "One week, everybody. One week!"

Rainey nods, but there's a hint of dare I say it...fear? Which is impossible. Rainey looks fear in the eye and laughs. Sighing, I take Serene's seat. Linking my hands together, I drape them across my stomach.

Rainey remains standing, facing the window. I'm afforded the view of her slender figure and sharp profile. As though she can sense me staring, she looks over her shoulder at me.

"I should leave, too. I told Momma I would help her—"

"You do not have to agree to this outrageous plan," I cut in.

Rainey crosses her arms. "Do you have any other plans in mind?"

"Yes."

"Well, are you goin' to tell me, or do I have to stand here in suspense?"

I rub my jaw as I carefully think my words over. "My plan is to find out the real reason you agreed to this bachelor farce because I don't believe you want to marry and have children."

Rainey juts her chin out. "Perhaps it is. You don't know

that."

"But it isn't," I say quietly.

Her mouth opens and shuts before she shakes her head. "Livingston…" Rainey stares at the floor and then back up at me. "I have no time."

The way her voice drops causes me to stand. I take a step closer. "Why not?"

Her dark eyes never waver from mine as she takes a deep breath and squares her shoulders. "My family is penniless."

I expected numerous explanations, but not this. "What do you mean?"

"There's no money," she says patiently. "Momma broke the news to me days ago that we are in financial peril."

Her sudden interest in finding a spouse and getting her dowry makes sense. Dread fills my stomach. This isn't what I wanted to hear, though, because the Pleasonton family has worked hard for their money. Like my family, their success wasn't born overnight. My brain can't accept that it's gone.

"What about the land?" I ask.

She shakes her head. "It's all gone."

"How?"

"It was sold to pay off debts."

"Has this been takin' place for years?"

Rainey nods. It seems out of the question to believe that Pleas would ever know about the family finances and not reach out for help. He had to know that Étienne and I would assist in any way. He knew that, right? Guilt gnaws at my conscience that this occurred, and I remained oblivious.

Furtively, Rainey glances in the direction of the hall and leans in. "I trust I have your discretion."

"Rainey, of course."

She dips her head, preventing me from seeing her eyes. Briefly, I cover my mouth with my hands as I try to think this over. Étienne is the brains of the family, but I've been known to be adept and reliable during trying times.

Suddenly, I lift my head as a thought occurs to me. "Who's your accountant?"

"I'm not certain. I believe Momma said his name was a Mr. Clarence —"

I groan and shake my head. "Clarence Sedwig?"

Rainey's eyes light up. "That sounds familiar."

"That old man can't tell the difference between a contract and a scroll. For all your family knows, there could be money left and you don't need to follow Serene with her bachelor plan."

It's a rarity to see Rainey quiet. But here she stands, steps away, nodding along with wide eyes. She's never looked more terrified yet equally hopeful in her entire life.

"I'll look through your family's books," I blurt because I never want to see her look like that again.

Without a thought, Rainey takes a step closer. "Truly?" she says in a hushed tone.

"Of course. I'll always do what I can to help your family."

It's then she launches herself into my arms.

Momentarily stunned, it takes me a few seconds to respond. The average span for a friendly hug is a few seconds. At least that's what I've been told. Rainey and I departed the friendly hug station the moment I wrapped my arms around her and splayed my fingers against her lower back, then squeezed tighter. The tips of my fingers brush against the sides of her ribs, and she sucks in a sharp breath.

And then a decidedly odd thing happens. I bend down and bury my head in the crook of her neck. Her entire body locks up, but she doesn't push me away.

Loudly, I clear my throat before I back away.

"I'll make sure you have all the ledgers. Anythin'. Anythin' you need," Rainey rushes out.

I think what we both need is for her brother to come back and provide us the answers of how any of this happened. Of why he gave her a dowry and made me the executor, or how the Pleasonton's fortune ever disappeared to begin with. Since that's impossible, I offer what I think is the second-best option: my help.

"We'll figure this out," I assure her.

Unlike last night when I told her I had a plan and didn't, this time I do. And it doesn't center around Serene's ridiculous bachelor charade in the slightest...

CHAPTER TEN

LIVINGSTON

One week later, the deadline to find bachelors for Rainey arrives.

My signature grin is firmly fixed on my face as I saunter up to the front door. Even the birds are chirping in the trees in encouragement. Nothing will bring me down. Ben opens the front door of Belgrave right on cue.

I smile at him. "My good man! Thank you!"

He seems baffled by my jovial mood. I know I haven't been my typical self since I came back from the Great War, but sometimes you have to make exceptions. Doesn't Ben know it's a perfect day to have a wonderful day?

Tucking my hands into my pockets, I whistle as I walk up the stairs. Serene may be upset that I didn't attempt to find Rainey any bachelors, but I had no options. I was the black sheep of my family. And a black sheep is typically friends with fellow black sheep. Hell, the only reason Étienne was my closest confidant is because we're connected by blood.

I make it to the second-floor landing with the mindset I'll explain to Serene there's no need for the urgency and desperation. We have sixty days, and sixty days is plenty of time for me to pore over the Pleasonton accounts and discover just how dire the situation is. Serene won't be happy with my explanation, but once she finds out the truth, she'll understand there was no need for the bachelors.

No need at all.

My grin widens as I walk down the hall, but as I approach the closed ballroom doors, my smile fades because inside, I can hear the rumble of voices. Deep male voices.

Serene wouldn't.

Without a second thought, I burst into the ballroom. No one notices my arrival. There have to be nearly thirty men in the room.

She did.

They stand in groups of threes, speaking to one another as though they're waiting for a race to begin. Although in this case, it isn't a horse they're betting on—it's Rainey. The outrageous part is some of the faces are familiar to me! Some I grew up with, others I drank with, and there's even one or two I've gone up against for stealing a woman they were sweet on.

Before I have a chance to have a word with any of them and ask who and what they were told, there's a sharp whistle and then a snapping of fingers.

The grown men quiet down like boys at boarding school and face the middle of the ballroom.

"Bachelors, if you will, please line up by height," Serene calls out in an authoritative voice.

She walks back and forth with a clipboard cradled to her chest. Rainey stands two steps in front of her, her posture erect and hands clasped in front of her. Although she appears calm and collected, I know she's anything but by the way her nails dig into her palms.

Scanning the room, I'm not surprised to find my brother leaning against the wall watching the scene play out in front of him with a look of boredom. His eyes are missing nothing, though. Immediately, he looks in my direction. My eyes widen, and I nudge my head toward his wife. He shrugs, a gesture that says, *you know how Serene is*.

I walk toward her and Rainey. Rainey's staring at the men with an unreadable look on her face, and Serene's talking a mile a minute. I tap her on the shoulder. "A word please?"

Turning my way, she smiles and says loudly. "Ah! You decided to show!"

I lower my voice. "What's this?"

She gestures to the men and then says just as quietly, "This is the plan that we agreed on. Remember?" She taps a finger against her chin before she leans forward. "Oh, wait! You dipped out on me and didn't recruit any men for Rainey."

"I don't recall agreein' to anythin'. Where did you find these men?"

Smiling triumphantly, Serene leans back. "Your brother and Asa."

I snort and glance in Étienne's direction. Impossible. He and Asa would never go along with this farce. The expression of guilt on my brother shows me my presumption was one more thing I was wrong about.

Serene steps away and looks down at her clipboard. "You're really dickin' with my bachelor spirit. You know that, right? Go stand by your brother and mumble over there."

Étienne takes that moment to walk over. He dips his head and whispers into his wife's ear although his voice carries. "Serene, I love you. I truly do. But are the cards necessary?"

She looks at him with wide eyes. "It's absolutely necessary."

I give the men a closer inspection to figure out what my brother is referring to. Sure enough, each bachelor has a tag with a number around their neck as though they're livestock at an auction. "Wait...why do they have those?"

Rainey clears her throat and walks toward the three of us. "If I may explain?"

"Please do," I say.

"Upon entering the ballroom, Serene made the bachelors put on tags. The numbers are linked to a certain bachelor to keep track of him."

"I made the suggestion," Étienne cut in.

I turn to him as though he's gone mad. He has been spending far too much time with his wife.

"I fashioned the tags with Alex's nanny late into the night," Serene chimes in excitedly. "And in fine print, beneath the numbers, you'll find the bachelor's name, likes, dislikes, location, and current employment status."

"I did not tell her to do *that*," Étienne heavily emphasizes.

Serene turns to him. "I know, but I really felt we were playing off each other, you know?"

By now, the men are all staring at the four of us and the spectacle we're creating. I regret coming here. The high spirits I had this morning have vanished now. There will never be any reasoning with Serene.

While defeat rocks through me, Étienne and Serene continue their debate about who had the better ideas. I wave a hand between them, attracting their attention. "Will the two of you stop? The details of the tag system are not important. Just say what you need to say to these men so they can all leave because right now they're all starin'."

Serene stands tall and looks at the bachelors as if she forgot they were here. Holding a fist to her mouth, she clears her throat. "Sorry for the brief interruption. I want to start by saying thank you for showing up." Serene looks at Rainey. "Rainey and I haven't been lifelong friends, yet it certainly feels like it. When she told me she was ready to find Mr. Right, I wanted to waste no time, and that's why you men are here. The thirty of you are easily the most eligible bachelors in the South, no?"

The men rapidly nod.

"Let's place everyone throughout the room so Rainey has the chance to speak with all of you. Bachelors one through five can go over there." Serene points to one corner of the ballroom. "Bachelors six through ten you can go there." She goes through her list until six groups of five are split up around the ballroom. Feeling satisfied that everyone followed directions, Serene continues, "Rainey will spend ten minutes with each group and converse with the bachelors. At the end, Rainey will choose her top fifteen."

My gaze shifts to Rainey. The entire time Serene speaks, she stares at the floor, avoiding the eyes of the bachelors before her. Doesn't Rainey realize this does not need to happen? I've begun looking at her family's ledgers!

"Before we begin, are there any questions?"

A bachelor raises his hand. In unison, all heads shift in his direction. He slowly lowers his hand and looks around as though he's having second thoughts. "There's been talk Miss Pleasonton's family is…destitute, and that's the reason she's in search of a husband."

Rainey's shoulders stiffen. As do mine. I don't know what stuns me more, that word has begun to spread about the Pleasonton's financial ruin or that this man had the gall to ask about it in front of everybody.

There's a heavy silence in the ballroom as we all wait for his question to be addressed. Serene narrows her eyes, trying to get a better look at his tag.

"A Southern lady never discusses such horrendous gossip," my sister-in-law says. I swear on all the money to my name she creates an accent that's almost as thick as mine. "But to alleviate everybody's worries, the Pleasonton family has no money issues. Rainey's intentions are pure." Serene smiles and slaps a hand against her clipboard. "Now you can keep talking to me, or you all can speak with this beautiful lady." Serene gestures to Rainey and holds Étienne's pocket watch in front of her, concentrating on the time. I wouldn't be surprised if she pickpocketed him while they were talking about the tags. "Round one of conversations starts…now."

"*Que dieu nous aide,*" I mutter beneath my breath. To say she was taking this seriously would be an understatement.

Everyone looks at Rainey expectantly. This can't start without her. Serene walks over to her with a tense smile. "Rainey, why do you look as if you're facing a firing squad? There are thirty handsome, rich young men in front of you. Did I mention they're rich? You would want for nothing. Hell, you could wipe your ass with a fifty-dollar bill for the rest of your life if you wanted. Go speak to them." Serene all but shoves her toward the first group of men.

Rainey walks forward but not before she looks over her shoulder with a frown. "I'm goin'."

Watching Rainey approach the men feels wrong. I have to stop myself from stepping forward and telling Rainey to come with me because then she'll stay just to make me furious.

I merely stand beside my brother and his wife, who looks particularly pleased with her work.

Étienne crosses his arms and looks at the men. "From thirty men to fifteen?" He glances at Serene from the corner of his eye. "I understand you want to move quickly but is all of this necessary?"

She rears back slightly and looks at him. "Does a bear take a shit in the woods? Yes, it's necessary! Rainey is finding her soulmate, and there's nothing greater." A steely determination enters her eyes. "However, this is a game. And. I. Play. To. Win."

"All right," Étienne draws out. "But you understand you cannot win because you're already married, correct?"

Serene reaches out and brushes her hand across Étienne's cheek. "Of course, I do." She steps back and looks in Rainey's direction. "This is so exciting. It's like I'm living my favorite show, *The Bachelorette*, through her."

"What show?" I ask.

Next to me, Étienne groans and rubs his temples. Serene has made tremendous progress to keep information about her time to herself. However, when she becomes excited, she can't help herself, and the words flow out. I've always said her tongue works faster than her brain, but that's the most endearing quality about her.

"Uhh…nothing. Forget what I said and stop distracting me." Serene turns her attention to the pocket watch. "I have to watch the time."

Étienne sighs. "We might as well go about our day. This will take a while."

"I'm stayin'," I say, my voice resolute. "God only knows what Serene will do next. Perhaps she'll give them a physical fitness test by makin' all thirty men run into town, jump into the Atlantic, and dive to the bottom for hidden treasure."

"Diving for hidden treasure is a bit much. But a physical fitness test isn't a bad idea," Serene says without taking her eyes off the pocket watch.

Étienne shakes his head and gestures toward a corner of the room. "If you're goin' to be stubborn, I'll wait with you."

"There's nothin' stubborn about me," I say over my shoulder. "Your wife is simply unpredictable."

"She's been unpredictable since the minute she came into our lives. You knew that, yet you asked for her help."

With my back against the wall, I cross my arms. "Remind me to never, ever ask for her help again."

"I would, but Serene has a way of placin' herself in others' lives when she doesn't need to be. She probably would've stepped in either way." Étienne directs his eyes at me. "Why did you ask for her help and not me?"

I focus on the floor. I can't tell him that I hastily told Rainey I had a plan when I didn't because I couldn't handle her tears. Never could. He'd find that rather interesting, and I don't want to explore interesting. At the time, Serene was the best route to take. I finally reply while I itch the back of my neck. "I came to you about the dowry, bein' her executor, and you didn't have a solution."

"No one would have. It's an ironclad legal document," Étienne cuts in.

"Nevertheless, I presumed you were busy, so I turned to Serene," I lie.

"Then this truly could have been avoided."

I grind my teeth together and give a blunt nod. "Yes."

The two of us grow silent and observe the spectacle that Serene has created with her bachelor idea. The cacophony of so many male voices in one room carries across this large space and echoes around me like an off-key tune. I can't help but wince.

The hesitance Rainey felt at approaching the first group of bachelors has all but disappeared as she continues speaking with the third group of men. She actively holds a conversation with them, and a few times, she makes some of the men laugh. She's...she's dare I say it...pleasant? The stories I could tell about this woman would have these men running in the opposite direction.

Serene announces that it's time for Rainey to move to the final group, and as Rainey takes her leave, the men's eyes remain hooked on her.

I cock my head to the side and stand a bit straighter. Why are they looking at her in such a fashion? She's a lady, not a piece of meat. Not to mention she's…Rainey. This isn't appropriate. Not at all. Has everyone lost their senses? Étienne places a hand on my shoulder. *"Reste tranquille. Vous êtes fâché pour rien."*

With outrage shining in my eyes, I look at him, then gesture to the men across the room from us. *"Tu vois ce que je vois!"*

Étienne shrugs and crosses his arms. *"La seule personne qui manifeste de la colère, c'est vous."*

My brother's words strike a chord in me as I look around the room because he's right. Everyone else is the very picture of calm. As for me, I feel as though I'm going to pop a vein. In fact, nothing would make me happier than to pick up the man nearest to Rainey and throw him out the window.

The next several minutes stretch out in front me like a road that has no ending. Right as I'm getting ready to push away from the wall and ask if the time is up, my sister-in-law clears her throat. "Okay," she drawls out as she stares at her clipboard. "That's the time!"

Rainey looks over her shoulder. I feel a sense of victory when I see that Rainey almost looks relieved that this is done, but then I'm concerned. Why is she relieved? Did someone say something inappropriate to her? She stands by Serene, and for the first time today, she looks directly at me.

I could tell by her wide-eyed expression that she wanted to discuss all the conversations she had with the bachelors. She wanted to leave the room as badly as I wanted to hear what she had to say.

I waggle my brows, drawing a giggle from her. That brings me a small sense of satisfaction. Could any other man in this room say they made her laugh? No. Only me. Serene lifts her gaze from the clipboard and looks out of the corner of her eye at Rainey. I wipe my face clean and look away.

There's a small pause before Serene speaks.

"See? It's over. No physical fitness test to be had."

I snort. "That we know of. Let's see what Serene makes them do when she narrows down the men."

"I understand that you're opposed to this bachelor idea, but Serene wants what's best for Rainey."

"And she believes this is it?"

"I helped my wife find some of those men. You know I wouldn't agree to Serene's idea if the bachelors weren't men of good character."

"Would they have been good enough for our sister?"

Étienne appears unamused by my question. "No one was good enough for our sister. Not even her husband."

I shake my head and mutter under my breath, "And look where she's at now…"

Nathalie's stuck in a marriage that may seem all right from the outside, but upon closer inspection, it's withering away like a flower without any sun or water. She would visit from Brignac House in Savannah as much as possible especially after Alex was born, but we've seen less and less of her. And I had a feeling her husband, Oliver, was to blame.

Étienne clucks his tongue and stares thoughtfully at the ground.

None too gently, I elbow his arm. "What is the problem?"

My brother patiently looks at me. "Hmm? Oh, I'm simply ponderin' why a man who would've done close to anythin' to rid himself of Rainey and bein' the executor not so long ago is now diggin' his heels in. Care to explain?"

Because none of this is necessary. I will find a way to make everything all right without Rainey having to marry a man she doesn't know.

"No," I say before my lips draw into a thin line. He will get nothing else from me.

Serene snaps her fingers, and the men quiet down. "All right. I think the time Rainey had with each group went off without a hitch. Now I just need you all to sit tight while Rainey and I deliberate."

While Serene wraps an arm around Rainey's shoulder and turns them around, several conversations break out amongst the men. Everyone's egos are starting to surface. No one wants to believe that they didn't make a good enough first impression.

"She didn't speak to me once!" I hear one bachelor complain. That makes me smile.

Meanwhile, Rainey and Serene remain unaware of the chaos building behind them. Their heads nearly touch as they speak in hushed tones. I don't think the two of them even stop to take a breath. They remain in that position for so long I'm beginning to wonder if they will ever come to an agreement, when finally, they pull away. The two of them share a look. It's impossible for me to read what passes between them. If women become good enough friends, they just have to look at one another to share their feelings. It's remarkably unnerving.

Holding her clipboard out in front of her, Serene begins the methodical process of striking through names. I squint my eyes.

"Are you attemptin' to see what name my wife's crossin' out?" Étienne asks.

"Yes," I reply as I continue to watch Serene go through the list. "My hope is Rainey realized they're all incompetent and wants none of them."

Étienne mutters under his breath just as Serene finishes. She lifts her gaze and smiles at the men.

"Whether you had stayed or left, I had every intention of findin' my way back here to watch this process," my brother says in a hushed whisper. He flings his hand toward his wife and grins. "Serene callin' out orders is where she truly shines."

I cringe. "I feel as though I've become privy to what goes on in your bedroom."

Étienne cuts me a dark look and crosses his arms, making himself comfortable against the wall. The same can't be said for Rainey. It's rare for her to be anything but confident and strong, but right now, she looks ready to jump out of the nearest window.

"Once again, I'd like to thank every bachelor for coming

here today," Serene starts off. "But as we know, we had to shorten the list of men because I think group dates might be frowned upon and perhaps a wee bit awkward."

Nervous laughter rises up throughout the room.

"If I call your number, you may leave." Serene's eyes begin to bounce back and forth between the clipboard and the bachelors. "Bachelor number twenty-four." She hooks her thumb over shoulder in the direction of the doors. Very rapidly, she begins to call out numbers, and the men begin to file out of the room slowly. Some are speechless, and others talk amongst themselves about what they believed went wrong.

As the crowd of men thins out, I watch with rapt attention. Now this? This I can get used to. Étienne was right. Serene is positively ruthless and doesn't stop to glimpse at the men. I don't suppress the grin I'm wearing as the bachelors slink away with their tail tucked between their legs. "Bachelor number two. It's been fun. It's been real. It's been real fun, but you're out of here."

The bachelor looked around him as though Serene said the wrong number before he reluctantly walks away. He moves past me and shoots me an irritated glance, as though I'm the one who delivered the terrible news. At the start of this, he was in good spirits. Not so much now.

My le savage *didn't choose you.*

Of course, I feel a sense of victory because I knew none of these men would be good enough.

Once Serene's finished calling out numbers, she lifts her head and smiles. "I believe that's all for today. For the bachelors standing before me, my husband and I will be in contact to set up social engagements so Rainey can better get to know you all."

"Oh, you'll be in contact with them," I say with enthusiasm to my brother.

Shaking his head, he rubs his temples. "My God no."

The men break apart, seemingly relieved they're potential bachelors and not on the chopping block...for now.

"Beaumont Legare?" Serene calls.

Raising his hand, Beau steps forward, his face is beet red. "I-i-it's Beau."

Serene arches a brow while Rainey looks him up and down with interest. With wide eyes, he stares back.

"What do ladies possibly see in this fellow?" I mutter to Étienne.

My brother shrugs his shoulders. "What do ladies see in you?" he whispers. "Impossible to know."

"I have personality."

"Well, it appears Beau has enough personality to hold a conversation with Rainey."

I have eyes. He doesn't need to tell me. Rainey is staring at Beau as though she's never seen the male specimen before. I've never seen that expression on her face before. Repeatedly, I clench and unclench my hands to release my pent-up frustration that's been building all day.

They would be a horrific match. Rainey wouldn't just have Beau wrapped around her finger; she would crush him beneath the weight of her confidence. Rainey needs a man willing to rise to her words and every challenge she gives. She needs a man who realizes she dresses herself with poise and courage.

The fools standing before her minutes ago are captivated by her smile, but none can handle her.

I shake my head; this won't do, and I seem to be the only person in the room to realize the truth.

Étienne and I walk toward Serene, and in the process, we hear the last part of Beau and Rainey's conversation. They're discussing their favorite hobbies.

"I m-must confess I-I s-spend far to-oo muc-hh time readin', a-and not n-near enough t-time outside," Beau sheepishly confesses.

"Neither do I," Rainey agrees.

I stop the snort that slips from my mouth. Utterly ridiculous! She lived outside as a child and still does.

Rainey whips her head in my direction and narrows her eyes. Beau looks over his shoulder at the rest of us and instantly turns red. It's as though he forgot we were there.

He looks back at Rainey. "I-I s-sh-hould go."

Rainey gives him a brilliant smile. "It was lovely to meet you."

"Y-you as well," Beau says before he leaves.

Rainey watches him go with the same daft expression on her face. I could repeatedly snap my fingers in front of her, and she wouldn't notice. What has gotten into her?

Once the door closes behind him, the spell has broken. She blinks at us, brows puckering slightly. She looks at me for only a moment, and when she does, her gaze hardens. Rainey knows what I'm going to say before I say it, and she doesn't want to hear it.

She turns to Serene and smiles. "I need to use the powder room."

"Please do. We'll be right here," Serene replies.

The doors to the ballroom have opened and shut so many times today I'm surprised they haven't fallen off the hinges.

With just the three of us, Serene heavily leans against Étienne, still clutching her clipboard. I'm not a violent person, but I want to snatch that infuriating object from her hands and break it over my leg.

"I think this could be a love connection," Serene confesses excitedly to Étienne.

Leaning forward, I stare at my sister-in-law. "Have you gone mad? They would be terrible together."

"What makes you say that?"

"They are the complete opposite of one another," I reply.

"Opposites can attract, Livingston."

"They can," I concede. "But in this situation, the results would be disastrous."

"They've only been speaking for a few minutes!"

"I know Rainey."

Serene stands up tall and lifts her brows. "If you know Rainey, then why don't you marry her?"

Her question dangles between the three of us. As they stare at me expectantly, silence fills the room.

"Because I know her," I reply.

"I do have one thought," Étienne says thoughtfully.

"If it's about my tag system, I stand by it," Serene replies heatedly. "Did you hear how fast I was calling out their numbers toward the end?"

"It's not about the tag system. It's about this bachelor idea as a whole."

Is it happening? Is my brother truly realizing the errors of this entire concept and attempting to reason with his wife?

It won't be easy, though. Serene's shoulders are already tense. "Yes?"

"These men have pride. How are you not certain they won't grow tired of bein' paraded around like cattle and then discarded when you and Rainey decide you have no need for them?"

Serene thinks over the question for several seconds before she answers. There's a spark in her eye that puts me on edge. "Because men love a good chase. They want what they can't have. Case in point, I had thirty men in this ballroom vying for Rainey's attention today. Why?"

"Because they were probably coerced here by you," I cut in.

Serene continues without batting an eye. "Because all around them were men who were vying for the same woman, and they all want to say they were chosen. They want to be the one to win it all." A wicked grin spreads across her lips. "That's why this will work and not a single bachelor will back out."

"My theory on why this won't work is Rainey may start out sweet and demure with the bachelors, but that veneer will fade and they'll see how opinionated and self-assured she is and immediately forget about this game you've created."

Both Étienne and Serene watch me with wide eyes. With every word I spoke, my voice rose until it echoed across the ballroom, but I wanted to get my point across. Serene clears her throat and speaks. "Cool it, buddy boy. Strong words attract a strong mind and offend a weak one. Whoever stands by Rainey is the right man."

It was of no use. No one was going to listen to me.

Frustrated, I turn and walk toward the door just as Rainey walks back in. I don't say a word to her, causing her eyes to widen ever so slightly.

Behind me, Serene rushes toward Rainey. "And then there were fifteen. Dun, dun, dun," Serene says ominously before she begins recommending that Rainey meet with Beau first. Nat spoke so highly of him. He was so handsome, and shy, and bright…and so on and so forth.

While my sister-in-law mentally picks out the perfect gown for Rainey to wear down the aisle, I storm out of the ballroom. I need some air. Everyone in my family has gone utterly mad. Serene's plan was drawn from boredom, and it's not reliable. Something is bound to go wrong. That's why my heart is pounding so rapidly, and fury courses through my blood.

Perhaps I should look into getting Nat on the first train to Charleston. With my sister home, maybe Serene can go back to being the levelheaded sister-in-law I've known her to be.

That is, if Nat agrees. As much as I blamed Oliver for limiting how often my brother and I were able to see our sister, there was no disputing the fact that he was decidedly different after he came back from the war. Everyone was, but the last time he visited, I saw the bleakness in his eyes. I couldn't fault him for that.

"There you are!"

Lifting my gaze, I find none other than Conrad Duplass lingering in the foyer. Conrad and I go way back. He was the black sheep of his family, could drink until the sun came up, and never encountered a party he didn't enjoy. I didn't see him in the ballroom, but it makes me wonder how many men I could've possibly known upstairs. But I can't very well ignore Conrad. He steps away from me. I suppress a groan and walk to him. No place is safe today. "Conrad, are you confused? Lacroix house is in Charleston," I say with a smile.

Throwing his head back, he laughs heartily. "I'm well aware of your address. I'm here for Miss Pleasonton. I'm one of the fifteen bachelors that made it through."

He says that with pride, as though he's won a high

achievement. What will it be like when it narrows down to ten and then five?

That will never happen, remember? You will find a better solution for Rainey.

"Are you still foxed from last night? There's still time to change your mind."

Because I'm Livingston. Because I'm the Lacroix brother who everyone can depend on to deliver a laugh, Conrad does just that. "There's no need for that. Étienne spoke to me two nights ago regardin' Rainey's search for a husband."

"You have seen her, haven't you?"

"Yes, I have. Have you?" he counters with a wink. I've shared many raucous quips with Conrad in the past. However, this time I do not laugh.

"What can you tell me about Rainey?"

My brows furrow. "Pardon?"

"Rainey Pleasonton. I want to know everythin' about her." Conrad leans in and smiles. "Everythin'."

I can think of many things I'd rather do right now than be pulled into Serene's little bachelor debacle.

Such as learning embroidery. Maybe become locked in a sitting parlor with mommas anxious to marry their daughter's off to the last Lacroix man. Perhaps drink paint.

It sounds severe, but if I open my mouth once to help a bachelor, I am positive they'll all come running. In the wrong hands, powerful information can be a dangerous thing. Besides, how can I describe a woman who has a face from heaven and a mouth from hell? That requires liquor, and a lot of it.

"I don't know if there's enough time to define Rainey, my friend," I say with a smile. There'd be no way to prepare any of the men. Rainey's too skilled with an arrow and her words. She reads far too many books and will discuss every detail she finds fascinating, even if you do not. Her sense of humor is as wicked as the curse words that occasionally slip from her mouth. "I'm afraid to say she's a wild animal that can't be tamed."

"Don't tell me you still harbor anger from when she shot

you in the leg all those years ago? I recall hearin' she used a gun?"

"My God, no. It was a bow and arrow, and how many people know that?"

"Everyone in Charleston, Lacroix. Now tell me everythin' about Rainey."

"I know just as much as you. She's still the same Rainey who chased after all of us when she wasn't allowed to play with the boys."

"Oh, but that's not true." Conrad leans in and lowers his voice. "She doesn't look the same, and this time, the boys want her to play."

As Conrad laughs at his own joke, my hands curl into tight fists. The smile on my face is strained, but it remains in place so Conrad is none the wiser.

If I don't find a new solution to Rainey's dowry fiasco, then the next few weeks will truly be torture.

God be with us all.

Especially the men because if Rainey doesn't shoot them with an arrow in a fit of anger, then I'm bound to kill at least one in a bout of rage.

The question is, who? And how long will it take?

CHAPTER ELEVEN

RAINEY

I must say this is highly unorthodox."

"Momma, I'm aware of that." You've only told me twelve thousand times. "But my hands are tied."

"And you're certain Livingston approved of this?" This is Momma's routine line of questioning ever since the bachelor game began.

"Yes. He approves."

Momma's lips purse into a tight line. She doesn't approve, and honestly, I'm uncertain of where Livingston stands. It was days ago when the bachelors convened on Belgrave, and the number went from thirty to fifteen. Since then, Livingston's been remarkably quiet, and I haven't heard much from him, something I find oddly unsettling. Livingston is many things, but quiet he is not

Truthfully, I'm unsure of where I stand. At the beginning, I resisted the very idea of finding a husband, but the men were not deplorable. Serene did a wonderful job of selecting each bachelor. And thus far, the experience has not been altogether unpleasant. As of now, I've had dinner with Philip or, as Serene called him, "bachelor number twelve." Conversation was pleasant, but whenever a quip slipped from my mouth, Serene and Étienne would laugh, and he would stare at me with a blank face. My words were lost on him. That wasn't a positive sign.

I strolled down The Battery during a pleasant sunset with

Franklin. Also known as "bachelor number three." At least, the sunset appeared pleasant. I wouldn't know. Franklin was personable, and his witticism had me laughing more than once, but Franklin liked to sing. A lot. High or low pitch, it made no difference to him. Singing was singing.

I wasn't creating my happily ever after, but I was open to the idea of discovering whether one of them would be a fitting husband. However, I drew a fine line at having no humor and constant singing at every turn.

"Who shall be there with you?" Momma asks.

My maid tugs on my hair as I sit in front of my vanity, causing me to wince. "Étienne and his wife."

Momma's brows lift in an elegant arch. "Oh?"

Only Leonore Pleasonton can place such heavy emphasis on the word, "Oh."

I look at Momma in the mirror. "Is that not satisfactory enough for you?"

"Étienne is a very respectable gentleman," Momma replies.

"But not Serene?"

Momma pauses before she says, "She's quite…crass. And no one who's so heavy with child should be in public."

I lift a shoulder. "Serene has been nothin' but gracious to me and instrumental in findin' such upstandin' gentlemen. I think once you get to know her, you'd be pleasantly surprised."

Momma doesn't reply as she watches my maid weave the headband through my chignon. "My Lord, Momma, it's a miracle you're not becomin' seasick with all your pacin'."

I hiss in a sharp breath as my maid tugs on my hair once again and focus my attention on Momma's reflection in the mirror. She waves a hand at me and makes another lap around my room. The last time I saw Momma walk this much was durin' a sale at a local store.

"You would understand my worries if you were in my situation. It's only a matter of time before people about town began to question why you're suddenly hangin' off every man's arm from here to Georgia!"

I bite down on my tongue to keep from saying that it's

certainly better than the alternative: losing everything we own. I give the maid a furtive glance and smile tightly at Momma. "Well, I guess if they say anything, you'll just have to tell them I'm ready to find love after all this time."

Momma gives me a less than amused expression. The maid takes a step back while my scalp screams in protest. I stand and walk to my full-length mirror in the corner to inspect her handiwork.

I'm willing to push the pain aside for a flattering hairstyle. Turning to the side, I give my royal blue dress a thorough inspection. The back dips lower than most of my evening dresses, but I happen to love the embroidery of this specific dress. The sash tied around my waist accentuates my curves, and the material swoops low, creating a train in the back. Momma loved it too when she went with me to get alterations. Now, she wears a leery expression as though this is my first season.

I thank my maid for her help and turn to Momma. "Serene and Étienne should be here shortly with my date, Mr. Legare. He's an upstandin' gentleman. His brother is a colleague of Étienne's. He comes from good stock."

The phrase "good stock" feels wrong coming from my lips, but I need to appease Momma and speak her language. Sure enough, her eyes widen, and I swear color comes back to her cheeks.

"A colleague of Étienne's?"

I shake my head as I grab my wrap and clutch from my bed. "You seem to have had a remarkable change of heart."

"There's nothin' remarkable about it," Momma says, trailing me as I walk out of my bedroom. "Your reputation, or what's left of it, needs to remain intact."

"It will."

"And I worry because —"

At the landing of the stairs, I turn and face Momma. "Don't. Please. There's already so much to worry about. Why fret over somethin' that's out of your control?"

Momma straightens and juts her chin forward, almost as

if she's getting ready to give me a tongue-lashing. Instead, she whispers, "Because you're all I have left."

For several seconds, all I can do is blink at her. There are many traits that set Momma and me apart, but one thing we don't do is share our true feelings. Swallowing, I tentatively lay a hand on her shoulder. I should say something kind and heartwarming. The words exist inside me, but they never seem to find the way out of my mouth.

There's a knock on the door, saving me from this strained moment. One of the servants opens the door and reveals Beau's perfect face. I spot the Lacroix car running on the street. Beau sees me and gives me a shy smile. I smile back and look at Momma. "I'll be home later tonight."

Placing a bright smile on her face, Momma faces my date as though she didn't just gut me with her words.

Being ever the gentleman, Beau holds out his hand for me to take. As I step out of the car and onto the street, I can't help but notice his grip is firm, but not too tight.

Everything about him is so…perfect.

Serene stands beside Étienne with her arm looped through his. Her eyes are as wide as saucers, and she has a smile from ear to ear as she looks at Beau and me. She's a cat who ate the canary, and I have no doubt that when we retreat to the ladies' room, she'll besiege me with endless questions about my thoughts of Beau.

The four of us proceed to walk toward the entrance of the theater. The Garden Theatre opened nearly a year ago. It made a name for itself in Charleston, so it's no surprise a small crowd has already gathered outside the doors.

While we wait in line, I watch as cars pull to a stop in front of the theater, the brakes lightly screeching. Drivers will step out and open the door for whoever is in the back, and then they'll drive away. Another car will replace its spot, and the process repeats itself. Downtown Charleston can't seem to handle the number of cars on the narrow roads. Every so often, I'll hear a driver impatiently honk their horn. Tonight, the noises and the crowds do not bother me. Standing beside Beau, I feel hopeful. Serene's bachelor plan could go better than I ever dreamed.

After several minutes of waiting, we receive our tickets and make our way inside. The entry was designed to complement the theater's name with a garden of flowers and trellises. If that wasn't enough, there are caged canaries. Their singing voices combine with the sound of women's heels echoing on the tile floor. Crystal chandeliers are hung, illuminating the shadows near the ornate archways.

As I look around at the multitude of people, it occurs to me it's been quite a long time since I've had a relaxing and enjoyable night. But the minute I see the familiar faces, and their eyes focused on me and my date, I immediately regret this night out. Expecting news of my bachelor ball not to spread across town would be delusional of me. The second I stepped foot out of my home with one of the bachelors, people started wondering, and since then, all eyes and ears have been on me and becoming more than bothersome.

Serene, on the other hand, is uninterested at everyone watching us and holds her head high. She's wearing a pale blue long-sleeved gown, with a high neckline, gold lace insertions, and a sash of the same color directly above her burgeoning stomach that she makes no attempt to cover. Confinement while pregnant is something Serene loathes. One of her hands freely rests on her stomach. Whether it's subconscious or on purpose doesn't matter to me. Serene is the same whether in public or in private.

"My God, it's hot in here," she mutters under her breath and begins to cool herself with her fan. "I don't know if I'll make it through the entire show."

"If I have to sit through this, then so shall you," Étienne says beside her.

Serene gently nudges him and turns to me. "I heard this silent movie is based on a book. Have you ever read anything by Jean Webster?"

"I haven't," I answer.

I can't remember the last time I sat down to read. Most likely before the war occurred. For my sixteenth birthday, Livingston gave me a book, *The Shepherd of the Hills* by Harold Bell Wright.

His inscription inside was:

I haven't decided which will be more damaging in your hands, your bow and arrow or this book.

I do know these words contained within haven't left me with a scar...yet.

Happy Birthday, le savauge.

I read the novel numerous times and still have it on my shelf. As the memory plays in my mind, a faint smile appears on my lips. Immediately, I mentally chastise myself. This isn't the time to become nostalgic or think of Livingston.

We take our seats in the first mezzanine, and as I smooth the material of my dress around my legs, I look around the spacious theater. The chandeliers are dimly lit in the auditorium as people walk the narrow aisles and begin to take their seats.

Directly in front of the stage is the small orchestra, preparing for the film by checking their instruments. The stage is empty, and the curtains are pulled back, revealing a bare wall for the silent film to show on. I feel a sense of anticipation knowing I'll see the actors, read the titles, and hear the beautiful music. I don't go to the theater enough.

Beside me, Beau clears his throat. "Y-you lo-ok lovely."

Turning to him, I smile. "Thank you."

He smiles back, and his features transform from handsome to breathtaking. But he manages to keep a sincerity in his eyes that I don't know if I've ever seen in a man before. "D-dare I say y-yo-ou a-are the p-prettiest woman here."

"Not everyone has taken their seats. Don't speak too soon," I tease.

"I-I stand by my w-words."

My smile widens. How can I give a wisecrack to that? "What did you think of the first bachelor event at Belgrave?"

"I'm g-grateful to be o-one of the fifteen men standin'."

"I'm grateful you are too."

"A-although I must confess I'm a-apprehensive to see what will be required of us next to win your hand."

I lean toward him and lower my voice to a conspiring whisper. "Not even I know that."

I notice when Beau becomes more comfortable in a conversation, his stutter significantly fades, but not entirely. Which I wouldn't want. I rather like how he talks. And perhaps, as the night continues and we talk some more, I'll discover there's more I like.

"Well, well, well…" Serene murmurs under her breath.

I look toward the focus of her attention and see none other than Livingston Lacroix. My heart drops to my stomach. What is he doing here? I can't count on one hand the number of times he's been to the theater. If there's no liquor in sight, there's no Livingston.

"Good evenin', everybody," Livingston greets.

At once, his eyes meet mine. I try not to flinch at the direct contact, and the intensity I see swirling in his hazel irises. His focus switches to Beau who had begun speaking to Étienne before Livingston walked up.

Livingston's eyes narrow, and his lips draw into a thin line. My word, what could he have against Beau? No one has a bad word to say about him.

Beau's remarkably shy and merely dips his head. I sit there, arms crossed, trying to figure out what Livingston is doing here.

"Hello, Livingston," Serene says.

Étienne leans forward, bracing his elbows on his knees, and chimes in. "This is an unexpected surprise."

"Why? I happen to love the theater."

"You've never been here. Not once. Ever. In your entire life," Étienne replies, his tone glib.

"Yes, but I've been to a theater," Livingston points out.

The four of us stare at him expectantly. It takes him a moment before he looks to his left and realizes a woman is standing beside him and has been for the entire exchange. In all honesty, I didn't know she was with him. I thought she was merely waiting to be seated. I watch her carefully and notice how Livingston places a hand on her back. Who is she to him?

"Please forgive me. Everyone, this is Rosalie."

I've never seen Rosalie before, thus proving my theory Livingston's had to branch out to other towns to find women. I look her up and down one more time. She's nothing like the moaning cow he was with weeks ago. I suppose that's a step in the right direction, but I still don't care for her.

"Hello," she greets in a breathy voice that makes you question whether it's real or a well-practiced action done in front of her mirror.

"I hope the four of you don't mind if we sit here?" Livingston asks. He looks at everyone but me.

"N-not at all," Beau says.

Much to my chagrin, I watch Livingston and his date occupy the two empty seats to my left. I expect Rosalie to sit beside me, but instead, it's Livingston. I try not to let my shock show.

The intention of tonight was to get to know Beau. He seemed like an upstanding gentleman. Serene says he's shy, but if a topic of conversation arises that he's passionate about, he turns into a different person. Étienne told me he enjoys reading. It was something we had in common.

Last night as I fell asleep, I envisioned us speaking of our favorite stories and the numerous lives we lived through our most cherished characters. Maybe, just maybe, we would share a mutual love for the same story. I wouldn't have to meet any of the other bachelors because Beau would be it.

It was a fanciful fantasy that would never come into existence. Especially with Livingston next to me.

As if he can sense me thinking of him, he glances at me as he makes himself comfortable. I can feel those hazels on me a mile away. "How are you, *le savauge*?"

I bite down on my tongue to keep from saying something harsh in front of Beau. He's so quiet and calm, and I want him to have a good first impression of me and not see me explode on Livingston. Not yet at least. That's always bound to happen.

I turn and give Livingston a dazzling smile. "Quite well. And you?"

His eyes narrow a fraction as he looks between Beau and me. I don't know why. Beau's engaged in a conversation with Étienne. The minute Beau's done, I will ask if he wouldn't mind switching places with me.

I know the question and the white-hot awareness of him won't abate until there's space between us.

I've run out of time, though, when the wall sconces become dimmed. Around us, voices fade, and in unison, heads turn to the stage, waiting for the film to begin. Somewhere in the theater somebody coughs. Another clears their throat.

The blank wall swallowing the stage suddenly fills with light. With every film I've seen, there's never been a steadiness, but that simply adds to the experience. The picture always appears to be moving even though it's not. I try to notice every single detail before the scene changes, even down to the opening credits.

A backdrop that appears is the shadow of a boat with numerous people sitting inside and the outline of mountains in the back. I begin to read the first subtitles. *Baby Souls, Kings of the Future, bearer*—

"An interestin' rumor has found its way to me."

Gritting my teeth, I keep my focus forward. Livingston is simply attempting to get a rise out of me.

"Do you care to know?"

Briefly, my eyes close. He's not going to quit until I reply. "Not particularly."

There's a pause, then Livingston whispers, "Very well. I'll tell you anyway. I've heard the bettin' books around town have made a game of your bachelors. A lot of people have become highly invested in your future husband."

Eyes wide, I turn toward Livingston. "You cannot be serious."

"When have I lied about a bet?"

"When you're losin'," I whisper.

Livingston shakes his head as the corner of his mouth lifts. "Believe me on this."

I don't reply and return my gaze to the film, but I'm thinking about his words. There are bets being placed on my future husband. I shouldn't be shocked. Yet I am.

"Do you want to know who is in the runnin' to win?" Livingston persists.

More than anything. "No, I do not."

"Sure?"

"Positive."

I attempt to read the subtitles and try to immerse myself in the film. How much have I missed? We're well past the boat scene; now the scene's one of a brick wall with trash cans that are filled to the brim. The ground is covered in debris. It's a stark comparison to the first scene.

"You're all dolled up tonight," Livingston says into my ear.

There's no possible way I can follow the film sitting next to Livingston. Not with him interrupting me every few minutes. The worst part is he's doing it to drive me mad. And it's working. I'm not going to let that show. Absolutely not. Beau is here, and I'm going to be the very picture of a Southern belle.

He shifts closer. "Is this attire all for Beau?"

Abruptly, I turn to him, my eyes ablaze. "It's impolite to speak durin' a movie," I hiss.

Keeping his eyes on mine, he holds his palm between our bodies. "Then let us write."

My eyes flick between his splayed fingers that leads to his palm and then back to his face. "You've gone mad," I whisper.

The rules of the write hand game are very simple and clear. One person will ask a question, and the other will answer by writing on the person's hand who asked the question. They will have three tries to guess what the answer is before the turn moves to the next. It's been years since I've played this. The last time was at Belgrave when I was nine. Livingston's parents hosted a party, and it was the first event Momma stepped out from mourning for. Miles and I still hadn't properly come to terms with the loss of Daddy, and unfortunately, we fought constantly. Momma made sure we were separated during that dinner by placing Livingston between us. I wanted to let my brother know how I felt. Keeping us apart wouldn't stop me, so I enlisted the help of Livingston. Maybe he took pity on me for the loss of Daddy because he agreed, and beneath the table, held his palm out to me and said, "Of course I will help you."

If I remember correctly, I never said thank you to him for being on my side that night and delivering all my messages.

Livingston shrugs. "Take your pick," he whispers back.

Sighing, I look to my right. Beau is transfixed by the movie. My eyes veer to Livingston's date, Rosalie. She, too, is absorbed in the movie. I had the same intentions, but I'd given up hope of keeping up with the subtitles and understanding the plot. Maybe another time.

"All right," I reluctantly agree, knowing that sometime at a later date, I will make Livingston pay.

Even in the darkness of the theater, I can see Livingston's wicked grin. It causes my stomach to flip. He rests his arm on the armrest and holds his hand out, palm up. I stare at his hand as though it's a trap. Ready to latch onto my hand and not let go.

"Your dress, it's new...correct?" he whispers.

I presumed we would discuss tonight's events. Not what I'm wearing. I take another deep breath. Reaching my index finger out, I lightly drag my nail against his skin, *YES*.

A small shiver rocks through me as I write the three-letter word. It feels indecent to be doing this in public. But this is a mere dare. A simple game. And we've been doing these for years. What's one more time?

"Did Beau notice?"

"It's my turn to ask a question," I whisper.

"I made amendments to the rules because you don't want

to talk," Livingston whispers back. "Now, did Beau notice?"

At the mention of my escort, I sneak another glance at Beau. He seems unbothered by Livingston's unprompted dare. My arm aligns with Livingston's as I write *NO*.

The wicked grin that was fixed on Livingston's face when we began this game begins to fade. The light from the screen plays across the angles of his face, showcasing his sharp cheekbones, and the perfect angle of his nose. I've said it once and I'll say it again, no man should be this handsome. Black brows slanted low over his light eyes, and his focus is devoted on his hand where my fingers still linger. Immediately, I snatch my hand back and place it on my lap.

"Do you think Beau is your bachelor?"

With that question, I pause. For one, it's impossible to write *I AM UNCERTAIN*, and two, I'm beginning to believe it's impractical to think one date can decide your fate with a person.

There has to be more time, more conversation.

"You're not answerin'," Livingston whispers into my ear.

"This is absurd. Let's watch the movie!" I hiss even though I make no attempt to move away from him.

Don't look at him. Do not look at him!

Mentally, I give myself a pat on the back for keeping my eyes trained forward. Out of the corner of my right eye, I spot Serene leaning forward, pointedly looking back and forth between Livingston and me.

I shove at Livingston's arm. "We're bein' watched."

Without delay, Livingston sits up straight. The two of us move our arms from the armrests. My hands fall into my lap, and my fingers become laced. Together, we stare serenely at the screen, as though we were two enraptured moviegoers and nothing else. In all honesty, I couldn't tell you what was occurring in the film for all the money in the world.

Serene settles back in her seat, and I tell myself my heart is beating erratically because we were caught not watching the film, and not because of how close Livingston is. The orchestra is playing music at certain times. When did they begin that?

After a moment of silence, Livingston slouches in his seat. His elbow settles back onto the armrests as he leans toward me. "Shall I continue?"

My eyes veer in his direction before they meaningfully roll toward Serene. He knows as well as I do that she saw us. I don't want to attract the attention of anyone else, especially Beau.

Livingston makes a fist and props his chin on top of it. "If you're apprehensive of bein' seen, does that mean you forfeit?"

Outrage courses through me. I forfeit nothing, and Livingston knows that.

Wordlessly, I tap his arm. It falls forward on the armrest, his palm facing up. With my eyes looking at the screen, I reach out and write on his palm, *NO*.

Then a thought occurs to me. "But what if I cannot answer your questions because my answers are far too long?" I ask in a hushed tone.

"The wound on my leg tells me you can be creative when you choose to be. So in the spirit of the game, get creative."

"Fine," I whisper back.

Livingston grins, and says, "Do you think you will see Beau again?"

This little game of Livingston's is highly uncomfortable because it forces me to acknowledge the lack of men I've conversed with in my life (with the exception of my brother's friends) and the multitude of men I'm about to speak with. I may not be entirely against this bachelor idea, but do I know what I'm ready for? I don't believe I am. But perhaps I need this type of excitement in my life.

My eyes shoot to Livingston's palm as I write, *YES*.

Once I'm done, I meet his gaze. His eyes widen as my answer dawns on him.

What did Livingston believe? That I would grow tired of the bachelors after three outings and refuse to see anymore? We both know I'm not afforded that luxury right now. He's still poring over my family's ledgers, a task I knew would be tedious and time-consuming, but I still found myself impatient.

Would he find miscalculations that could potentially save Momma and me from financial ruin, or was there nothing to be done? I needed answers for so many things, and this was one matter someone was willing to help me resolve.

"You'll see him again...so is he at the top of your bachelor list?"

My index finger hovers above his palm, prepared to write no when I hesitate. He wants creative? I will show him creative. Very slowly, as to not make too much noise, my fingers curl around the edge of Livingston's jacket. I can feel his eyes on me. My heart beats so rapidly my hand nearly shakes as I draw the material up his arm. It snags around the middle of his forearm. Light from the movie is cast across our arms, showcasing the contrast between the two. Powerful and slim.

Starting at the inner corner, I write across his skin and veins, *I DO NOT KNOW.*

He's quiet for a long second. I can picture him piecing together every letter and structuring each word. As the seconds slip by, I look at him from the corner of my eye. The material of his jacket and sleeve remain bunched around his forearm. Livingston stares forward, his black brows dipped low over his hazel eyes.

He should've understood my reply by now. I lean into him. "Should I write it again?" I whisper.

"No," he says. His voice is choked.

Livingston shifts in his seat, as though he's uncomfortable. What's going through his mind right now?

Because I know what's running through mine, and it's him and his silly date. Tonight, will he take her home after he's spent all night next to me, speaking with me in the dark? If he does take her back, will they go upstairs to his room? If they go to his room, will they be intimate like he was with the nameless woman I caught him with?

As I think this through, I drag my finger up and down the armrest. I don't understand the way that woman held onto him for dear life and made those noises. And to be honest, I still don't want to understand because I do not want to need something so much. Whether it hurt or felt pleasurable, it was far too much at that moment.

Is that a side effect of love, or lust?

Must be lust.

Has to be lust.

I've loved many people in my life—my parents, brother, close friends—and not once did I throw caution to the wind for that love. The option never arose.

If that was a requirement to be with Livingston, I pity each woman who has ever pined after him. I truly do.

So why does the bitter aftertaste that only comes with jealousy fill my mouth and coat my heart?

"Rainey?"

The deep timbre of Livingston's voice against my ear brings me back to reality. I blink away my thoughts as I slowly turn toward him. He's so close that our noses nearly touch. "Yes?" I whisper.

His eyes pointedly veer between my face and the armrest. I follow his gaze, and my eyes widen when I see our fingers are linked, and our hands now comfortably rest in his lap.

As though we're a couple. As though this happens often. The scariest part is my hand fits perfectly in his. The tips of his fingers rest on top of my knuckles, and my heart twists at the sight because it appears so harmless yet possessive.

Dear Lord, I wasn't touching the armrest. It was Livingston the entire time. Idly tracing the prominent veins in his arms. It's no surprise he appeared so uncomfortable.

"Do you forfeit?"

His words repeat in my head. Eyes wide, I stare at him. As I try to compose the explanation to my actions, the audience breaks out into a hearty applause. Livingston turns toward the stage. While he's distracted, I break from the mysterious embrace our hands forged and all but clutch my fingers to my chest as though they're wounded. It tingles in a thousand different points.

The sconces on the walls light up as Rosalie sighs and looks at Livingston. "What a lovely movie."

Livingston smiles at her, the sleeve of his jacket is still drawn up around his forearm, and the only person who seems to notice is me.

We missed the entire show.

Livingston stands and offers his arm to Rosalie. I remain sitting, and my heart is still pounding for some reason. I watch Livingston discreetly shake his arm so the bunched-up sleeve languidly slides down his arm and rests at his wrists. He flexes his right hand, almost as though erasing the touch of my words.

Immediately, I turn away and face Beau's direction. Livingston suggested the write hand game, and I was stupid enough to agree. Beau is already standing, patiently waiting for our eyes to meet. When he holds out a hand for me to take, I don't hesitate to take it.

"D-did you e-enjoy yourself?"

In alarm, I look at him. Did he catch me with Livingston? His innocent expression reveals he didn't.

I look down at the ground as we make our way to the aisle. "I did. It was good."

We turn into the narrow aisle. The theater has become a mass of bodies, but that doesn't stop me from searching for Livingston. Has he already left? Probably has. If he came here to ruin my opportunity to have a pleasant night with Beau, he succeeded.

I need to salvage what time I have left.

As we wait for the people in front of us to move forward, I look at him. "I was thinkin'...I don't go to the theater near enough."

Beau merely stares at me with wide eyes.

"Do you?" I gently prod.

He shakes his head before he thinks better of it and replies. "N-no."

As the theater thins out, we make progress toward the foyer. As for Beau and me, the only way we'll be able to make headway is if I ignore everything Momma has ever told me and be forward. "Perhaps we should go together again."

At last, Beau understands the direction of the conversation.

"I w-would like t-that very much."

In the foyer, the voices of everybody carry toward the high ceilings. All conversations that were placed on hold the second the movie started have promptly resumed under the bright lights. We stop and wait for Étienne and Serene. There's still no sign of Livingston. He's probably pulling up in front of the Lacroix house at this very moment and getting ready to open Rosalie's door.

We find Étienne and Serene and proceed toward the front doors. Serene dives into her thoughts about the movie. I can only nod because I watched just the first ten seconds. The fresh air feels amazing against my cheeks and clammy hands when the four of us step outside.

Serene stops and takes a deep breath before she leans against Étienne's arm.

The hairs on the back of my neck stand, and the feeling of being watched sweeps through me. I scan the faces nearby, nodding my head while Serene continues speaking. Ahead of us, I see Livingston with his date on the sidewalk, waiting for his car. I feel relief.

So they haven't left.

However, my relief melts into dread once I realize they're leaving.

Why should it matter to you?

It doesn't. But Livingston impeding on a date with one of my bachelors matters greatly to me, and that's precisely what he did tonight.

"And then my midwife said I was pregnant with triplets," Serene says.

"That's nice," I say, my eyes never leaving Livingston and Rosalie. Ever the gentleman, he holds the door open for her. Once her back is to me, he finds my gaze. Those incredibly light eyes are searing and intense, and even with the distance between us, they send a white-hot heat through me. Exhaling a shaky breath, I tighten my grip on Beau's arm.

"And each kid is said to weigh ten pounds."

"How lovely. I'm so thrilled for you," I murmur.

Livingston remains as still as a statue. I can't decide whether he's going to join Rosalie in the car or make his way over here. I rather wish he would so I could confront him on why he appears so disgruntled with me. As though I spoiled his night and forced him to speak with me during the film. Abruptly, Livingston turns and walks around the car to the driver's side, and all I'm left with is the outline of Rosalie's and his profiles as they drive away.

I quickly look away, blinking rapidly, and focus on Serene. "I'm sorry? What's that?"

Serene lifts both brows and tilts her head to the side. "You had no idea what I was saying, did you?"

Scoffing, I casually toss my hand between us. "Of course I did. You were speakin'...you were speakin' about the movie."

"Not even close. I made up some farfetched lie about my pregnancy, but you were too busy watching Livingston like a hawk."

I don't bother denying her observation. With the cacophony around me, and Beau and Étienne deep in conversation, I feel free to voice my thoughts to Serene. "Have you seen Rosalie before?"

"Have I?"

I nod, my gaze intent.

"No. I haven't, but maybe Étienne has. I can ask for y—"

"Absolutely not," I say a little too harshly.

Serene's eyes widen.

"There's no need to ask your husband," I explain patiently. "I'm merely curious. I've never seen his date before. That's all."

Serene nods and idly pats her stomach. "God only knows where he found her. Probably branched out of Charleston in search of her."

"I nearly said the same thing!"

Serene winks. "Great minds think alike. But tell me, since we're on the subject of Livingston...what were the two of you doing during the movie?" she innocently asks.

For a second, I think my heart stops beating, and the color drains from my face. My mouth opens several times as I try to forge the best reply. "What do you mean? We were simply watchin' the movie as was everyone else."

"Yeah...and this baby was conceived by immaculate conception," Serene replies dryly.

"How did you—"

"At this stage in the pregnancy game, no seat is comfortable for me. I was squirming back and forth the whole time and saw that you and Livingston had your heads hunched together a lot. A lot, a lot." Serene taps her index finger against the corner of her mouth. "Now why would that be?"

"We were talkin'."

"Oh, of course. I've always admired how well you and Livingston can talk."

Before there's a chance for me to give a rebuttal, I'm interrupted.

"I apologize for the delay," Étienne says. He stands beside Serene. Their hands are like magnets and find their way back to one another. "Beau and I were discussin' a recent business opportunity of mine."

"No worries. It gave Serene and me time to talk...about the movie."

Étienne narrows his eyes at his wife but doesn't say a word.

"A-are w-we ready to go?" Beau asks.

When I turn to him, a happy if not wistful smile graces my face. Perhaps I had high expectations for tonight. All right, I absolutely did. But Beau Legare was a handsome, shy, delightful man. He should be perfect for me, and I'm willing to try again.

Together, the four of us walk to the sidewalk. I leave feeling slightly dispirited, but I remind myself that the next time Beau and I see one another, we'll have to be far away from *his* presence because that's a distraction I can't afford. If our next date isn't a success, then I will move on to the next bachelor.

As Beau helps me into the car, my stomach remains in knots. The driver pulls onto the road. Idly, I look out the window for several seconds before I look down at my left palm and stretch my fingers.

I played the write hand game with the wrong man.

CHAPTER TWELVE

LIVINGSTON

My blade catches the sunlight streaming into the room as it makes a smooth arch and powerfully clashes against Étienne's. Smiling, I ignore the sweat dripping into my eyes and make sure to keep my legs braced apart. My controlled, smooth, and precise strikes are exactly what I need right now. Fencing requires you to push aside any distractions in your life. How your muscles ache and your lungs burn become irrelevant because you are incredibly present in the moment.

Right now, I need that more than anything. Most of my nights are spent plagued by the horrors of war. If I don't drink enough, the solitude of silence creeps upon me, and I can hear the cries of every man who didn't make it back home. In the morning, I wash away my regret and am immediately forced to think of Rainey's predicament. In the beginning, I kept waiting for the moment when she'd pound on my front door and announce this bachelor farce Serene concocted was no longer for her. But as the days ticked by, it became apparent that was not to be.

Rainey couldn't possibly enjoy these men being paraded in front of her, could she?

But yesterday, I thought of something. These men saw what they thought was a stunning woman. If I showed up and evoked the real Rainey, the bachelors might think twice about pursuing her. Then I wouldn't have these buffoons in my life and a situation such as last night.

I met Rosalie at a gathering two days prior to attending the theater with her. She was in town visiting friends or family. I can't recall. All that matters is she was beautiful and lush and didn't have a hot retort for every word I said. And she was available last night and eager to attend the theater.

What I said to Rainey about the betting books was true. At my favorite drinking establishment, I discovered Rainey was the raucous topic of conversation. I attempted to push all thoughts of her aside, but their debauched words lingered in my mind and made me see red. I know she's not a child, but when did the rest of the men start to see that?

And if I didn't know any better, I'd say Rainey enjoyed the attention. She had a mesmerized look on her face when she spoke to Beau in the ballroom, and that didn't change as they sat beside each other in the theater. She was beguiled by the man.

I knew what my intent was when I sat beside Rainey. She undoubtedly thought it was to drive her mad. To an extent, she was right, but as I sat there, my stance changed. I felt protective of her and found myself looking at her and Beau from the corner quite often. But there was something different about the protection I felt last night. I've been protective of her as a child even when she drove me mad. Only I could be the one to retaliate against her.

I should have tried to understand why there was an imbalance between us before we played the write hand. Because that ended up being the biggest oversight of the night.

Never in all my years of taking part in the write hand game has it ever been so...erotic. Rainey wasn't aware. Why would she be? The write hand game was a rite of passage between the Lacroix and Pleasonton children. Several times we had sent messages or tried to uncover what the other was saying with our parents being none the wiser. That's what I set out to do last night. Find out if Rainey truly intended to see Beau again.

I did not plan on becoming aroused by my sister's closest friend. It was a mere touch, but I think it showed how desperate

I was for female companionship because when her fingertips dragged up my arm, I focused on the touch. I barely breathed when her nails lightly dragged against my skin; all I could think was how they would feel moving down my back. The image flashed in my head so quickly there was no time to fully process who I was thinking about until later.

The last time I attempted to be intimate with a woman, Rainey stormed into my room with her damn bow and arrow.

I left the theater with Rosalie on my arm, and in a rare act, I did not take her back to my home. I gave her a chaste kiss on the cheek and left with Rainey in my thoughts.

Instead of nightmares of war and echoes of screams, I dreamed of the Belgrave ballroom. Rainey stood in the middle of the room. I stood to the side, but she didn't see because she was staring at the selection of bachelors before her. Just as she would narrow down the list, the bachelors would multiply, until the entire room was filled with men vying for her attention. It was a nightmare all on its own. When I woke up, I was undecided which was less alarming—my nightmares of war or this entire bachelor event.

"Livingston," Étienne pants out, breaking my train of thought. I look at his red face. "We need to take a break."

Our fixed distance becomes broken as Étienne takes several strides backward. His clothes are soaked in sweat like mine, and his hair clings to his temples.

"We've been in here for quite some time," he says.

Have we? It feels as though we'd barely begun. This type of exertion brought my mind relief. I could think clearly when I was finished, breathe better, feel the blood coursing through my veins. Although respite has an expiration date, that did not stop me from trying again and again to find the momentary bliss.

I seemed to be forever chasing after peace, and I didn't know how to stop.

"We can cease...for now. Let's continue in fifteen minutes," I say.

Étienne shakes his head and walks to the chairs that are

lined against the ballroom wall. He places his sword down, picks up the towel he brought, and dries off his face.

Reluctantly, I follow him and stand beside one of the windows looking toward the long, winding driveway. There is no Rainey to pay us a call. Or her long line of bachelors. It's probably for the best. If I did see one of them, I might attempt to drive the tip of my sword clean through their heart.

"You seem more focused than usual." Étienne looks at me from the corner of his eye. "Is there somethin' on your mind?"

Stepping back from the window, I shake my head. "Nothin'. Other than this bachelor debacle."

Étienne snorts and drops his towel. "You do realize you were not invited to last night's engagement, correct?"

"I did not know you four would be at that theater."

"Charleston is not that large. How many theaters do you think this city has?"

"I'm not goin' to answer that. My date was eager to see said film, and I obliged."

"Clearly," Étienne murmurs. "Tell me, was your date Rosalie or Rainey?"

My head whips in Étienne's direction so fast that I swear I pull a muscle. Étienne grins, but I don't return the smile. "I don't understand what you're implyin'. Perhaps you're gettin' them confused? Might I suggest you wear your readin' glasses more often?"

"I could see just fine last night. Your date was to your left, and she was the one you overlooked. And Rainey was to your right, and she was the one you continued to speak to and stare at."

"I did not stare. Why would I stare?"

"You did. And that is a good question. Why were you starin' at Rainey?"

"For the last time, I did not stare. And if I did look in Rainey's direction, perhaps I was ponderin' over her choice of escort for the night."

Étienne crosses his arms and leans back in his chair. "Beau is an upstandin' man."

"But not for Rainey." I know my brother is far from finished with this discussion, and as much as I want to exert more energy fencing, sitting down and gathering a deep breath isn't so bad.

Placing my sword next to my chair, I sit, crossing one ankle over the opposite knee. We're quiet for several moments. Voices from inside the house filter through the cracks around the double doors. There's the faint yet undeniable sound of a giggle.

The corner of Étienne's mouth curls upward.

Marriage, love, whatever you prefer to call it, has changed my brother into a man I barely recognize. Even the elite of Charleston have noticed the slight difference. The general consensus on Serene isn't favorable, but no one can deny she is the woman who's tamed the untamable. For that, she gained a certain level of respect.

Étienne clears his throat, pulling me from my thoughts. "Rosalie seems...lovely."

I give a noncommital shrug. "She is."

Étienne looks at me from the corner of his eye. "You will not see her again, will you?"

"No. I don't believe I will." I pause. "She wants commitment."

Étienne dramatically gasps. He's been spending far too much time with his wife. "A woman wants commitment from another human being? My God. The nerve. Did you alert the police?"

I fling my hand in the air. "I don't understand what happened to casual datin'."

"I'm afraid that is somethin' of the past. At your age, settlin' down with a woman might appeal to you."

The mere thought causes me to shudder. I have far too many scars from my past and questionable ways of coping with them. I have no desire to bring someone into my personal life. Indefinitely. "Why would I want to settle with one woman?"

"Because we're made of sugar and spice and everything nice. So kiss my ass." Étienne and I turn in time to see Serene walk into the ballroom.

I gesture to my sister-in-law. "Here walks Exhibit A. Dear God, you're still pregnant? It's been almost two years."

"Do not get me started. This child is bringing the noise and bringing the funk on my bladder."

Étienne stands and grabs a chair lined against the wall, and places it next to ours.

"What brings you here?" Étienne asks as he helps his wife sit down.

Serene links her hands around the underside of her stomach as she makes herself comfortable. For all her bellyaching, I believe a small part of her truly enjoys being pregnant. "No reason. The two of you have been in here for a long time."

My brother looks my way. "It's Livingston. He wouldn't stop. I almost stabbed myself to make it end."

Furrowing her brows, Serene looks at me. "Why the intense fencing game?"

My brother leans back in his chair. Arching a brow, he smiles at Serene. "Because of Rainey."

"Oh, of course." Serene slaps her palm against her forehead. "I should've known that. This pregnancy is seriously throwing me off my game."

"I'll have the two of you know that me fencin' has absolutely nothin' to do with Rainey."

The two of them stare at me with bland expressions. They don't believe a word I'm saying.

"I'm serious," I insist.

Serene nods, her eyes wide. "Of course."

I look around the room before my gaze ventures back to Serene. Do I dare ask the question that's been hounding me since last night? Oh, why not? This is Serene we're talking about. Somehow, someway, she finds out everything.

"Has she expressed interested in seeing Beau again?"

Serene looks at Étienne before she answers. "No, not to me. But for the sake of transparency, Beau told Étienne he wants to see Rainey again."

I snort. "I'm sure he does." I push myself out of my chair as a sudden surge of adrenaline courses through me.

"Has it ever occurred to you that these men might want to be with Rainey for Rainey?" This question comes from Étienne.

"No. And you know why? Because I'm a male, and I understand what they're thinkin'. Trust me when I say gettin' to know the real Rainey is the furthest thing from their mind."

Serene stops rubbing her stomach and gives me a thoughtful look. "But what if it is?"

As I sit there thinking of the bachelors having genuine intentions, something unheard of courses through me. It isn't jealousy, anger, or fury, but something between the three. It's hot and powerful, and makes my hands clench several times. My mouth opens and closes, yet I can't seem to muster a reply to Serene's question.

"Chan-Chan! Chan-Chan! Don't run!" Alex hollers in the hall, impeding my aggressive thoughts.

Serene slaps her hand against her knees and attempts to stand. "Ah, crap. I gotta go."

Wordlessly, Étienne holds his hand out, and Serene takes it. She launches herself out of her chair and waddles toward the doors. Once in the hallway, Serene yells for Alex to slow down.

I look at my brother. "There's never a dull moment in this home, is there?"

Étienne shrugs, but a tiny smirk covers his lips. "I find it pleasant. Belgrave was quiet for far too long. A home of this size needs to be filled with children."

"Precisely how many children?"

"As many children as Serene wants to give me."

"My Lord," I groan. "Belgrave doesn't have enough room for the number of children the two of you will produce."

With that said, Étienne laughs heartily. Some of my pent-up aggression fades, but it won't completely disappear until I know Serene is done with this bachelor charade. This is going to drive me mad.

Sighing, Étienne looks at me. "If you want to remain a

bachelor your entire life, so be it. I will no longer browbeat you."

I nod. "Thank you."

"And in terms of Rainey, if you're truly disgruntled with Pleas's will, then perhaps we can have our attorney look through it and see if there are any holes in it."

"That would be good," I reply noncommittally. I appreciate the offer, but I'm certain Pleas's will was ironclad. I think of a conversation Rainey and I had the day Serene proposed the idea of having a bachelor ball, and how Rainey privately confessed her family's financial peril. I promised my discretion, and she has it. However, that doesn't mean I can't help guide Étienne in the right direction. "And I'll look through the family's financial documents," I blurt.

Slowly, Étienne turns to me. "Why?"

"To make sure all is well. Rainey mentioned they are between accountants, and I know Pleas played an important role in their finances. It's just to make sure everythin' is okay."

Étienne absorbs my explanation. "Very well, then. If you need help, let me know."

"Thank you."

Étienne gives a blunt nod and stares straight ahead. "But it goes without sayin' that the process will be tedious and can take quite a long time."

"I know," I say empathetically.

I understood that more than Étienne realized. The examination through the first set of ledgers Rainey gave me was not going how I anticipated. Miles took painstaking care to list everything that came into the Pleasonton household and everything that went out. The daily expenses were neat and orderly, as was the cash account, and the two were always on separate pages. It was evident that Miles had been attempting to hold the creditors back, for years, to the best of his abilities by taking loans from one bank and paying them off from another loan through an acquaintance or friend. On one of the cash account pages, toward the bottom, was Étienne's name. There was a date the loan was taken out and the amount. There was no date listed for any payment. I don't know if that was because Étienne refused for the loan to be paid back or Miles didn't have the funds. But seeing my brother's name in the ledger brought a sinking feeling to my gut.

"She should continue seein' each bachelor," Étienne says, his tone frank.

The mere word bachelor causes me to grind my teeth. There has to be a better description for these buffoons pursuing Rainey. "Even though this entire arranged marriage process is futile and inane?"

"To place your concentration in one area would be foolish. There's no harm in socializin' with these respectful men," Étienne rationalizes.

It's hard to say if years of marriage or being a father has turned my brother this way. He's still the terrifying Étienne everyone knows him to be, but there's a genial side. Right now, I need the terrifying side, who sees these men for what they really are. I have more respect in my pinky finger than any of those men.

"I'm placin' my focus in one area because I already know what will happen. The bachelors will discover Rainey's tenacious personality and run for the hills. And then Rainey will sour from the experience."

"And does all your focus require you to arrive to each event Rainey's at with one of her bachelors?"

"No."

My brother's face remains expressionless save for a single arched brow.

"You don't have faith in me. That's fine," I say.

"It's not that. I just believe you should speak with Rainey and be honest. Far easier than chasin' after her from place to place."

Étienne has a valid point. Perhaps, I can remind Rainey, very calmly, that I'm still reviewing the ledgers, and she doesn't have to continue with this madness. However, I'm not about to mention that to my brother. I stand and give Étienne a confident smile. "Soon you will see I'm correct in this."

"Absolutely," Étienne mutters behind me. "Because even a stopped clock is right twice in a day."

CHAPTER THIRTEEN

RAINEY

Last night after Étienne, Serene, and Beau dropped me off at home, Beau was ever the gentleman and escorted me to the front door. He settled for kissing the knuckles of my left hand, and I felt...nothing.

Not a single thing.

My heart quickened more when I traced words on Livingston's palm.

I wasn't willing to bid adieu to Beau Legare. He seemed so perfect, and it's not as though I dedicated the whole night to get to know him as I should have. Most of my time was compromised by Livingston.

As I laid in bed last night, I mulled over each bachelor. I didn't know all of them by name. Some of them I did. Rather, I recognized them by their faces. Which made me feel ostentatious, but maybe it was better this way. My date with Beau made it abundantly clear that sometimes my mind can get ahead of itself. Perhaps, after the second date, then I can learn their name.

It sounds harsh even to my own ears, but I desire a spark. I desire chemistry. I merely desire the rush of desire.

Like with Livingston, I think to myself and immediately take back the thought. My God, where did that come from? The two of us are like oil and water, as opposite as black and white. What tingled one night might not be there the next.

"Rainey, dear, are you listenin'?"

Blinking rapidly, I stare down at the stitching hoop clutched between my hands. Over breakfast, I gave Momma the shock of her life when I offered to embroidery with her this afternoon, but I had ulterior motives. I was desperate to give my mind a respite from this bachelor/dowry situation. Thus far, it wasn't working, and I have poked the tips of my fingers at least ten times.

Lifting my head, I find Momma lookin' at me expectantly. "I'm sorry, what did you say?"

"You were lost in your thoughts, weren't you?"

"Of course not." I look at the needle clutched between my thumb and forefinger. "I was simply engrossed in my embroidery."

Momma tugs on the hem of my cloth so she can get a better look at my handiwork. Her eyes widen. "Mercy me, Rainey. What is that? A doll or a candle that's caught on fire?"

"I don't follow patterns, but my imagination and this"—I point at the yellow mass in the middle of the cloth— "is the sun. Because I like yellow, and the sun reminds me of happier times in my life."

My hope is that my false truth of a story tugs at Momma's heartstrings, but as the seconds tick by, she remains expressionless. I shrug and all but toss my embroidery onto the ottoman in front of me. "I believe I need to take a break."

"Wonderful. Because now you can answer my question from before. How was your...time with Mr. Legare?"

For all her reservations regarding the bachelors, Momma is still inquisitive by nature. She can't help herself. I take a deep breath, and I swear she leans in with wide eyes.

"Just as I told you last night, he was a kind gentleman, and we had a pleasant time at the theater." Although, as I say those words, moments from the night before run through my mind. It's not Beau's beautiful face I see, but Livingston's heart-stopping grin and the image of my hand touching his.

"Did you get to know him better?"

"Not as well as I hoped." But I learned that slowly tracing letters on Livingston's palm is enough to make my breathing accelerate. "There's always a next time," I say with false enthusiasm.

"You'll see Mr. Legare again?"

"Perhaps."

"And will you do this with the rest of the men? Time is of the essence."

"If need be, yes."

Momma resumes her needlework. Apparently, the important questions are out of the way. "You'll certainly be an occupied woman for the next several weeks."

"I will," I agree. "But Serene has a rigid timeline. I'll be seein' numerous bachelors each week."

"How wonderful. And what if a bachelor wishes to see you more than twice in a week?"

"Momma, what is it you truly want to say?"

Her eyes turn serious as she looks at me sharply. "Rainey, I don't believe Miles intended for you to go about findin' husband this way."

"Well, no one knows the way he wanted me to find one. This is the route I chose."

"And while I'm glad you're acceptin' of your dowry, Livingston as the executor, and not usin' your bow on a single soul in the past two weeks, seein' these men in such a way..." Her lips become pursed as she shakes her head.

Angling my head to the side, I smile. "Are you scandalized by me?"

To her credit, Momma appears dismayed by my question. "Of course not. But you should know that folks about town might find this all very objectionable."

"It has crossed my mind," I lie.

This was now the second time someone has made mention of the conversations buzzing throughout Charleston about the bachelor arrangement. The chatter didn't bother me, but I would hate it even more for Momma to lose this home and everything inside it. That would be something everybody in Charleston would discuss for quite some time.

"If you're worried about me bein' in a compromisin'

position with one of the bachelors, you shouldn't."

"Because you will have Livingston as a chaperone?"

I bite down on my tongue. That's the last person I want to see while I'm getting to know the bachelors, especially after last night. "No," I say slowly. "Because Serene and I will be vigilant with every outin' and event that there's no chance of bein' compromised."

She sighs and looks in the direction of the window. I know her well enough to know she's still not content with the arrangement. None of this is how she envisioned it occurring. And it makes me wonder, not for the first time, if she whispered nonsensical things into Miles's ear about me to get him to change his will and add in the foolish dowry.

A light knock on the sitting room doors thankfully puts a pin in the conversation. I don't think I've ever been more relieved. The butler clears his throat. "You have a caller."

Momma sends me a furtive glance, as though I'm a child she's watching over and quickly stands. She speaks with the butler for a moment and then turns back to me. "Livingston is here to speak with you."

In an instant, my relief turns to dread. That should have explained the sudden bounce in Momma's step and the spark in her eye. I will never understand how he's able to bewitch nearly every woman he meets.

"Why is he here?" I quietly ask myself before I stand from the couch. "Very well. I'll make this quick."

Momma places a hand on my arm, stopping me at the doorway. "Go gentle on him, Raina."

"Momma, he's not a baby deer."

Believe me, my expression says. Momma wrings her hands together and watches me with doubt. I sigh and walk out of the sitting room. For the first time in my life, I'm mournful to leave the embroidery behind. As I walk down the hall, my mind runs with endless questions. What could Livingston possibly want? Is he here to discuss last night? Or perhaps he has found extra funds in our family's account that our accountants missed. My heart soars at the possibility. Every little cent counts.

Livingston is in the library, slowly sauntering around the room with his hands behind his back. Every Lacroix has a commanding presence. Each in their own unique ways. They were born in high stations; they have high expectations. Étienne is always so blasé about what he sees. Nat is gracious, and always smiling. Because of that, people are drawn to her, anxious to absorb a bit of her happiness. And Livingston…his presence is undisturbed. There's not a lot that affects him. Why would it? When you want for nothing, you wish for nothing.

Lately, though, he appears restless. His shoulders are always tense and alert. And while he maintains the carefree Livingston, there are moments a mask covers his eyes, and I don't recognize the face in front of me.

My heart aches for him. For no other reason than him fighting some unspoken battle. That is all.

Right?

Clearing my throat, I enter the room. Slowly, Livingston looks over his shoulder at me. Once again, the guarded expression cloaks his eyes. What was he thinking about before I interrupted him?

I take a deep breath and glance at the clock on the fireplace mantel. "Two in the afternoon. Shouldn't you be havin' your breakfast in bed?"

Livingston closes his eyes and dramatically clutches at his chest. "Once again you wound me with your words."

"What part offended you?" I ask as I approach him.

"The breakfast part. Everyone knows I only drink coffee. It must be as black as my soul."

"Ah." I dip my head, but it's only to hide my smile. When I look him in the eye, I'm back to being straight faced. "My apologies then."

Livingston faces me, rocks back on his heels, and arches a single brow. I know he's waiting for my manners to kick in and to offer him to sit down, but I do not want to do that. It's best if we aren't near one another because I'm still trying to grapple with what I felt last night. Even now there's an unexpressed energy between us that neither one of us refuses to speak of.

I hide the slight tremor in my arms by crossing them, and tell myself the tingles I feel underneath my fingertips is from the needle constantly pricking me.

"What can I do for you?" I ask.

He gestures to the ledger on the desk in the corner. "I'm here to return the first ledger. I went through everythin' and I'm ready to look through anythin' else you may have."

"Oh."

There truly is a reason for his unexpected visit. When I gave Livingston the first ledger, I trusted him to give his thoughts to me when he was finished. I didn't have the best patience, and a lot of times, I would force myself not to ask how the process was. But the very thought he could have potentially spotted an error or extra funds causes my heart to wildly beat.

"Did you find anythin'?" I blurt, my words blending together.

Livingston's eyes soften, a sign that what's to come out of his mouth is never good. "No. I haven't. But I've just started. That can all change."

Nodding, I look away even though I've started to lose faith that anything will change. I can only keep meeting with each bachelor, and once Livingston looks through all the finances and I have my second opinion. Then I will know I exhausted every option.

"I can start examinin' what ledgers you may have left," Livingston suggests.

His words pull me out of my thoughts. "Oh, yes. Right, right." I spring into action, and walk to the desk. I open the middle drawer and grab the key to open the drawer to the left where the rest of the ledgers would be. I place them one by one, and in total there are three. How long would it take for Livingston to inspect these ledgers? Idly, my gaze looks over the desk surface. Taking note of the lack of belongings and clutter that once lined the sides when I was a child. Before Daddy died, he would often work in the library. He said the view of the garden was relaxing. For Miles, it was his favorite place to work, too. I can't fault either of them. I love it too.

Lifting my head, I look out the window the desk faces. I adored playing in the garden even more.

A faint smile causes the corners of my mouth to lift as I think back to a memory when I was seven. I coaxed Nat into being my assistant while I treasure hunted in my backyard. I used a stick as my sword, and also as a crutch after I was gravely wounded battling evil pirates, and wild animals.

Apparently, I appreciated theatrics as a child.

It would take some time but Nat would gradually become an active participator. Our shrieks and laughter would become loud enough to earn the attention of our brothers.

Miles would help make our game better by recommending which live Oaks to climb and which branches were sturdy enough. Étienne would have little to no involvement, and sat off to the side, reading a book. Their younger brother Julian was filled with energy and because the boys were showing an interest in our game, it became good enough for him. He would join in, climbing the trees at impressive speeds even I had to admire his skill. He kept a lookout for any sneaky raiders.

And Livingston would imbed his opinion at what seemed to be the worst times. I needed to sharpen the end of my stick if I was going to use it as a sword. And how did I wound my arm in battle but limp around the garden with my left foot instead? If Julian was keeping watch in the tree, then why was Nat attempting to climb the tree and griping about Julian taking her spot.

Livingston was the killer of all joy, and so I announced he was one of the raiders who snuck past Julian's watchful eye. Julian let out a war cry and Nat forgot about getting her way. The two of them turned on Livingston. Like faithful soldiers they charged him while I looked on for several seconds and then ran into the attack.

I close my eyes and exhale a shaky breath. I bite down on my lower lip to stop myself from crying. Far too many memories have been created here for it to all slip away.

"Rainey?" Livingston says behind me.

I open my eyes, blinking rapidly. The garden is pristine.

Just as it should be. I know most people would prefer it in this condition, but I loved it best with errant flowers from kids' footfalls. I turn, with a smile fixed on my face. "Here we are. I believe these are the rest of the ledgers."

I hold them out for Livingston to take. He makes a small grunt when he takes the brunt of all the weight. "Do you know Pleas kept a very detailed account of the financial records?"

Sadly, I smile. "I'm sure he did."

Livingston looks away momentarily and then back at me. More uncomfortable silence. As quickly as possible, I think of anything to fill the void. "When he was at college, he tried his best to keep order of everythin' but it was too consumin' so Momma had our accountant take over. It was the same for when he went to war."

"Makes sense considerin' *he* is the accountant."

I smirk. "Miles was a very patient, yet a controllin' man. He wanted to do everythin' his way. In any case, let me find the ledgers that were balanced by the accountant." I grab the first ledger from the top of the stack, but I instantly recognize Miles's handwriting.

I lean closer to Livingston until our shoulders are pressed together and open the ledger at the top of the stack. As I flip through the pages trying to find the any evidence of our family accountant, Livingston's dips his head and...did he smell my hair? I freeze, mid-turn of the page, blindly staring at the numbers below. He smelled my hair. I know he did. I heard the slight inhale. The brush of his nose. Why did he do that? Better yet, why is my heart beating like a drum?

Livingston's body becomes rigid beside me, as though he realizes he was caught. Slowly, he pulls away from the crown of my head. I continue to look at the ledger as if nothing occurred but now it's all I can think of. The numbers on the pages look like a different language.

"I spoke with Étienne today," he blurts.

I can't help but arch a brow. Livingston speaks with his brother every day. "Oh?"

His jaw clenches and unclenches, as if he's struggling to

say his words. I become alert. "We both think it's imperative that while you pursue Serene's absurd bachelor idea we have our lawyer look at Miles's will. See if there's a chance there are loopholes."

I don't mind the bachelors. I'm not against the attention. It's quite nice having men wanting to fawn all over me, while Livingston turns into a big ball of fury. He believes I do not notice.

I do.

I notice everything about him, even when I try my hardest not to. I believe he attempts to do the same with me. Even now, he's going out of his way to find a better opportunity for me to receive my dowry without marrying. But something about his statement doesn't seem right to me. Étienne's stoic, and at times blunt. He wouldn't have Livingston speak for the two of them.

"Question, were Étienne's exact words, absurd bachelor idea?"

At that, Livingston averts his gaze and scratches the back of his neck. Several seconds go by before he answers. "No. But it was heavily implied."

"Of course," I say, deciding to go along with this charade of his. "And why does he not care for the bachelors?"

Livingston places the heavy ledgers on the chair beside him, crosses his arms, and narrows his eyes, while I stare on with an innocent expression. "Because he believes they might pursue you for monetary ambition."

"And does that truly matter? I myself have monetary ambition. Perhaps our ambitions can be the one thing we bond over."

Livingston leans in, light eyes ablaze. "Greed is not somethin' you want to bond over. Trust me on this."

I mimic his actions. "It's not greed, but desperation. And I'll trust you the minute you admit that he is not Étienne, but you."

Livingston takes a step back and throws his hands in the air. "All right. Fine. I believe this is absurd, and I haven't concealed that. Figured I'd say my brother was in agreement with me so you would change your mind. It's apparent I was wrong. You'll continue to see these men no matter who asks you not to."

"You thought Étienne's opinion would change my mind?"

"Perhaps. You seem to do the opposite of everythin' I say."

"I've always done that."

There's got to be a better way of savin' your family from financial ruin than virtually sellin' yourself."

My cheeks turn red from anger. "I am not sellin' myself."

Livingston looks me straight in the eye. "I've said this before, and I'll say it again. This is not the way to go about everythin'."

"I wish there was a different way."

"Well, there could be. When I visited Étienne, I asked him to look at your family's finances." My shoulders become tense. Livingston quickly speaks. "This means the process can move faster. And I know I told you, you had my discretion and I meant it, but I promise you, Étienne has a remarkable eye with findin' error. It won't take him long to discover the outcome of your finances." He pauses, watching me carefully. "Are you comfortable with that?"

Right now, I need all the help I can get. Livingston doesn't need to solicit his brother's strengths. I know his twin's business acumen is unrivaled. This is for the best. I give Livingston a genuine smile. "Of course. I trust Étienne."

Livingston taps the ledger on top and nods. "Then I'll give one of these books for Étienne to look through as soon as I can."

"Thank you."

Livingston dips his head and looks away. Within seconds the silence fills the room is strained. Whenever Livingston and I have extended conversations that are cordial we don't know what to do with ourselves. It goes out of our typical area of comfort.

"Excellent. I will be on my way then." At the door, he looks over his shoulder at me, as though he's forgotten something.

"Since Étienne is willin' to help, I'm more than happy to tell Serene that this bachelor charade is over."

Oh, that sneaky little bastard. "Absolutely not!"

He stares at the ceiling and shakes his head. "You still want to proceed with this bachelor charade?"

"I have no choice, Livingston."

He holds the ledgers between us, slightly blocking his face from view. "I'm givin' you a choice now."

"Can you or Étienne find a way out of this financial ruin tomorrow? Can you guarantee that I will not have to marry a man or use this dowry to keep the home I grew up in from bein' taken from my momma?"

The sound of his silence is the only answer I need. I sigh. "That's what I was afraid of. Now, if you will excuse me, I have to get ready. A bachelor will be here shortly to take me on a walk through the park."

"I can loan you the money."

Livingston's words cause me to become frozen. Arching a brow, I remain silent as I process his words and attempt to think of the best reply.

"I think we both know there's no possible way for me or Momma to pay you back," I say honestly.

"There's no timeline to this loan," Livingston immediately replies. His eyes are solemn. He means every word.

"Don't you think there's nothin' favorable to come out of loanin' friends money, no matter the amount?" I ask, my tone soft.

"Yes, but I'll make an exception this time." Livingston gives me a crooked grin that most women can never say no to. For me, though, I've seen it so many times I feel only a small flutter in my stomach. I know better.

Sighing, I reach out and pat him on the arm. I shouldn't have done that because almost immediately, I feel a jolt in my fingertips and the heat that spreads across my palm. Almost a punishment for thinking I'm immune from his charm.

I snatch my hand, hiding it behind my back and continue speaking as though nothing is the matter. "I appreciate the offer, but I was raised under the belief that if money is loaned out, it should be paid."

"I respect that, but let me do this…for your brother."

For your brother.

His words aren't meant to cut to the quick. I know Livingston is being kind. But the three words don't sit well with me because they're said to me, but they're for someone else. He's doing this for Miles. I know the fact he doesn't want to be the executor of my dowry plays a tremendous role. Am I that much of a burden to him?

Livingston dips his head. "I will take your silence as a no."

Lacing my fingers together, I stare at the ledgers held between his hands. "It's better this way. And I'm confident that between you and Étienne reviewin' the accounts, Momma and I won't need to worry about the creditors knockin' on our door. It might not happen tomorrow as we wish, but we'll have the answers soon. Maybe you will find money hidden somewhere, and I won't have to accept this dowry," I say with a weak smile.

Livingston's brows become furrowed as he looks at me. His mouth opens and closes several times. "Rainey—"

I hold up a hand because I don't want him to say something else out of obligation or pity. "And if you don't find a thing, that's fine, too. I have my dowry." I never once thought I'd be saying those words aloud. Yet here we are.

"And the bachelors," Livingston mutters.

"And the bachelors," I agree faintly.

Livingston becomes silent, carefully watching me. "You mentioned you have a bachelor takin' you for a stroll around a park this afternoon. Which one is it?"

"What's it matter to you?"

Livingston scoffs "It doesn't matter. I'm merely bein' polite. Which bachelor is it?" he repeats.

"Oh…" I try to think of a male name, any name, but nothing comes to mind. Livingston tilts his head to the side as he waits for my reply. "I'm uncertain."

"Wouldn't it be best if you know who you're seein'?"

"It would," I concede. "But I'm usin' the Livingston

Lacroix method with the bachelors. Recognize them by faces. Never by their names."

At that, he arches a brow. "Is it Beau?"

"I said I'm uncertain," I reply.

Livingston can poke and prod all he wants, but I'm not conceding to anything. The truth is, there is no need for me to freshen up because no bachelor is escorting me around the park. I said that to get Livingston to leave, and for him not to know when the next actual event with my bachelors will be. I don't want another theater fiasco on my hands.

"Uncertain?" he questions with a quirk of his brow.

I merely nod.

Livingston leaves, maintaining his half-smirk and a look in his eyes that said, *I know you're lying.*

"Have fun with Uncertain," he calls out behind him.

I shake my head, trying to be annoyed but I can't stop myself from smiling.

CHAPTER FOURTEEN

LIVINGSTON

I must say this roast ducklin' is superb."

"Thank you. I worked very hard on this dinner," a female voice says. Has to be Serene.

I press my face closer to the key lock until my nose is nearly smashed against the door to get a better look inside the room. All I can see is one side. Fortunately for me, it's in the direction where Rainey and Conrad are sitting.

"Did you?" Conrad says.

"No, the cook made it," Serene replies.

Everyone in the dining room laughs. I snort, and stop myself from rolling my eyes when someone or something tugs at my jacket. I shrug it off, and continue staring into the dining room. Is it my imagination, or is Conrad moving closer to Rainey? He's nearly sitting on her lap. My left hand curls into a fist. I stop myself from bursting into the room and demanding him to back away. It's supposed to be a dinner, and he's far from being respectful what with the heated glances he's giving her. I know those glances. I've given those glances. He's thinking of bedding her.

"Bastard," I mutter.

"Uncle Liv?" a child's voice sweetly says beside me. There's another tug on my sleeve.

When I look down, I find Alex staring up at me with her almond-shaped eyes.

"Go play with your cat, Chauncy," I say dismissively. Can't

she see I'm in the middle of something?

"His name is Chandler. I call him Chan-Chan. Have you seen him?"

"They're both ridiculous names."

"Uncle Liv," she repeats, this time more urgently. "Have you seen Chan-Chan?"

My God, doesn't this child have a nanny? What happened to proper childcare?

"No, I haven't. I'm a bit preoccupied," I whisper and watch as Conrad turns toward Rainey preventing me from seeing her face.

"Dammit, move," I hiss.

"Dammit," Alex echoes perfectly.

Wide-eyed, I face the child as she begins to skip in circles, saying a word that will undoubtedly be linked back to me. Giving her my undivided attention, I kneel in front of her, and stop her by placing my hands on her shoulders. "You cannot say that. Uncle Liv was wrong." I mock slap myself. "Bad Uncle Liv."

Alex giggles and slaps her cheek. "Dammit." She points a finger at me. "Your turn."

This hellion thinks it's a game! She's going to ruin this for me.

I happened to discover this dinner by sheer luck. I came to Belgrave to drop off some of the Pleasonton ledgers for Étienne to peruse, and instead was drawn toward to the kitchen by the delicious scent of food. I tried to take a bite of one of the biscuits. But when the cook, Pearl, has been part of the staff longer than you've been alive that's not easy to come by, and she promptly whacked my hand and said, "Shoo, boy. This is for Mr. and Mrs. Lacroix and the dinner they be hostin'."

I asked who would be at the dinner and Pearl said she knew Miss Rainey would be there but that's all she knew. It didn't take long for me to grasp that I'd been hoodwinked by Rainey. There was no walk in the park with a bachelor. She simply wanted to distract me from this dinner.

I must give her credit for such a well-thought-out lie.

"I can't find Chan-Chan," Alex whines.

"When I go into town I'll find a stray cat for you. We'll call it Chan-Chan number two."

"No, I need Chan-Chan."

Impatiently, I look down at my niece. "You need your nanny. Better yet, why aren't you in bed?"

I can't decide what it is I said to cause her eyes to well up with tears. All I know is her lower lip begins to quiver right as the voices from inside the dining room approach the doors. There's no time to offer her condolences or bribery. Promptly, I bend down and sweep Alex into my arms. The door opens and I turn to my niece and smile as if I didn't corrupt her by teaching her first cuss word. "No, my sweet Alex, I love you."

The four of them stare at me with confusion. After a few seconds Rainey tilts her head to the side, crosses her arms and narrows her eyes into thin slits.

"Livingston? What are you doing here?" Serene asks as she strides toward Alex and me.

"I came here to…talk about finances."

"At eight o'clock at night?"

Gladly, I give her Alex. "I take great offense to that question, Serene. Finances have always been incredibly important to me. I think my brother would agree with me."

All eyes turn to Étienne, but he's staring at me as though I've grown three heads. The only time I've expressed interest in my finances is to pay off gambling debts, or a bill at Vincent's Chicco's from the night before.

"Well, okay then," Serene draws out as she pats Alex's back. "I'm goin' to lay Alex back down in her bed."

They're almost to the staircase when Alex yells, "Oh, dammit!"

What is the child, a parakeet?

Serene stops in her tracks and turns on her heels, and gives me a questioning look. "Did my daughter just say dammit?"

At that, Alex giggles once again and slaps her own cheek. "Dammit," she repeats.

I hold my hands out in front of me. "It's remarkable what

kids acquire at such a young age, but this one." I wag my finger at my niece. "She just might be a genius. You and my brother should truly be proud."

"Uh-huh," Serene finally says, in a flat monotone voice. She's far from moved. The only advantage with Conrad being present is Serene is on her best behavior, and isn't demanding to know all that I said to Alex.

While she goes upstairs, I turn to Étienne, Rainey and Conrad. "Havin' a pleasant dinner?"

"We were," Rainey remarks.

"I think now is the perfect time to retire to the sittin' room. Shall we?" Étienne says diplomatically.

"Wonderful idea," Conrad says. He steps back and gestures for Rainey to walk in front of him. As she does, I can't help but notice how he places his fingertips on the middle of her back. It's a gesture I've done when I'm intimate or comfortable with a woman. As far as I knew this is the first time Conrad and Rainey are having dinner together, but I'm having second thoughts. He should be locked away for showing any interest in her. She's too young for him. If Conrad had the sudden desire to find a wife he needs to look closer to his age. Not at Rainey.

Briefly, my eyes meet Rainey's. It doesn't last for longer than a few seconds. She stares boldly back at me until I look away. That's always been the fascinating thing about Rainey. While most women blush and play coy, Rainey chooses to be direct and straightforward. What you see is what you get.

"Livingston, you're more than welcome to join us in the sittin' room, unless you need to speak with me privately?" Étienne asks with one brow arched.

The real meaning behind his words: why are you here?

"You know, I do believe I will take you up on your gracious offer. Thank you, dear brother."

Shaking his head, and muttering words under his breath, Étienne walks down the hall with Conrad. They begin discussing one of Étienne's newest business acquisitions and through no fault of my own, I'm left with Rainey.

"I need to speak with you before you leave," I say, keeping my voice neutral.

Rainey looks at me from the corner of her eyes. "About what?"

"My finances," I say, placing emphasis on the last word.

She doesn't stop walking, but her shoulders stiffen. "You came here to speak about that? Couldn't that wait until tomorrow?"

"It could. But I had important questions. Meet me in Étienne's office."

"But—"

"Meet me in Étienne's office," I repeat, my tone brokering no room for argument.

I turn and walk away, knowing full well that this time, she's stopped in her tracks and is staring daggers at me because no one ever tells her what to do and lives to tell the tale, and two, she will meet in the office because her curiosity will get the best of her. She wants to know what I have to say.

In the office, I make sure the heavy ledger is where I placed it on the desk and make my way to the sideboard to pour myself a stiff drink. I don't know how long the rest of the night will go on for Rainey and Conrad.

Out of all my miscreant friends, is Conrad the worst for Rainey to possibly have a future with? No. In fact, some would say if you placed my pitfalls against his, I'd be considered the immoral one. I'm not trying to win Rainey's hand, though. But I see nothing wrong with trying to avert her attention away from the men who are no good for her.

There's a small knock. I turn in time to see Rainey slip into the room, and quickly shut the door behind her.

She takes a deep breath and points at me. "Stop sabotagin' me, Livingston."

"Good evenin' to you, too, darlin'."

"Good evenin'. Now stop it."

"I'm not sabotagin' anythin'. Belgrave happens to be my childhood home. I come here often."

"Did the garden theater happen to be your childhood

theater, too?"

"That happened to be a coincidence."

She walks deeper into the room, rubbing her temples in the process. "Livingston, what did you discover about our finances that you just have to tell me tonight?"

Now that we're alone, I take her in, and my brows nearly connect. She looks different tonight. I cannot decide if that's for the best or worst. Her hair is half up with the dark strands hanging to her waist. And what is that on her cheeks? Rouge?

The hem of her sleeveless, gold lamé and peach insert gown grazes her calves. It's a drop waist that I've noticed is becoming popular as of late. Unsurprisingly, the style nearly hangs on Rainey's lithe frame. But it highlights her collarbones, the elegant curve of her neck. For all her stubbornness and strength, she's still incredibly delicate and incredibly female.

Clearing my throat, I gesture to the ledgers and put a mask of indifference on. "I've begun the process of lookin' through your family's finances."

Rainey hurries forward, her eyes filled with concern. "And?"

"Just as I thought, the accountant your momma hired after Pleas's death is a halfwit."

Her face falls, and at that moment, I want to take back my words. But when have Rainey and I ever been anything but honest with one another? It's one of the things I can never fault her for, and vice versa.

"What do you mean?"

"Mr. Clarence Sedwig?" I say. Rainey nods. "How long has he been your accountant?"

"For several years. There was a short time that Miles had taken over all the accounts."

"For how long?"

"It was years ago. All I remember is Miles sittin' in the study, his head bent as he intently poured over the ledgers as though his life depended on it."

I nod, encouragingly.

"But it's my understandin' that his son Gerard was quite

skilled with numbers and would help him." She averts her gaze. "Before he too perished in the war."

"Ah. I understand." I bow my head, mulling over my next words. Because even though I'd just begun looking through the ledger's there were numerous errors that anyone with two working eyes would notice. "Well, Mr. Sedwig has been muckin' up numbers, and the Pleasonton fortune went into bad investments. Would Pleas sign off on this?"

"Before the war? I believe so. Durin', I think Momma took over. Perhaps Mr. Sedwig encouraged her to invest."

Like a hungry lion, I pounce on her words. "What companies were they?"

"I don't know. I can search in the study. See if I can find any important documents."

"Thank you. Anythin' can help. It doesn't make sense why the ledgers are so terribly flawed. How this man had a career as an accountant is most remarkable. Your family might've been his only clientele."

Rainey's nostrils flare as she looks away. "I will kill Mr. Sedwig myself."

I stop myself from smiling, but inside I'm thinking, "There's my girl."

"Well, *le savauge*, I regret to inform you that your little bow and arrow are of no use. He died two weeks ago."

Her eyes widen. "From what?"

"I'm not sure. Old age? The man was ninety-two."

Rainey mutters a curse beneath her breath that has the corner of my mouth tilting up. Wonder what Conrad would think of Rainey if he could see if her in her raw, natural element. To me, this is when she's at her finest. Cheeks become flushed, eyes wide, and there's a small part between her lips. She'll lick her lower lip every so often as though she's deliberating over her answer, or the destruction of her opponent.

I cross my arms and lean against the fireplace mantel, watching her pace the floor. "Did you ever meet him?"

"Yes, once. Very old man. Could not hear a thing," Rainey replies.

"Not surprised. You should have asked him what it was like to be alive durin' the Old Testament."

At times my humor can be crass and inappropriate, and other moments it's a much-needed transition for the uncomfortable. For Rainey and me, these wisecracks can go both ways. I hold my breath and wait for a reply. She stops pacing. She becomes silent for a millisecond before laughter spills out of her mouth. No one in the world has a better laugh that Rainey. It's infectious. When you hear it, you stop what you're doing and seek the source of the sound, smile in spite of yourself, and try to find out what is so very funny. You want to laugh with her.

So I do, because even my dark soul deserves a moment of solace every so often.

"Oh, the stories he could have told," she says wistfully, as her laughter dies off.

"He would have made for a great dinner companion."

She looks down at the floor, stabbing the foot of her shoe into the Persian carpet over and over. "I'm still quite furious," she says after a beat of silence.

"As you should be. This is your family's money we're speakin' of." My gaze flits between the ledger and Rainey's tall, regal frame. I want to find a way for her to get out of this situation. Just because she's Pleas's little sister. Because she's a close family friend. Because I want nothing more than to wash my hands of this dreaded dowry.

That's it.

"Did you enjoy yourself tonight?"

Rainey lifts her head and looks at me from beneath her lashes. And it feels as though I've been punched in the gut. "It was dinner, Livingston."

"I've heard people can fall for one another around the dinner table, no?"

Rainey crosses her arms and grins. "Is that so?"

"It's possible," I say cryptically.

"Anythin' is possible.

"Will he be fillin' anymore of your dates?"

"My calendar is full of other men at the moment."

The last time Rainey and I were in close proximity she caused me to be aroused by a mere touch. It's in both our best interests if I leave the room. I did what I needed to do, which was tell her what I discovered so far in the books.

It's not as though Rainey is the only woman available. If I leave now, I can go to Charleston and have a woman of my choosing in my bed within the hour. It's happened before, and it can happen again. But there's no challenge in that.

"Any more questions you have for me?" Rainey asks.

"I'm not certain."

"Let me know. I can write them on your palm."

She smiles wickedly at me. Undeniably, she thought she was delivering a challenge, but I wasn't thinking of her as Rainey. There was a millisecond her words made my blood pound, and adrenaline course through my veins. I began to take a step forward to get a better look at her, this woman in front of me. But then I blinked, and it was Rainey.

I cleared my throat. Son of a bitch, what has gotten into me? "No need for the write hand."

"If that will be all, then I think I should go. I don't doubt my absence is noticed."

There's nothing left for us to speak on, yet I don't want to go, and I don't want her to leave. I have no desire to go home to an empty home. For the past few days, the Pleasonton ledgers have been a wonderful distraction from my nightmares, but I can only look at so many numbers until they all begin to blend. I suppose I could drink. I can't think of a time liquor has ever disappointed me. However, even that doesn't seem tempting. "Conrad seemed quite forward with you in the dinin' room."

"Forward?" Rainey's brows pucker as she stares at the floor momentarily. Then, her eyes widen. "Are you alludin' to him touchin' my back? With that logic, Étienne and Asa have been forward with me several times in the past few years. I think you should speak with them."

"They are irrelevant right now."

"Are they, though? Because it seems to me no man is safe."

"They've grown up with you," I cut in.

"As have you yet, remarkably, I don't feel safe right now."

My eyes narrow into thin slits. "Is that so?"

"Certainly. Everywhere I look there you are, and you can claim you're attemptin' to keep me safe, but I think that's not true. I think you're a bit resentful."

Her words are laughable. "Resentful?"

"Yes, resentful. Resentful that maybe your *le savauge* isn't so savage after all, and other men notice." Rainey leans closer, her deep brown eyes staring into mine. "Maybe they find me desirable."

She doesn't realize it, but she paints an alluring picture. Smartly, she grins because she thinks she's about to win this round. My lips curl upward because the point goes to me. *Le savauge* isn't an insult. Never has been. I like her savage and wild. It is her title, and what sets her apart from every other woman.

I won't tell her, though. She needs to discover that for herself.

"Don't be at my next date, Livingston."

Like Rainey, I can never back away from a challenge. Intrigued, I tilt my head to the side and cross my arms. "And if I am?" I counter.

The two of us stare at one another. We've done this so many times throughout the years. Provoke, incite, and placate only to repeat the process over and over again.

Just kiss her.

The thought stuns me, but once I think the three words, I can't erase them from my mind. God, I wish I could. There's a slight hitch in Rainey's breath. Her eyes widen. She feels the shift in the room. I dip my head closer. Rainey doesn't stop me and that fills me with anticipation. She wants this, too.

Just kiss her.

"Knock, knock."

I jump back, nearly launching myself across the room to get as far away from Rainey as possible. Serene peeks her head into the room. She looks between Rainey and me with raised brows. "Am I interrupting?"

I give my sister-in-law a smile. "Not in the slightest. In fact, you just missed me turnin' down Rainey's proposition to come on her next date with one of the bachelors."

I turn to Rainey in time to see the dazed look in her eyes change into annoyance. Whatever almost happened before Serene came into the room was a mistake. Things are back to how they should be. "I'd love to, darlin'. But I just can't." Gently I tap her under the chin. The gesture is playful, but I can't help but notice how smooth her skin is, and the way her eyes brighten with defiance.

Rainey swats my hand away, her cheeks turning red.

"I don't believe you for a second, but that's not why I'm here." Serene steps into the room with her hands filled with a large stack of cream paper and envelopes.

"What's this?" I ask.

Very carefully, Serene places the stack of paper on the desk and takes a deep breath. "These are going to be what the invitations for the bachelor ball are written on. I wanted to ask if you could help Rainey address them in several days time, but I didn't know if you'd left yet?"

"Oh, that's not necessary," Rainey interjects before I have the chance to reply. "I can manage on my own."

"It's a lot," Serene says. "By invitation number fifty your hand will resemble a misshapen claw."

Rainey appears to be weighing her choices: accept my help or take the risk and have a disfigured hand for the rest of her life.

"It appears as though Rainey is more than okay walkin' around with a gnarled hand for the rest of her life," I say.

A frustrated groan slips from Rainey. She throws her hands up in the air. "Fine! He can help."

"Excellent," Serene replies. "You two can address all two hundred invitations at Belgrave?"

"My God," I mutter.

"Wait? Two hundred? What happened to the guest list of seventy-five people?" Rainey asks with shock.

"What happened is the word has spread about this ball, and no one wants to miss it," Serene says. "You would be surprised the amount of people I've had to turn away."

"Enlighten me," I challenge.

"Sixty people," Serene replies, enunciating each word very slowly.

Rainey's eyes widen. "My word."

Serene nods, looking very pleased with herself. "Whether people like my idea or not is irrelevant. All that matters is they're talkin'."

"But how are they talkin'?" I'm quick to point out.

Serene pointedly ignores me.

"And before I leave, I've taken the liberty of updating the bachelor list for you. Just in case you forget who's who," Serene says with a smile.

"Oh, there's no need for that when one has you, Serene," I say dryly.

Her eyes narrow into thin slits as she looks in my direction.

Rainey murmurs her thanks as she accepts the list and begins to look through it. Her eyes intently scan the names on the list as though she's studying for an exam.

I snatch the paper out of Rainey's hands and try to get a glimpse of the names, but Rainey yanks the list back, tearing a small corner of the paper in the process. "Give me that."

At the beginning of the sixty days she seemed reluctant, almost shy to meet the men. But as each day passes, she grows comfortable with each date she has with one of the bachelors. I think she's been spending far too much time with Serene.

I peer around Rainey to try to get a glimpse of the names. The next elimination is soon, but names have been crossed through making it abundantly clear who Rainey wanted to continue to pursue and who she didn't. I read the names that aren't crossed out, but there's one that catches my eye and causes me to burst into laughter.

I laugh so hard my sides hurt.

Rainey lowers the list to her side and straightens her shoulders. "What is it?"

I take a deep breath long enough to say, "Taylor."

"What about him?"

I wipe the tears from the corner of my eyes as the last of my chuckles escape. "For starters his last name is Hiscock. Do you want to be Mrs. Hiscock?" I grab the paper from her, lift it in the air, and peer closely. "This has to be a typo." Moments later, I lower the paper and grin. "No. He's still Mr. Hiscock and you're still Mrs. Hiscock."

"Stop callin' me that," she hisses.

"Rainey, no respectable woman would be Mrs. Hiscock."

She plucks the paper from my grip. "His last name is of no relevance to me."

"I'm just tryin' to help," I offer.

Rainey clucks her tongue. "Are you, though? Because if you were tryin' to help you wouldn't be so arbitrary."

I shrug. "I don't know what to tell you. The men are unsavory."

"No, you're unsavory so you believe every man is unsavory."

"All the more reason to value my opinion. I can spot fellow bastards better than most."

I continue to look over her shoulder. "Grady? What kind of name is Grady?"

"Grady is quite a common name. The better question is, what kind of name is Livingston?" Rainey shoots back.

"It is a family name!" I object.

Rainey shrugs a small shoulder and resumes looking at the list. "My God, is Duncan's last name Hyman?"

She twists around and appears far from amused. "It's Hageman."

"Wow." I whistle. "That was close."

"You are incredibly vulgar," Rainey huffs.

I wink at her. "Thank you, darlin'."

"Do not call me darlin'."

I lean toward her. "Why not? I've called many women darlin'."

Sighing, Rainey gives me her full attention. "Maybe that's why I don't care for the endearment."

"But the endearment can and will be used when a man is flirtin'. What are you goin' do when a man calls you sweetheart?" I challenge.

Rainey's body freezes, and her eyes flit to the names. After a few seconds, she replies. "I would permit it."

My blood ices over at the thought of another man calling her sweetheart. It's not jealousy, but it comes close to it and I don't care for it. I give her a crooked grin. "Then you should perfect the art of flirtin', Red Rainey." I move closer when I know I shouldn't. "You're red because you're embarrassed."

She looks at me from beneath her lashes. If she was an accomplished flirt she'd realize that action right there was a coquettish act, and enough to get any red-blooded man's interest piqued. "Oh, please do enlighten me on how to seduce my future husband," she says, her words dripping with sarcasm.

My tongue and my brain don't seem to be working, and my eyes have a mind of their own and can't seem to stop staring at Rainey's lips. Has her bottom lip always been so plump and soft? And is she wearing rouge? Women don't have lips such a natural color.

Abruptly, I lean back in my chair, and clear my throat. My thoughts are going down the wrong path. "I'm afraid you'll have to task out another man for the job," I grin at her. "I'm already preoccupied."

Grinding her teeth, Rainey fixes her eyes on the paper. "Oh no, whatever will I do?" she replies dryly.

The idea of Rainey seeking someone else to teach her how to properly seduce a man doesn't sit well with me and leaves a bitter taste in my mouth. "Which one of these lucky fellas will you see next?" I ask, anxious to change the subject.

"If you must know —"

"Since I'm in charge of your dowry, I must," I cut in.

Rainey gives me an irritated glance. "The next bachelor I will see is Duncan."

"And what is it you'll be doin' with Duncan?"

Rainey avoids eye contact by repeatedly straightening the

papers in her hands. "I'm unsure."

"Shouldn't you know?"

"I think the better question is should you know?"

I snort. "I don't want to know. I'm merely askin' in case I should leave my car runnin' where you're located should my ward need a getaway if Duncan is less than savory."

Crashing her hands on the table, Rainey faces me, eyes ablaze. "Stop callin' me your ward."

Lifting my hands in supplication, I take a step back and lean against the wall. "My apologies. I was simply givin' you an option out of seein' this bachelor."

I was merely jesting when I said I'd be a getaway for Rainey. It's just fascinating to watch that porcelain skin turn all rosy when she's uptight. All the same, it might not be the worst idea I've had. Seeing so many men isn't safe. One of them is bound to try to take advantage of her, and even though she has Étienne and Serene with her, I know how the two of them can become swept up in their own world and not notice anything around them.

"Your opinion is not needed. I've spoken to Duncan before, and he's been nothin' but a gentleman."

I push away from the wall and stand tall. Her answer doesn't sit well with me. A lot of her answers as of late haven't been sitting well with me. "When?"

"Two days ago. I was shoppin' with Serene and just happened to see him."

"I bet you did," I mutter beneath my breath. "Since Duncan sounds like prince charmin' are you plannin' your life with him? Is your first son going to be named after him, or perhaps you'll go with Milton in memory of your beloved fish?"

On cue, the corners of her lips curl upward. She fights it. She always does. But she loses and then she laughs. It's a sound that always strikes me in the gut. A sound I can hear no matter where I'm at. A sound to pull me out of any darkness. If that isn't the very definition of pure laughter, my God, I don't know what is.

"I can guarantee you none of my children will have the

name Milton. No one can compare to Milton, and the name Milton for a child?" She scrunches her pert nose. "It's a very stiff name. Fit for someone who's a butler for a large English estate."

The corner of my mouth curls upward. "I believe you're right."

Rainey smiles back, and whether she realizes it or not, she leans in. There's no question in my mind, Conrad could burst into the room and she wouldn't be able to call him by his first name for all the money in the world.

Her plump lips part.

Say you've changed your mind. Say you will not see Duncan.

She doesn't say anything, though. Instead, she folds up the list into quarters and tucks it into her dress. The action allows me a small glimpse of her cleavage. Rainey's skin is smooth and glows in the room. My blood heats at the small action; so many times I've seen her as Pleas's little sister, and then she does that, and it shows how much she's grown. Rainey slowly bats her eyes at me, and a half-smirk appears that speaks to every red-blooded male.

"How can I thank you, Livingston, for everythin' you're doin' for me?"

"*Dieu aide moi,*" I mutter, once I catch my breath.

She taps me on the nose as though I'm a little boy. "And that is how you properly flirt."

With my heart racing much too fast, I watch the gentle sway of Rainey's hips as she walks out of the room. Perhaps Serene should consider changing the name of the bachelor ball to The Hunting Season because these men will not make it out with their hearts intact.

Not a one of them.

CHAPTER FIFTEEN

LIVINGSTON

She's been with him for almost an hour.

Sixty whole minutes.

Approximately thirty-six hundred seconds.

And during that time the infuriating woman cannot go fifteen minutes without inserting her opinion. The fact she's lasted this long is proof miracles can and do happen on a regular basis.

What are they talking about? I've spoken with Duncan. He's not terribly fascinating. Not a thrill-seeker like Rainey. Or bold like Rainey. He doesn't have strong opinions like Rainey.

But he does have one thing that Rainey requested: he comes from money.

The common denominator all the men have is money. I don't believe that's a coincidence. And I cannot fault Rainey. When she said her family was in financial peril, she was being generous.

There were four weeks left until Pleas's deadline, and unless a rich mysterious relative of Rainey's swooped in to save her and her Momma, they were facing the risk of losing everything, including the house that had been in her family's possession the minute fortune fell into their lap nearly one hundred and fifty years ago.

Even I couldn't deny the appeal of Rainey's dowry. It would be the obvious, and painless way. I don't have the best morals like Étienne, but watching Rainey marry a man she doesn't love and who's intentions are less than honorable doesn't sit well with me.

"Livingston, we've been here for quite some time. Can we leave?" my date asks.

For a moment, I forget why she's here, and then I remember. I asked Georgina to be my dinner companion. I invited her as a distraction and hoped that later, she'd come home with me. If I could be aroused by a mere touch from Rainey and tempted to almost kiss her, perhaps I was cured from my lack of sexual activity. Maybe if I finally slept with a woman, any woman, I wouldn't be seeing Rainey in the way I have. And everything can go back to normal.

Georgina and I have had dinner before, but tonight, I've hardly spoken two words to her. That's because our table is at the perfect place, angled in such a way where I can watch Rainey with Duncan and hidden from sight where Rainey won't notice. Although I swear there was more than once were Rainey abruptly looked over her shoulder. Almost as though she could sense my stare. I would shrink lower in my seat and wait until she faced forward.

I knew I couldn't stay here all night. Besides, their food just arrived, and there's nothing captivating in watching Étienne devour his food as though it's his last meal.

I told Rainey I'd stop disrupting her dates, and with her, I always keep my word. In all honesty, I can't fully get to the bottom of my actions for coming tonight. I want to keep an eye out for Rainey, but with Étienne and Serene overlooking tonight, I can't justify my actions.

I don't want her to see me or even know I was here.

There's no reason in sitting here, attempting to absolve myself for being here. All that matters is Rainey doesn't catch sight of me as I make my quick exit.

I finish off the last of my drink and give Rainey and her date a final glance before I look at my own. "We can leave."

I still have the opportunity to spend the evening with a beautiful woman, and I won't let any more time go to waste.

"Did you hear me?"

I look down at Georgina's fingers crawling up my stomach. She gives me a look that's meant to be seductive but merely translates as desperate.

As I try to think of what I last heard her speaking about, the clock on the fireplace mantel loudly ticks. How long have we been sitting here? Because I swear it's been hours, and if it wasn't for the drink in my hand my body would be far more stiff from sitting here. By now, I expected the two of us to be in my room, but my mind continues to stray. Have Rainey and Duncan left the restaurant? They must have. It's far too late. But they appeared to be having an enjoyable night, so does that mean Rainey will want to see him again? After all the bachelors were chosen, I discovered Duncan was an acquaintance of Étienne's. My brother said Duncan hailed from a prestigious family. Graduated from Columbia University in 1904. Started out as an office boy for his family's small but prosperous business, Blue Stone Industries. I'm half convinced Étienne likes him because he knows Duncan will be good conversation for himself. A fellow businessman to discuss the economy and strategies with...what is not to love?

What I want to know is, if Duncan's so wonderful, why hasn't anyone proclaimed him as their own?

He sounds like another bachelor on the never-ending list that isn't good enough and has suspect motives.

I take another drink to stop the constant barrage of questions running through my head. Between me and my date, we have drank far too much. Yet I have a strange suspicion that nothing will be powerful enough to withstand Rainey.

"Livingston?" my date drawls. "Did you hear me?"

Lazily, I smile at her. "My apologies, darlin'. Can you repeat yourself?"

Georgina places her drink on the table before focusing on me. "I said we must never go this long without seein' each other."

"I agree, but I've been busy."

She mock pouts. Rainey would never pout. She would much rather throw herself in front of a car than pout and appear featherbrained. "With what?"

I lift a shoulder and take a drink. With the number of drinks I'm consuming tonight, it's going to take three able-bodied men to help me up to my room. But I don't need my room. I can sleep anywhere. The floors, filthy trenches, in the back of a Liberty Truck. It only took me the ravages of war to learn that sleeping comfortably in the silence with clean sheets, is a luxury most fail to appreciate.

"Livingston!" Georgina whines, but there is a glimmer of frustration in her eyes.

"I'm sorry. I'm sorry." I lean in close and smile. "I'm merely prolongin' this evenin' so you won't leave."

In reply, she giggles, leans back into me, and all is forgiven.

"The word about town is you're with the Pleasonton girl." Georgina taps her index finger against the corner of her mouth. "What's her name?"

Resting my head against the settee, I look at Georgina from the corner of my eye. "You know her name is Rainey."

Instinctively, my hand tightens around my glass. I don't know what Georgina has to say, but it's impossible for me not to become defensive on Rainey's behalf.

Georgina scoffs and glances at her nails. "I certainly do not. We didn't precisely run in the same social circle. When I was intent on makin' my debut, she was teachin' the rest of the debutantes curse words."

I'd never heard that story, but it sounded so remarkably Rainey I can't help but chuckle. Georgina raises both brows, so I focus on our conversation.

"Is it true?" she asks.

"Is what true?"

"That Rainey is in search of a husband?" Georgina whispers excitedly.

As much as I loathed this entire bachelor fiasco, there wasn't a single part of me that wanted to discuss this with

Georgina. She was here to keep my mind off Rainey, not on her.

"A husband? Is that what the gossipmongers are sayin'?" I say, feigning indifference.

"Not just the gossipmongers, but everyone."

Upon hearing that, my heart picks up. I don't believe Rainey would take issue with all of Charleston discussing her bachelor scenario. In fact, I was the one to tell her about men placing bets on her bachelors. The people who needed to be informed were. The truth was bound to be unveiled. Far more shocking liaisons have occurred throughout the years. But what could possibly be shocking for the people of Charleston is the Pleasonton's financial struggles. That would upset Rainey more than anything.

"Is this how you want to spend our time? Talkin' about hearsay?"

Georgina's lips curve into a smile, and when she leans forward, it's deliberate so I can look down her dress.

I'd be a fool not to take what she's offering.

At last.

But as she tilts her head to the side, and her lips almost touch mine, I smell her perfume. It's not overpowering. Nevertheless, the scent makes me pause. It's a sweet scent that's distinctly artificial. Rainey's scent is nothing of the sort. She always manages to smell like fresh flowers. Even her hair smells like it.

Quit thinking about Rainey!

Closing the distance between Georgina and me, I kiss her. My mouth moves, and my head angles to the side, but not once does my heart rate pick up. Frustration starts to build so I move my tongue against hers. I need to give this time. Georgina molds herself against me and enthusiastically kisses me back.

I feel nothing. Not one damn thing. I was more enticed by a single drag of Rainey's fingernail against my palm than this kiss. It's no use. This was all for nothing.

Before the kiss can go any further, I pull away, curling my

fingers around her forearms. Georgina's eyes are still shut, and her mouth's pursed together. When she realizes my lips are no longer on hers, she looks at me with confusion.

I extend my arms over my head and dramatically yawn. "It's late."

She arches a brow and leans in. "I know."

This one is not going to make things easy.

"I have business to attend to early in the mornin'." Slapping my hands against my knees, I stand and hold a hand out for her to take. She's temporarily aghast at my polite yet firm rejection. With flushed cheeks, she slowly stands, accepting my hand. She agrees she must be leaving, and how we must do this again, and at the front door, she leans in one last time. I oblige, giving her a long, deep kiss.

Still nothing.

"Livingston, we must never go this long without seein' each other, all right?" she breathes.

Nodding just to get her to leave, I'm delighted when she hails a cab. I close the door, and heavily sag against it. Dragging my hands through my hair, I stare at the floor. I'm positively certain that if I go outside and ask Georgina to come back in, she will.

I have no desire to.

Pushing away from the wall, I walk to the sitting room and pour myself another drink. I drop down into one of the chairs and stare blankly at the wall across from me. I don't know what I'm turning into. Before the war, I didn't have nightmares and nearly drank myself into oblivion. And before Rainey, I could freely be with other women without the image of her haunting me.

My circumstances with Rainey would eventually change. There would be a solution to her problem, and I would see her less. And my nightmares would slowly become distant memories. I'd drink less to forget and more out of remembrance.

Until then, all I need to remember is that sooner than we know, every after becomes a before.

CHAPTER SIXTEEN

LIVINGSTON

The smell of soot and gunpowder wafts into the air, intertwining with the rancid scent of sweat and dead bodies. The combination can make your eyes fill with tears and your stomach churn.

I lay on the cool ground, staring up at the sky. Clouds cover the sun. I can't think of the last time I saw the sunshine. It seems as though even the sun is reluctant to enter No Man's Land. I have only my fellow soldiers and the animals in the thicket of trees not far from me for company. But no one is making a sound.

My ears still ring from consecutive gunfire. All at once, it seemed to cease. I blindly reach for my Chauchat and find it near my right hip. Slowly, I sit up and see I'm in a dirty field with bodies all around me. Some move, others don't.

My breathing increases as I come to sit up on knees and search the faces around me. I don't recognize the lifeless bodies. I stand, my shoulders rigid and my rifle clutched between my hands.

Somewhere close by, a man gasps for air. It's a sound that cannot be disregarded no matter how fearful one is to move. Cautiously, I step forward. There's a heavy fog that seems to be closing in around me as the seconds tick by. I don't know which direction I should go. The ground is so frozen, the grass crunches beneath my worn boots as I walk forward. I look at the bodies in search of anyone who still might be alive.

I seem to walk for miles without encountering a single living soul.

Why am I still alive?

The question echoes in my head as I keep walking through the empty field. I look down at one of the bodies lying on the ground and see the face of Rainey's father, Malcolm. I stop so quickly my boots slip on the mud, and I almost fall forward. He's nothing of what he used to be. There's no laughter causing his stomach to rumble, or a well-timed wisecrack pouring from his mouth.

Swallowing, I take several steps backward before I turn around. I can't get away from the sight of his corpse and the smell of decay quick enough.

I stumble forward, my legs wobbling beneath me. I should stop and take a deep breath, but I'm afraid if I do, I might turn around and see the image of Miles and Rainey's dad. So I continue. I wish I didn't. I wish I had stopped and looked anywhere but to my left. Because it's there that I see my father lying next to my mom. My younger brother, Julian, right next to them. It's then my breathing becomes choppy. I don't come any closer, but I'm afraid to leave them. I should because this is wrong and morbid. I still remember the day they were buried. I couldn't bear to look then, so perhaps that's why I can't tear my eyes away now.

My heart feels as though it's stuck in my throat. I don't know whether to cry out in fear or muster the courage to speak.

When you lose someone, you think of what you'd say to them if you saw them one more time.

"Pourquoi es-tu mort?"

No one answers me.

Words felt from the heart can hurt just as badly spoken aloud. They disappear into the fog that surrounds me, but the remnants of them still linger and cling to the earth around me.

The sights and smells make my eyes water. I turn in every direction, trying to find a way toward safety.

As I continue walking, I look at each body I pass. I don't want to. I'm terrified of what I might see.

I pass by a wounded soldier and immediately stop. Because the wounded soldier is Miles Pleasonton. He lays on the ground with a single gunshot in his upper chest. The material of his uniform absorbs the blood, creating a circular pattern. And on his right hand, blood coats his fingertips, forming a small story of the seconds after he was shot. On impact, he fell to the ground. He feels pain, but shock controls his movements. He lifts a hand to the wound, believing the touch will stop the heavy bleeding, but nothing could've saved him from the fatal shot.

"Pleas?" I whisper.

As I bend down, his eye sockets became endless black holes. And his skin begins to eat away around his mouth until all I can see are his teeth and gums.

Rats crawl out of his eyes. The same ones that lived in the trenches and they're coming toward me. Ready to attack me, eat my eyes, and—

In one giant rush, I sit up, clutching my bedsheets as though I'm a little boy. Frantically, I look around my room. It's silent and safe. But I don't feel safe.

I drag my hands through my hair and squeeze my eyes shut. It's my own damn fault for believing I could fall asleep without the past chasing after me.

Swinging my legs over the side of the bed, I walk across my room and to the armoire. Even in the pitch black, I know precisely where my liquor is located. The second my fingers curl around the bottle, some of the panic I feel subsides.

I twist the top off and let it fall to the floor. The first and second drink burn as it travels down my throat, but it becomes tolerable by the third and fourth.

Lowering the bottle from my lips, I look over my shoulder at my bed. Georgina not staying tonight turned out to be the best decision. Never thought I'd see the day where I'd be relieved not to have a woman in my bed, but it's better than having her witness my nightmare. Can I call what I experienced a nightmare? It felt merciless in its details and unfeeling in its delivery.

Going back to sleep isn't a possibility. I'm afraid to close my eyes and come face to face with the people I've loved and lost one more time. I sit in the seat in the corner of the room and stare out the window.

I volunteered to join the Army before the draft, and my family didn't understand. Étienne was exempted from joining because of his poor vision. Nat's husband, Oliver, was eligible and, much to his dismay, did what was asked of him. Pleas waited until a week before he was to leave before he told his close friends. I could envision Rainey using a rifle to protect herself and the people around her with relative ease. I couldn't with Pleas. He believed in third, fourth, and fifth chances. Didn't care much for the annual fox hunts. He preferred resolution in a peaceful manner that didn't require bloodshed.

The night before he left, I spoke to him and asked him what made him want to join. For several seconds, he was quiet. Like always, he remained calm and collected. He looked over at me and lifted a shoulder. "This is the right thing to do."

I joined to find my worth. To find what I'm meant to do in this world. I joined to find a bit of myself because after my accident years ago, I haven't been the same. I don't remember that time. I don't remember being attacked and left for dead. Or the time I spent at Belgrave recuperating. I simply know because my family told me.

I discovered I wasn't going to find my answers in France in trenches. I probably wasn't going to find it here, either. And now I was left to figure out what I was going to do next with my life.

Many times, I've wondered where I'd be right now if I hadn't joined the Army. Would I be drinking so profoundly? I'd like to think no. Would I have intense nightmares? I know for certain I wouldn't.

Placing the liquor on the floor, I let my hands dangle between my legs and close my eyes. *"Pourquoi suis-je toujours là?"*

The jostling of the car makes me groan as I press the brakes to park in front of the steps leading to Belgrave. Wearing the same clothes as yesterday, I take the steps two at a time and immediately regret the fast-moving action. I know I'm late. Incredibly late. If I don't get an earful from Serene, I certainly will from Rainey.

On cue, Ben opens the door, and in spite of my splitting headache, I manage to say thank you. Étienne's office door is open. He's at work, and the first floor is relatively quiet save for a few servants moving here and there. Serene is nowhere to be found, and for that, I'm grateful.

Might as well find Rainey and get this over with.

The intent of last night was to forget all about Rainey and have a warm body in my bed. Instead, I had the worst nightmares since I came back from the war and drank until I passed out. I don't have nightmares every night but quite often. At times, the setting would transform. Trenches, smoke-filled fields, and a forest with trees all around. But there was always the sight of blood coating my hands and the echoes of screams of no one I could save. They left me tense, shaken, tired, and afraid because I knew they were never going to stop.

This morning, I woke up sprawled across the library floor and drooling on the design of the house I started months ago but never finished. I had ample amount of time to do what I loved the most, but I only seemed compelled to pull out my designs when I couldn't think long enough to change my mind. Very few people knew of my secret hobby that had turned into my only passion, and I intended on keeping it that way.

"If you're searching for Miss Pleasonton, I believe she's in the ballroom," Ben provides for me.

"Once again, you come to my rescue, Ben," I say and dip my head.

My feet are heavy as I walk up the stairs. It seemed like a good idea when I told Serene I'd help address the invitations. Anything to drive Rainey mad, right?

As I heavily lean on the banister for support, I begin to regret ever saying yes. My witticism isn't up to par, so I won't stand a chance today. It will be a miracle if I don't get sick in one of the large vases in the ballroom.

I exhale loudly when I make it to the second floor. My feet plod against the floor. Why am I putting myself through this misery? It's simple. There's a small part of me that's utterly terrified to be alone. I used to believe my demons only found me at night, but now I'm not so sure. And I'd rather spend the day with a headache and looming sickness and Rainey as company any day than experience the bad dreams I had last night.

The ballroom door creaks in protest when I open it. It's a noise that I routinely ignore, but today, it makes me wince and earns Rainey's attention. She stops organizing the invitations placed on the table in front of her long enough to look me up and down.

"Well, well, well...the king of the South decided to show up," she says, her tone droll.

With my temples pounding, I step deeper into the room and immediately regret it. Citrus oil fills my nostrils and makes me want to hurl. A servant must have been in here earlier. Normally, I wouldn't mind the scent, but today, it's repugnant. I wince at the bright light filling the vast space and rub my temples. "My God, has this ballroom always been so bright?"

She straightens her spine and narrows her eyes at me. "Are you foxed?"

"No. I was foxed last night. I now have a headache, and you hollerin' does not help one bit."

"I do apologize, I've merely been waitin' here for nearly an hour."

I take my time walking across the room. To the unknowing eye, it's a slow stride. For me, I'm reminding myself the sickness shall pass in an hour's time. "Where's Serene?" I ask.

Rainey perfectly aligns the four pens in the middle of the table, not bothering to spare me a glance. "I'm not certain. I wasn't scheduled to meet her. I was scheduled to meet you."

The corner of my mouth attempts to curve into a crooked grin. I simply don't have it in me to be the jovial Livingston she knows me as. "Well, I'm here, so let's get to it."

Sighing, Rainey grabs the pen in front of her. I've been late numerous times before, yet today, she's unnaturally angry with me. Did last night not go well? Did Duncan make unwelcome advances after I left the restaurant? No, he wouldn't. Étienne would have informed me if the bastard did. Besides, it's none of my concern.

I clear my throat. "What is it you need me to do?"

Impatiently, Rainey lifts her gaze and turns in my direction. The action sends a whiff of her perfume in my direction. "I need you to address these invites for the ball in your best penmanship. Can you do that?"

"Are you askin' if I can write? Yes. Yes, I can," I respond stoically as I sit down.

Unamused, Rainey returns to addressing each invite. I look at the stack of empty envelopes and the invites. Once again, I'm baffled by all of this. Is this a ball or a wedding?

"The guest list is right here." Rainey taps the paper between us with the tip of her pen. "After you write the name and address, just cross them out and move to the next."

"Can you explain that to me once more?" I ask flatly. "I don't think I quite understand the directions."

Rainey shakes her head, her lips moving to a firm line before she gets to work. Judging from the small list of names already crossed out, it seems as though Rainey got a head start. I grab an envelope and start at the bottom of the page. We work in silence with only the sound of our pens scraping against the paper to cushion the stillness. I must admit, this task is methodical and almost relaxing. For a few moments, I almost forget my temples are pounding.

And then, out of nowhere, Rainey blurts, "Where were you last night?"

My pen stops, causing the ink to bleed onto the envelope. Did she see me last night? Quickly, I finish writing out the last name and look at Rainey from the corner of my eye. "At home. With a date."

Both brows rise, and her eyes flash with…jealousy? The heat is there and gone before I can comment on it.

"Her name is Angostura, and she's never let me down."

Rainey absorbs my words and shakes her head. "I'm sorry I showed interest."

"If I didn't know better, *le savauge*, I'd say you're…" Leaning back in my chair, I tap a finger against my unshaved chin. "Almost envious."

She folds the invitation in half and nearly shoves it into the envelope. "I'm not envious. Envy would imply I long for somethin' that someone has, and that's not true. What I care about is my time bein' wasted."

I whistle as I shake my head. "My, my," I drawl. "You're very disagreeable today. Did you not get enough sleep last night after your date with Duncan? If so, perhaps I should speak with your momma about implementin' a curfew because you're my ward and it's in your best interest."

Rainey's cheeks grow redder by the second. She rubs her temples and mutters curse words that would have any soldier blushing. If only her devoted bachelors could see her now.

After a few seconds, she drops her hands and takes a deep breath. "No curfew is necessary. Duncan had me home at a proper time."

I was angling to find out how her night went, but I wanted specific points, not vague details.

"Will you see him again?" I ask, keeping my tone disinterested as I cross a name off from the guest list.

"I believe so." Rainey keeps her gaze forward. Her penmanship is fluid and graceful. The first letter of each name is always done with a bold loop that almost leads you to believe the name she just wrote was hers. I don't know how she manages to write so beautifully.

"You believe so," I repeat under my breath.

"Mmmhmm."

For reasons I cannot understand, Rainey is uncharacteristically upset with me. More so than usual. She received her wish. I did not impose on her time with Duncan. What is churning inside that stubborn mind of hers?

If I didn't have such a wicked headache, I might ponder over this a bit longer. Yet right now, all I want to do is walk out of the room, take a shower, and then pass out. And the only way that will happen is if we finish the task at hand.

Rainey doesn't need my help. She needs an assistant.

"While I was...on my way, did you make much progress with plannin' the ball?" I ask.

"Oh, I did so much!" Rainey says with false enthusiasm. "Because as we both know, I am very well-trained for these events."

"You cannot say I didn't try to prevent this, *le savauge*," I point out, gesturing to the papers scattered about the table.

"You've made it apparent you don't want to be here, and neither do I. If we work together, we should only be a few more minutes, all right?" Rainey reasons.

At random, I pick a name from the guest list and nod. "Fine by me."

One hour later, I throw my hands in the air. "I cannot do this any longer. How about you have anyone who desires to go to this ball place bets, and the people with the highest numbers get an invitation. Or perhaps, we can do a game of chance and place thirty names in a bucket. Draw ten, and those are your guests."

Rainey pinches the bridge of her nose and throws her pen onto the table. "Be serious."

"Oh, I am."

"We have ten more names left on the guest list. That's all. Serene says the invitations need to be mailed immediately. Once we're finished, you can take your leave."

"How kind of you," I drolly reply.

"I am not precisely thrilled about this either, Livingston," Rainey grumbles as she picks up her pen and gets back to work. Her eyes remain glued to the envelope in front of her.

Her words ricochet through my head so badly it feels as though my skull is going to break in half. Normally, my headaches disappear by this time of the day, but I don't think it's the amount of alcohol I drank last night that's causing the tension to build. My nightmare hit the small part of my heart that wasn't wounded and putting on a façade.

Reluctantly, I grab my fountain pen. The muscles in my arm ache in protest with every glide of the pen. Who knew writing could exhaust you so much? Or perhaps, it's been an incredibly long time since I've sat down and held a pen between my fingers.

It makes me think of all the drawings in my office, hidden

from sight. In France, I'd dream of locking myself away in my office and drawing endless houses until my imagination ran dry. Instead, I pulled all the curtains in the house closed until it resembled a dungeon and roamed the halls like a ghost with only liquor and questionable acquaintances to keep me company.

"Precisely how long shall this go on?" Étienne's question rings in my head.

"How's this?"

Rainey lifts her gaze long enough to look at my handiwork. "Good. We'll simply tell Mrs. Mattigola that Serene and Étienne's daughter wrote her name."

I give her an irritated look and continue through the list of names. By the third invite, my hand cramps terribly. I drop my pen and shake my head. "I officially quit. There's no longer any feelin' in my hand."

Standing up, I shake my hand out and begin to pace. Even with a healthy distance away from the table, I can hear the steady scratch of Rainey's pen against the envelope. Blood has begun to rush back to my hand, but I don't stop pacing. I'm still irritated for reasons I cannot explain. I should've stayed at home.

I stare at my hands and I see dirt packed beneath my nails and around my cuticles. Holding my hands in front of me, I spread my fingers. In and out, my hands go from being clean to filthy.

In the distance, I can hear Rainey calling out to me, but her voice is overshadowed by the sound of screams and moans, and the smell of gunpowder.

Impossible. Breathe. You need to breathe!

I should've bathed. I always bathe. Why didn't I bathe? I was determined to get here on time and not allow a glitch in my normal routine to throw me off. That's why.

Explain the situation. Rainey will understand!

I don't want her pity and sympathy. I'd much rather have her condemnation.

As I look at Rainey in the eye, trying to formulate

the correct words, she stands there patiently. She knows something isn't quite right. I find myself moving toward her. Pain understands pain on a fundamental level. Perhaps, that's why we consistently seek solace when we're hurting even though we know we'll regret it later.

"I have things to do."

Rainey remains quiet.

"Better things," I say, my voice rising.

She nods. That's it.

"You understand that, right?"

At that, she lifts a brow. She's not saying anything. I need her to respond.

"The last thing I want to do is to fill out invitations for a bachelor ball," I say, my words dripping with disdain. For such a large room, it feels as though it's closing in on me rather quickly. I need to go home and take a shower to wash the dirt beneath my nails. I need to get away from everyone.

Rainey takes a step forward. "Are you okay?" she asks as she reaches for me. I pull back.

"I'm fine. Leave me alone."

"No, wait."

When I move to the left, so does Rainey. I quickly dodge to the right, but Rainey is fast and anticipates my movements. She looks me straight in the eye. There is no condemnation. No humor. Just concern. I'd much rather have the humor.

"Livingston, tell me what's the matter," she says quietly.

My chest rises and falls rapidly.

"You will be okay, and every breath you take is strength for tomorrow. You can make it through today. You're Livingston Lacroix," she whispers fiercely.

I don't deserve Rainey's kindness, but I'll accept it because there are terrifying moments in my life when I need something to hold onto. But I don't want to have to hold onto her. I want to be able to shake off her arm and say that I'm okay.

Grabbing her by both arms, I'm ready to tell her I simply can't do this today, and she can find Serene or someone else better qualified. But when I do, Rainey's dark eyes go wide, and this close I smell her scent.

She smells...clean and refreshing. And her eyes are wide, fringed with dark lashes. When she parts her lips and takes a deep breath, I notice how plump her lips are. When did that happen?

Frustration mounts as words become tangled in my throat and my body continues to betray me. It doesn't help that Rainey isn't saying a word, either.

"Just...just."

Those are the last words I say to her before I groan and kiss Rainey Pleasonton. My best friend's sister. I kiss her to silence the fear rocking through me, an urgent need for everything to be calm in my world.

At first, her body is as rigid as her lips. My fingers are locked around her forearms, keeping them pinned to their sides because Rainey's wild. I can never hold her in one place for long. I'm afraid if set free, she'll run or punch me in the face.

The longer the seconds go by, Rainey responds in a way I don't expect. She's hesitant, almost shy. My tongue repeatedly glides against the seam of her lips, but she doesn't open her mouth, and that's probably for the best. One of us has sense. I've clearly become unhinged.

I'm persistent and patient as I give her closed-mouthed kisses. Very slowly, I feel her body become pliant. I release her arms to cup her face, and her palms fall against my stomach as she tilts her head to the side. And then her lips part for me.

I don't let this opportunity go to waste. When my tongue moves against hers, she breathes in deep through her nose but doesn't pull away. I don't know what she's thinking. But I know what I'm thinking, and it's that Rainey tastes amazing.

So amazing. A soft moan tears from her throat and rocks through me. Progressively, Rainey grows bolder. Her fingers spread and trail up my chest as her tongue touches mine.

Panting, I rip my lips away from her and stare at Rainey with shock. For once, we wear the same expression. And for once, we're both stunned into silence.

Now it's my turn for my hands to fall to my sides. I shake my head from side to side. What did I do? "I-I'm sorry," I breathe and take a step back. It's imperative that I do. Right now, my brain isn't functioning properly.

Rainey's hands snake out and curl around my wrists. I freeze and stare at her slender fingers as they make soothing caresses on my skin. Swallowing, I look back at her. "No. Don't be sorry. I didn't want you to stop," Rainey says softly. She tugs ever so softly, pulling me back. With my eyes fixated on hers, I go willingly.

When she's close enough to hold, she lets go, and it's as though our bodies instinctively know what to do. She steps back into my arms, and I instinctively wrap them around her waist. Rainey gently holds my face. The hem of her gown brushes against my boots. She inspects me, as though I've spoken to her in a language she doesn't understand. Then she leans in, and her nose brushes against mine. Her lips are inches away. She stays still, her fingertips stroking my cheek. It's sweet and gentle and unexpected from Rainey. I find myself leaning into her touch.

Her touches cease as her lips brush across mine once, then twice. So soft, I question if I imagined them. But each one grows with intensity. By the fifth kiss, her grip on my face tightens, so she's holding me in place as she kisses me deeply. My control is starting to break. Something close to a groan escapes my mouth.

Slowly, go, slowly, I remind myself.

Rainey is inexperienced but eager. I attempt to take control, my tongue moving against her bottom lip. Pressing her flush against me, I gather the fabric of her dress in my fists. Anything to get closer to her. To her bare skin. I feel Rainey everywhere, and it doesn't feel close to enough.

She's untamed and nothing I've ever held in my arms.

What were we precisely doing before this? Is it daylight or night? Where are we? Don't know, don't care, doesn't matter. I hear nothing and feel nothing but Rainey.

She arches against me, allowing me to feel the outline of

her body. Her small breasts rub across my chest, and it takes all of my power not to touch them.

Curling her fingers around the collar of my shirt, she jerks me toward her until there's no space between our bodies. She stands on her tiptoes until we're nearly the same height and sucks on my tongue.

My God, what have I unleashed?

She hums her approval. Her hands are wild as they unbutton my vest and the top three buttons of my shirt. I attempt to help her, but she bats my hands away and continues to fumble her way through. My shirt gapes open. The tips of her fingers touch my chest. My heart jumps as though this is the first time I've held a woman.

Although this is the first time I've ever held a savage woman. Any man with sense would be terrified, but I lost my senses the second I kissed her, so I let her have her way. Her hands trace each line and groove on my stomach so quickly she leaves behind scratches.

I intended to go slowly. I am capable of kissing and walking away. At least I have been in the past. But I can't seem to stop and neither can Rainey. She grows bolder with each second, using her hands and lips.

Her back hits the wall. I wasn't aware we were moving.

Unable to stop myself, I gently suck on her neck. She shudders but doesn't crumple or become weak at the knees. No, not Rainey. Not my *le savauge*.

I'm certain she will match me kiss for kiss.

Touch for touch.

Passion for passion.

And it gives me something I haven't felt for some time. Excitement. What courses through me, inflating my lungs and making my hands shake. My grip on Rainey tightens as though she'll unexpectedly be ripped from me.

She's desperately holding on, and I'm desperate to hold someone. My hands skim up her body, feeling the rigid grooves of her corset. I hear the hitch in her breath. Her fingernails dig into the skin around my hips. I don't have to ask her if I'm the first man to touch her like this because I know I am. That makes me move a bit slower and savor the moment.

My lips find their way back to hers. And right as my thumbs brush the underside of her breasts, the door bangs against the wall. At once, I pivot so my body's looming over Rainey's, blocking her from sight, but I know it's too late. Whoever is standing in the doorway saw us. Looking over my shoulder, I see my very pregnant sister-in-law and my niece standing there. Alex smiles widely, oblivious to what she's walked in on. Serene's mouth hangs open while her face turns as red as her hair.

Is this payback for the time I walked in on her and my brother after they had sex in Étienne's office? Perhaps.

"Uhh…" Serene says.

With one hand firmly around Rainey, I continue to look at my sister-in-law. "We were just —"

"No explanation needed," Serene cuts in. She holds her hand out for Alex to take and immediately turns back toward the doors. "We saw nothing."

As they leave, I hear her say to my niece in a sweet voice, "Alex, honey, this is what I like to call bad timing."

With my heart fiercely pounding, I watch my sister-in-law walk my niece out of the room. Serene gives me a knowing smirk before she shuts the door. Turning back to Rainey, I close my eyes and sigh.

When the two of us separate, my body becomes cold. The way you feel when something warm has abruptly been ripped away from you. My fingers clench and stretch as I fight the urge to reach for her. Immediately, Rainey sets to work on her clothes. I follow her lead, buttoning up my shirt and tucking the hem back into my pants. Rainey makes a point not to look at me. I can't say the same for myself. I can't remember the last time I kissed a woman and responded in that way. I'm still in a daze and watch as she attempts to fix her hair. Both hands lift to her hair as she adjusts the pins, and her blouse stretches against her breasts.

Dear God, what's wrong with me? I want her again.

Clearing my throat, I take a step back. "I'm late…" Blindly, I point toward the windows facing the driveway. "For a meetin'."

Slowly, Rainey lowers her hands. And for once, she nods. "Of course, of course."

"All right, then." I dip my head in her direction and blindly point toward the doors. "I should be goin'."

"All right."

My head tilts to the side as I inspect her. Has her lower lip always been so soft and plump? I swear I would've recognized that before.

"Uh, Livingston?" Rainey says, interrupting my thoughts. "You said you had a meetin'?"

"Right, right." I start to walk backward toward the double doors. Once I'm in the hallway, I take a deep breath, and hurry toward the stairs.

What happened between the two of us?

Better yet, who is Rainey Pleasonton? Her aim with kisses is unparalleled and strikes harder than any bullet. I'm beginning to recognize just how dangerous Rainey truly is.

Rather than leaving, I head to the east wing toward Étienne's office. When I go to knock on the door, it swings opens. I jump, slamming my back against the wall as though I've been caught kissing Rainey all over again. Étienne's head jerks up from the paper in his hand, and he looks at me with confusion. "Oh. Hello."

"Hi," I say with a hint of guilt.

My brother frowns at me. "Is there anything I can do for you?"

I pass by him, heading directly to the sideboard. I need a drink. Right away. "Can't a brother visit his brother?"

"I suppose so. But normally you aren't in the business of bein' up at"—Étienne pulls his pocket watch out to look at the time—"eleven in the morning."

I pour myself a generous drink of scotch. "I was with Rainey."

"Ah, yes, your ward."

"Can we not call her that? Why must people continue to call her that?" I say, my words flowing together in one giant rush before I tip back the scotch. It burns going down, but the adrenaline coursing through me is causing my hands to shake. All because of a kiss.

Étienne arches a brow. "For the very reaction you gave me?"

I swallow loudly and place the empty glass on the sideboard. I want another drink, but I need to pace myself. I drop heavily into one of the seats across from his desks, resting my elbows on my knees, and drag my hands down my face.

My brother walks pasts me and chuckles. "You seem distraught. I would ask why, but I've been in your position many times."

Lifting my head, I watch as he leans against his desk. "My situation is not similar to you and Serene."

"Of course it isn't. But it's interestin'…I was in denial when I first met Serene, the very same way you are now."

"I don't deny a thing. Because there's no attraction between Rainey and me."

Lie.

All I can think about right now is whether she's still in the ballroom and how quickly I could run up the stairs and kiss her again. Groaning, I run my hands through my hair.

Christ. What have I done?

"Are you certain nothin' else is amiss?" Étienne asks after a few seconds of silence.

I lift my head and look him in the eye. "Absolutely."

Lie, lie, lie, lie…LIE!

Étienne stares at me for a moment longer. "Very well. I was goin' to take a much-needed break and go to the stables. Would you like to come?"

"You're takin' a break?"

Étienne pushes away from his desk, looking unamused. "I take breaks. Only when they're needed. Now come with me. Whatever you went through with Rainey…" My brother looks at me carefully. "You need a break."

I stand and pat him on the back. "I couldn't agree more."

CHAPTER SEVENTEEN

RAINEY

I gave my first kiss to Herman Findley when I was thirteen. Even though we were the same age, I wasn't particularly close to him. But Herman didn't mercilessly tease me about my thin frame and ungainly limbs. He was kind and courteous and made me smile. One night after a gathering at his family's home, we kissed in the garden.

Our lips mashed together in a sudden rush, and it was far too wet. My teeth knocked against my lip so hard I was convinced it broke skin and bled. It didn't help that I was taller than him. However, I was taller than most boys my age. My eyes were squeezed shut, trying to emulate the woman I once caught in the embrace of a man at a party. Although, as the seconds ticked by, and nothing of importance happened, I opened my eyes. I couldn't understand why people found this so appealing. Six years later, I found myself in the same position but with a different boy. The kiss wasn't as inelegant as my first, but I felt nothing. My heart didn't beat wildly in my chest. There were no butterflies in my stomach.

Women speak more about marriage, family, embroidery, clothing, and parties. When we gather, there's an infinite amount of topics we speak about, and it's not limited to the opposite sex. When men are the subject of conversation, I listen carefully because while I do not consider myself a wilting wallflower, I still don't know so much about men.

Through conversations, I've discovered that the woman

I saw in the embrace at the party was the expectation, and the desire to want to be her wasn't disproportionate but truly possible.

Since then, I've been seeking the heart-stopping sensation that accompanies the perfect kiss. I knew someday I would find it. I just never expected that kiss would be delivered by Livingston Lacroix.

He left the ballroom minutes ago, but my lips continue to tingle. It's a visceral reminder of what happened. Softly, I brush my lower lip with my thumb and walk toward the table, intent on resuming the tedious task of finishing the invitations, but it's futile. My focus is elsewhere.

Before the kiss, something came over Livingston. Something I've never seen before. He became a different person. Almost as though a curtain was draped over his eyes he was no longer filled with self-assured hubris, but became a bedraggled, frightened man. I didn't know what to make of it, and I still don't.

Did something occur last night to make him act this way? Is that why he didn't disturb me while I was with Duncan? During my dinner, a part of me held a candle of hope that he would burst into the restaurant with an absurd explanation for being there. Rather than being mollified by his absence, I wondered where he was. Was he with one of his admirers? Because of that, I could barely hold a conversation with Duncan. By the time he escorted me to my door and wished me a good night, I realized that Livingston didn't have to be present to still win.

I was irritated when I first saw him walk through the ballroom doors. Irritated that he was beginning to consume so much space in my head. As the day wore on, I realized something wasn't right with him. There was a moment before he kissed me when the pain, frustration, and torment broke free in his eyes. I wanted to wrap my arms around him and protect him from the world.

I have flaws. I have deep-seated pain residing in my soul that will never abate. Who am I to prod into Livingston's life?

Who am I to demand he cut open a vein and tell me everything he saw while at war?

The truth is, it will never happen.

I've always remained steadfast in the belief that you cannot change someone or mend their pain. But you can be a solid support for them. If Livingston needs me, I will forget everything and be there.

Sometimes I think my blind devotion to Livingston stems back to our families. Yes, that must be it. I feel an obligation to make sure he's emotionally stable. And we've experienced so much heartache together. Heartache that most people can't comprehend. I knew Livingston hasn't been himself since the war, but I didn't know he was fighting with his demons this bad.

Especially with Nat in Savannah. They've always had a close relationship, and with her absence, who can he confide in?

"Rainey, I want your opinion."

Halting mid-step, I backtrack—not before I give the front door a longing expression—and stop in front of the sitting parlor doorway. I find a very pregnant Serene standing in the middle of the room with all past Livingston and Lacroix relatives around her.

It's a family reunion of the past.

Serene waves me impatiently into the room. "Come, come."

Hesitantly, I step inside. I was all too ready to flee Belgrave as quickly as possible after my kiss with Livingston, but it was clear Serene was having none of that. I examine the paintings with mild interest. I have my own somber ancestor paintings staring down at me each time I step inside my home. They judge me for being twenty-eight and unattached. I'm failing my family. Bills are not being paid. The home will go into disrepair. Momma will have to sell the house.

How were you the catalyst, though? You cannot fix what you don't know.

I know now, though. And time is of the essence. There are moments I cannot get out of my own way.

"What are your thoughts on these paintings?" Serene asks, pulling me out of my thoughts.

"What are my thoughts?" I repeat.

She nods, her gaze volleying between each stoic face.

"I...uh, I think they are all upstandin' men who–"

She whirls around. "Oh, I don't need that whole song and dance about their character," Serene cuts in. "I want to know how they look. Don't bullshit me, either."

"Oh." I'm a bit taken aback by her request. "Well, to be honest. The paintings are a bit...intimidatin'."

She throws her hand in the air and smiles victoriously. "Thank you!"

"Why do you ask?"

"Because at least one has got to go. I told Étienne his great-great-grandpa"—she points to the pock faced man with a shock of white hair and green eyes that almost seem to be peering into my soul—"looks so serious he resembles a North Korean dictator. Alex says he scares her. Honestly, she's not too far off the mark." Serene continues to stare at the paintings thoughtfully. "The dining room is comfortable. And the rest of the home is haunted by angry relatives."

"For most Southern families, that's how it is," I say with a smile.

"Fair enough. I just want the least terrifying ancestors on the wall."

As children, Miles and I would scurry from room to room as fast as possible, pretending our ancestors were beasts chasing us. If we were able to make it to our room without being chastised by our Momma or Nanny, then we defeated the beasts. It made us feel victorious and helped with our fear.

Sighing, Serene shakes her head. "I'll make the decision soon enough." With her mind momentarily appeased about the paintings, she looks at me with a little gleam in her eye. "Are you off so soon? It seems as though you just got here."

Even though Livingston hid me from Serene's line of sight, I know she saw what happened between us. She's a smart woman. And she wasn't going to talk to me without bringing the topic up. But I cannot explain it and don't want to attempt to.

Looking at my linked fingers, I exhale a deep breath before I lift my head. "I apologize for what you walked in on," I say suddenly.

Serene waves her hand in the air. "No apology needed. I'm the one who barged on in."

I nod, feeling uncertain of what I should say next. "T-that's…I mean, it's never happened before."

"Of course," she replies gently.

By this point, my eyes are wide and my voice is imploring. "It was a mistake."

I need those words to be spoken into existence for my sake and no one else's. Because someone can kiss you, but that doesn't mean you have to respond. And I reacted in a way to Livingston that resembled all the women who have ever fell for him. He's a beautiful man. A beautiful man with a devastating smile…who kisses remarkably well.

That is it.

Serene smiles at my words. "Certainly didn't appear that way. I mean, Livingston was going to town, and you weren't stopping him."

Serene's blunt words can at times be too refreshing, confusing, or embarrassing. Today, I'm embarrassed because it doesn't take a genius to piece together what she's referring to. I say nothing and simply look at her.

Tilting her head to the side, she reaches out and clutches my arms. "Oh, Rainey. I know that look."

Jutting my chin, I step back. I brush a hand across my skirt and clear my throat. "Everythin' is fine."

"Of course it is. You just gave your heart to a Lacroix man."

With those words said, my head jerks up, and my heart skips a beat. Breathing becomes difficult. I swallow several times, trying to phrase my words the right way, but my tongue feels far too big for my mouth.

What is wrong with me?

Serene winks. "You can relax. I won't tell a soul. But it's

time you bust out the heavy artillery."

The day I fall for a Lacroix man is the moment I become a successful debutante, and I want to say just that, but I'm more curious to know what Serene is referring to.

Finally, I gain control of my tongue. "What are you speakin' of?"

Serene rolls her eyes as though I'm an errant child who hasn't been paying attention. "Lacroix men are terribly stubborn and can't see what's in front of them. And he's a man, and sometimes common sense isn't so common for them."

"I still don't understand what you're gettin' at."

Serene smirks deviously. "You will at your bachelor ball." Before I can ask her what she means by that, she continues speaking. "How did the invitations go?"

"Livingston and I finished them all."

"Excellent. I'll have them delivered at once." She looks at her belly and gives it a loving pat. "Did you think last night's date with Duncan went well?"

"Yes. It's made me even more certain of the final bachelors."

My confession brings a wide grin to her face. "Don't tell me! I want to be surprised the day of. That reminds me…" As her voice drifts off, dread trickles down my spine, causing me to sit up straight.

"Yes?" I prod.

"There's a chance Étienne might not be able to attend because of work. And because of social etiquette." She pauses to roll her eyes. "I might need to ask another person to step in and take his place to oversee the event."

Before she can finish her sentence, I know who she's referring to. "Please tell me it's your butler, Ben."

"I'm afraid not."

Every step I take, there is Livingston. As remarkably frustrating as that may be, I can't help but note that perhaps his unpredictable arrivals to my dates and the words that come out of his mouth are a welcome distraction from the immense pain I feel from the loss of Miles.

Serene takes my silence as a sign of anger and places a

hand over my hand. "Now don't get mad. Étienne just can't make it."

Livingston never mentioned this. I shake my head ever so slightly. I can't explain to Serene that it's apprehension not anger I'm feeling at the idea of seeing Livingston. I don't know what will happen to us after our kiss. "You can, though," I point out. "You are the perfect chaperone."

"You're right. You're right. I can make it. But what if one the bachelors is suddenly all up in your business? What can I do? Waddle after him, and whack him with my belly?" Serene shrugs. "All in all, I'm glad Livingston is stepping in at the last second."

Last night, I was disappointed that Livingston didn't show up to my date with Duncan, but that was before our kiss. I didn't know how I was going to react when I saw him again. I knew it wasn't going to be our customary repartee.

"And if he says something that gets under your skin just know he can't help himself."

I find myself leaning in, desperate to hear her answer. "Why can't he, though? I don't understand his actions."

Serene lifts a shoulder. "You know the saying, 'If it looks like a jealous man, walks like a jealous man, and talks like a jealous man, then it might just be a jealous man.'"

"I don't believe I've ever heard that until now."

"Really? Well, there's a first time for everything."

When I arrive home, Momma is pacing the foyer with her hands tightly woven in front of her.

The second she spots me, her eyes widen with excitement. "There you are, dear."

"I told you I'd be at Belgrave."

"Workin' on the invitations for the ball, correct?"

Slowly, I take off my hat and look at her skeptically. "Yes, you're correct."

She nods and smiles off into the distance. "Wonderful."

"I must say, I'm baffled by your reply. You've made no

effort in hidin' your dislike for the bachelor ball."

"No need to split hairs, Rainey. All that matters is people cannot stop speakin' about this ball."

"I know. And you didn't care for that."

"That was before it became a runaway success! I've had two matriarchs from Charleston's most prominent families visit today inquirin' about the ball. Of course, I'm still in mournin' so I had to politely turn them away." Momma barely stops to take a breath. "Three bachelor's mommas have sent invites to have tea. I daresay, this will be the event of the year!" Before I can say a word, she places her hands on my shoulder blades and all but pushes me into the sitting room. We stop in the open doorway. My eyes widen and my mouth drops as I take in the room. The fragrance is nearly overwhelming, but it doesn't compare to the colors before me. It's a sea of flowers. Every surface is covered, and around the furniture and Persian rug are even more flowers, creating a small maze.

"All from your bachelors, dear."

"Oh, wow."

Momma nods, her eyes alight with excitement. "I haven't seen this many flowers since Nathalie Lacroix's weddin'."

"What do we do with all of them?"

"Appreciate the sight and smell and be a courteous Southern lady and write thank-you notes."

This was quite a lot to take in. I don't think I've ever had one bouquet sent to me, let alone a room full. Yet not one was from the man who could kiss me speechless.

"Did you finish all the invitations?"

"Hmm?"

"The invitations," Momma says, pronouncing her words slowly. "Are they finished?"

Shaking my head ever so slightly, I shift toward Momma. It takes me a moment to figure out what she's talking about. "Yes. Yes, they're done," I rush out.

"Wonderful." Momma's so roused by the attention of the upcoming ball she doesn't notice my reaction. It's time for her restorative beverage, but before Momma leaves the room, she holds one of my arms and gestures to the wild array of colors before us. "Just think, somewhere in the midst of all these flowers is a bouquet from your future husband."

"Uh-huh," I say numbly because my lips continue to tingle from my kiss with Livingston.

CHAPTER EIGHTEEN

RAINEY

If there's any benefit to having a momma with expensive taste in all areas of life, it's that I've never once lacked for a topic of conversation during each date with the bachelors. Even I learned a thing or two from my tutors and when I was a debutante. The second is there's no absence of dresses to choose from in my closet. The seconds before I dress, I shed my true skin, and with each button sliding into place or zipper tightening the material around my body, the pain of Miles's death retreats for a time. I focus on the present and the goals, which is making sure Momma and I don't lose this house. Time was running out, though, as the topic of conversations ran thin and the list of bachelors grew smaller.

At the beginning of this, I didn't love the bachelor idea, but it certainly wasn't the worst. But soon, it distracted me. I found myself anxious to take off one attire and dress in another. I didn't get dressed for today's outing with much aplomb, though.

Did it have to do with Livingston being there? Most certainly.

I haven't heard from him for the past two days. And I wasn't thrilled about that because I absolutely didn't want him to bring up the topic of the kiss during the bachelor event. It needs to be addressed but in private. Away from prying eyes and listening ears.

I needed more time to think on the matter, too. Not that

I wasn't diligently thinking every detail over until there was nothing left to inspect. I wanted a heart-stopping kiss? Well, I received it. Livingston kissed like a man with nothing left in life but one last breath. He made every thought in my mind go dark and my muscles become lax, but under my skin, my nerves were alive, dancing throughout my body, searching for a way out. It was an exhilarating feeling, but I knew I needed to be prepared to see Livingston today, and for anything he might say. For us, a conversation is never simple. There are many routes, and I never know which one he might take.

"I must admit, it's been quite some time since I've had a picnic," says Taylor, one of my bachelors, pulling me out of my thoughts.

A small laugh escapes me as I hold the opposite end of the checkered blanket. Once it's straightened out, we lower it to the ground. "It's been many years for me, too. But change is nice, wouldn't you agree?"

The idea came from Serene, but to be honest, I think Alex's governess might have suggested it. She's always going on picnics with Alex. I was afraid we were going to resort to writing ideas down on paper and pulling one out from a hat.

"Oh, I certainly agree," Duncan says next to me.

"Me too," Conrad chimes in.

The rest of the bachelors murmur their agreement, and I can't help but think, if playing this bachelor game is what it took to have men agree with me, perhaps I should've done this years ago.

Everyone politely talks with one another, but after several minutes, the lack of food becomes apparent and so does Serene and Livingston's absence.

"Where are Mrs. Lacroix and Livingston?" Conrad asks.

Taylor lifts his gaze toward Belgrave and points. "There they are."

Turning my head, I cup my fingers over my eyes and squint. I can distinctly see the outline of Serene and the sun blazing down on her red hair, and beside her is the man who gave me the greatest kiss I've ever had. Livingston.

Why, oh why did it have to come from him?

I think that's what I can't stop thinking about. There are endless men in this world, and my heart-stopping kiss came from Livingston.

I didn't know how to accept that. Did I pretend it never happened?

There's a fluttering in my gut as he walks closer. In any light, Livingston Lacroix is truly a sight to behold. Livingston's not dressed for a picnic. Livingston appears to have rolled out of bed, half-heartedly buttoned his shirt, and grabbed the first vest he saw in his room. His sleeves were rolled up. His stride was slow to keep in time with Serene. With the sun shining down, strands of his coal black hair turn chestnut brown.

He turns his head toward Serene and laughs at something she says. His brilliant white teeth stand out against his olive skin tone. That smile seizes my attention, pulling my eyes to his lips. He has good lips. Much softer than I expected. I wouldn't push him away if he kissed me again.

I shake my head softly to rid myself of the thought and quickly look away as he approaches our group. I glance at him from the corner of my eye and find him blankly looking at me. His eyes move away, and I feel as though I've been dismissed.

"Don't fret, Hiscock. We have everythin'," Livingston says as he places the picnic basket on the ground. He rests his hands on his hips and looks around at the bachelors the way a king would at his peasants. With that scowl on his face, the resemblance between him and Étienne is impossible to deny. "Wouldn't want you to lose your spot next to Miss Pleasonton." There's an edge to his tone that has Serene lifting both brows.

I stand along with everyone and dust my hands and keep a dignified smile on my face. "May I speak with you for a moment, Mr. Lacroix?"

"Ma'am, I would love nothin' more," he replies with his charming smile. My heart may skip a beat, but I don't fall to his feet like the rest of the women have.

Livingston falls in step beside me immediately. His arm brushes against mine. Given the chilly reception he gave me, I expect him to move away, but he doesn't.

I look over my shoulder to make sure we're a healthy distance away from the rest of the party. Taylor's become a reformed gentleman and is now helping Serene sit on the blanket. The other bachelors are talking amongst themselves. Although, Conrad is looking this way. Quickly, I turn away and face the thicket of trees. "I remember the days where you weren't at the theater or interruptin' a lunch or dinner I was at," I say wistfully.

"I remember the days when I wasn't contractually obligated to see over your dowry. Are we finished with this trip down memory lane?"

I take my hat off and errantly tap it against my leg. "You need to be civil today."

Livingston looks mildly surprised. "I am civil. In fact, I'm the most charmin' Lacroix in my family." He finishes his words with a smile. His dimple appears, and my pulse quickens.

Nothing is amiss. This is the same banter you always have. Keep your composure, Rainey. Don't think about the kiss, and don't talk about the kiss!

"I presume your charm doesn't extend to Taylor because he's not a woman?" I ask.

Livingston snorts. "No, it's because Hiscock is a cretin."

Narrowing my eyes, I link my hands behind my back. The ribbon attached to my hat brushes against my legs. "Harsh words for someone you've never spoken with."

"Don't need to. My intuition tells me he's a cretin. Now if we're done, I believe I'll join everyone else." He dips his head and turns around.

I don't want to discuss Taylor. Or any of the bachelors. All I want to discuss is the kiss, but I can't. Livingston is the very picture of calm and cool, and the kiss seems to be the furthest thing from his mind. I need to appear the same.

"Don't impede on my time with them," I blurt.

Livingston stops and looks at me over his shoulder with a dangerous gleam in his eyes. I know this man quite well, and he doesn't take kindly to being told what to do. We're alike in that way. Slowly Livingston walks back to me, maintaining a healthy distance between us. But I almost wish he was an inch away. Chest to chest. The fire in his eyes feels far more intimate. "Correct me if I'm wrong, but I did not impede on your time with Duncan, did I?"

Wordlessly, I shake my head. At this point, I'm tapping my hat against my leg rapidly.

"You had every chance to get to know your bachelor. If you did not, that is your responsibility. Not mine."

I open my mouth, but he steps forward, and now we're standing with only inches between us. He speaks first.

"Come now, Rainey," he says, his voice coaxing, "I think you realize by now there will be some people who you just know you will connect with, and others you won't. You can have twelve dinners with these bachelors, see all the movies that are available, and allow them to escort you around Washington Square until your legs can no longer move, but if there's no connection, you can't place the blame on me. When you know, you know."

I know with a certainty he's not referring to the bachelors in the slightest. His words cause my hands to tremble. The temptation to kiss him returns with an intensity that takes me by surprise. Exhaling a shaky breath, I look away from Livingston and stare toward the trees.

I can feel his eyes on me. They're trailing across my cheeks, lips, eyes, and down my neck. I take a deep, shuddering breath. Then I feel the slightest graze against my wrist. At once I stop tapping my hat and freeze. I take measured breaths in and out as his fingers drift down my palm. The touch feels like a feather against my skin, making my skin break out in goose bumps. Before he has a chance to pull away, my fingers curl around his. Lifting my head, I look at him and see a stark hunger in his gaze. "Rainey, I—"

Immediately, he lets go and steps away from me. Turning around, I see why.

Serene, with one hand on her stomach and the other shading her eyes from the sun, is walking toward us. "Are we going to eat soon? The baby and I are starving, and the longer I stand here watching the two of you spar with your words, the more Livingston's head is beginning to resemble a sandwich."

Livingston shifts back, giving Serene an alarming glance and gestures in front of him. "Well, I would hate to keep you waitin'."

Serene nearly runs toward the plaid blanket. I don't think I've ever seen her move so fast.

Livingston and I follow her in complete silence. We both realize that we were almost caught for the second time being far too close. "We need to discuss…"

He arches a brow and gives me his devilish half-smirk. "Yes?"

"We need to discuss what happened in the ballroom," I say in one giant rush.

So much for not discussing the kiss.

Livingston appears momentarily surprised before he nods thoughtfully. "We do."

The moments when we agree are so few and far between. It's like seeing a shooting star. You can't help but savor the moment so you can think back to it during a gloomy day.

"However, your bachelors are lookin' forward to your return so at a later time." Anytime the word bachelor spills from his mouth, it's bitter and hard as granite. Our peaceful moment is gone so swiftly.

Livingston gives the men a look filled with annoyance before he turns back to me. "That's why Serene arranged this picnic, so you could better get to know the bachelors, right?"

Before I can answer, or even ask when we can talk about our kiss, he walks away.

"Wait, Livingston—"

Frustration fills me as I watch him saunter away. Why did I ever naïvely think we could have a conversation about the kiss? He has doubtlessly kissed more women than I can ever begin to imagine. What was memorable for me would hardly bury itself in his memory.

By the time I reach everyone, Livingston's sitting beside

Serene and playfully picking at the food on her plate. She elbows his arm and narrows her eyes before she continues eating, causing him to grin.

Frowning slightly, I sit down across from him, next to Conrad and Taylor. Is this how it will be from here on out between us?

"Arrogant bastard," I mutter under my breath.

"I'm sorry, did you say somethin'?" Conrad asks.

I freeze for a moment and glance at him with wide eyes that I hope come across as innocent. "Pardon?"

"You said somethin'. I didn't know if you were talkin' to me?"

"Oh...I- no." I look around as I grapple with a reply. "I was talkin' to...myself?"

Taylor, along with everyone else, arches a brow. I even have Livingston's undivided attention.

"I believe in positive affirmations," I supply with a straight face.

Taylor nods. "That is a wonderful quality."

"Mmmhmm." I continue to smile while studiously refraining from looking in Livingston's direction. He's undoubtedly suppressing his laughter.

*Arrogant, arrogant bastard...*I repeat, this time in my head as I stare at Livingston. And I was the foolish woman who kissed him. Better it was just a kiss and nothing else, right? I still have my dignity and the ability to push the kiss into the darkest corner of my mind.

"Now what did that poor chicken do to you, Rainey?" Serene asks, pointing at my plate.

I look down and see the shreds of meat scattered across my plate. Between my hands are the remains of the chicken leg. Pity it wasn't Livingston. Rationally, I knew it wasn't anger I felt but hurt that Livingston could so easily forget. In order to move forward, I should want that, though, right? The truth is, the kiss should've never happened.

Knowing the truth didn't make the situation any better. Because the truth is, I wanted the kiss to happen again, and again, and again. Placing the chicken leg on the plate, I wipe my hands on my napkin.

"I like my food to be in small, cut-up bits before I take a bite out of it." I eat a piece of meat while I stare at Livingston.

There's a heavy silence. Serene looks back and forth between the two of us with wide eyes.

With his elbows braced on his knee, Livingston tilts his head to the side and observes me for several seconds before he leans forward. His eyes gleam not with anger but with hunger.

"Miss Pleasonton, I believe you're referrin' to prey," he says.

"Food and prey can be one and the same, Mr. Lacroix."

Nobody around us says a word. Livingston narrows his eyes. I lift a brow. And then Livingston smirks at me because my temper isn't something he hasn't seen before. He knows me far too well. And maybe that's why I'm scared and lashing out. This person who's been a consistent and, at times, an annoying presence in my life is someone I desire.

Distantly, I hear someone clear their throat. At once, I break eye contact, anxious to look anywhere else.

"This is quite a spread," Taylor says graciously.

"Thank you," Serene replies.

"Mrs. Lacroix, did you make this?"

"Yep. I was in the kitchen all morning," Serene says without missing a beat.

He takes a bite out of his food and chews for a second before he says around the bread, "Rainey, did you know the sandwich was invented by John Montagu? I believe he was the 4th Earl of Sandwich."

I nod and direct all my attention to him. "Is that so? I did not know that."

"Oh, yes. It's said he requested his valet to place meat between two pieces of bread."

"Fascinatin'," Livingston murmurs although his eyes dance mischievously.

He takes a break only to wash down his food with some Coca-Cola. Holding the glass bottle away from him, he looks at the label. "Of course, the Coca-Cola's story isn't quite as interestin', but there are some pieces of information you might care to know. Rainey, did you know Coca-Cola was originally intended to be a nostrum? And Rainey, did you know…"

And so began a string of information delivered in the form of, "Rainey, did you know…"

Taylor knew unimportant facts, but they were highly detailed. And he said them with such conviction I couldn't help but nod along even though no one could get a single word in.

Livingston just sat there, placing his weight on his palms as he leaned back and watched it all unfold in front of him. A bemused expression danced on his face.

By some miracle, Serene manages to insert herself into the conversation. "You know a lot of facts, Taylor."

"I do, I do. But armin' ourselves with facts is very important."

"I agree," I say merely because he didn't say "Rainey did you know…"

These minute details kept me busy from lifting my gaze and looking at Livingston.

"Serene, do you want another sandwich?" Taylor asks.

"I shouldn't." She pats her stomach. "Otherwise I'll be farting up a storm."

Livingston and I are used to Serene's blunt words and crass humor. Taylor, however, isn't. His cheeks turn beet red, and his thin lips draw into a line so small they nearly disappear.

"What's wrong, Taylor?" Livingston asks.

"I'm taken aback. When I marry, my wife will do no such thing."

"You mean fart?" Serene asks, fighting a smile.

The red from Taylor's cheeks has spread through his entire face. It's hard to say whether it's from embarrassment or anger.

"Wait." Serene winces. "I meant to say flatulence."

"I understand it's common and will happen, but it's very unrefined."

Serene's eyebrows lift so high they nearly reach her hairline. She remains quiet and merely nods and smiles, but if I'm annoyed by Taylor's remark, I can only imagine what Serene's thinking.

Livingston, on the other hand, is positively beaming. He understands me well enough to know Taylor's ludicrous and antiquated opinion is all I need to cross him off my list.

After that, lunch quickly sours. Livingston continues to keep the conversation going, but Taylor keeps looking in my direction, and I swear he's sniffing the air discreetly as though he's waiting for me to break wind.

And then, the conversation takes a swift turn when somehow one of the bachelors makes mention of the war.

"I must say, it's good to have you with us, Lacroix," Grady says.

Livingston smiles, but it's a sharp smile. Meant to cut anyone who gets too close. "Thank you. It's good to still be here."

"We lost far too many great men in the war," Conrad remarks.

At that, I look down at the blanket. Everyone murmurs their agreements. And for a reason I'll never understand, Grady says to Livingston, "What was it like there?"

Livingston's shoulders tense. I brace myself for his reply. In life, there are particular questions you don't ask. You may think them, but manners stop you from saying your thoughts aloud.

My gaze meets Livingston, and for some reason, I think of the moment he came home...

Momma didn't want to go to Charleston Port, better known as Army base terminal, and welcome home Livingston's unit. It was said roughly a thousand men were to be expected. Word still hadn't arrived if Miles was one of those men, and Momma's nerves were frayed.

I couldn't stop myself. I had to go.

I still remember what the Charleston Evening Post *said on November 11, 1918,* "This morning the cloud of war lifted from Europe and the agony of more than four years which Germany brought upon the world ended."

This homecoming is something I couldn't ignore. Even though I had a pit in my stomach about Miles because there was one person who would be stepping onto the platform. Livingston.

In the heavy crowd, I stood by Nat and Serene, with Étienne behind us. The conversations around us only heightened the furor for this momentous occasion. Standing on my tiptoes, I tried to peer toward the empty tracks as though a train was going to suddenly appear.

A large "Welcome Home" banner had been hung between two small buildings. Several people hold small flags in their hands. In the large crowd, there are mommas soothing their babies in prams or bouncing them in their arms to keep them from crying. Then there are the mommas repeatedly telling their rambunctious kids to stay away from the tracks.

"What could be takin' so long?" Nat huffs impatiently.

"I believe they were stoppin' at Camp Jackson first. It shouldn't be long."

Days ago, Livingston's ship, USS Mercury, arrived at port, and his unit was taken by train to Camp Jackson to demobilize. It was frustrating yet exciting to know Livingston was hours from us.

Before Étienne could finish his sentence, a rumble can be heard from the tracks and then the sound of the train whistle cuts through all the conversations occurring in the crowd.

Nat grabs my arm. Her eyes nearly filling with tears. "They're here!"

Everyone cheers. People lift their hands. Flags start waving in the air. Young kids find themselves on the shoulders of their relatives.

The next few minutes feel like hours as everyone in the crowd waiting for a loved one pauses with bated breath. There may be familiar faces in the horde of people, but most are strangers. On a day such as today, that doesn't matter because all of us understand each other. The wait, fear, and apprehension are something that will connect us. The same way the soldiers on the train will be connected by the darkness of war.

Tragedy can be interesting that way. It always has a way of bringing the unlikeliest of people together.

The train doors open, and at last, the soldiers begin to walk off the train. The cheers that erupt from everybody make my ears ring. But I'm one of those people. I've regressed to being a child, and I'm holding

Nat just as tightly, and all but jumping up and down with only one interest: finding Livingston.

It doesn't take long for family members to spot the soldiers they know. Soon, the platform becomes so crowded with bodies it becomes impossible to take a step forward without bumping into someone. Soldiers continue to disembark the train, but they're all stepping onto the platform so quickly it's impossible to tell if any of them are Livingston. Serene, Nat, and I stand on our tiptoes, looking for Livingston, before Serene slaps her husband's arm and points at the train. "You're taller than anyone here. You do the searching for us."

He obliges and scoured the crowd. And suddenly a somber Étienne said with enthusiasm, "There he is!"

To our left, breaking through a throng of people, is Livingston. He was different from the polished, gorgeous man everyone knew him to be. His clean-shaven face has been replaced with dark whiskers that pepper his cheeks and chin, and only pronounce his sharp cheekbones.

When we all gave our goodbyes one afternoon in May of last year, Livingston cut a striking figure in his uniform. The olive wool was clean and crisp, with his unit patch on his sleeve. His first lieutenant shoulder straps were perfectly straight. The bronze eagle buttons on his uniform shined, and around the collar, when I saw the distinct letters US, I felt a sense of pride.

Those buttons were now dull. The material around his shoulders shows strain, probably from months of carrying a heavy haversack.

As Livingston stands in front of us, he drops his haversack to the ground and greets us with a half-smirk. There are bags around his eyes. How long has it been since he's gotten a good night's rest?

His first hello was to his brother, followed by Serene, then Nat. And then there was me. When Livingston set his sights on me, I felt a jolt rock through me. Sometimes when you haven't seen someone for so long, you forget certain characteristics.

He takes off his cap and holds it to his chest and gives me a wink. He clearly hasn't been robbed of his charm.

"No hug?" Livingston shakes his head in mock disappointment. "I shaved and dressed for this occasion."

Looking over my shoulder, I arch a brow at Nat. "Should I hug a doughboy?"

I turn back to Livingston. He tries to appear unamused, but one corner of his mouth stubbornly tilts upward. "Do you know where that nickname came from?"

"I don't think anyone does."

As I lean into Livingston, his family laughs and speaks to one another. My hands curve around his shoulders as his arms rest around my lower back. The voices around us blend, becoming a suppressed sound. All I can hear is the pounding of my beating heart, and all I can smell is the scent of Livingston. He smells of sweat and man. It was disturbingly appealing. We held on for a heartbeat longer than necessary until the sound of a crying baby brings us to our senses.

We begin to pull apart, and when we do, he gives me a small squeeze and briefly leans into me. I would've held onto him if no one was watching.

"I'm sure you're tired and hungry," Étienne says.

Livingston blinks rapidly at me before he looks away. It's several seconds before he turns toward Étienne, and replies, "Yes, yes, very hungry."

"Serene has some food prepared at Belgrave if you're ready?"

Livingston places his cap on his head, covering his dark hair, gestures toward the ground before him, and smiles at everyone but me. It's almost as though I imagined that hug and the way he lingered toward the end. "Lead the way."

Livingston grabs his haversack and slings it over his shoulder as though it weighs nothing. Étienne, Serene, and Nat lead the way. Nat talks about what they'll have for dinner and how happy she is to have everyone in one place. I step in place beside Livingston, noticing the jealous stares from the women around us. For a second, I bask in the moment and smile victoriously at the ladies. Because Livingston is walking with me, hugged me, and talking with me.

We begin to fall behind and walk past numerous homecomings. Fathers are holding their babies for the first time. Families are remaining still as someone takes photos with a Kodak Brownie. Neither one of us attempts to catch up to his family. He keeps glancing at me from the corner of his eye, looking at me strangely.

Is there a bug on my forehead? Hair caught in the corner of my mouth? Narrowing my eyes, I look at him. "What?"

He shrugs and glances forward, giving a clear view of that perfect profile of his. "You look different, le savauge, that's all."

I shake my head. "I'm not different."

"Start wearin' dresses?"

"Never stopped."

"Lose the trousers?"

"Still in my armoire," I say, without breaking my stride.

Livingston grins, and butterflies build in my stomach. Yes, I certainly forgot about his grin. How could I possibly forget that grin? No one can forget that grin.

Ahead of us, someone honks their horn. I turn and see Étienne waving our way wildly while Nat and Serene lean against the car. I wave back. Livingston does none of the sort. His entire body has locked up. If there was a rifle nearby, I'm sure he would've grabbed it. If a bunker was behind him, he would've dived for cover.

After a few seconds, Livingston looks around. He blinks rapidly, taking in the heavy crowds, and looks at me. In his eyes, I can see when he settles back into reality, but also when he realizes I saw everything. Shame causes red to stain his cheeks, and he looks away.

Rather than asking if he's all right and bringing more attention to his reaction, I say, "I'm glad you're home."

Livingston's shoulders imperceptibly sag as though the air has been sucked from him. He smiles at me gratefully. "Thank you."

"Come here, you two," Nat says, raising her voice over the noise.

While she begins to tinker with her camera, Livingston groans.

"Livingston, don't you dare say a word. This is a special memory that needs to be captured. We need a family photo."

"I can take the photo if you'd like," I volunteer.

Nat stares at me as though I've begun to speak in a different language. "Nonsense. You'll be in the picture. And when Miles returns, we'll take another photo altogether."

"I can't say no to that," I say with a smile.

Nat searches for someone in the crowd for several minutes.

"It's a simple photo, not an oil painting," Serene mutters and plucks the first person who passes by us.

Nat hands the man her camera as though it's a delicate piece of china.

"Nat, dépêche-toi s'il te plait," Étienne grumbles.

Frowning, she lifts her head. "Sois patient!"

Once she's certain the man knows what to do, she all but skips back to us. I stand on Livingston's right side, and she takes the space to his left. With Étienne by her, Serene moves close to Nat. As for Livingston and me, we look at one another with a hint of tension that's never been there between us before. He's the same Livingston, but something has changed about him.

"You two. Hurry up and get close for the picture," Serene demands.

Silently, Livingston spreads his arm wide for me to step closer. I move into the space he's offering. In such close proximity, I can feel the side of Livingston's body against mine. I link my fingers together in front of me and maintain my composure for the picture. Inside, my heart is doing interesting things. Pounding in my chest before it feels as though it's tumbling all the way to my stomach. There's nothing I can do to stop it. And there's something exhilarating, yet utterly terrifying about the action.

Take the picture. Take the picture! *my heart pounds with every second that ticks by.*

And the longer I stand there, the hotter I become until I'm convinced my clothes are going to disintegrate into thin air, and my skin will meld with Livingston's body.

Once the picture is taken, I step away as though I've been burned. Nat gathers her camera, and Serene begins a conversation with Livingston, inevitably pulling him away from me. Every few seconds, he looks at me, giving me the same strange look he did earlier.

If things feel different, it's because they are. Time has moved forward. That is all.

That is all.

Unhurriedly, we all begin to get into the car one at a time. I can sense Livingston standing behind me while Serene and Nat figure out the seating arrangement. I'm willing to strap myself to the roof to make this all end when I feel a tap on my shoulder.

Turning around, I look expectantly at Livingston. He stands there with one hand gripping the stained strap of his haversack, and leans into me. "I'm glad to see you, too, le savauge…"

The memory breaks apart, disappearing into thin air.

What's left is a man who refuses to face his past, and strangers oblivious to what he's experienced. Livingston's eyes move to the ground. His cheeks are stained red, and his lips are drawn in a tight line. It's so uncommon to see Livingston at a loss for words, so I react without a second thought.

"I heard it was wonderful there," I blurt. "Five-star dinin' and the sleepin' arrangements were superb."

Everyone appears shocked by my reply, especially Livingston. Then the small chuckles erupt throughout our small picnic, and the bachelors begin to tease Taylor for asking such a question in the first place.

Livingston looks at me from beneath his lashes. For once, he's not smirking or wearing an all-knowing expression, and without it, he looks raw, almost boyish. I don't know what to make of it. But there's no mistaking what I see in his eyes: he's grateful for what I said.

It's time to wave the white flag. This picnic failed miserably.

Serene dramatically yawns and looks at the three of us. "Well, this lunch was riveting, but I'm getting tired. Is everyone ready to go?"

It's hard to say which one of us jumps up first: Taylor or me. But the ending of this lunch date seems to be the only thing we'll be able to agree on. It takes us record time to clean up everything, place the leftovers back in the wicker basket, and fold the blankets.

As we walk back to Belgrave, Serene walks with me, and says out of the corner of her mouth. "I do believe we missed the mark with Captain Can't Crack a Rat."

Regretfully, I nod.

"Was it just me or did anyone else want to punch him in the face?" she asks.

"It wasn't just you."

Sighing heavily, Serene pulls out a folded sheet a paper from her blouse. Has that been there the whole time? On the paper is a list of the bachelor's names. "I guess that leaves Duncan, Beau, Conrad, Grady, Elijah, and Sean."

"You truly have that bachelor list memorized, don't you?"

Livingston says from Serene's right. I didn't hear him come up on us.

"Of course," Serene replies without taking her gaze away from the paper. "I'm the curator of said list. I know their names, occupations, dates of birth, and if it wasn't out of line to get a vial of their blood, I would."

"You mean, knowin' the birth date of every bachelor isn't out of line?" he counters.

Serene shrugs. "Not in the slightest." She lifts her, eyes wide as saucers. "Oh, God! My notebook is in the wicker basket. Hey, Taylor! Where's the fire? Wait for me. I need to talk to you!" Serene hollers in the most unladylike manner. If Momma was here, she would drop to a faint.

I watch her half-waddle and half-run toward a confused Taylor and several other bachelors. Once she's halfway to him, I look at Livingston from the corner of my eye.

"This is the part I despise," I confess.

"Truly? Because this part is my favorite."

Swallowing, I slow my steps and look anywhere but ahead of me while Serene tells several bachelors that I will no longer be needing their company.

"I'm sure you're pleased with how the picnic went."

Livingston appears to mull over my question before he replies. "I am. You saw me offer the last sandwich to Serene before I ate it. I was ravished, but my manners remained intact."

"I'm not speakin' about the sandwich, and you know it. I'm talkin' about Taylor."

Livingston's brows lift in feign surprise. "Oh, is this about his stance on passin' gas?"

"Yes."

"You can't expect me to believe that you think I told him to say that, do you?"

"Why not? It's not a far reach. You've done worse."

"Yes. I've been plottin' this for years," he says dryly. "After all this time, your ultimate downfall would end up bein' flatulence." Livingston shakes his head. "You're merely frustrated that the lunch didn't go as you expected, and Taylor is one more bachelor to cross off your absurd list."

His words make my blood simmer because he's absolutely right. And I hate that he's right.

"And I think we both know the closer I approach my sixty-day deadline, the more appealin' that list begins to look."

"I can't wait to hear what you'll accuse me of next. Before the picnic, I was not allowin' you the time to get to know the bachelors, and now I'm tellin' the bachelors what to say."

"I won't say anythin' because I'll be findin' my perfect match amongst these bachelors to prove you wrong, Lacroix. Just you wait and see."

Abruptly, he stops walking. "Is this all the bachelors are for? To prove me wrong?" Livingston doesn't give me a chance to answer before he continues. "Because I must say, you're goin' to be sorely disappointed in the end."

If I don't marry one of the bachelors, Momma and I stand to lose everything. If I do marry one of the bachelors, I lose my freedom and a chance of truly finding my soulmate. It seems to me, the ending will be disheartening no matter how I look at it, but I have to make the best of it.

Livingston clears his throat so loudly I'm surprised people on The Battery don't hear him. Arching a brow, I give him my full attention. He keeps his gaze rooted on the ground as we continue to walk. "I need to tell you thank you...for what you did with Taylor at the picnic."

He flings his hand toward the path behind us as though that will prompt my memory. But I knew the moment he said Taylor's name.

"Like you said before the picnic, Taylor's a cretin," I say, attempting to put Livingston at ease. He nods and laughs. It's the type of laugh you give when you're embarrassed. I can count on one hand the number of times I've seen Livingston truly vulnerable. Very swiftly, the protective feeling I had for him earlier returns.

"There's nothin' to thank. He was bein' foolish and had no right to ask."

"Ah, but some people think they do," Livingston says.

"Most people haven't experienced what you have," I point out.

Livingston slowly nods in agreement and goes silent.

"Not all moments were terrible there," he says suddenly.

I'm so stunned by his omission, I say nothing.

"At first, everythin' was overwhelmin'. I couldn't understand this was my life. But gradually..." His words fade, and he shrugs. "You make the best out of your circumstances." Livingston looks at me from the corner of his eye and gives me a half-smirk. "Comin' home was certainly nice. Probably one of the best moments throughout it all."

Linking my fingers together in front of me, I faintly nod and look at him. "It was nice to see you."

"You have that picture, *le savauge*?"

Shortly after his return, Nat showed me all the photos she took before she left for Brignac House. Photos of Belgrave and attempts to take pictures of Alex in the garden with her mom, Livingston, and Étienne together in his office. Étienne was unsmiling, and so was Livingston. The energy and life that typically danced in his light eyes wasn't there though. I didn't care much for that photo. Toward the end was the picture we took at the Army base terminal. We all stood together. I knew how I felt at that precise moment, and it made me inspect every detail of the picture. The small space separating Nat and Livingston was natural as though they'd stood for a picture beside each other.

There was no space between Livingston and me. Whether we realized it, we leaned into one another like two magnets. My hip nearly in line with his hip and my shoulder below his.

Nat left the picture with me, and I never returned it. It was tucked into the corner of my vanity mirror. I looked at it every day.

"Don't be ridiculous." I roll my eyes and scoff. "Of course I do."

Livingston laughs so loudly the sound makes me gasp slightly. I faintly smile because that sound holds so much life. It's rich with memories. Of happiness, tears, smiles, and laughter. It's part of Livingston. But I haven't heard him laugh like that in so long. I almost forgot about that laughter.

My heart unexpectedly flips again. I have the sudden urge to reach out and brush my fingers across his cheek. Livingston's laughter fades as he sees the look in my eye.

Our moment of peace is interrupted by a collective sound of voices moving toward us. Livingston smiles as the remaining bachelors approach, but the smile doesn't reach his eyes.

"I'll leave you with your bachelors. But thank you again."

He leaves my side before I can say a word. Conrad replaces his spot and immediately heads straight into a conversation about how impolite Taylor was. I nod, but the entire time, I watch Livingston walk back to Belgrave.

It hits me then, the image of Livingston sitting at the picnic with the stark, desperate look in his eyes when Taylor asked him to discuss the war. At that moment, my heart felt strong enough for the both of us. I would've said anything to make things right for him, even if they were wrong for me. The revelation rattles me. What else am I capable of doing for him?

Once Livingston disappears from sight, I try to focus on the final five men. I'm getting close to the end. Less dates to have. This should alleviate my worries. If anything, I feel more urgency than when there were thirty bachelors to choose from.

"All right, all right. Let's allow Miss Pleasonton some breathing room," Serene says with a clap of her hands.

The men break apart for Serene, and I can't help but breathe a sigh of relief. Serene tells the bachelors it was a pleasure having them at Belgrave. I give my good-byes, and as they walk away, some of the tension leaves my body.

Serene silently stands beside me for several moments before she asks, "How do you feel?"

"Overwhelmed," I confess.

"I want to tell you that you shouldn't be. But that would be a lie because things are about to get remarkably interesting," she says with a mischievous grin.

CHAPTER NINETEEN

RAINEY

That night, sleep doesn't come easily. I toss and turn, dreaming about the one person who causes me to act as mad as a March hare. I think of our conversation today and the heated looks he gave me during the picnic.

With a groan of frustration, I sit up and punch my pillow, pretending it's Livingston. If we didn't kiss, perhaps none of the uncomfortable tension would exist between us.

It's then I hear a loud noise at my window. Suddenly alert, I stare at the window and see a dark shadow. The lock wiggles. Frantically, I look around my room for something to use as a weapon. I only have my curling iron at my vanity table to use as a makeshift weapon.

Jumping out of bed, I snatch the iron, clutching it as though I'm getting ready to hit a baseball. My eyes never waver from the window. Hinges creak as the windows move upward. Someone clutches the window frame. Their body dips in. I take quiet, tentative steps toward them. Whoever is breaking in is just as quiet as I am but is dedicated to the task. They don't see me sneaking up on them.

Too bad. That works in my favor.

My God has one of the bachelors lost their mind and is trying to get inside my room? That's the only possible explanation. Never did I think this would happen. My grip tightens on the iron as my heart rate quickens.

The large frame is still hidden by the shadows, but there's

no mistaking it's a male. I lift the iron, ready to take a swing, when the intruder speaks. "Rainey, put the weapon down."

In an instant, I recognize the voice. Slowly, I lower my weapon and squint as though that will help me see better. With the window open, the streetlamps outside bring a weak glow into my room. "Livingston?" I hiss.

"Of course it's me. Who else would it be?"

"I didn't know." I scramble to my nightstand and turn on my lamp. A dim glow illuminates the room and reveals Livingston standing there with the same clothes he wore during the picnic. He seems larger in my room. The planes and angles of his face and wide shoulders are more pronounced. His male vitality is impossible to ignore. "I don't have guests waltzin' into my room in the middle of the night."

Livingston snorts. "It's hardly the middle of the night." I watch him pull out his pocket watch. "It's a quarter till one."

"That's the middle of the night for me," I reply.

"For me, it's the beginnin'." He grins and then looks me over. "Were you gonna shoot me again?"

I look at the curling iron and walk to my vanity. "Quite possibly."

That is a fabrication on my part. I don't have arrows laying around my room. My last one was left at Livingston's. I hope it's still embedded in the armoire, and he looks at it every single morning and thinks of me. I hope he's reminded I will never conform to what the world expects of me.

"Find a better weapon."

"Find a better entrance," I point out and place the iron on the vanity with a solid thwack.

A corner of Livingston's mouth curls up.

"Now what did you need that couldn't possibly wait until mornin' time?" I cross my arms over my chest. I'm not fully awake and prepared for Livingston's presence. That's why my heart races the way it does. Nothing else.

Livingston doesn't answer and instead walks around my room. Growing up, he saw my room in passing when the door was open. I would try to avoid that, though, and the second I heard his voice, I would jump up from whatever I was doing and shut my bedroom door because I didn't put it past him to pull any shenanigans.

My bedroom has changed, and Livingston notices. He peruses my rows of books stopping to read the titles on a few spines before he continues. He looks over his shoulder at me. "People have libraries, you know."

"I understand that, but I prefer to have my bookshelves nearby."

"Why?"

"Because bookshelves are a journey for your eyes. To remember the places you've experienced, the characters you've encountered. The laughter and heartache each writer has given you is incalculable." I lift a shoulder, suddenly feeling foolish for my fanciful explanation. "I could stare at my bookshelves all day."

Livingston smirks, his eyes dancing with amusement. He turns his attention back to the shelves and continues to peruse at a leisurely pace as though my room was a bookstore and he was a paying customer. I know the second he spots *The Shepherd of the Hills* on the shelf by the way the corner of his mouth curls up. Did he presume I wouldn't keep the book? I'm far more nostalgic than anyone would think.

Livingston hasn't spotted the picture from the day he came home on my vanity, but if he continues to thoroughly look around the room, he will.

I clear my throat. "Again, to what do I owe this unexpected, late-night, and very much inappropriate visit?"

Turning toward me, he sweeps his eyes up and down, deliberately resting on the collar of my nightgown. All of my nightgowns are modest, but he makes me feel as though I'm wearing nothing. Beneath this, I'm not.

His eyes lift to mine. Sharp and hot. "I wanted to speak with you about the picnic."

"What about it? Do you take issue with the final five bachelors?"

"I've taken issue with all of the bachelors," Livingston

says without missing a beat. "No, I wanted to talk about your conversation with Taylor. I believe in positive affirmations?" he says, doing his best imitation of my voice.

"What is wrong with positive affirmations?"

"Nothin'. But you wouldn't recognize positive if it was directly in front of you. Now negative is a different conversation."

I grin. "Good. Because I'm about to give you a handful of them."

"There she is," Livingston murmurs and takes a step closer.

Today didn't go quite as planned. I wasn't on my best behavior. My temper reared its ugly head, I spoke out of turn, and thought about Livingston and our kiss more times than I can count. I don't mind that Livingston is deliberately goading me. I want to spar with someone. That my adversary is the very person I can't stop thinking about makes it all the better.

"There she is? I've gone nowhere. But you certainly did when I wanted to discuss our kiss."

Livingston spreads his arms wide. "Well, here I am now."

"How convenient for you. What if I didn't want to discuss it anymore?"

"How convenient for you," he retorts with a half-smirk.

"I wanted to make certain that the kiss wouldn't affect our friendship."

"It won't," Livingston answers at once. "The kiss was a spur-of-the-moment thing and won't happen again."

Rapidly, I nod. I should be relieved, right? It's in both of our best interest that the kiss was a one-time mistake. So why do I feel disappointed? "Good, good."

Livingston quirks a brow. "Is that all you wish to discuss?"

"Yes."

No. I had many, many questions I wished to talk over with him. But the sooner he left the room, the better.

The two of us are silent. Livingston rocks back on his heels, then lifts his gaze to mine. "But it certainly was memorable, wasn't it?"

It was all I could think about. "It was good," I reply.

Livingston's eyes widen and then immediately narrow. "Good? Just good?"

"Contrary to what you might believe, I don't make it a habit of kissin' the bachelors. My area of expertise doesn't lie in the art of kissin'."

"Whether experienced or not is irrelevant. A memorable kiss is felt and never forced."

I didn't need him to tell me that. I felt every inch of that kiss in the ballroom from the crown of my head to the tips of my toes and all the way to my soul. But I shrug a shoulder. "If you say so."

"You truly believe it was simply good?"

The sharpness of Livingston's words has me raising both brows. "Are you upset? I didn't say it was bad. I just—"

Abruptly, my words are cut off as Livingston lunges for me. His hands curl around my upper arms. He stares at me with a baffled expression in his eyes, and before I can ask what's wrong, his lips meet mine.

The kiss is urgent and picks up where the last left off.

He has been thinking about this, too.

I make a sound from the back of my throat. Something close to approval. My fingers curl around his biceps.

His tongue sweeps into my mouth, and his grip on me tightens the way it did in the ballroom.

The two of us walk backward. I feel the footboard touch the back of my legs but only for a moment. I leave my frustration from today on the floor as my body travels up the bed. Livingston's lips never leave mine as he follows. When my head touches the pillows, my lips part, giving Livingston the entrance he's been seeking. He groans. It's a sound that vibrates through me and brings me a shiver of warmth. His lower body sinks into me, and I feel the hard length of him against my thigh. My fingers curl around his bicep.

My hands remain at my sides; I'm afraid to touch him. I'm afraid that once I start, I will not stop. My emotions are already frazzled tonight. If our first kiss has shown us anything, it's that the two of us cannot be trusted alone.

I find the strength to push back, my palm resting against Livingston's chest. His eyes are half-mast as he gives me a dazed expression. I try to take a deep breath, but I can feel him, all of him, against my leg. I've never been this close to a man before, but I'm not scared.

Because every rapid beat of my heart moves in tandem with three simple words: *you are alive. You are alive.*

I search for that in everything I do. In order to survive, pain makes you numb to the world. But the glorious, heart-racing awareness and excitement coursing through me is unlike anything else. I can feel every touch and the abrasion of our clothing every time our entwined limbs move. The clean scent of him wraps around me, making me hold him tighter until it becomes too much.

"What are we precisely doin'?" I breathe.

"Well, days ago, we kissed. And then Serene interrupted, so we stopped. And now I am resumin' the kiss to show you it was more than just good. *Si je puis?*"

This is my chance to say no. This is my chance to tell him he needs to leave and that I'm not one of his many paramours. I do none of that, though. Instead, I curl my hands around his shirt, pulling him closer.

"May I resume?" he asks against my lips.

With my eyes closed, I nod.

In the privacy of my room, where no one can find us, Livingston gives me everything. I taste war on his lips and pain on his tongue. I'm no match for him, but that doesn't stop me from trying to heal him. I've always craved a challenge.

His hands move to the buttons of my nightgown. The first button is open as my eyes flash open.

He looks at me from beneath his lashes, his hazel eyes nearly glowing. "Do you want me to stop?"

I don't answer. Instead, my eyes rove over his face. In the dim lighting, it's hard to see every perfect detail of him.

"Rainey?" he urges.

My eyes meet his. For once, he looks uncertain of himself and desperate for my answer. "No," I say.

"Are you positive?" One button slides free, then another. "Because I'll only say this once. A kiss is a kiss, but a touch can break you."

I stretch beneath him, languishing in his words. I love the shiver of anticipation they give me even when I know they shouldn't. "You can't break me."

It's not a challenge but a mere fact. I won't let him break me. I won't be like all the other ladies who fall for him.

Livingston still doesn't seem convinced. "I won't be the man standin' on the front porch waitin' for you," he warns. Perhaps, this is his final attempt to dissuade me.

But after each kiss we have, I crave another and then another. I want them to last longer than the last. And now I have a new thought: what else can he show me?

"Oh, Livingston, I won't be the woman askin' you to stay."

My reply causes a groan to tear from his throat. My reply is as good as yes.

You're playing a dangerous game.

Livingston presses himself closer as he slants his head at an angle. My fingers curl around the back of his neck and drag through his hair.

My need for Livingston is so incredibly strong that I suck in a sharp breath and hold him tighter. He holds me back just as tight.

For a moment, I give it full control of my body, and with my eyes still closed, my hands drift to the buttons of his shirt. One by one, they give way when my hands slip through the opening to touch his chest. Livingston's lips move down my neck. I wait for his mouth to replace his hands, but it never does. It continues to build, and I grow wetter between my legs and move restlessly.

I'm never at a lack for words. But for once, I don't know how to articulate what I want. I just desperately need to assuage this growing desire. It's growing inside me, trying to find a way out with every touch of Livingston's.

Then his hands slip from my breast. His fingers hook around the hem of my nightgown and drag the material up my legs. A shiver rocks through me as my bare legs are exposed. My breath catches in my throat when his palms drift down, and his fingers trailing behind, making goose bumps appears on my skin.

When he doesn't come into contact with the material of my undergarments, he pulls back, a questioning look in his gaze.

"I refuse to have anythin' diggin' against my flesh when I sleep," I say with defiance.

He stares down at me with a glazed look in his eye. "*T'es la mienne. Mon beau sauvage.*"

I've never been looked at and held in such a way, but Livingston is making me want to. Again, again, and again. With my hands curled around the lapels of his collar, I pull him down to me and kiss him.

His hands wrap around my waist, and his palms boldly cup my buttocks. He presses me flush against him, and while his tongue slides into my mouth, I feel his cock press against me. Over and over, he repeats the act until I move with him.

He rips himself away, his chest rapidly moving up and down. He looks like a man on the brink of losing all control. "More?"

Breathless, I nod. Livingston looms over me with one palm on the mattress, next to my shoulder, and the other hand curled possessively around my knee. His eyes slowly rove my body.

He slowly slides a finger inside me. My fingers grasp the material of his shirt so tightly it wraps around my knuckles. I gasp and lift my hips.

Pressure fills me, but it isn't unpleasant. Far from it.

His strokes are slow, almost teasing. Gradually, they become faster, and the tension grows. And as the heat builds in me, I move against his hand. A second finger sweeps against my curls and parts my lips. I'm so sensitive that I grip his shoulders, and I'm certain I'll leave marks.

"You're so wet, Raina."

His bold words send a shot of pleasure through me. I hold him tighter.

"Please," I whisper.

This is Livingston's area of expertise. I have no control, and we both know it. I have to follow and trust him the entire time.

His fingers are proficient and fast as he leans down to whisper into my ear. *"Allez-vous crier mon nom quand vous viendrez?"*

The sultry sound of his words mixes with the feel of his fingers, and all the heat and tension that's been building inside me becomes unbearable. My heels dig into the bed, and my back arches.

Before I cry out, I have enough sense to crash my lips against Livingston's as I spasm around his finger. I feel nothing but molten heat rush throughout me. It's slow-moving, but it finds a way to reach every limb until I feel paralyzed. He swallows my screams and swallows his name as his fingers continue to expertly move in and out of me.

My feet drop heavily to the bed like weights, but my body continues to shudder. Gradually, the shudders abate, and I feel Livingston's finger slip out of me. The warmth of his body moves off me. I'm in such a daze and so coated with sweat I don't argue. He lays right beside me, his arm touching mine.

"My God," he pants.

Staring up at the ceiling, I can only nod. I'm not entirely certain what just happened, but similar to the first kiss Livingston gave me, I want it to happen again. My body feels pliant and relaxed. I couldn't move even if there was a fire.

For several minutes, the two of us lay there, staring at the ceiling, trying to gather our breaths. I roll to my side, my nightgown still in disarray. Even though the tremors have subsided, my heart won't stop its furious pounding. I feel lightheaded and disoriented and don't try to fight the smile pulling at my lips as I look at Livingston.

I don't tell him to leave, or that this was a mistake and he should never come here again. Rather, I place a hand on his chest, lean in, and reveal what's in my heart. "Come back tomorrow night."

Livingston rears back an inch, and his eyes widen. He sits

up, resting his weight on his elbows. There's a pregnant silence between us before Livingston replies, his voice gruff. "Excuse me?"

"Come back tomorrow night," I whisper.

The weight of my words settle around the two of us. Livingston doesn't answer for several seconds, and when he does, there's a lot of guffawing on his part. "I think you've gone delirious!" he says on a laugh.

"Yet you're the one who sneaked into my room," I point out.

Livingston knows I'm right. The laughter stops. "And we shall do what?"

"I propose we do precisely what we were doin' five minutes ago before you stopped." My heart pounds. I can feel Livingston's eyes on me. I haven't been this nervous in quite some time and begin to drag my fingers along the collar of his shirt. "Our time in the dark will never be spoken of in daylight."

"Of course not," he murmurs.

I keep speaking because it's far easier than thinking of him saying no. "Our time will also be good practice for me and—"

"Practice?" Livingston sits up, causing my hands to fall away from his shirt.

I sit beside him. "Yes, practice. For when I'm married. The day we kissed at Belgrave, you were quite confident in your skills to seduce a woman. Surely, you can continue to teach more to me."

That's not entirely true. There's an imbalance starting to bloom between Livingston and me. I want to learn more. Understand what he likes and doesn't.

"When it comes to seduction, I'm more than confident," he replies, insulted I would question his capabilities. "In fact, I've never been more sure of anythin' in my entire life."

"Right," I continue before shooting him a dubious look. "And tonight seemed…enjoyable for the both of us, so why not continue?"

Livingston has never been so quiet. Has he gone deaf?

Maybe he thinks I'm jesting because he continues to stare at me as though I'll say, at any moment, "I had you for a moment!"

"Livingston?" I gently prod.

Turning away, he shakes his head slowly. "I'm thinkin', I'm thinkin'. I never expected you to make a proposition such as this."

"But now I have." As the seconds tick by, I feel myself becoming vulnerable. Why did I ask him if we could continue?

Tucking my hands beneath my thighs, I take a deep breath. "I enjoyed myself, but I made the error of bein' presumptuous. Perhaps it wasn't enjoyable for you. If that's true, we can pretend tonight never happened."

His head jerks my way. "It was enjoyable." His hazel eyes blink but remain steadfast on me. "It was very enjoyable."

The gruff tone of his words sends a thrill down my spine. I can only nod and wait for him to give me an answer to my proposition.

And then, finally, he does. "I'll agree. Under one stipulation."

My eyes narrow. I should've known there would be a stipulation. "And that would be?"

Livingston faces me. "As much as you may want to, you can't fall in love with me."

I can't help the unladylike snort that slips from my mouth. "There's no problem of that happenin'."

It almost happened once before. I can fight it a second time. "You seem confident."

"I've never been more sure of anythin' in my entire life," I reply, using his own words.

Playfully, Livingston taps me underneath my chin. "You sure 'bout that, darlin'?"

"Lacroix, you climbed through my window. It seems to me that you're in danger of fallin' in love with me."

"Yet you want me to keep comin' back," he counters.

"I won't fall in love with you," I say, making sure to utter each word slowly.

There's no sense in denying the attraction between us, but

love? I won't let it happen. For Livingston, it's not out the question to expect a woman to fall in love. It happens time and again for him.

"Shall we shake on it?" I propose.

The corner of his mouth curves up into a half-smirk. "Shake?" Without another word, he leans in and kisses me soundly. I hum my approval. This is much better than shaking hands. When he pulls away, he brushes his finger against my lower lip. "Can't go back now, *le savauge*. You kissed on it."

Why does my heart beat a bit faster at those words? Why do I find myself leaning in closer?

Right then, Livingston looks at my pillows behind us. His body betrays him as he yawns, and his eyes fight to stay open. Sitting up straight, I look at him closely. "Tired?"

Sighing, he sinks his hands through his hair before they drop heavily between his legs. His head swings in my direction. He gives me an exhausted smile. "I haven't been sleepin' properly."

"Does properly mean not at all?" I ask with a small smile.

Livingston chuckles. The sound gives me butterflies. "Yes, it does."

Nodding, I look away, carefully choosing my next words. Several times, my mouth opens, then shuts. Words are ready to roll from my tongue, but I stop myself.

Livingston stares intently at the floor as though the answer to all his problems are between the cracks of the floorboards. I've stared at this floor many times myself. The resolution isn't there.

"You can tell me what is on your mind." I pause. "If you desire to do so."

For a long time, it's been apparent something's wrong with Livingston. Him confessing he doesn't sleep confirms it. I don't like to see Livingston hurt or fighting his inner demons because I don't know how to fix the problem.

I remember when I received the news that he was left for dead on a sidewalk in Charleston. I thought for a fearful second I was going to lose someone far too important to me.

"Thank you, Rainey." He places his hand on my leg and gives my knee a reassuring pat. But then his hand stays put, fingers splayed across my knee. I can feel his palm nearly burning a hole through my nightgown.

He looks down, staring at his large hand on my thigh. I stare with him. I know too much about him. I know how he earned the scar on the middle fingernail of his right hand. Étienne and Miles accidentally slammed it in a barn door on Belgrave property when they were ten. If you asked Livingston to tell the story, he'd end it by saying he never cried. Étienne and Miles would say differently. When his nail grew back, there was a small depression in the nail bed and a longer scar on the inside of his finger.

I know too much about him for this to mean nothing. I need to rescind our agreement.

My lips remained closed. I don't move. I don't breathe because I know when I do it's going to break this moment, and then he will leave, and tonight will be over. I'm not prepared for that yet. Being alone with him, in the dark, is peaceful. How I felt in the ballroom when he kissed me is the emotion that came over me the minute he stepped through my bedroom window.

There are no bachelors to choose from, no looming debts to pay, and the pain of losing Miles doesn't feel as sharp. And I think, for Livingston, that whatever haunts him persistently is alleviated. As he sits beside me his hair is in disorder from my hands running through it. Strands fall over across his forehead, but the tension around his brows and around the corners of his eyes aren't as pronounced. He looks peaceful and collected. Almost boyish. The longer we sit here in silence, my heart breaks.

Tell me what's wrong. Tell me how I can help you.

As though he can sense my thoughts, Livingston pulls his hand away. His eyes are uncharacteristically solemn as he briefly looks at me, almost pleading for me not to say anything, and stands up. "I should be goin'."

"Yes, yes," I rush out and stand after him. "It's late."

With my hands linked behind my back, I walk him to my window as though this sort of thing occurs frequently. Before he opens the window, Livingston turns back to me. The short walk across my room has given him a chance to retreat back into himself.

"I will see you soon?" he asks.

The corner of my mouth lifts. "Yes. I hope so."

"Good night, *le savauge*." I can imagine the impish gleam in his eyes right before he says those words and disappears through the window.

Smiling, I close the window behind him and walk back to my bed feeling dazed and out of sorts. Sleep is out of the question, but I make myself comfortable and bury myself in my sheets as tonight replays through my head.

In every possible way, Livingston and I are a terrible match. I wake up early, and Livingston sleeps the day away. He shirks his duties, while I prefer to be on time to every event. Livingston is Charleston's number one womanizer. I am Charleston's untamed debutante.

For some reason, though, there is an attraction between us. I denied the first kiss and the second.

God help me for anticipating the third kiss.

CHAPTER TWENTY

RAINEY

The next night, I pace my bedroom floor with my robe billowing behind me.

Livingston agreed to come, but what if he's changed his mind?

There's a significant chance he's thought this over and realized what a terrible idea it is. I know I couldn't stop thinking about last night, but did I have regrets? Did I want to abort tonight? Absolutely not. My heart raced at the very idea of seeing him, and I thought about it all day. Even during my dinner with one of my bachelors, Sean Atwood. He was kind and kept a steady flow of conversation. Slightly pompous but had an amiable sense of humor. I did my best to remain present during dinner, and right when I thought Livingston was off my mind, I would see a man out of the corner of my eye in the restaurant who I swore looked identical to Livingston.

I was beginning to feel unhinged because even though there's always been a level of anticipation whenever we sparred with our words, this was different. This was consuming my mind.

Wordplay was in the heat of the moment everything about tonight felt deliberate. I kept the lamp on because I wanted to see him better, and I wanted him to see me.

I even took great care to pick out my least modest nightgown and came to the conclusion that I dress like an eighty-year-old spinster, complete with the braid. I had no desire to be one of

Livingston's conquests, but I certainly didn't want him to see me as an undesirable old maid. Or most importantly, like the young girl he once knew.

I worked with what I had and chose a sleeveless empire nightgown made of muslin. Hand-embroidered flowers trim the V-neck with pale pink ribbons keeping the sleeves together.

If I had a bigger bust, it would look a bit more seductive and far less...sweet. I didn't want sweet. There's nothing captivating about sweet. I stop in front of the full-length mirror in the corner of my room and give myself a thorough look. I brushed my hair until my hand began to ache. The dark strands flow down my back, with the ends touching my waist. I didn't braid it like I always do each night and question myself. Should I braid it? No. Leave it as it is. The neckline appears too high and demure. It firmly shelves me next to every childhood friend Nat grew up with.

Furtively, I look around and undo the first button. Spurred by my bold actions, I pull the plain neckline down. No. Too far. I pull it back up and take a deep breath.

"Stop it, Rainey," I mutter to myself.

One button is as far as I can go.

For the hundredth time, I glance at my clock. It's five past twelve. I should go to bed. It's apparent he's not going to show up tonight. At least one of us has sense. I give the window one last look and walk toward my bed. When I bend down to turn off my lamp, I hear the *tap, tap, tap* against the windowpane.

By the time I turn, Livingston has the window open and is crouching his head down to slip inside.

My fingers become tightly linked in front of me. The butterflies that have been tightly caged in my stomach break free as I watch him stand to his full height. "Hello."

Livingston begins to take a step forward. "Rainey, listen, if you were caught up in the moment last ni—"

Before he can finish his sentence or wipe the dust off his pants, I lunge myself into his arms and kiss him. If mouths could talk, mine would say, "What took you so long?"

I momentarily take Livingston off balance, but he rights

himself and wraps his arms around me. It feels good to take the lead. But seeing this is our third kiss, I feel confident in what he's shown me. Now I want to know what else he can teach me.

We break apart and his half-smirk appears, as does that dimple. "Should I continue with my question?"

"I don't believe that's necessary."

Livingston begins to lean in for another kiss but abruptly pulls back and steps away. He doesn't appear unsettled so why is he holding back?

"How was your day?" he asks out of nowhere.

"How was my day?" I repeat.

Livingston nods as though this is a routine question he asks. Perhaps other friends do, but not us. We're continuously preparing for what the other will say next.

For a moment, I'm taken aback. "Today was...dull."

"Why's that, *le savauge*?"

A month ago, that blasted nickname would've made my blood boil, but now it makes my heart race. This is why you don't kiss your brother's best friend. Everything can change in an instant.

"I-I had a dress fittin' with Momma," I say as though it's my first time forming words. I make sure to keep the part about my date with Sean out of my reply.

Livingston's brows lift, and his eyes sweep down my body and back to my face. My arms become covered in goose bumps. It took the seamstress nearly thirty minutes to get all my measurements, yet I'm certain he obtained them with one simple look. "Sounds fascinatin'."

"Oh, I couldn't contain my excitement," I say with a straight face.

Livingston smiles.

"And how was your day?" I ask.

With his hands behind his back, Livingston takes a stroll around my room, much like he did the night before. I think he's purposely placing this distance between us, prolonging what he came for and why I've been pacing my room for the past hour.

Livingston can shrug with indifference and proclaim Étienne is the one between the two of them who has an interest in business, but he's being dishonest. I know Livingston's smart. His mind was constantly in motion, and he read more books than I did. There's no one who isn't inspired. They simply haven't found what sets their soul on fire.

"A chess set?"

Oh, no.

My heart beats against my chest. After dinner with Sean I passed the time by playing chess. I forgot to put the game away. I watch him carefully as he picks up one of the queens, inspects it, sets it back down and then goes for the king.

"You want to play a game?"

"No," I say a little too forcefully.

With both brows lifted, he looks at me and slowly lowers the king onto the set. "Do you have a sudden aversion to chess?"

"No. I normally don't play at such a late hour."

"And I normally don't climb trees at such a late hour to sneak into rooms." His mouth quirks. "Do you want me to be rebellious on my own?"

I've played chess since I was a girl. The only worthy adversary I've come across has been Livingston. He may appear jovial, but he was as shrewd as his twin. When he played, he played to win. And if he lost, he continued to play until he won.

After Livingston's attack, the people closest to him didn't know how to proceed. He didn't have his memory and such a crucial part of him was missing. The many pastimes he enjoyed before the attack he no longer partook in, but chess? He couldn't resist the challenge of chess.

We played so many games after the attack it started to become a form of recovery. We would play late into the night. When everyone else had retired for the night, we were hunched over the small table brought into the sitting room, all our focus on the chessboard. Sometimes, we didn't say a word to one another. Other times, I would reminisce about the past, and I was truthful. The opportunity to change history by lying was there, but I spared no detail. I knew I was a menace as a little girl, chasing after him, Étienne, and Miles.

I knew there were times he was dubious, but I had him lift his pant leg, revealing the scar on his calf. He wasn't doubtful after that.

Perhaps it was naïve thinking on my part, but through those conversations and chess games, I thought I saw a glimpse of the real Livingston. For all anyone knows, maybe our private tête-à-tête gradually brought his memory out of hiding.

That's not what happened, though.

What came to pass was hope expanding inside me only to be crushed by false hope.

"Perhaps another time," I offer, my voice becoming a tinge bit desperate.

"Then what should we do?" Livingston asks in a lazy drawl.

Looking everywhere but at him, I gather the courage to say my words, "Well, last night we agreed you should teach me more about affection. Correct?"

"Correct. Is it called affection, though?"

"What would you call it?"

He moves in, and my heart races. I know this man. He can read a nursery rhyme and make it sound wicked. "From last night, I would describe it as your devotion to me."

"Try again."

"Rapture?"

I shudder. "No."

"A frenzy for what's to come."

That makes me hesitate.

"We should continue with that, yes?"

"But I have one rule."

He arches a brow and patiently waits.

"No words or trite phrases you might say to one of the ladies you're commonly with."

Livingston holds a hand to his chest and appears shocked. That doesn't stop him from moving closer. "That hurts. You believe I would do such a thing?"

I blink rapidly at him.

"I can't say, 'I'm poor with words, but rich with affection. Let me show you'?"

I lift a brow. "Yes, that's precisely what I was referrin' to." Even so, the thought that he would give his attention, even for a second, to another woman fills me with jealousy. I know it's wasted. This is Livingston I'm considering, but I want everything he says to me to be original.

"Of course last night I showed you some affection, and I plan to continue...for education purposes," he quickly amends.

"Of course," I agree just as quickly. He's only two steps away. "Education is important."

"I've never agreed more with you."

It's hard to say who kisses who or who meets who. His hands become tangled in my hair, and my arms wrap around his neck.

I love that his kisses are never soft. They're needed and necessary as much as the very breaths he takes.

He groans before he pulls away, holding my face between my hands. "You shouldn't bite."

"And why not?"

There's nothing but silence for several seconds, then, "Some men might not like it."

"Is that why you just groaned?"

I may be a virgin, but I'm not a nitwit. That groan wasn't born from pain.

"No," Livingston replies his tone gruff.

"It seems to me that kisses should be like words. Soft at times or with rough edges, but they should never be planned." I lift my head and stare at him. "No?"

Livingston brushes a finger across my lower lip. The corner of his mouth lifts, albeit reluctantly. "No. Never planned."

What I secretly love about our conversations is the direction they move. There are curves and loops that neither of us sees coming but always try to. Blood courses through me at the idea of the same technique being used for this. My hands land on his hips and travel up. His stomach is tense, muscles bunched. He's anticipating the same thing as me.

Livingston clears his throat and tries to resume control. "Now if I'm to teach you anythin', it's—"

My fingers are set in their ways and trail across his belt, brushing against his cock. For the barest second, I feel the long length of him. Last night, he more than touched me. And I wanted to touch him back. Through his slacks, I boldly curl my hand around him. My touch is light, but Livingston's shoulders slump forward. He slams a palm on the wall behind me.

"Rainey—"

"Never planned, right?"

His mouth opens. His eyes are bright and alert.

"Miss Rainey?"

The two of us freeze at the sound of my maid. I made sure to lock my door, so no one is getting inside this room, but Livingston doesn't know that. He begins to disentangle himself. I fiercely shake my head and hold on tightly. Livingston's eyes widen. I place a finger to my lips.

"Say somethin'," he whispers.

"Yes?" I finally say although it comes out squeaky. As though I haven't had water in weeks.

There's a pause. "Is everythin' all right?"

Livingston dips his head. His lips connect with my neck. My eyes close as I feel his teeth and tongue against my skin and small pulls. If he doesn't stop, there will be a mark. I softly moan.

"Ma'am?"

My eyes flash back open, but Livingston continues. I realize this is Livingston's retaliation for me not allowing him to step back when he wanted to. If this is the punishment I get, I'll never let go of him.

"I'm fine. Go!" I shout more loudly than I intend.

Livingston lifts his head, his hazel eyes dancing. My eyes narrow back at him. It's his fault.

"Are you sure?" my unsuspecting maid asks.

"Yes." I take a deep breath. "That will be all for tonight."

Livingston and I wait, listening carefully for my maid's footsteps to fade down the hall. Once we're certain she's gone, we move for one another at the same time. The space we carved out near the door is no longer safe. While our lips and tongues move against one another, Livingston guides us away. Within seconds, I feel the soft surface of my mattress beneath me and Livingston on top.

He sits up and hurriedly unbuttons his shirt. He takes it off and blindly throws it behind him. I take the moment to soak him in. His shoulders are broad, and his muscles seemed to be etched from stone. The black chest hair gathered around his defined upper body isn't too thick and nearly disappears around his stomach. Above this belt, a black trail of hair begins and disappears beneath his slacks. I'm tempted to follow the path, but my eyes catch on the grooves above his hips and the lines they form. To my eyes, it almost appears to be the letter V. Slowly, my fingers trace the veins.

Livingston doesn't move, but he's as rigid as a block of ice. I know it's taking all of his control to remain perfectly still.

Reluctantly, I pull my hands away from his perfect body and lean back on my elbows. "What should I do now?"

Livingston blinks languidly. His eyes rooted on my lips. "Hmm?"

"After this"—I gesture between us with a single finger—"what should I do?"

Livingston's Adam's apple bobs as he swallows. He looks away, his gaze settling on my nightgown. "Well, as you said, kisses should never be planned. And neither should anythin' that comes after."

My breath hitches in my throat as he leans forward and curls his hand around my neck. He dips down, and I willingly close my eyes. When my lips press against his, I'm more than comfortable at this point. I want more, more, more.

I'm essentially waiting for his next move. There's a heat growing inside me that causes my pulse to race and my hands to shake. I know what I desire, but I don't have the gumption to say it. I want him to touch my breasts. Last night, his touch was fleeting, barely lasting a second, but I felt it to my very soul. It made my body come alive, and I couldn't help but crave more. His touch was turning out to be just like his kisses.

Livingston breathes deep through his nose as he guides my head to the side. My legs spread farther as I arch upward. That searing heat has now reached my fingertips and the tips of my toes. It's searching for a way out.

Livingston groans deep. His hands move from my hips, and I nearly sigh with pleasure as they drift up my body. His nimble fingers pull on the ribbon keeping one sleeve together. Slowly it falls, and the material splits apart revealing only the upper slope of my breast. I feel Livingston's lips trail down my jaw. He momentarily sucks on the inner slope of my neck, causing me to shift restlessly.

Breathing deep, Livingston pulls away and looks at his handiwork. Immediately, I can feel my nipples pucker.

There's a moment of silence, almost as though he's debating whether he should take the next step. By now, I'm nearly panting and close to pulling my nightgown down and boldly placing his hand on my bare breast.

His eyes meet mine, and the burning heat makes them change colors and appear dark green. They remain locked with my gaze as he curls a finger around the material of my nightgown, and tugs. The air touches my breast, but that's not what makes goose bumps appear across my skin. It's how he's staring at me. As though I'm the most desirable woman he's ever seen. The look in his eyes is so convincing that I almost believe him.

Our kiss in the ballroom was rough and wild, so I braced myself, not knowing what to expect. My chest rapidly rises and falls as he bends his head. His tongue is surprisingly gentle as he licks at my nipples. My eyes close and a gasp escapes me. This sensation is indescribable. Without thinking, my hands rake through Livingston's hair, holding him close.

His attention doesn't stop. Gently, he pulls on the tip with his teeth. My legs find themselves wrapped around Livingston's waist as I move against him. There's a tension building deep inside me. Livingston wraps an arm around my waist and flicks his tongue against the tip of my nipple. Gasping, I lean into and simultaneously moan with relief and cry out with frustration because I can't take a whole lot more.

He continues his ministrations, switching between breasts until I'm holding him tightly to me. When he stops, I feel the cold air touch my sensitive breasts and nearly cover myself. But I don't and open my eyes to find Livingston panting, staring at me with wide eyes. Breathless and spent, I smile at him.

"Fuck," he pants.

"I liked that. That felt good," I blurt.

Rapidly, Livingston nods. His eyes continue to stare at my chest, and when I look down, I know why. From his handiwork, my nipples are hard points. My breasts feel tender and swollen, and after what just happened, I should be covering myself up but I like the way he's staring at me.

I think power can come from any position. It merely depends on the person. But there seems to be something very alluring about being on top and dominating. At least it appeared that way. I wanted to find out for myself. I push against Livingston's shoulders, and with a crooked grin, he willingly falls against the mattress. He tucks his hands behind his head as though he's amused and waiting to see what I'll do next. My nightgown becomes hiked around my thighs as I straddle him.

My hair falls around us, creating a dark curtain. We've created a world where it's only us. Every touch, every word, every caress will only be known by us.

"*Dieu aide moi*," he murmurs.

I will not pretend that his silky words don't have an effect on me. But how many women has he has spoken those words to?

Doesn't matter. Right now, he's only staring at you.

I placed myself in this situation. I invited him here. I need to make the most of this opportunity because soon it'll be morning, and he'll be gone, and we'll be back at each other's throats.

"And him? I assume he'll like to be touched?" I ask.

Livingston stills below me. His grip on my waist tightens. "Yes," he croaks and quickly clears his throat. "Yes," he repeats. This time more firmly. "He'd like that."

My gaze meets his. "Where?"

"Where do you want to touch?"

I stare at him as though his body is a map. The grooves and indents of his stomach are mountains, smooth skin is the sea, the dark line of hair disappearing beneath his pants is a trail.

"Touch anywhere," Livingston bites out.

I stop staring at my self-declared map and give him a questioning look.

He huffs out a breath. "You can touch anywhere, and it will feel amazin'," he explains in a quieter tone, although I'm finding it very hard to concentrate on what he's saying because when he raises his head briefly from the pillow to look at me, his abs contract, instantly placing them on display. My mouth goes dry at the sight.

Stomach. I'll begin with his stomach.

My touch is whisper soft and languid. Starting at his collarbone, I move to his sculpted pecs. I trace the lines of each defined muscled beneath his olive skin, loving how he jumps beneath my touch.

And then I reach the trail of hair on his lower stomach. I hesitate for a moment before I begin to unbutton his pants. My wrist brushes against his cock, and my pulse spikes.

He grabs my hand, his eyes flashing with stark desire.

"Christ, Rainey."

I arch my brow and wait for further instruction. Livingston remains stiff as a board, but he lets go, his hands falling to the bed. He wants me to keep touching him.

I'll never quite understand how we can disagree on everything, and our personalities are the opposites, but the minute our bodies touch, they align perfectly, and it feels as though I'm on fire. My life has swiftly become a gossamer web of confusion. So translucent you can barely see it, but once you step into the web, you're trapped. There are no misunderstandings in Livingston's arms. I think we both know this is purely physical.

I tug on his pants. He lifts his hips, and with one pull, his pants are pushed to his thighs. My eyes widen at the sight of him. I felt him against my leg and touched him through his pants, but I didn't anticipate this.

He's thicker than I expected with veins running the long length of him, toward the bulbous tip. I reach out, almost hesitantly, and curl my fingers around him. His skin is far softer and pliant than I thought.

But what do I possibly do now?

As though he can sense my hesitation, Livingston curls a large hand around mine. I look at him, but his eyes are closed. His dark brows are furrowed, and his cheeks are red.

"Up and down." His words are terse and brief. He drops his hand away, and I'm left on my own.

I move slowly at first, but continue to repeat his words in my head.

Up and down, up and down, up and down.

Before long, Livingston's breathing becomes rapid. I'm not adept, but I catch on, finding the correct rhythm, and when I do, my speed increases until I get a slight ache in my hand.

Livingston thrusts into my hand and groans. I wanted to please him, but I didn't expect for this to please me. I feel myself becoming wet, and my heart racing in my ears.

"*Je te veux plus que tout.*"

I lift my gaze and find him staring me with an intensity that makes my rhythm falter.

How many women has he spoken those words to?

I look down and increase my speed. My arm aches in protest, but I don't stop. I hold tighter, watching his reaction. He grips the sheets, bares his teeth, and throws his head back. And white ropes of liquid shoot out of him.

Shocked, I stop and begin to remove my hand, when he places my hand back on him.

"No, don't stop," he pleads. His eyes flash open, and I see the desperation there.

I continue, resuming the pace I had before. I watch with rapt attention as his body jerks and spasms uncontrollably. More white liquid shoots out of him, landing on his stomach, and even on my hand.

Gradually, I slow down before I eventually let go. Livingston lays splayed on the bed much like I did the night before. Greedily, he sucks in air while wearing the most content expression across his face.

I want what's eating him inside to be forever erased. I want my old Livingston back. His eyes flutter open and meet mine. Afraid he might sense the intensity of my thoughts, I crawl off him and sit beside him, trying to form the right words. "That was…that was…"

"Yes." Livingston exhales before he sits up.

I nod as though Livingston's reply makes sense. Right now, it does. My mind has lost the ability to string words together. Even though I wasn't the one who lost control, I almost felt like it was. I wanted to be able to give Livingston that again and again. He sees the mess he's created on himself and stands, in search of something to clean himself.

"Is intimacy always like that?"

Livingston's shoulders briefly tense as he bends down to pick up a piece of clothing. When he comes back to the bed, I see a muscle along his jaw jump. "No. It isn't."

He appears almost reluctant to admit that. He looks me over, studiously cleaning his hands before he reaches down, cleans himself, and then tucks himself back into his pants. He wads the chemise up and winces before he tosses it toward my vanity. "I'm sorry, but it was all I could find."

I smile. "Don't be. I'm the one who did it."

The two of us stare at one another. I didn't know what to say. Each time he came to my room, my explorations went further, and he taught me more than I imagined. What do I say now, though? Thank you for letting me orgasm in your arms last night, and for teaching me how to properly hold a cock?

No, even I didn't have the gumption to say something like that. I busy myself by attempting to tie the sleeves of my nightgown together. It's much harder than it looks. Livingston shoos my hand to the side and gestures for me to move closer. I sit cradled between his legs, and my hands shake as I stare forward. This feels oddly intimate, and something I'm not prepared for.

"Will you be at the lunch tomorrow?" I blurt.

Livingston pauses his tying. I can feel his frown even from where I'm sitting. "What lunch?"

"Étienne and Serene are hostin' a lunch for the bachelors and their families. I believe it's essentially a shrewd way for Serene to narrow down the list. The power is going to her head," I say teasingly and glance at him. Livingston's furrowed brows form a tight V the moment I said bachelor. I want the frown gone. I want to take back my words.

"I'll go," he answers after a moment of silence. He moves to the next shoulder. "I love to watch Étienne writhe and become socially inept."

"Very well. I suppose I'll see you then." I turn around and face him.

"I suppose you will."

We both knew this was the moment he's supposed to leave. In fact, I'm counting on it. The problem is, Livingston wasn't leaving, and I didn't want him to go. After what we just did, why would I?

"You can stay for a bit," I say nonchalantly. For good measure, I add, "You look tired."

I make multiple circles on the sheets as I wait for Livingston's reply. After a few seconds, I look over at him.

Livingston leans back and tucks one hand behind his head. His eyes are fighting to stay open as he mumbles, "Need to go."

I pet his cheek, loving the feel of his whiskers against my palm and watch as his black lashes fall against his cheeks. He looks so boyish and peaceful, and I don't want to wake him up.

"Get some sleep," I whisper before I roll onto my back and get comfortable. I'm not tired in the slightest. In an hour, I'll wake him up. Sighing, I stare up at the ceiling

What Livingston and I did is only making matters more

difficult. I'm supposed to be picking a bachelor and Livingston is undeniably not one of those men.

Livingston stirs and rolls toward me, his head resting between my breasts and one arm secured around my waist. *"Puis-je te garder pour toujours?"* he drowsily murmurs.

There's something about this moment that is so personal and intimate it nearly spurs me into waking him up. Because I know, if I'm not careful, it can grow into something else.

But when's the last time Livingston slept this soundly? I think it's been a long time. I rest my head against his, and my eyelids begin to flutter shut.

In an hour, I'll wake him up...

"Miss Rainey?"

"Mmm?" I say against my pillow.

"It's time to wake up, and your door is locked."

At that, my eyes flash open, and it's not my pillow I come into eye contact with, but a naked male chest. Disoriented, I try to pull back, but then realize there's a heavy arm around my waist, and my leg is wrapped around a very warm body.

Everything about last night comes back in a flash, making my cheeks turn red. My stomach twist into knots as I think of the sounds I made. I don't have regrets. I would do it again.

"Miss Rainey?" my maid repeats.

With a soft push, I sit up and think of a quick reply. "Please come back. I...I...I need you to get me some warm tea. My throat aches."

There's a long pause. I've never been one to lounge in my bed unless I was violently ill. "Of course," my maid replies.

Closing my eyes with relief, I breathe deep, and then I realize what a mess Livingston and I have made and how close we were to being caught. That's not true. There's still the matter of getting Livingston out of my room.

"Oh, Lord." I drag my hands through my hair and then down my face as I try to think of a plan. "Oh, Lord."

"Livingston," I whisper-shout. When he doesn't reply, I

gently shake his shoulder. Within seconds, his eyes flash open. He goes from sound asleep to wide-awake just like that and sits up in bed.

He briefly looks around my bedroom, at me, and then back at me. I can see the moment when last night's events dawn on him by the way his eyes widen ever so slightly.

All I can do is nod, a gesture that says, "Yes, we did that."

Livingston scratches the back of his neck as his eyes sweep across my body. His gaze lingers a heartbeat longer on my breasts.

"What time is it?" he asks.

"Eight. My maid just knocked on the door."

"Shit!" he hisses and whips the sheets off.

I follow him and watch as he frantically rummages to find his shoes and shirt. "Why did you let me fall asleep?"

Grabbing my robe, I put it on and hastily tie the belt. "I didn't plan on this. I accidentally fell asleep myself!"

Finally, Livingston spots his shoes clear across the room. He sits on my vanity chair to put his boots on and stands back up to keep searching for his shirt. I hope he never finds it; a bare-chested Livingston is a sight I could stare at all day.

"How do I get out?" he asks as he continues to hunt for his shirt.

"The same way you got in?"

"Someone could see me outside," he points out. He spots the shirt halfway hidden beneath my bed.

"The chances are far less likely than someone seein' you in this house."

Livingston quickly buttons up his shirt. I don't tell him that it's uneven. Everything about him is chaotic, including his disheveled hair and wrinkled pants. He's still incredibly handsome.

"You should go now. My maid will be back up here any time."

"All right, all right. I'll go." He grabs his jacket and gives me a quick kiss before he strides toward my window.

"*Le savauge?*"

I turn, expecting him to say he forgot something. Instead, he curls one hand around the back of my neck and gives me a firm kiss. The spontaneity of the moment causes me to smile. At that second, I'm so happy I become off-balance and grab Livingston's arm. He pulls back seconds later, one side of his mouth curling up. "You look good in the mornin'."

He disappears out of the window before I have time to reply. The curtains billow into the air as Livingston begins his slow trek down the tree.

My shoulders touch the wall. I toy with the collar of my nightgown as a secretive smile causes my lips to curl up.

I just couldn't seem to help myself.

Besides, this is just an attraction between two people. There's no love. I know what I have to do to save Momma and me from ruin.

The two of us could walk away from my outlandish offer without either one being hurt.

But that was the truth. If Livingston was the king of the South, I was the queen of lies. From my deceit and his charm, we could build a kingdom that would last for centuries.

Je te veux plus que tout.

How many women has he spoken those words to?

My heart knew the answer to the question.

To the wrong women? Far too many to count. But to the right one? Just once.

And she was me.

CHAPTER TWENTY-ONE

LIVINGSTON

Many forms of torture have been used throughout time. Hippolytus de Marsiliis is noted for creating a water torture method where water falls onto your forehead in intervals. While you, restrained, slowly go mad. My sister-in-law's methods aren't quite as barbaric. However, they are no less painful because even though I'm not restrained, and there's no water dripping onto my scalp, I have the uncomfortable pleasure of feeling every single lady's eye on me who's sitting at this table. And there's far more than I expected.

This lunch is intended for the remaining bachelors and their families to attend. Not their family's family, and friends of the family. I haven't seen Belgrave this crowded since my sister's wedding.

It was a mistake on my part to come to this lunch. Why did I agree? Oh, yes. Rainey laid beneath me with her nightgown half-open, petting me as though I was Adonis in human form. The moment she uttered the word "bachelors" I felt a blind fury build in my chest and spread throughout my body. I said yes without a second thought. I said yes because her body fit against mine, and so she was mine.

And now here I am. Freshly shaven, in a new suit, and sitting across from none other than Rainey Pleasonton.

She carries on a conversation with Serene as though we didn't spend the night together. In fact, she has looked at me only twice, and that was only because I asked how her momma was faring, and if she was enjoying the cool weather Charleston was experiencing. Her replies were polite. Every time she looked at me, I attempted to catch her gaze for longer than a second but was unsuccessful.

I came to only one conclusion: Rainey would make a remarkable poker player.

Did it bother me she didn't appear affected by last night? I don't know. But I do know she's the only woman I've ever spent the night with and not slept with, causing me to take care of my own needs in my bedroom this morning, like a fourteen-year-old boy who's hot around the collar.

If Pleas was alive, he would kill you for thinking about his little sister in such a way.

Not for the first time I shift uncomfortably in my seat, clear my throat, and lean in toward Étienne. "After this lunch, your home will be a breedin' ground for all the mommas of the South lookin' to marry off their daughters."

Étienne snorts and gives me a resentful look. "Yes, and I have you to thank for that."

I arch a brow. "Me?"

"If you didn't enlist Serene's help over the dowry dilemma, these bachelors would not be sittin' around my table."

I dip my head. "Fair enough."

"Then does that mean you'll be the first bachelor Serene can arrange dates for?"

I shudder at the thought. "Absolutely not."

"Yet here you are. On a Thursday afternoon."

"I'm like most people, Étienne. I have to eat. Would you prefer I starve?"

"I once asked if you'd be interested in attendin' a meetin' with Asa and our business partner, and you told me you would love to but you couldn't because your afternoon was booked. At home. In your room. While you slept off the effects of your drunkenness."

"It wasn't a lie. My afternoon was booked. Like food, I also need sleep, too."

I grin, but my brother is unamused. "My point for that story is these events are somethin' you never look forward to."

I look away and take a sip of my drink. "Once I heard what was on the menu, I knew I had to be here," I lie.

"You're a lover of fillet of sole au Vin Blanc?"

"It's a new passion of mine."

"Hmm," Étienne's replies.

At that moment, Rainey laughs. I wish she hadn't because I'd done a wonderful job of not thinking about her or looking her way. And now I do just that. The bachelor sitting beside her is the source for her laughter. I believe his name is Elijah.

Fuck Elijah and his words.

She hasn't had a date with him or any time to get to know him. In her eyes, he still has a chance of being the one to give her everything.

I narrow my eyes. What did Cameron say to her? Rainey doesn't laugh for nothing. She's not that type of woman who giggles coyly and bats her eyes whenever a man looks her way. You have to earn her laugh, but when you do. Damn. The sound is unabashed and free.

"Stop starin'."

I turn and find Étienne giving me a pointed look. "Pardon?"

He takes a sip of his drink and says out of the corner of his mouth, "You've been starin' at Rainey since the moment we sat down. If you don't stop, one of her many bachelors will notice."

"That would require them to stop fawnin' over her," I mutter under my breath.

Étienne hears me, though, and the corner of his mouth tilts upward. "Why, Livingston, you're lookin' rather green with envy."

I scoff and grab my drink. "No."

One of Rainey's insufferable bachelors asks Étienne a question. He's someone I've never seen before. "Who is the man you were just speakin' with?"

"I have not the slightest idea," Étienne truthfully answers. "Would you like a detailed guest list the next time Serene hosts a dinner party at our home?"

I grunt in response and continue eating. Étienne chuckles. "You're in a rather peculiar mood today. Did you have a particularly rough night?"

My food becomes lodged in my throat. I gasp in air, but that causes the piece of food to become further stuck. Étienne whacks his palm heavily against the middle of my back, and as painful is it feels, the food comes out.

One of the bachelor's mommas across the table murmurs, "Mercy me!"

Embarrassed, I wipe my mouth with my napkin, then reassure everyone around me I'm all right and there's no need to send for a doctor. I was just thinking about the woman who fell asleep in my arms last night.

It's then, at that moment, Rainey chooses to lift her head. The guard she's had up since lunch is lowered as she looks at me with concern. My throat burns from the bile, but Rainey looks ready to leap across the table and help in whatever way possible. That's the most confounding thing about this woman. One minute she wants nothing more than for me to leave her presence, and in the next, she looks as though she'd do anything for me. Fight any battle for me if I ask her to. Her loyalty is unmatched, and one of the many attractive qualities about her. Because there's more than one, and I'm discovering something alluring about her every time I spend time with her.

As I finally catch my breath, I gladly accept the water Étienne offers to me. All eyes turn in her direction, and it's as though Rainey becomes aware of her surroundings.

Slowly, she settles back into her seat. With her beautiful fingers, she delicately drapes her napkin across her lap and focuses her attention on the bachelor next to her.

Serene and Étienne stare at us.

"Do you need more water?" the guest next to me asks.

"No, no. I'm quite all right," I say with a friendly smile.

The only thing I need is for my life to be set to rights. Everything is displaced, and I could direct the blame at Pleas, but he's gone. I can't place responsibility on Rainey's shoulders. Climbing through her window (both times) was my own choice.

I was losing my mind. Whether that culminated from lack of sleep or the nightmares of war, I didn't know. I just knew I couldn't stop. I felt helpless.

For the first time, I was becoming dependent on a woman. Each day, I counted on Rainey's smiles, laughter, and our conversations.

I wondered, did Rainey even know she had me under her thumb? Did she know last night was the first time I've slept peacefully in months? No nightmares. No fear.

Nothing.

It was the best feeling in my life. I could easily see myself becoming devoted to that feeling. But it should've never happened and can't happen again.

After a moment, conversation slowly resumes around the table. Much to my relief. As for my brother, he won't stop staring at me suspiciously. "Is there somethin' developin' between you and Rainey?" Étienne asks quietly.

I keep my gaze on my plate. "If you're askin' if she's less bothersome, then yes."

"That's not what I'm askin'."

Finally, I look at him from the corner of my eye. "Then I don't know what to tell you."

"Do you care for her in the way I care for Serene?"

"You love your wife."

Étienne gives me a meaningful look. "Precisely."

I look my brother square in the eye. "I do not care for Rainey." Yet the moment I say the words, I want to take them back.

For several seconds, my brother doesn't look away. His sharp gaze is speculative, trying to find any clues I might be lying. Then he nods. "Very well. I will take your word for it."

"Thank you, now can we change the topic of conversation?"

"Of course." Étienne pauses. "I had my attorney examine Pleas's will."

Now this is a conversation I'm willing to have. Just not

sitting at table with strangers around us. After looking around, I lean in and lower my voice. "What did he find?"

"It is ironclad. There is no possible way to get around the dowry. And from the ledgers I've been searchin' through…" Étienne's voice fades. He gives me a meaningful look, but I don't say a word. I want him to finish the rest of what he's saying. "The mistakes are erroneous and too many to count."

"It's been the same for me."

Étienne solemnly nods and looks around. "This isn't a conversation for the table. We'll talk about this more in depth later. But have you thought it best to leave everythin' as it is?"

"No," I reply before my brother has a chance to finish his question.

This time, Étienne glances around the table. "Serene may have unorthodox ideas at times, but this one might be her best one yet. Look around you. Better yet, look at Rainey."

From the corner of my eye, I do just that as Étienne continues to speak.

"Rainey is happy, and as her executor and brother's close friend, that should make you happy. She's been through far too much in life."

Much of what he's said has me nodding. I understand the words. I do. But they don't sit well with me. "I do want her to be happy. But she's too stubborn. Rainey…Rainey won't be happy with these fools."

"Let Rainey be the judge of that."

I never have the chance to answer Étienne because Serene stands and announces it's time to retire to the sitting room. Napkins find their way to the table, chairs are pushed back and voices are raised as everyone begins to move toward the foyer. I have no desire to stand around in the sitting room, watching the bachelors fawn for Rainey's attention. I'm out for number one. I want the attention for myself.

My eyes stay trained on Rainey as she walks ahead of me with people surrounding her. Numerous conversations are occurring. She has a friendly smile, but she looks inundated by the attention.

When we're all in the foyer, I weave through the bodies to expertly sidle up next to Rainey. She's speaking to one of the bachelor's mommas, but I know she senses me by the way her body tenses up. Once they're done talking, I shift toward her so our shoulders are touching. Rainey freezes in place.

"Go to the east wing," I say against her ear. "No one will be there." Rainey briefly nods, and I slip away before anyone has a chance to notice our brief interaction.

Anticipation rushes through me as I walk down the hall, knowing that I'm leaving behind the voices and loud laughter and heavy perfume. I just want to breathe in Rainey's scent and hear her voice. Everybody else can cease to exist.

Just as I expected, the east wing is quiet. I wait for several minutes before I hear the sound of heels clicking on marble floors. Smirking, I flatten myself against the wall and wait.

A long shadow stretches across the floor before she turns into the hall. "Livingston?" Rainey asks in a hushed whisper.

I watch her walk deeper into the hall as she searches for me. Once I'm sure that no one has followed her, I step away from the wall and press my body against hers so she's flush against a side table, and my palms rest on the cool surface.

Her eyes widen. Once she recognizes me, her shoulders sag. "My God," she gasps. "You scared me."

Without a second, thought she wraps her arms around my waist and tilts her head back.

"I've missed you," I say against her lips.

"You saw me this mornin'," Rainey replies with a smile and kisses me back.

I drag my tongue across her lower lip. I love how plump and smooth it feels. And when I gently bite down on it, Rainey moans.

Her hands glide up my chest and around my neck. I keep my hands on the table, afraid that if I touch her, I won't stop. We barely stopped last night.

I lift my head. "Did I? Seems as though it was last night."

She smiles and pulls me back to her. I start to lose myself in the kiss, but then there's the sound of servants' voices. I rip myself away from Rainey and plaster myself to the opposite wall. Panting, Rainey and I stare at one another. Two servants walk past the east wing hall, thankfully heading toward the servant's stairwell. They're too busy talking to notice two figures in the shadows. Once they're out of earshot, I go back to Rainey. Our bodies and limbs take the same positions as before.

Possession rises in me. My tongue moves against hers urgently. Rainey is momentarily taken off guard but quickly matches my passion. She's a quick learner, and all the time we've spent in her bedroom has made her so skilled in the art of kissing that she could teach me a thing or two.

A selection of men are here for her, yet she's with me.

I've never been one to lack confidence, but at that moment, I need that reminder. I need to feel her in my arms. No one feels and fits as good against me like Rainey.

My lips move down her neck. Sucking and nipping a small path to the curve of her shoulder. Rainey tilts her head back and holds me close.

My hands curl around the lip of the table as Rainey's body draws me in. I thrust my cock against her leg.

She stops, her breath hitched in her throat, and grips the lapels of my coat. I move against her a second and third time, and the moan that comes out of her is soft and filled with desire. Her left leg wraps around my waist, and if there wasn't the barrier of clothes, I could slide right into her. The very thought causes a strangled groan to slip from my lips. She felt amazing last night, but today…it's as though she's made for me.

Abruptly, I pull away just enough so there's an inch or two between our bodies. Panting, I try to gather my breath, and instead, I'm pulled back into Rainey's web. "If I keep goin' I'll spill inside my pants like a schoolboy."

Rainey smiles, her cheeks rosy, and reaches blindly behind her in search of my hands. She finds them almost immediately and links her fingers with mine. In this position, her breasts thrust out to me like an offering.

"You behavin' like a schoolboy?" Rainey's lips wickedly

curve up. "Whatever would your loyal subjects say about their king now?"

"They would make me abdicate," I say and kiss my way up her neck.

"Doubtful. You'd charm your way back to your position."

Right now, the only position I'm interested in is being on top of Rainey, surging inside her. She would be wild, like she always is. I just know it. The very thought makes me thrust faster against Rainey. I capture her lips to mine so unexpectedly she breathes through her nose.

"*Dites-moi que vous avez besoin de moi. S'il vous plaît,*" I murmur.

Rainey's eyes meet mine, and her mouth opens. Then something behind me catches her attention. "I think I hear your brother."

I'm in such a daze, it takes me a moment to fully understand her words. But when I do, I stand straight. Rainey begins to smooth her clothes and fix her hair as best as she can. Before she can slip away, my hand meets the table, blocking her path. We stand hip to hip, and even though I'm supposed to be clearing my mind of Rainey, I can feel a fresh wave of desire coming through me. "I'll see you tonight?"

"Absolutely," Rainey replies without a second thought. My hand falls back to my side. She quickly walks away without giving me a second look.

I've seen business transactions take longer than our conversation, but I received the answer I wanted. What more should we speak of? Moreover, if we're spotted having a cordial conversation that doesn't have Rainey vowing to get even with me, people would become suspicious.

It's difficult to walk away from her.

Rainey takes the first step, dipping her head slightly. "It was nice speakin' with you, Mr. Lacroix," she says loudly for anyone listening to hear.

I follow her movements, the corner of my mouth lifting upward. "You too, Miss Pleasonton."

Swallowing, she gives me one last look before she walks away. I watch her, making sure I keep a lighthearted smile on my face.

Discreetly, I adjust myself, but my efforts are ineffective because the silhouette of Rainey is toward the end of the hall. Her hips sway with each step, and her heels echo on the marble floors. My fingers flex involuntarily to feel her hips.

Something that should never and can never happen. Remember?

Who am I trying to kid? I will go to Rainey tonight. I will go to her every night if I have to.

It's almost a relief when she rounds the corner out of my sight. I start to walk down the hall toward the sound of the voices. By the time I reach everyone, no one should notice my...condition. At least that's what I tell myself.

"That was quite a friendly interaction between the two of you."

At the sound of my brother's voice, I turn and see him round the corner. I forgot all about him. His hands are behind his back as though he's taking a leisurely stroll down the driveway.

"My God, Étienne. When did voyeurism become a hobby of yours?"

"When you became so secretive." He steps out of the doorway and moves closer. "I know you said earlier that you do not love Rainey, and I'm tryin' hard to believe you, but it's apparent the two of you have become less...bothersome to one another."

I sigh and try my hardest not to look in the direction of Rainey. Is one of the bachelors speaking to her? My God, I've become unhinged. "Where are you goin' with this, Étienne?" I ask impatiently.

My brother looks me in the eye. "You can run your hand through her and feel the warmth, but don't hold still. Rainey will light you on fire. That girl will singe what's left of your soul."

"If I didn't know better, I'd say you don't care for Rainey."

"Quite the contrary. I care very much for her. I've watched her grow up. And that's why I can say confidently that the man for Rainey needs to be strong enough to stand by her."

I'm not that man. I don't want to be that man. But having someone, especially my own twin, place such little doubt in me makes me want to prove I could be that man.

"I'm not strong enough?"

"After the war?" Étienne pauses and shakes his head. "No. You're not. You both need to be careful."

All I can do is nod because it's too late for that. I could've used his warning the day I kissed Rainey in the ballroom. But I've become a cautionary tale of what happens when you kiss your best friend's sister, and for the first time in months, you start to feel alive.

CHAPTER TWENTY-TWO

RAINEY

The lunch at Belgrave was intended to meet the bachelor's families and better get to know them. And to a certain degree, that happened, but only on a surface level because everything that was said to me, I replied with a perfunctory smile. I can't remember the conversations I had or who I laughed with, but I know where Livingston Lacroix was throughout the meal, who he spoke to, and each time he laughed. I remembered every moment my heart sped up, trying my best to remain indifferent to the man across the table from me.

A man who spent the night with me and was now coming back for the third night in a row.

This wasn't a routine. Routines and habits take time to develop. No, this was a...learning experience. I know I'm not skilled in the bedroom, and our time in the dark is simply bolstering my confidence for when I'm married.

I'll know what to expect. The hand of a man securely wrapped around my waist will feel safe instead of shocking. Just thinking about how I woke up in Livingston's arms causes my blood to warm.

Maybe this is why people get married. Maybe they don't want to feel alone in life. The protection and warmth I felt this morning was something I've never experienced before but wanted to again. In my mind, I think of this morning and keep substituting Livingston's face with one of the bachelor's, but it's wrong and unnatural. Ultimately, Livingston's features returned.

It was unsettling how appeased my heart felt. Unsettling how desire gripped me every time we were alone. We could have been caught in the hallway at Belgrave today, but all I could concern myself with was the man who held me tightly.

Don't allow him into your room, my heart warns.

Yes, routines may take time to form, but the memories between Livingston and I had been constructed several years ago. And each night Livingston comes to me, each night we build upon those memories.

I'm growing increasingly fond of him. It extends past a fluttering of my heart or butterflies when I see him. Something deeper and more powerful.

"If you know I'm comin', can't you at least create a makeshift rope to throw down every night?"

Whirling around, I find Livingston standing in front of the open window dusting off his pants as though it's perfectly normal to be entering through the window.

I take a deep breath and give him a faint smile. "I left the window open," I point out.

"I'm also not a child anymore. The branch almost cracked underneath my weight. I feared for my life," Livingston says.

"Well, I'm pleased to see you made it inside without a scratch. We wouldn't want a king like you to get a tear in one of his shirts," I say dryly.

Slowly, I edge my way toward him. We had to be careful at Belgrave. There seemed eyes were everywhere, and when we did speak it was barely two words. Several times, I saw Étienne look at us suspiciously, and I swear he knew something was occurring between Livingston and me.

I don't want tonight to come to an end abruptly like the nights before. His presence was almost uncovered by my maid. Yet that brush with danger didn't stop him from coming back or me from leaving the window unlocked.

And I knew it was only a matter of time before one of us came to our senses and called off these late-night meetings.

There was an expiration on my dowry and debts that needed to be paid.

"Speakin' of kings, where's that chessboard of yours?"

My God, this man has a sharp memory. I thought the subject of chess was put to rest last night. Evidently, I was mistaken. "I put it away because I'm not playin' it right now."

"And why not?"

"Because our games go on for hours! And you cheat."

"I believe you've confused me with yourself."

My eyes narrow into slits. Stepping closer, I jab my finger at his chest. "I don't cheat. Perhaps, you are a sore loser. Ever think of that?"

Livingston smirks, and one of his dimples appears. "You cheat."

My temper flares. "I do not."

"Play a game with me, and I'll be more than happy to prove it."

Apprehensively, I scratch the side of my neck and look away.

"No more than five minutes."

What will one game hurt? It's a simple chess game.

I regard him once more. "Five minutes?"

Livingston's smile broadens. He knows he's won this challenge. "Five minutes," he agrees.

"Very well. Even though it's late, I can beat you at any hour, but let's speed this along, shall we?" I toss over my shoulder as I walk over to my armoire where I stored the chess set.

"Do you have somewhere to be?"

With the set in my hands, I close the armoire doors and studiously avoid Livingston's gaze. "No. But I am quite familiar with your strategies." I straighten and walk to the bed. Before I place the set on the mattress, I stare at him cautiously. "The time remains five minutes?"

"If I say five minutes, five minutes it shall be."

I finish arranging the board, my lack of certainty clear. "All right then. Let's play."

Livingston doesn't bound for the bed like I expect him to.

He gazes at the chessboard pensively, and then his eyes slowly widen. I've seen that expression on his face many times before.

At once, apprehension fills me.

With his arms crossed he meanders over. "You want to make this game a bit more…interestin'?"

Wary, I watch him. "How so?"

He stops right beside my bed and cocks a brow. "Ever played strip chess?"

"Of course. Every night with my maid."

Livingston leans in and waggles his brows. "Really now? Is this the same maid that knocked on your door last time?"

I nudge his knee with my foot. "You're impossible."

"So do you want to?"

"What are the rules?"

Livingston smiles. "Whenever a bishop, rook, or knight is captured by the opposin' player, that would be me, then the angry, sore loser, that would be you, has to remove a piece of clothin'." His light eyes glint wickedly. "Of my choosin'."

I lift a brow. "But if I capture your bishop, rook, or knight, which will undoubtedly happen, then that means *you* will have to remove a piece of your clothin'. Of my choosin'."

"Ah, you're a very quick student. What do you say?"

I chew on my bottom lip. There's a part of me that's more than intrigued and fascinated by how risqué this game sounds. That means I should probably say no.

"I'll play," I say. "But only for five minutes."

"Of course," he agrees.

The two of us take our places on my bed. We sit with our legs crossed and the chessboard between us. For several minutes, he adjusts some pieces and gets comfortable. Livingston rolls his neck and pops his knuckles as though he's preparing for the fight of his life. "Ready?"

"Ready to watch you lose. You?"

"I'm ready to watch you cheat."

I fling an impatient hand toward the board. "Start, will you?"

Years ago, we played a chess match of all chess matches.

The privilege to be able to go first indefinitely. The game was bloodthirsty, lasting for twelve hours. We took breaks only to go to the washroom and did without food. When all was said and done, Livingston won that game. He relished in his win for the weeks to come.

He stares at his white pieces with something close to reverence before he sharply scans the pawns. I watch him closely.

This isn't going to be a five-minute game.

And I'm right. Our pawns move forward, and rooks in lines, but neither of us goes in for an attack. We're both waiting for the other to let their guard down and building our own defenses.

"What were you discussin' with Elijah?" Livingston asks, his voice indifferent.

I'm in the process of moving my rook. I freeze and lift my head. "Hmm?"

"At Belgrave. You were speakin' with Elijah, no? Or perhaps I've mixed up your bachelors?" Livingston keeps his tone neutral, but there's an intensity in his eyes that's not typically there. He wants an answer to his question. I want to keep my mind on the chess game.

"Do you see a future with him?" he persists.

I hesitate to answer the question because the future is impossible to predict. "I'm unsure," I finally reply and make my move, swiftly taking one of his pawns. "Now would you be so kind as to give me your shoe, good sir?"

Looking less than pleased, Livingston does as he says. I catch the boot with one hand and gently place it on the floor. Serves him right for asking me that question.

With a look of pure concentration, Livingston focuses on the chessboard. "What I meant to ask was, do you want a future with him?" he asks several seconds later.

I swallow. "Right at this moment? No."

Without warning, his rook captures my knight. Livingston wickedly grins. "You're lookin' flushed there, darlin'. You can remove your dressin' gown."

I look down at my body, and the lack of clothing cover me. "This isn't fair. I have fewer clothes."

Livingston shrugs. "*Le savauge*, I don't make the rules. Now don't be a spoilsport. Hand over the gown."

Muttering words under my breath, I sit up straight and untie the belt. The material at my waist immediately gives.

Livingston's shit-eating grin briefly fades as he hungrily watches every move I make.

"Happy?" I ask as I wad the silky material into a ball and shove it toward him.

"It's just a dressin' gown," he replies, although gruffly and takes it.

With my fingers steepled in front of me, I think of the fastest, smartest attack to Livingston's king because I will not lose this game.

An hour later, we remain across from each other. Livingston is without his shirt, and the top button of his pants undone. We came to a compromise for the lack of clothes I had. My nightgown remains on, but every time my pieces are captured, I have to slip free a button. There's only one button remaining, and all that will be left to remove is the nightgown itself.

I stare at the chessboard and shake my head. I know I'm going to lose, but I hold Livingston responsible. He hasn't stopped staring. He distracted me, particularly when he removed his shirt. I think my mind went dark for a moment, and I forgot my name.

And now he's going to win. I can foresee the opportunity, his future checkmate. Sighing with defeat, I briefly close my eyes and tip over my king.

I look at Livingston. He has a predatory glint in his eyes as he waits for my next move.

All that is left is my nightgown. My nerves are about to take over, and I can barely breathe. The only person to ever see me naked is myself when I'm changing for bed. I've never revealed myself to another person. But a game is a game, and

I lost fair and square.

Taking a deep breath, I push myself onto my knees. As if he's in a trance, Livingston follows suit. The chessboard remains between us, but he feels so close. I'm aware of every shift his body makes, every hitch in his breath as though they're mine.

"Nightgown, Raina," he says.

My thumb hooks beneath the material of one sleeve. I drag it down my arm. Even though my heart is racing the entire time, my eyes remain on Livingston's. I slip my arm free, feeling the air exposed to my breast. When I move to the next sleeve, my fingers are shaking. The sleeve snags on my elbow. One tug and it's down and now my upper body is free. My nipples pucker. I shudder as the nightgown falls down my body, leaving a trail of goose bumps.

It lands at my knees.

There's a pregnant silence in the room. Livingston breathes deep through his nose and flexes his fingers.

I jut my chin out as though it's common for me to stand before Livingston naked every night. In truth, I think I'm going to be sick.

Livingston remains unmovable. He's so still, he looks like a statue. The only thing that moves are his eyes. Up and down, they trail across my body, never lingering for long.

"Game over," I say, breaking the silence.

Livingston's eyes flash as though this moment is about to be over. "Like hell," he mutters as he pushes the chessboard onto the floor and lunges for me. I land flat on my back with him on top. He leans into me and gives me an open-mouthed kiss. The seconds that pass by are filled with the sound of rustling as we both hurry to remove the rest of his clothing.

I regard him with wide eyes. His skin is olive everywhere. His cock juts out from his body, and for a moment, I hesitate.

He joins me on the bed. His knee brushes against my outer thigh as he moves above me. Once he's comfortable, I nearly groan at the feel of his naked body pressed against mine. So warm and solid.

His hands cup my breasts almost as though he's weighing them. I'm no fool. Compared to other women, I'm quite small. His thumbs make repeated circles around my nipples. My breath quickens and turns into pants as he draws a nipple into his mouth and gently bites. As he moves to the other breast, he lifts his head and gives me one of his devastating smirks.

"You don't want me to stop, do you? You're so sensitive I could make you orgasm by doin' this." His head dips back down, and he draws a nipple into his mouth, giving a long pull.

I cry out and manage to nod. Heat travels through my body in several different places. This is different than the last time he touched me. All barriers are gone. We're skin to skin, and there's no turning back.

I can feel the beads of sweat gathering at my temple. What he says is right, and if he doesn't stop, I'm going to break into a thousand pieces. I manage to slip a hand between the two of us. He feels my fingers traveling down his body and tenses.

"You're so sensitive," I coo. I wrap my fingers around his cock and stroke the satiny skin. "I could make you orgasm by doin' this."

A ragged groan tears from his throat. He fights to maintain composure and control, but in the end, he thrusts himself into my hands.

I smile and brush my fingers against his tip. Livingston knew what to bargain for with me. He doesn't call me *le savauge* because of my refined ways.

When I've tortured and teased him into the same frenzy he put me into, I pull away. Livingston's hands are gentle as they touch me, his lips soft against my neck, but as his body aligns with mine, I know what's going to happen. I would be lying if I said my heart wasn't racing.

His arms are bracketed near my head, and his lips move back to mine. My eyes close as I relax. My arms curl around his biceps as he hovers above me. I feel the silken tip of him repeatedly rub against me.

As amazing as this feels, I stiffen because I don't know how painful this will be. But Livingston doesn't go further from there. Over and over, he repeats the action until my hips lift.

And then he stops. My grip on his bicep tightens as his forehead touches mine. feel the gentle prod of him, and it's then Livingston looks me in the eye. With a deep shuddering breath, he slowly slides deeper. I suck in a sharp breath.

"Dieu me pardonne ce que je m'apprête à faire," Livingston murmurs against my lips before he embeds himself fully into me.

Have you ever felt pain so bad you writhe away from it, attempting to fold in on yourself until it dissolves? In this situation, Livingston is the reason for my pain. I cling tighter to him and shift my bottom, trying to get comfortable, but that doesn't seem to help.

His eyes nearly roll into the back of his head. "Christ, Rainey. Don't."

I remain still while my body stretches around him. But the abrupt pain I once felt is dissipating into a dull ache.

Perhaps this isn't as bad as I initially thought.

At a slow pace, I move my hips from side to side, ready for more of him. A choked groan spills from Livingston's lips. He grabs both of my hands and holds them above my head. My eyes widen as they make contact with his. He stares at me with rapt concentration. "I'm tryin' my hardest to go slow, but if you move against me one more time, this will be over far too quickly."

I nod, and his nose brushes against my cheek. Ever so slowly, he begins to thrust in and out of me. I sigh and close my eyes as he sinks deeper into me. Every time, it feels better than the last.

Livingston is patient with me, guiding my legs around his waist. His hips swivel in a slow, torturous rhythm, and a prickling sensation spreads throughout me. A small gasp slips from my lips. I don't know whether to grab Livingston's arms or push away from him. This feels almost too good. Better than our kisses or when he touched me nights ago. I want to sink into the sheets and mattress, and just feel every little thing he does.

"Move with me."

Above my head, Livingston keeps his hands linked with mine. Once again, our foreheads touch and breaths mingle as we find the correct rise and fall of each other's bodies.

The middle of my back lifts from the bed as I meet his thrust. A rumble of satisfaction is heard from Livingston, spurring me to keep going.

He whispers wicked remarks against my neck, "You are so tight...I've thought about this for so long..."

It makes the heat inside me become excruciating. Livingston's thrusts are becoming faster and harder. Enthusiastically, I arch against him, and I can't stop. Pleasure begins to build until I feel myself tightening around him.

And then, in one sudden rush, I fall apart. I don't care about my surroundings, or who might hear. I call out Livingston's name loudly as my body spasms and jerks, and I feel hot and cold all at once.

"Fuck. I can't...I can't last," he gasps. Livingston's beautiful face contorts into one of pain as he slams into me. His hold on me is so tight I have to take small breaths.

Some part of me instinctively knows to tighten my legs. I grip his shoulders and limply hang onto him. My bed gently hits the wall from the ferocity of Livingston's thrusts.

One of his hands curls around my waist, lifting me at an angle, and he slides even farther if that is possible, while he tilts his head back. A wild, primitive look fills his eyes as he bites out, "Christ."

He moves faster and deeper. My nails dig into his back. His sweat drips onto my skin. He convulses, and his hips jerk. "Raina."

He chants my name as though it's a prayer he's been saying his entire life. I hold onto him until his voice grows hoarse, and his body slows.

He collapses on me, gasping for several minutes, and then moves away. I feel a brief sense of panic. Is he leaving? Will he come to regret this later?

He walks about the room, disappears into the bathroom,

and comes back, the mattress dipping from the weight of him. In his hands is a damp washcloth.

"For a moment, I thought you were goin' to leave," I confess.

His lips quirk. "Commonly, I leave a room with my clothes on." He moves the washcloth between both hands before he shifts toward me. His eyes continuously rove across my face for any signs of distress.

"I've never been with a…a—"

"A virgin?" I supply.

Rapidly, he nods. It's rare to see Livingston so unsure of himself. He almost appears shy. Gently, he nudges my legs apart. It takes me a moment to understand what he's about to do. I reach forward, but he holds the washcloth out of my grasp. "I can do that," I protest.

He shakes his head, brows slightly furrowed.

The washcloth is cold against my skin, but I don't say a word. I let Livingston clean my blood from my body. What he's doing is deeply intimate and personal.

I feel the fissure in my heart as I watch him. I notice the sharp cut of his cheekbones, the perfect line of his nose, the very faint lines around the corner of his eyes and lips that inevitably come with life. He's still the same, but everything has changed. Just then, a dark strand falls across his brow. And he looks at me from beneath those dark lashes and smirks at me.

Oh, dear.

The realization of what I've allowed to happen sinks in. I muster a weak smile at him. No sheets cover my naked body, but I feel hot all over. My heart pounds furiously as I sort through my racing thoughts.

Livingston stands and walks back to the bathroom while I take deep breaths in and out.

How did I let this happen?

"Are you all right?" he asks. There is a thread of concern in his voice.

I turn and see him staring at me carefully. I sit up and

move over so there's room for him. "I'm fine."

"Are you certain? You can tell me if I hurt you."

He lies beside me and pulls me toward him. Our legs intertwine, his olive against my pale, smooth flesh. I sigh and try to disregard the relief I feel with him next to me. "I promise you didn't hurt me," I say.

Livingston gathers the sheets around us, and we lie there peacefully. My head rests against his chest, and I listen to the steady beat of his heart, but I need a better confirmation he's real and beside me. I rest my hand across his and watch the steady rise and fall of my hand for so long my eyes burn. Livingston combs a hand through my hair.

Slowly, my eyelids start to flutter shut. Until Livingston quietly says, "I'm startin' to care less and less at the idea of bein' away from you."

My eyes flash open. I swear my heart stops beating. Lifting my head from his chest, I swallow and gather the courage to speak. "You don't have to leave tonight."

"Somebody will catch me."

"My door is locked."

If Livingston wanted to go, he would have left the first chance he got. Of that, I'm certain. He wants to stay just as much as I want him to.

"I don't want you to go," I quietly confess.

His hold on me tightens before I can finish my words. I watch his Adam's apple bob as his eyes sweep across my face. "Then I'll stay," he replies gruffly.

I smile and lower my head back to his chest.

"Good night." I say, finishing my words with a yawn.

"Good night, *le savauge*."

Livingston rolls toward me, wrapping his arms securely around me. My body is tucked into his with his chin resting on the crown of my head. I breathe in the scent of him while his eyes grow heavy.

"Everything I do seems wrong. But you? You are the only thing that feels right," Livingston murmurs before he falls asleep.

I stare at his chest, replaying his words. A small shudder escapes me. I'm beginning to realize that as the sun falls, so do Livingston's walls. He becomes the man I've chased after my entire life.

Weeks ago, in a dark theater, I played the write hand game with the wrong man. Which led to a kiss I couldn't stop thinking about. And tonight, I gave him my virginity.

And now I know, I'm in love with the king of the South.

CHAPTER TWENTY-THREE

LIVINGSTON

I have experienced many things in my life, but nothing paralyzes me more than children.

Specifically, little children.

They highlight the lack of progression in my life.

When Alexandra was first born and I held her, she opened her eyes and promptly let out the loudest wail known to man. It's as though she knew she was being held by someone who not only couldn't feed her, but who's happiness hinges upon people's approval.

Only hours old and my niece knew I reeked of failure. What would my nephew see in me? My God, after war the options were endless. This morning, I shaved and made sure I wore my finest suit as though I was meeting the king. In a way, I was. I was meeting the prince, soon-to-be king to carry on the Lacroix name. And if he's anything like Étienne, he'll learn to execute a firm business-like handshake before he's five, build an empire as tall as the sky before thirty, and have the perfect family before forty.

Upon entering Belgrave, the energy is alight with tangible excitement. The staff all have an extra pep in their step. I don't have to wonder why. The beaming smile stretched across Étienne's face is infectious. As he greets me, I find myself smiling back and embracing him. "I hear congratulations are in order."

Étienne pulls away and gives me a blunt nod, although he

smiles broadly.

"*Ton bonheur m'apporte de la joie.*"

My brother appears momentarily surprised. "*Je vous remercie.*" He gestures to the second floor. "Would you like to see him?"

"Umm…of course," I say although it comes out more as a question.

We're quiet as we walk up the stairs. Once we reach the second floor, Étienne looks over at me. "I'm truly surprised you're here today."

"Did you think I would cancel?" I ask.

"That's exactly what I thought would happen."

"Well, I would never miss the chance to see the newest addition to the Lacroix family," I reply when, in fact, that was precisely the case. I was informed of my nephew's birth the moment he was born. And I used every excuse I possibly could until the excuse well ran dry.

Once we reach Serene's private quarters, I pause in front of the closed door. "Are you sure it's proper for me to go in there?"

"The baby was born yesterday morning. Serene's been restin'. She's in good spirits if that's what concerns you."

No, that's not what concerns me. Nonetheless, I dip my head as if that's the direction of my thoughts.

"I just want to make certain mother and baby are comfortable."

"Trust me, mother is the most comfortable she's been for the past nine months," Étienne replies wryly and then opens the door.

Étienne walks in front of me and lightly knocks on the wall as we step into the room. "There is a visitor for you."

Serene is sitting up in bed, holding my nephew. Her hair is pulled back, and she's wearing a nightgown with a dressing gown over it. She looks exhausted, but there's a radiance about her.

"Hello," Serene whispers so lightly I can barely make out the greeting.

I clear my throat and shift from foot to foot. "Good afternoon."

Serene rolls her eyes and gestures with her free hand for me to come closer. "I thought you got lost on your way here," she says as I kiss her cheek.

"Nonsense. I've had some business that needed attendin' to," I say with a grin.

Serene's eyes twinkle. "Oh, I bet you did," she replies smartly, as though she knew exactly where I'd been last night.

Impossible. Unless...she'd spoken to Rainey. Had I narrowly missed Rainey today?

I shake my head of all thoughts of Rainey, and with my hands behind my back, I lean my body forward and peer closely at my nephew. Thankfully, his eyes are closed. No inspection from a newborn.

"Livingston," Serene whispers, her eyes never leaving her son's face. "I'd like you to meet your nephew, Julian Trace Lacroix."

The baby squirms. His face scrunches and turns red. I can't tell if he's soiling himself or is preparing to cry. But thankfully, all he does is yawn with one of his tiny hands curling into the tiniest fist and resting out of his swaddled blanket. I breathe a sigh of relief. I remember Alex's cries as a baby. She was capable of breaking the windows at Belgrave if she tried hard enough.

"Hello Julian Trace, you're quite strappin'." I carefully scan his small face. Overall, he looks quite similar to Alex when she was an infant. "Lacroix chin and frown. You have your mother's nose, thank God."

Étienne snorts.

"I cannot tell, but I presume you have blue eyes?"

"Gray," Serene inserts.

"Gray. Gray eyes," I quickly correct. "Which is unexpected, but perhaps they'll change." I pause momentarily and nod. "You will do, good sir."

Étienne steps forward. "My God, Livingston. He's an infant, not an elderly man."

"I will not do that cooin' and awwin' you and Serene do."

"I've done no such thing," Étienne fiercely protests.

"You do," I say.

At the same time, Serene says, "You really do."

"Would you like to hold Julian?" Serene asks, holding the small bundle out to me.

For seconds, my eyes move back and forth between Serene and my nephew as though he's a bomb that could explode at any moment.

"Right now?"

"We went through this with Alex." Serene laughs.

"I know, and I'm not entirely certain she's not an adult trapped in a child's body. The words that she says…I'm concerned."

Serene shakes her head. "It could be because she spends time with you."

I give that theory some thought and shake my head. "No, that's all Alex. I wish you the best of luck as she grows into a young adult."

"I refuse to think about any of my kids growing," Serene says as she stares down at the baby. "Not right now."

Even though I just arrived, I begin to think of a reasonable justification to take my leave. Étienne chooses that moment to take his son from Serene and place him in my arms. "Here. Hold your nephew."

I do just that but in the most inelegant way. It's as though I'm carrying heavy sacks of potatoes.

Serene watches me and laughs. "I can't wait to see you with your own kid."

"I don't think that will happen, Considerin' the two of you mate like rabbits, you'll have enough children for a village." The mere thought of being in my brother's position, standing beside my faceless wife and staring down at our newborn baby, brings about a wave of panic inside me. There's a fleeting moment, though, where my faceless wife suddenly has features and looks remarkably like Rainey. I become so nervous I'm going to drop the baby that I abruptly shove him into Serene's arms. "That's enough for now."

"Okay," Serene drawls out slowly as she adjusts the baby. Étienne stares at me as though I've gone insane. If he knew what image suddenly appeared in my head, maybe he'd understand.

"How have you been Livingston?" Serene asks, never taking her eyes off the baby.

"Fine," I reply cautiously before I think better of it. "Why?"

Serene lifts a shoulder. "I've been seeing you around Rainey more often, and you've been less of a Boozy Suzy. Why is that?"

"I don't know what Boozy Suzy means, and truthfully, I don't believe I want to."

"You don't," Étienne chimes in.

Serene's eyes flick in my direction. "So why is that?"

"I've decided to no longer partake in alcohol." I grin at my sister-in-law. "Consider this my resignation."

"If that isn't a lie, I don't know what is," Étienne says.

"It's true, brother," I continue. "I've taken to heart all the profound conversations you've had with me. It's time for me to change."

Étienne mutters curse words under his breath.

"That's not the question I was asking and you know it. Why have you and Rainey been spending so much time together?" Serene persists.

Both she and Étienne stare at me intently. Particularly my brother. I take no issue with discussing the ladies I've been with. However, not once did I think one of those ladies would be Rainey. But if they imagined me confessing to what happened last night with Rainey, they were imagining wrong because I myself wasn't entirely sure. I'm not filled with regret even though I should be because I was making a bumbling mess out of things. Rainey was someone I couldn't stay away from. Rainey and I had a long intricate history that was impossible to deny.

"I'm not certain that's any of your concern," I say stiffly.

Serene tilts her head to the side as though I was speaking

French. "So Livingston Lacroix has been spending time with a woman, and he won't comment on it...how very singular."

I pinch the bridge of my nose and sigh. They weren't going to stop until they had the answers they wanted. As much as that frays on my nerves, I will not tell them a single detail about Rainey and me.

Serene glances at Étienne. "How was that? Did I sound like someone from this time?"

"Yes, you did."

Serene raises her hand midair and gives what she calls an "air five" to Étienne. Since Serene has become a permanent part of this era she has made a conscious effort to tweak her vocabulary and stop saying popular sayings from her time. Typically, it ended up with a lot of malapropisms on her part.

"Are we finished with this conversation?" I ask.

It doesn't take long for Serene to control her laughter. She solemnly looks at me. "In all seriousness, don't you ever get lonely in the Lacroix house all by yourself?"

"Are you askin' if I want a wife?"

"Absolutely."

"No, I don't."

"Why not?"

I start to tick the reasons off on my fingers. "Because I prefer the vastness of space as my own and don't want to share it with anyone else. I become uninterested far too quickly, and I cannot care for myself, let alone another human."

For years, those selfish reasons have been my justification for being a bachelor. As for right now, the only reason that rings true is the last one. I don't know if I would want to put anyone through the nights I go through, and the shame I wake up to. If I was to marry, I'd only give my wife misery.

"What about Rainey?" Serene says.

"What about Rainey?" I shoot back.

"She's a woman."

"That's debatable," I murmur, but it's a lie. The image of her dropping her nightgown to the floor and boldly standing naked in front of me flashes through my mind.

If I left Belgrave right now, how long would it take me to get to her home? Subtly, I shake my head. I can't sneak into her home during the day.

"You weren't debating it when you were kissing her like a sailor on leave," Serene retorts.

Étienne laughs and covers it by coughing into his fist.

Looking at Serene, I shake my head. "Whatever happened to discretion?"

Serene shrugs. "There's no such thing as discretion in this family. I remember you having a lot of fun with Étienne and me when we first…got together. Of course I'm going to give you a hard time."

"That was quite different."

"In what way?"

"The two of you…" I pause, searching for the right words. "The two of you have a mutual attraction."

Serene and Étienne continue to stare at me as though I might have more to say. I stare back, obstinately standing in place. In every respect, the circumstances surrounding Rainey and me are different from Serene and Étienne.

Right?

Right. They loved each other. There was no love between Rainey and me. Just the strong desire to be intimate.

My brother clears his throat. "I'm uncertain why we're even discussin' this. Rainey is eleven years younger than Livingston."

"Your wife is nearly 100 years younger than you," I point out.

At that, a three of us become silent. Smirking, Serene looks at Étienne. "Care for a rebuttal?"

Étienne looks at the floor. "No, no…" His voice fades before he impatiently flings a hand in my direction. "This conversation doesn't pertain to me. It's about Livingston and Rainey!"

Once again, they look at me. Tired and ready to leave the room, I do what anyone else would. I cave. "If you must know, Rainey and I have kissed once," I lie.

Serene is unmoved by the announcement. "You and Rainey kissed."

"When you gave birth, did you lose your hearin'? Yes, we kissed."

"I was screaming so loud, it's a possibility," Serene replies. "Now keep going; we already know about the kissing part. If you recall, I interrupted the two of you."

Of course, I recalled. If Serene hadn't walked into the ballroom, the kiss would've continued. "There's nothin' to go on about." I avert my eyes. "We kissed. The end."

Serene watches me carefully. "No, that's not the end. But I have more questions so I'll let that go. What are you going to do about this?"

I look at Étienne whose gaze is conveniently on his newborn son. I have no one to support me. "There's nothin' to do. Believe it or not, a kiss can simply be a kiss."

"I'm aware of that. However, when you have the history the way you and Rainey do, it isn't simply 'a kiss.'"

Rainey and I were far past a simple kiss.

"I'm starting to think that perhaps..."

Serene's words fade, and as she tries to think of the right thing to say, I cut in. "Startin' to think what?"

"That as much as I think this bachelor idea will pay off in the end, Rainey's beginning to feel like..." Serene repeatedly snaps her fingers before she points at me. "Like Consuelo Vanderbilt!"

Ah, Consuelo Vanderbilt the American heiress who married the 9th Duke of Marlborough in 1895. It was a union bound by money and titles, and one I didn't follow too closely. Nat did, and she was all too happy to divulge the information she read about in the papers. From my sister, I knew Consuelo and her duke had separated.

"And what happens to Ms. Consuelo?" I ask merely to humor Serene.

Serene narrows her eyes. "She has a brother-in-law who's a pain her in ass. The brother-in-law doesn't see the truth is right in front of him, so she whacks him over the head with a two-by-four."

"If I tallied the amount of times you threatened Étienne and me bodily harm, I'd be the richest man on earth."

"And the luckiest," Serene retorts smartly.

Serene has a quick tongue, but there's no bite. She's as gentle as they come.

"I can't help but notice you're smiling, Livingston," Serene remarks. "You may roll your eyes at me, but you and Étienne would be lost without my smart-ass tongue. You know who also happens to be a smart ass and keeps you on your toes?" She doesn't give me time to reply. "Rainey."

I should've known this was where the conversation was going. Serene has never believed in pointless discussions. Every word that comes for her mouth takes aim.

"Listen, I know you've had a proverbial skank train in your life since you realized Livingston Jr. could rise all on his own—"

"Lovely, Serene," Étienne interjects.

My sister-in-law continues. "But maybe it's time you find someone who fits you."

"You think I've been settin' my sights on women who I'll never end up with?"

"I think that's exactly what you've been doing."

"If this is the trajectory of the conversation, I believe I'll take my leave." Bending down, I kiss Julian's head and head toward the bedroom door.

"Livingston, do you plan on bedding her and then being done with her?" Serene blurts.

Serene and I have always had an excellent relationship. In her, my brother has met his match. And even I have to admit that the things to roll off her tongue have me laughing, but I am not laughing now. Suddenly, I stop walking and turn around.

My brows slant low. "Never."

"You seem upset with me."

"I am not."

"You do." She brushes her fingers across my nephew's cheek and glances at Étienne. "Does he seem upset with me?"

Étienne nods. "He seems upset with you."

"I cannot tell you how wonderful it is to come visit the two of you and have these invigoratin' conversations," I say drolly.

"And I cannot tell you how wonderful it is to watch you come to the realization that you love Rainey Pleasonton."

"Have you gone mad? Étienne, your wife is unhinged." I stab a finger in Serene's direction. "I do not love Rainey. The two of us have been at war since she was a child!"

Étienne grunts. "Yes, and two people who hate one another can never fall in love. Right, Serene?"

"Oh, of course." Serene smiles back at my brother. "It never happens."

"I need a new family," I mutter as I leave the room.

"A new family, you say?" Serene calls. "That's funny, because Rainey's in the market for a husband!"

The two of them are ridiculous. I do not love Rainey. Desire? Perhaps. For some reason, the feeling won't fade but grows stronger by the day. As unnerving as that may be, I've desired women before. Not to this degree, but I'm sure it will dwindle soon. It's probably because we've been forced to spend more time with one another, and I haven't had as many female companions as I normally do. That's the problem. Well, tonight, that all changes. Tonight, I won't go to Rainey's. I'm halfway down the stairs debating on which woman I'll call on when Étienne catches up to me. "You left in a rush."

"I have business matters that need attendin' to," I say, not bothering to break my stride.

"That was your alibi for not visitin' earlier. Think of somethin' else."

"My apologies. I don't know what you'd like for me to say. I am a very busy man."

"I don't need your many alibis. What I'd like is for you to explain why you've been sneakin' into Rainey's room."

At once, I stop walking. My heart stutters for a moment as I process my brother's words.

"How did you—"

"Rainey visited Serene this mornin'. Serene got the truth

out of her."

A string of curse words pours from my mouth as I drag my hands through my hair. It occurs to me Rainey didn't tell Serene everything. If that was the case, my brother would be choking me on Pleas's behalf.

"What do you think you're doin' fallin' asleep in her room?" Étienne asks, his voice low.

Ah, that's what he thinks. Deplorable, but not near as scandalous as taking Rainey's virginity.

I knew what I did was wrong, and the last thing I needed was for my brother and his wife to know the full extent of my wrongdoing. Dragging my hands through my hair, I take a deep breath. "I don't know, all right?"

My brother watches me as I begin to pace. "I went there to discuss her family's accounts. My intentions were honorable. Sometimes we play a game of chess or talk and enjoy one another's company."

The rest of the time is spent in Rainey's bed as I teach her all I know about pleasure.

"You can talk and play chess in the daylight, too," Étienne remarks wryly.

Not the chess we played.

Which was the wrong way to think because Étienne stands tall, his cheeks become drawn as he sucks in a deep breath. He begins shaking his head. "My God. You didn't."

"I have a perfect explanation."

"Tu ne peux pas garder tes mains pour toi?" Étienne explodes in French.

I go to answer him but an image of Rainey sitting on her bed comes to mind. She's slipping free the last button of her nightgown, smirking at me as though she knows the effect she has on me. As though she knew I was seconds away from ripping the nightgown off with my teeth.

"Well?" Étienne demands, his voice cutting through my fantasy like a knife.

I clear my throat. "Apparently not."

Étienne takes a step forward and lowers his voice. "If this

gets out, it could cause a scandal. You need to do the right thing and marry her."

A harsh laugh escapes me. "In my life, Rainey has shot at me twice for embarrassin' her. Imagine what she'll do if I propose to her out of duty."

"If Pleas was here, he would kill you. He would kill you dead."

"You don't think I know that?"

"So why did you go to her?"

I stop pacing long enough to turn and stare at my brother with wide eyes. "I don't know!"

The truth hangs between us for several seconds.

"If you care for her at all, you will stop goin' there."

"Of course I care for her. I am not devoid of emotions. She's Nat's best friend."

"All the more reason not to see her!" Étienne roars.

"Again, I am not a heartless monster. I have no intentions of hurtin' Rainey."

Étienne appears far from convinced. "Once, when you were with a woman, she went to the washroom and you grabbed your shoes and jacket and escaped on the rose trellis so you didn't have to say good-bye."

I shrug. "I saw my exit and took it. Besides, it's worked before in the past. I don't see why it wouldn't then."

"The last time you fell and injured yourself."

"Ah, but I learned my lesson and no injuries happened."

"For one moment, I need you to be genuine." With his steepled fingers pressed against the tip of his nose, Étienne stares at the floor for several seconds before he looks at me with serious eyes. "Rainey is one woman who doesn't need to be in your bed."

I dip my head, but it's only to hide my anger. "Agreed," I say tightly.

In truth, Rainey's lithe body has never stretched out across my bed. Her head has never touched a single pillow of mine. I'm the one who's been going to her. Over and over and over.

Rainey is years younger, but no one should let her age fool

them. I've said it once, and I'll say it again. That woman is dangerous. She's the one they need to be speaking with. Not me.

I'm certain Étienne interprets my silence as an acknowledgment of my guilt. He can believe what he wishes. I'm not about to reveal that I seek Rainey's companionship because she's the only person who can quiet down my nightmares.

"I apologize if my words are harsh, but I'm simply lookin' out for her," Étienne says.

My gaze cuts in his direction. "I am lookin' out for Rainey."

"By keepin' her under you?" Étienne challenges.

I can feel heat flood my cheeks. I'm not embarrassed, but furious. Furious that, for my brother, it's remarkably easy to group Rainey with the rest of the women I've been with.

I'm mere seconds away from lunging at my brother when we're interrupted. Étienne appears mildly annoyed by Ben's appearance, but I'm grateful. I turn away and take a moment to take a deep breath. My God, what is happening to me? I almost hit my brother, and for what? Over what he said about Rainey?

Twisting around, I open my mouth, intending to apologize, but stop when I see the expression on Étienne's face as he reads the small paper in his hand.

"What's wrong?" I ask.

He's stoic by nature, but this is different. The energy around him is barely contained, and something he's not altogether comfortable with himself. Sighing, he hands the letter over to me before he averts his gaze. I give him one last look before I read the brief telegram.

I've never read a telegram faster in my life. "My God," I mutter.

Slowly, I lift my head. This can't be true. It can't. But I know it is; Étienne would never jest in this type of manner.

Nathalie's husband, Oliver, is dead.

CHAPTER TWENTY-FOUR

RAINEY

W hen one has no money, should one be gettin' fitted
for a new wardrobe?" I ask.

Momma stops scanning the array of dresses,
blouses, and skirts in my armoire to look at the stack of dresses
on my bed. "When one is in search of a husband, yes. And do
keep your voice down, Raina."

I look around my bedchamber. "Momma, there's no one
here," I say, making a point to whisper back. "The seamstress
won't be here for another fifteen minutes."

"Please continue to practice whisperin'. I know you like to
make a habit of bellowin'."

I frown. "I do not bellow. I raise my voice in order to be
heard."

Momma chooses a dress lying on the bed and thoroughly
inspects it, shakes her head, and tosses it back onto the bed.
"It's not ladylike to raise your voice."

"But how will anyone know they're wrong?" I say teasingly.

At that, Momma looks at me with disapproval in her eyes.
"Honestly, Rainey, I do not know what I'm gonna do with
you," she huffs.

"I know what you'll do. You'll marry me off to the first man
you see," I mutter under my breath, but apparently, it's not
quiet enough because Momma lifts her head and looks at me.

"Are you still goin' on about that? I've told you I had
nothin' to do with Miles's will!"

"Forgive me if I still have my suspicions." My voice drips with sarcasm.

"Sweetie, you can mull over your brother's will until you're blue in the face, but it's only goin' to cause you more pain because you won't find the answer you're searchin' for. In fact, you won't find any explanation at all."

"I'm quite aware of that."

Most days, Momma's the one who's erratic and emotional. Today, it's me. This morning, I woke up feeling awry, and my mood hasn't shifted. It has everything to do with the knowledge of knowing I'm in love with Livingston Lacroix.

Livingston.

My worst fears have come true. I'm in love with a womanizer.

This discovery weighed heavy on my heart; nothing good was bound to come out of this, but I had to tell someone. Certainly couldn't be Livingston. Definitely not Momma. She would be writing out the guest list to our imaginary wedding before I could finish my sentence.

So I've kept silent. Especially with Momma in my personal space. In the past, I'd turn to Miles when I'm sad, and with his stable energy gone, I feel as though I'm falling with no one to catch me.

What I need is privacy so I can cry. If I've learned anything from the losses in my life, it's that a good, long cry can make me feel surprisingly better.

A soft knock on the door interrupts our bickering. Immediately, Momma's demeanor changes. Her eyes soften, lips curl upward.

Fight? What fight? We're simply a mother and a daughter spending quality time together.

"Come in," Momma calls out.

One of the maids peeks her head into the room. She appears undaunted by the mess Momma has made and looks at me. "Ma'am, there's a Mr. Lacroix to see you."

Momma and I glance at one another in confusion. What is he doing here? I have no bachelor to see, and there's no important discussions we need to have.

I smile at the maid. "Thank you, I'll be down shortly."

She closes the door, and I fix my blouse and skirt.

"Did you know he was payin' you a visit?"

"No." But I'm glad he is.

"Then what does he need?"

"God only knows," I say as I walk out of the room.

"The seamstress will be here in ten minutes!" Momma calls out behind me.

"I know, I know," I call out.

My footsteps echo in the foyer as I nearly fly down the stairs. I try to slow down. I haven't seen him since the night we made love. I've missed him more than I should and couldn't stop thinking about the next time he would come to my room.

I step through the doorway and see the figure he cuts in his suit. I can't fight the smile that pulls at the corner of my mouth.

"Hello. This is certainly a surprise," I say.

Livingston turns. "We need to talk."

There are certain expressions one makes that will stop you dead in your tracks. The somber look in Livingston's eyes and the strain around his lips cause me to do just that.

"What is the matter? Who's hurt?" I rush forward until the tips of my shoes brush against Livingston's. "Is it Serene? I know she just had baby Julian, but has somethin'—"

"No, no," Livingston cuts in. "I just left Belgrave. Serene and the baby are fine."

I sigh with relief and then immediately become suspicious about what caused that look on his face. "Then what?"

Perhaps it was me. Maybe he's here to show regret over what we did. Please don't let that be true.

"As I was on my way out, Étienne received a telegram." Livingston pauses. "Oliver passed away last night."

I rear back, not because I'm shocked or devastated, but because for the small moment, as I process the news, I'm relieved it isn't Nat. That makes me a terrible human being. My closest friend just lost her husband.

"My word," I whisper.

Livingston nods. "I wanted to inform you before the news spreads through Charleston."

I shake my head and stare down at the floor.

Livingston hesitates over his next words. "Nat said she attempted to call you, but she was unsuccessful."

I would love to say Momma was opposed to modern advances, but given the fact Livingston had undoubtedly passed the rotary phone in the hall numerous times, there was no way I could say that. We had to curtail our spending as best as possible, and since it was clear Momma wasn't willing to reduce her time spent at the shops, I took matters into my own hands. I never thought the subject would come up.

"Hmm…I don't know why I didn't receive her call." I furrow my brows and feign confusion. "I just made a call yesterday."

Livingston slowly nods, appearing unconvinced. "It's fine. She was unable to speak with Étienne and sent him a telegram."

I begin to fuss with the collar of my shirt. I want to speak with Nat right this second, see her. Let her know that everything is all right. "When is the funeral?"

"I'm uncertain. All I know is Oliver is dead, and I need to get to my sister."

Rapidly, I nod. "When are you leavin'?"

"Tomorrow."

"I'm goin' with you."

At that, Livingston lifts a brow. "And leave all your bachelors behind?"

I thought we could have a moment without the bachelors being mentioned. Apparently, I was wrong. Impatiently, I fling a hand in the air, ready to change the subject. "They aren't important right now. I'll go with you."

Crossing his arms over his chest, Livingston looks at me. "It's August 23rd. There's only a week and a half left to spend time with your remainin' bachelors."

"I understand there's a time constraint to find a husband, but I want to go with you. I need to be with you and Nat."

Livingston remains quiet. Giving the open doorway a quick

look, I step forward and slide my arms around his narrow waist. I lay my cheek against his chest and inhale the clean scent of him. At once, my restlessness dissolves in his arms. Slowly, Livingston's arms band around me. I feel his chin rest against the crown of my head.

We stand like that for several seconds, simply embracing one another.

"All right," he finally says, his voice gruff. "We'll go together."

CHAPTER TWENTY-FIVE

LIVINGSTON

Almost immediately, plans were set in motion.

Bags were packed. Calls and telegrams were sent. Train tickets to Savannah, Georgia, were purchased. The adrenaline I feel the night before we leave is akin to what I felt while I was in France.

Because Serene had just delivered Julian, she and Étienne were staying in Charleston with their children. I overheard Serene telling Étienne to go, but he said he couldn't leave her and the kids.

Instead, I would be traveling with the most unlikely of companions.

At seven in the morning, I used the brass knocker and waited for someone to answer. A servant answers, steps aside, and immediately dips their head as though they've been expecting me. "Good mornin', Mr. Lacroix."

"I'm here for Mrs. Pleasonton and Miss Rainey."

"Of course," their butler, Stanley, says. "Please come in."

I know the Pleasonton house as though it's my own home. I've hidden in the cupboards, ran through the narrow halls, slid down the banister, and received a tongue-lashing of the century from Mrs. Pleasonton. And most recently, I climbed the tree outside Rainey's room to see if our carnal kisses were all in my imagination. It turns out, they weren't. For whatever reason, there was a spark between Rainey and me that neither one of us anticipated. Perhaps, when you dislike someone long enough, the animosity can burn bright enough to start a fire. That's what I've been telling myself, and what I will continue to tell myself for this entire trip. Otherwise, the small morsel of sanity I have left will kick in and tell me how foolish it is to travel with someone I desire so much.

At that moment, I hear Rainey and Leonore talking upstairs. They round the corner and begin to walk down the stairs. Whatever they're discussing must be consuming because neither one notices me standing beside the front door. When they reach the first floor, Rainey sighs and sets her valise on the floor.

Leonore takes the opportunity to give her a good look. "Raina, did you dress in the dark?"

Rainey looks down and smooths a hand across her navy blue blouse. "There is nothin' wrong with my attire."

"If you wear the skirt one more day, the material is gonna tear."

I think she looks exquisite. I didn't come to her last night. I thought it'd be best if I let her rest before the journey, but I missed her. God did I ever.

She will choose a bachelor soon! You can't keep her forever.

But could I? Not for the first time have I thought of what it would be like if she was mine. Rainey would never settle as a mistress. I would find another arrow being directed at me if I made the proposition. And this time, she wouldn't miss her mark.

All the same, the bachelor debacle has shown one thing — Rainey truly desires a family. A life of her own. She deserves that, and I don't know if I could give her that. But the thought of her laying with another man…it sends me into a tailspin. My calm demeanor disappears altogether and I feel as if I might rip every bachelor limb from limb.

"We wouldn't want that, now would we?" Rainey murmurs beneath her breath, pulling me out of my thoughts.

Leonore opens her mouth, but immediately stops when she sees me standing in the foyer, and her demeanor promptly brightens. "Livingston."

I smile at her and step forward. "Mrs. Pleasonton, it's a pleasure to see you."

"Please forgive us for carryin' on. I wasn't made aware you were here."

"I came early."

"Lord have mercy." She places a hand on her chest over her heart while their trunks are carried to the car. "My heart breaks for your dear sister and your family's loss."

Rainey stands beside her mother. She doesn't say a single word, but she does look at me from out of the corner of her eye for a scant second. I take that moment to greet her. "Rainey, good mornin'."

"Mornin', Livingston." Her reply is calm.

I try to catch her gaze once more, but she busies herself with her hat. Leonore remains unaware, as she's already begun giving orders to the servants to take the bags to the car.

Rainey and I follow Leonore outside. In the early morning, the humidity hasn't had an opportunity to claim the outdoors. Within a few hours, it will be impossible to walk outside without becoming coated in a thick layer of sweat.

Rainey sighs. "It's a lovely day to travel."

I glance at her from the corner of my eye. "Indeed."

Are we having a conversation about the weather? As though we're two acquaintances who have fortuitously met one another on the street and have nothing else to speak instead of.

Before Rainey can get into the car, I step into her way. Patiently, she stares at me. She doesn't blush, and she certainly doesn't giggle or send me a coy smile. It's as though we never kissed, touched, or made love.

It is most interesting.

"I trust you're doin' well?"

She dips her head. "Quite."

I watch her carefully. "Did you sleep okay?"

"All things considered." Right then she lifts her gaze. My heartbeat stutters and stops. "Did you sleep all right?"

I slept as though my bed was a pile of bricks. No matter what I did, I couldn't get comfortable, and it was because I didn't have a wild savage whose loyal companion was her bow and arrow. I slept a grand total of two hours. Eventually, I gave up the fight when the sun began to rise, and with a sober head, I wished I was in her bed. "As well as can be," I reply.

"Well then. We both had a pleasant night of sleep. Most remarkable."

I don't want to stand there and speak of pleasantries. We both have perfected the art of Southern charm. What I truly want to do is take her in my arms and kiss her, and ask if she thought about me last night as much as I thought of her.

"I believe we have a train to catch?" Rainey says.

Shaking my head slightly, I step to the side and gesture for her to move in front of me. "After you."

Rainey smiles at me. A smile that's been given hundreds of times, but now feels remarkably intimate. She gives that smile after she's made love. My heart stops and stutters again. When did I become a panting schoolboy for her?

Dear God, this is a going to be one hell of a trip. I've survived war, but I don't know if I will survive Rainey.

As I get into the car, I observe the woman who's been unwittingly making my nights better. All this time, I thought I knew her. But who is Rainey Pleasonton? I think I could look at her a thousand times, talk to her in a million ways, and still find something new.

And for some reason I can't explain, that's utterly terrifying to me.

CHAPTER TWENTY-SIX

RAINEY

The trip to Savannah is wrought with tension.

I cling to my momma's prattling like a lifeline while Livingston sits across from us. When he isn't reading the paper, dozing off, he's looking at me with eyes half-mast. I feigned indifference as though I was the same Rainey who continued to view Livingston as she always did.

But after the nights in my room, that's no longer an option.

Like one of the love-sick women who pines for him, he's frequently on my mind. I thought about what he was doing and who he was with. The nights we had together weren't enough. I felt starved for more.

My emotions were altogether unsettling. Sooner than later, I would become sated and filled. Until then, I would try my best to be cordial. Friendly, almost. There's a good chance it came across as stiff, but I was determined for the world to know that I was not falling in love with Livingston Lacroix. A man known to leave a trail of broken hearts.

For all anyone else knew, Livingston and I were still enemies, and words were our weapons.

But I knew the truth. I knew I loved this stubborn, arrogant man.

How could I ever let this happen? I should've been more diligent. More careful. I should've safeguarded my heart better. At what moment did it happen? Last night, when he didn't come to my room, I had an ample amount of time to think this over. Perhaps it was our first kiss in the ballroom? Or maybe when we played the write hand at the theater? The picnic with the bachelors?

My gut tells me it's none of those choices. It goes back further than that. Much further. I think I'd find my answer if I searched hard enough, but a part of me is afraid to find out.

How it happened is unimportant right now. How to carry on with my life is because if I continue this amicable façade, I'll surely explode.

When we arrive in Savannah, I nearly kiss the platform. I've never been happier to see a train station in my entire life. Livingston escorts Momma and me off the train while a man retrieves our luggage. As we weave in and out of the crowd, avoiding passengers on the way to the platform, my body presses against Livingston's side. Awareness trickles through me.

Don't look at him. Do not look at him.

By the time we step outside, I nearly push myself away from Livingston, open my handbag, and furiously begin to fan myself. We stand there for several minutes before Livingston gestures to the empty benches in front of the train station entrance. I sit on the very end, hoping Momma will sit beside me, but she doesn't. Livingston's large male body takes the space in the middle. His long legs don't have enough room, so he stretches them out in front of him.

While we wait for the driver Nat sent to pick us up and drive us back Brignac House, I sneak glances at Livingston. In this heat, beads of sweat have quickly gathered around his hairline. After sex, when he was spent and exhausted. He laid on top of me, and I licked a droplet of sweat running across his shoulder. It tasted like salt.

I shift and cross my legs again. When I do, my calf brushes against Livingston's leg. In a flash, he turns toward me, and I suck in a sharp breath. His eyes are bright but strained. The muscle along his jaw jumps.

"Oh, I think that's our driver!" Momma says, breaking through our tension-filled bubble.

He stands, and I nearly sag forward with relief. My intentions to travel with Livingston were pure. I needed to be with my best friend during this time. She was always there for me. But I didn't take my current situation with Livingston into account.

Livingston begins to help the driver with our luggage while Momma and I fan ourselves.

"You were quiet on the train."

"I was thinkin'."

"About?"

"Well, Momma, I was thinkin' on how to be a proper Southern lady." I close my fan together long enough to tap the ends against Momma's arm. "I want to make you proud."

Momma sniffs and continues to fan herself. "I think the heat has gone straight to your head. You need a glass of sweet tea immediately."

"Sorry to interrupt you ladies, but the car is ready," Livingston says.

"Wonderful." Momma stands and places her fan into her handbag. Before she takes Livingston's proffered arm, she looks at me. "Oh, and dear? I was young once. I see right through the both of you."

The speed of my fan slows, but my heart speeds up. Momma's words make me feel uncovered; I thought I was convincing in my performance. Were my feelings so apparent?

Quickly, I gather all my belongings while Livingston lavishes Momma with charm and helps her into the car. Once she's inside, he turns to me, sweeping his hand toward the door.

I give him a stiff smile and wait for him to step aside and let me in, but he doesn't. We stand there in the blazing sun. I rock back on my heels, feeling Livingston's eyes on me. Luckily, my fan's still in my right hand. To keep myself busy, I nervously fan myself. Livingston's hazel eyes burn so bright, the gold around the pupils nearly gleams. He clears his throat, drawing my attention from his beautiful eyes to his beautiful lips. "Rainey, you wouldn't be evadin' me, would you?" he asks, his tone quiet

"Nonsense. Why would you think that?"

"You would not meet my gaze on the train."

"Didn't think there was a quota I had to fill," I reply.

He doesn't flinch or bat an eye. His control is remarkable. "And you hardly said two words, which is a rarity for you. You're either agitated with me about somethin', or you're uncomfortable after our...night together."

"My God. No, no, no. I'm not uncomfortable," I quickly say. But Livingston couldn't be closer to the truth. I was uncomfortable by what Livingston brought out of me when we were alone at night. It wasn't normal to crave someone this much. I'm certain if I confided in another woman, they would stare at me as though I'd just grown horns and a tail.

"No, certainly not," I firmly assert.

"Indeed, it is."

"Can we have this conversation later?"

"I don't know, can we? My intent was to speak on the train, but instead, I had the lovely honor of speakin' to your momma."

I can't help but smirk at that. "For that, I am sorry."

"Did you know her dear friend Lucy from the First Baptist Church, not to be confused with the Lucy who goes to St. Patricks, is havin' their friends over for tea on the same day your momma hosts their monthly book club meetin'?"

"My, my what impertinence."

"Oh, that's not all."

"All right, all right." Laughing, I hold a hand up. "I acknowledge your sufferin'."

He broadly smiles. The dimple in his left cheek pronounced. There's a tightness in my chest that squeezes my heart so tightly I can barely breathe.

I love you. I love you so much. Tell me how to fix you.

Livingston's smile vanishes as though he can read my mind. For a minuscule second, there's a flash of yearning in his gaze. I'm almost tempted to say my feelings out loud just to take that expression off his face. But then he blinks, and his signature blasé grin is back in place. His eyes are completely blank. "Right. Well, we should be leavin'."

Inside the car, I grab my fan, unable to ignore the stifling heat. The only breeze drifting into the car comes in through the open door. It doesn't help matters when Livingston slides in beside me. He could sit beside the driver. There's plenty of room beside him, but no. Apparently, the back seat is far more appealing.

The length of Livingston's leg presses against mine, and even through the fabric of my traveling suit, I can feel the searing heat of his skin. Flashes of him looming over me in my bed, his arms bracketed around me, and his hips thrusting between my legs run through my mind.

I cannot continue to have these thoughts while we're here. This is about Nat. Abruptly, I move toward Momma. Her left shoulder becomes pressed against me at an uncomfortable angle. I find myself selfishly uncaring, because for a minute there's a few inches between Livingston and me, and I can breathe. Maybe not fully, but enough to gather my composure.

Momma turns to me, and with sweat gathering on her upper lip, she looks at me as though I've lost my ever-loving mind. "My God, Rainey. This travelin' suit is not light. You layin' on me like that will cause me to faint!"

I wince while Livingston smirks.

"I apologize." I move an inch, but that places me in Livingston's personal space, plastered against him.

I close my eyes and take a deep breath.

It is a few days. A few simple days.

I have been through worse.

CHAPTER TWENTY-SEVEN

RAINEY

When we turn into driveway of Brignac House, we spot the slew of servants outside the plantation. Starting from the door and leading down the porch steps, the servants stand, all fifteen of their faces somber, their hands linked in front of them. Standing by the door is Oliver's momma and Nat. Nat looks forward. Her face impassive and eyes unsmiling. The severity of her features feels like a jolt. I've never seen her so solemn.

"Oh, my," Momma remarks.

I simply nod.

"Is there a reason they have a brigade of servants?" Livingston asks rhetorically.

I shake my head in disbelief. "Has Nat ever mentioned that before?"

Livingston thinks over my question, his eyes sharp on his sister's small frame. The closer we get, the more defined she becomes. "Perhaps in passin'. I simply didn't think much of it. In person, it's quite excessive."

"That's an understatement."

As we get closer to Brignac House, the servants almost create a human arrow toward Nat and the woman standing beside her. Both of them are wearing black gowns, but the woman who I recognize as Oliver's momma, I can't place her name. I want to say it starts with an M? Mary, perhaps?

Momma and I exchange glances and then look at our

own attire. This might be the only time in my life I've ever felt underdressed. Momma brushes invisible lint from her skirt and juts her chin in the air. "I'm quite fond of my travelin' suit."

Livingston leans forward and rests his elbows on his knees. He grins at Momma. "As you should. Purple looks lovely on you, Mrs. Pleasonton."

Momma stops waving her fan long enough to tap the edge of the fan against his arm. "You're too kind to me, Livingston. Too kind."

While they strike up a conversation about the arrangements of the train, I can't help but notice Livingston is leaning closer and closer to me. His elbows remain on his knees, and now my forearm is pressed flush against his rib cage, and my elbow is conveniently placed directly by his hip.

My heart is threatening to burst out of my chest, and my breathing becomes erratic. On my lap, I link my fingers together and try my hardest to ignore Livingston. Which has never gotten me far in life.

"I say, sweetheart. You're lookin' very red. Do you need my fan?"

"No, thank you. I have my own," I croak. I begin to toy with the latch on my handbag as though this is the first time I've used my hands. I bend forward, the purse finally opening, and my elbow brushes against his lower stomach, far too close to the buttons of his slacks. Livingston tenses up. I begin to wildly fan myself as though the gates of Hell are steps away. Judging from my wicked thoughts, that isn't too far of a reach.

Livingston looks at me from the corner of his eye and arches a single brow. I take the opportunity to smoothly elbow him in the side. He grunts, and the corner of his mouth tilts upward.

Thankfully, the car stops in front of Brignac House, ending my torture. Before the driver has a chance to open the door, one of the servants does.

Nat and her mother-in-law walk down the steps of the impressive mansion. Livingston whistles as we take in the stately plantation. The twenty-one columns that wrap around the home have flecks of paint missing. As do the black shutters that flank the front windows. But those small flaws add charm to what would be immaculate property.

"I thought you've been here before," I remark.

"Neither Étienne nor I have visited Brignac House." The edge to Livingston's reply causes me to stop gathering my belongings and look at him. Livingston's always been incredibly close to Nathalie. What would prevent him from visiting her? Was it Oliver, or something else?

Livingston steps out of the car and turns to help me, I take his hand and ensure my skirt stays in place. Once I'm standing, my lungs greedily expand, inhaling the fresh air.

Nat and her mother-in-law are mere steps away, and I've yet to think of her name. I think my bafflement is written across my face because Livingston leans toward me.

"Her name's Matilda," he whispers in my ear.

I nod and suppress a shiver at the close contact. As Livingston proceeds forward to greet his sister, I stay back and wait for Momma. She's not too far behind me. When she's within earshot, she says, "After that insufferable drive, I do believe this travel suit is utterly ruined. I must say it's lookin' rather beneficial the amount of servants at Brignac House. They'll need a small militia to wring out the sweat in my suit."

My lips fight to stay in a straight line. Leonore Pleasonton can have a rare, unexpected sense of humor when she chooses. Livingston heads toward us with Nat, and Matilda next to him. I take the moment to quickly remind Momma the name of Nat's mother-in-law.

Momma is the epitome of a Southern lady as she greets Matilda. Her words flow with grace, and her eyes are filled with genuine sympathy. Nat hasn't spoken much of Matilda, but it's clear to see the raw pain in her eyes. She readily accepts Momma's condolences.

Nat continues to remain emotionless. She stands between Livingston and Matilda. She's not sobbing into a handkerchief, nor is she smiling and embracing me.

Only tragedy brings such a range of emotion out of people.

Not one person's reaction will be the same.

Stepping forward, I hug my best friend. There's no energetic embrace that's generally expected with a Nathalie hug. It's as though the very life has been depleted from her.

"Nat, I am terribly sorry."

She nods and squeezes my hands. "Thank you for comin'."

"If there's anythin' you need while I'm here, anythin', you just let me know, and I'll get it for you."

Once again, she nods. I get the impression Nat isn't fully registering most of the interactions occurring around her. My heart sinks even further because I know it will be that way for quite some time.

"Nathalie, will you show our guest their living quarters?" Matilda says.

"Of course."

While the servants walk to the car for our luggage, we follow Nat inside the spacious Brignac House.

Upon stepping inside, it's a struggle to keep my face impassive. The fetid smell clashes with the extravagant plantation. It's the scent of body odor mixed with sweat. It could be solved with airing the house out. As I peek into the sitting room and see the windows nearly boarded up, I realize that's not an option.

My gaze meets Livingston's. He looks like he's holding his breath and treating each inhale as though it's his last.

If Nat notices the smell, she doesn't show it. She continues to walk up the stairs while the three of us follow her.

"My...this home has remarkable character," Momma comments diplomatically.

Character is certainly another word for stench. But all I can wonder is how does Nat manage to live here day in and day out?

"It does," Nat replies. "I'm certain Matilda will tell you even durin' her time of mournin'." Her tone is derisive yet manages to be vacant.

I give a furtive glance at Momma and quickly speak up. "It's much like Belgrave."

At the top of the stairs, Nat whirls around. For the first time since we've arrived, her eyes become alive. Unfortunately, it's with anger. "Brignac House is nothin' like Belgrave."

The three of us stop and gape at her. Even Livingston, her own brother, looks taken aback. And then she dips her head, her eyes veering toward the ground, and sweeps her hand to the left. When she looks back at us, a tense smile is back. "Mrs. Pleasonton, I have placed you in the west wing of the home. If you follow me, I believe you'll find your room quite acceptable."

"Of course, dear."

Nat begins to walk down the hall without waiting for the three of us. Once again, we all look at one another before Momma hurriedly follows after Nat.

"What happened?" I whisper.

Livingston slowly shakes his head. He's as bewildered as I am. We both know this display from Nat isn't solely from the loss of Oliver. The traits she's always possessed have slowly been chipped away, patiently and methodically.

Nat shows Momma to her room, a lovely space that has plenty of bright light. Momma hums her approval.

Silently, we walk toward the other end of the second floor. Nat opens the first door to the right. "Rainey, you'll be in here." The guest room is lovely with a large bed to the right and a gold chenille coverlet spread across the mattress. The room has all the prerequisites for visitors: a single armoire, a desk with a stack of pristine white paper and a pen, an upholstered armchair is angled in one corner of the room and fresh flowers are placed on the end table.

Perhaps what's notable is the curtains are open along with both windows, allowing fresh air to permeate the space.

"Praise God," Livingston murmurs into my ear.

I suppress a grin and pretend I didn't hear him.

Nat gestures to the door opposite of mine. "Livingston, you're across the hall from Rainey."

I'm sure for Nat it was a matter of simplicity. Place the guests all in one wing. For me, it's close to torture. Like placing

CALIA READ

forbidden fruit in front of me and expecting me not to try to take a bite.

Livingston clears his throat. "Thank you. Sounds nice."

"I need to go downstairs and see how I can help Matilda elsewhere." With her shoulders rigidly set, Nat walks out of the room without sparing a good-bye or giving her signature bright smile. I knew she would be in mourning, but I didn't know she'd be this bereaved.

I take a step forward to go after her. "Should we —"

Livingston shakes his head. "No. Right now, it's best to leave her. I know my sister." He says he knows her, but there's a furrow between his brows that says differently. Livingston's never seen her quite like this before either.

"Well," Momma sighs as she looks around my room. "I need to lie down before dinner." Before she leaves, she gives Livingston and me a pointed look. "Make sure you keep your windows open," she half-whispers, as though the entire staff and Matilda are listening in the hall.

I make sure to keep my face straight when I nod. "We will."

Momma starts to walk toward the door but stops when she realizes Livingston's not behind her. She looks over her shoulder at him and arches a single brow, the implication clear in her eyes, *Why are you so comfortable being alone with my daughter?*

Livingston smoothly steps in behind her. "I should go to my room. Make sure the windows are open, too."

Momma nods her head approvingly, then walks out of the room with Livingston in tow. Doors click shut as people go to their proper rooms. Sighing, I give the bed a stare filled with longing.

I get the sense I'm being watched when I hear, "Psst."

Whirling, I see Livingston standing in my doorway. My stomach dips, and my pulse thrums. I shouldn't be this excited to see him. He hasn't been out of my sight for no more than a minute. Nonetheless, I rush over to him, unable to wipe the smile from my face.

"You're supposed to be in your room."

Livingston tucks his hands into his pockets and angles his body closer. "I know. Your Momma made that very clear. I stayed back because I wanted to bring a conclusion to our conversation at the train station."

Crossing my arms, I lean against the door. "I thought that conversation was finished?"

"No. It was interrupted."

His hooded gaze looks me up and down as he gives me a lazy smirk. My fingers itch to pull him closer. But one glance from the corner of my eye reminds me this isn't my room, and anybody could walk by and see us in this open doorway standing awfully close.

I straighten, trying to gather my composure. "We can't... here."

Livingston nods. "Of course not."

"*Le savauge*?"

My head snaps up, ready to tell him once again not to call me that, when he leans forward. His large hands frame my face as he dips his head for a quick kiss. Momentarily, I'm taken off guard but it doesn't take me long to respond. My hands curl around the lapels of his jacket, savoring his lips on mine and having him close.

It lasts no more than a few seconds, but it's all I need to cling to him like a second skin. Livingston blinks rapidly, his black lashes touching his cheek. He gives me a smirk and brushes his finger across my lower lip. There's a small tremor to his touch. He might appear untouched by the interaction, but he isn't.

"I wanted to do that all damn day."

CHAPTER TWENTY-EIGHT

RAINEY

On the day of Oliver Claiborne's funeral, there's clear skies. Sunlight streamed through my window, and I even saw a bird chirping in the trees. The second I left my room, I felt as though I was descending into a cave. Matilda kept all the curtains closed. Everyone in the house felt the absence of sunlight and spoke in hushed whispers in the hallways. The weight of today makes the air on the first floor thick and grimy.

The parlor room was emptied of its large pieces of furniture to make room for rows of chairs. It didn't have the appearance of a funeral. More like a church service or wedding.

Nat didn't utter a word while Matilda made demands from behind a black veil that looked far more theatrical than mournful. Every so often, she would look toward the windows, narrowing her eyes at the light that managed to peek through the curtain panels. Not even the weather was cooperating for her today. When her husband said the casket had to be ushered through the parlor doors, she was appalled because, "the living entered there."

She didn't understand why their home didn't have a death door, and then immediately began to sniffle. Matilda's pain has been palpable since the moment we arrived. She doesn't attempt to hide her grief. Initially, my first instinct was to respect that trait. Many women I know are raised to bury their emotions deep inside them and put a veneer on their lives. After less than a day with Matilda, and watching how briskly her moods would change, I think her veneer was lost and the more people to watch her, all the better. She clutches a handkerchief to her mouth and begins to walk out of the room. She stops beside Nat and stares at her with her bottom lip quivering, and barely suppressed anger gleaming in her eyes. "This family is cursed with pain."

Moments later, she left, her weeping echoing in the hallway. Nat stood with her back against the wall, unmoved by her mother-in-law's emotions or words.

"Lord have mercy," Momma said quietly before she stood and followed Matilda.

Matilda's husband easily managed the responsibilities and apologized on her behalf. There was no way else for Oliver's casket to be placed in the room but through the parlor doors, and so in the end, that's what happened. The pallbearers slowly ushered the casket through the main doorway. Nathalie didn't bat an eye. My heart broke for her because I knew my caring, genial friend would never be the same after this. There's no comforting words I can soothe her with and no gifts to alleviate her pain. We've both been through this before. When her parents and brother passed away, Nat folded in on herself. Not quite in the way she's reacting now, but close.

Over time, the room begins to fill with mourners. Nat remains as solid as a rock, accepting condolences and hugs as though there's nothing she would like more.

During the funeral, I sit on one side of her and Livingston on the other. As the priest quotes scripture and talks of Oliver's life, I look at Nat from the corner of my eye. Her hands remain linked on her lap, but repeatedly she picks a cuticle with one of her nails over and over until she draws blood near the nail bed.

I turn my attention back to the priest for the rest of the funeral. When he finishes, there's a natural procession of people giving their final good-byes. Many of them stop by Nat and give her one last "sorry for your loss." Ladies I've never seen reach out and briefly grip her hand. I knew my best friend would create a new existence in Savannah, but to see it directly in front of me is a bit unsettling.

After the mourners leave, there's only the five of us. The priest, Nat, Oliver's father, Livingston, and me. The priest stands to the side, allowing the family to say their good-byes.

When Oliver's dad, Robert walks toward the casket, I look at Nat. "I think I should leave," I urgently whisper.

As she continues to stare forward, she reaches out and clutches my hand. "Stay."

"Nat, this doesn't seem approp —"

"Stay," she stresses.

I stay, but I keep my head down, feeling ill at ease the entire time. When Robert walks back to his seat, I anticipate Nat getting up. Does she want me to go up there? I haven't said good-bye to Oliver. We weren't close to begin with. However, if my friend needed me to be there for her I would.

Nat remains seated. She's emotionless with her eyes staring straight ahead.

"Matilda's right," she says after several minutes of silence and loudly enough for everyone in the room to hear. "This family is cursed."

"She didn't mean that," Livingston replies in a hushed whisper. "She's unsettled by the tragic loss of her son."

Nat shakes her head. "No, she's always in that state."

At that, Livingston and I lean forward and make eye contact. How did Nathalie manage to live with Matilda without going mad herself?

Perhaps, she already was.

Right then, the topic of our conversation walks back into the room. I thought Matilda would return while the mourners still lingered in the room. I envisioned wails that bordered on histrionics. But Oliver's momma is composed for the time being, tightly clutching a handkerchief to her chest as she walks up to his casket.

Nobody watches her more closely than Nat as she stands there with a hand on the glossy wood. And then she leans down and drapes herself over his body.

Nat turns her head and stands. Livingston and I stand with

her. "Let's go. We need to give Oliver's great love time to say good-bye."

For the second time, Livingston and I look at one another. What funeral did we walk into?

In the South, there are many traditions. Some preposterous and others we learn at a very young age. When it comes to funerals, we gather around the family that has lost a loved one. They won't lack for food for a month, houses are spotless whether there's a team of servants at their disposal or not, and children will be cared for.

Why do they do this? Because death will happen to us all, and you can only hope this care and attention will be extended back to you.

After the funeral, the Claiborne family opened their home to everyone who paid their respects. This is the part I never quite understood about funerals or memorials. I understand it was a celebration of the deceased's life, but the flow of conversation and laughter that occasionally rose into the air felt wrong to me. I know life moves forward, but it always felt too soon.

Nat's cold display of emotion in the parlor vanished as she circulated throughout the room. And was it my imagination or were people here not to console the grieving family, but to watch the grieving family?

"That was..."

"Different?"

Livingston nods approvingly. "That's the perfect word."

Matilda joined everyone after they were finished eating and talking to one another. I think the whole time she was with Oliver. She continued to keep the veil over her face. From my vantage point, I saw how people tentatively approached her. It's the same way kids in Charleston would approach Toy Altwood's front door, an elderly woman who was known to use her cane to push people out of her way when she was impatient and holler when anyone was in her garden.

The people of Savannah were scared of Matilda Claiborne. I tilt my head to the side and continue to inspect her. But why? From one night here, it's discernible that she's troubled. The reason isn't clear, though.

"I wouldn't be surprised if Matilda has him embalmed and put in a glass case in the dining room so she can see him every day," Livingston says in a hushed whisper.

I shudder at the image he paints. "What do you suppose Nat meant by callin' Matilda his great love?"

It's Livingston's turn to shudder. "I don't want to begin to imagine."

"This place is peculiar," I quietly remark as I look around the room.

That's not true. The Claiborne's are peculiar. And they've reconstructed this former plantation to fit their idiosyncratic life.

"Oh, don't restrain yourself, *le savauge*, we both know peculiar is bein' kind."

I turn toward him with a smile when I see Nat walking toward us with her mother-in-law, my momma in tow, and a blond woman I've never seen before. Nat has a miserable look on her face. It's the expression someone would wear if they've resigned themselves to a life of servitude.

"Rainey, Livingston, I'd like for you to meet our neighbor Rea Breymas. Rea, this is my close friend, Rainey Pleasonton."

On principle, I don't like Rea, and I know it's wrong to judge someone based on their looks, but she is simply gorgeous. I can almost smell the self-involvement wafting from her light blond hair. Her hazel eyes are fringed with the thickest lashes. Even I find myself becoming envious. She can bat those doe eyes at every man in the room, and they'll all fall to their knees.

My stomach fills with knots as Nat introduces Rea to Livingston. Here it comes. Here comes his famous charm. Here comes his devastating smile, accompanied by his dimple.

However, none of that occurs. Livingston is polite, courteous as he reaches out and shakes her hand. He scarcely looks twice at her.

Even his own sister glances at him curiously. Who is this man standing beside us?

Did he not get enough sleep last night? I could hear him pacing his room like a caged animal until the early hours. I knew it was best we stayed in our respective rooms. We're here for Nat. We're not lovers or a couple. We have no definition. There's nothing intertwining us. Except for Miles's will.

The very thought of the dowry brings about a wave of restlessness. I may be away from Charleston, but my problems will follow me wherever I go. The bachelor ball will be here far too soon, and I'll have to make a choice I'm still undecided about. I shouldn't be bothered by how many women bat their lashes at Livingston, or who he speaks to; I have more pressing matters to worry about. But I can't seem to help myself. After my recent discovery about the depth of my feelings for him, I feel more than protective for Livingston. I'd claw out the eyes of every woman in this room if I thought they had the one thing I want more than anything: his love.

Tell him the truth. Tell him before it's too late.

"It was lovely to meet you both, but I must be after my brother," Rea says, breaking apart my thoughts. "He's here somewhere."

Once she leaves, Matilda turns back to us. Her smile has disappeared as she leans toward Momma and me. "She has some nerve to show her face," Matilda huffs.

Momma and I exchange glances. I was taught to sense deep Southern gossip a mile away, and there's a reason everyone in the room gives this stunning creature a wide berth. What is the problem? Was she Oliver's former scorned lover? Did a breeze pick up and cause her calves to show?

I don't know, but I want to.

As badly as I want to unravel the story behind Matilda's anger at Rea, I know I can't. Momma and Matilda drift into the crowd with promises of returning. Nat and Livingston are standing beside the closed windows, quietly talking to each other. It's been quite some time since they've seen one another, so I don't want to interrupt.

"You're curious, aren't you?"

I turn at the sound of the male voice behind me.

One word comes to mind: *wow, wow, wow.*

I'm curious about many things, but my curiosity disappears the minute this man steps beside me.

His light brown hair is cut close on the sides and longer on top. I'm not a fan of mustaches. They can have a Machiavellian look to them. But this man appears very distinguished with one.

I realize I've been staring for several minutes and rapidly blink. "Curious?"

"About Rea." He gestures to the beautiful blonde. Thankfully, she's nowhere near Livingston. "Rea was once the perfect Southern belle of Savannah until several years ago."

He knows her in some capacity. In what way doesn't matter because I have so many questions, and maybe this man can answer them.

"Did she do somethin' to hurt Matilda or her family?"

He thinks over that question for an awfully long time. "Not that I've been made privy too. But Matilda Claiborne is an… uncommon individual."

"My word," I manage. He didn't have to tell me Matilda was uncommon. One night spent at Brignac House, and I more than understood. The handsome man nods and looks straight ahead.

"Are you goin' to tell me how you know this?"

He smiles at me, and I swear on the good Lord above the angels in heaven sing. "I thought you would never ask. I'm Rea's younger brother." He holds his hand out to me. "Loras." His smile widens. "And your name?"

I shake his hand. "Rainey Pleasonton."

"You're not familiar with my sister so you can't possibly be from Savannah," he says.

I smile faintly, unsure on how to reply. Most Southern ladies would politely move the conversation onto another topic, but I'm curious. "I suppose that means she has a reputation that precedes her."

"Possibly."

"If I was to ask people what her reputation is, would they all say the same thing?"

Loras stares out into the crowd, contemplating my question. "Depends on who you ask."

I nod, thoughtfully and then lift a shoulder before I lean in. "Then it appears I'm still in the heart of the South."

At that, Loras tilts his head back and laughs loud enough to earn the gaze of several people standing around us, including Livingston. He's standing beside Nat across the room. When he sees I'm not far from the source of the laughter, his light eyes narrow into thin slits. At once, he excuses himself and walks across the room.

From afar, when you see Livingston, you notice a strikingly handsome man with not a hair out of place and impeccably dressed. But he begs for a closer look. When you're given that inspection, those arresting green eyes tell a far different story. They're bold and impish as though he knows all your darkest secrets. And he wants to inform the world but doesn't because the wicked side of him likes knowing how you really are.

How Livingston gazes at me right now is intimate. The way a lover would, and he makes no effort to hide it in front of Loras.

This is a day of mourning and remembrance for Oliver, and here Livingston is, nearly undressing me with the heat in his eyes. I momentarily turn away and try to gather a deep breath, but that's essentially impossible with Livingston standing so close.

"Hello. I don't believe we've been introduced." Livingston addresses his words to Loras, yet I can't help but notice how he shifts his body so he's nearly standing in front of me.

Loras regards Livingston, his gaze cool and distant. "Don't believe we have."

"Livingston, this is Loras Breymas, Rea's younger brother."

Livingston, however, is undaunted by Loras and solemnly dips his head in Loras's direction. "Livingston Lacroix."

"Lacroix." Loras wags his finger at Livingston. "You must

be part of Mrs. Claiborne's family."

"Yes, I am. And I'm also one of Miss Pleasonton's close friends."

Loras arches a single brow. I shake my head at Livingston. He isn't a possessive person, but he's certainly acting that way.

Loras turns his attention to me and smiles. "I hope we meet again."

I dip my head, my lips curling up at the sides. "Me too, Mr. Breymas."

I watch him go, and the entire time, I can feel Livingston's eyes burning a hole into my profile.

"May I speak with you?" Livingston whispers into my ear.

Before I have the chance to reply, his hand curls around my elbow. He steers us out of the room, somberly dipping his head at strangers who have come to pay their respects. Once we're in the foyer, I expect him to say his truth and go on his way, but he continues walking until we're at the back of the house, nestled in a small corner where no one can see us. My back becomes pressed against the wall as Livingston stands incredibly close to me.

"What has gotten into you?" Livingston demands, his eyes serious.

I cross my arms. "What are you talkin' about?"

Livingston gestures toward the hallway. "Do you make it a pastime of yours to bat your eyes at every man durin' a funeral?"

"No. Loras happened to be one man, not every man, and I did not bat my eyes at him. He spoke to me."

"Don't tease me, Rainey." Now that I'm standing this close to him, I can see the prominent dark circles beneath his eyes.

Provoking aside, I furrow my brows. "What's the matter?"

"I didn't sleep well last night."

"I didn't sleep well either!" Excitedly, I lean in, and whisper-shout. "It's this house, right? I swear I heard footsteps outside my room! I'm startin' to believe it's haunted."

"Every plantation in the South is rumored to be haunted, but no, that's not why." His hands settle on his hips, pulling his jacket away from his body and revealing the gray vest that fits his lean body perfectly. He stares at me for a moment longer, before he lowers his voice. A lock of dark hair falls across his forehead. "Can I see you tonight?"

Our nightly visits has become a dangerous routine as we both become increasingly comfortable with this ritual.

Livingston stares at me intently, waiting for my reply. When he wants to, his presence can be far more foreboding than one expects.

My eyes drift toward the hallway, thinking over my reply when Livingston's hand gently curls around my wrist. When my eyes meet his, he has the look of desperation almost as though he's afraid I'm going to leave. He wears this expression far too often. Where can I possibly go? Where have I ever gone? I've never known a world without Livingston Lacroix. I blink, and the look is wiped clean from his face.

Briefly, I nod. "Yes."

It's hard for me to decide if there's relief in Livingston's eyes or casual indifference. He nods once and lets go of my hand only to wrap his arms around me. My hands slide around his shoulders as though we've done this for years. I nearly sigh at how complete this one touch makes me feel.

I think we both know that our covert time spent at night can't continue, and to prolong our rendezvous won't help either of us. What else am I to do?

I love him.

CHAPTER TWENTY-NINE

RAINEY

After every mourner has left, I wait. After the sun begins its descent into the sky, I wait and continue to wait even when every light has been turned off in the house. The silence in Brignac House tonight borders on eerie. Dinner was a light array of foods graciously given by neighbors or mourners. Nat and Matilda were noticeably absent during dinner. It left Momma, Livingston, and me to sit in the dimly lit dining room. Livingston and I stole glances across the table like two love-stricken adolescents. To an extent, it wasn't an incorrect portrayal of me. One moment, I was at war with Livingston, and the next, I was here, loving him and under the spell he cast over me. Could he love me back? There have been times I've caught him staring at me, his eyes unreadable, and I think maybe the possibility isn't so far out of reach.

Think you could love me?

Those hushed spoken words flit through my mind. It's been years, but I still think of them. Still think of what could have happened. It was absurd. He didn't remember, and neither should I. It's pathetic really, when you think about it, how this one memory can still control me.

Livingston's had more control of my life than he's aware of. Never more so than at night when we're together. The more he teaches me, the bolder I become. I think of what I'd do to him if I went a bit a further than just with my hands. I know the second I tell him I love him, everything will change. The balance will shift, those walls he's slowly dropped will go back up, and the opportunity to do as I wish will be taken away.

Impatiently, I walk to the door and rip it open. I look back and forth, but there's no one in the hall. Where is Livingston?

"Are you lookin' in the hall because you're expectin' more company?" a male voice asks behind me.

I nearly jump out of my skin and look over my shoulder. I find Livingston sitting in the dark corner of the room. He has one leg crossed over the other, and his face is hidden in the shadows, but I know it's him.

Closing my door, I turn to him, beyond baffled. "What…I mean, how long have you been here?"

"Not long."

"Not long," I repeat.

Nodding, Livingston sits forward, his elbows resting on his knees. "Long enough to watch you lock and unlock the door. *Le savauge*, were you tryin' to keep me out?"

Even with the shadows cast on his face, I can feel his eyes on me. I boldly stare back. Looking away means there's something to hide. This is my room, and I was getting ready for bed.

"No, I wasn't tryin' to keep you out. If I remember correctly, you asked to see me." I hold my hands out in front me, a gesture that says, "Here I am."

Livingston is undaunted by my words. I can feel his eyes sweeping down my body. He leans forward, and the light on one side of his face reveals his dimple and that devilish smirk that promises so much. "Here you are indeed," he murmurs.

Don't utter a word. You are fine. This is only Livingston. Mere minutes ago, you were boldly imagining all the things you wanted to do to him! Be bold!

"I trust your room is within your likin'?" he asks.

Like a nitwit, I simply nod. But I don't have to feel too bad, because Livingston nods back, and we stand there, resembling two ventriloquist puppets, with our every move being controlled by some unseen force that we can't explain.

When I don't say a word, Livingston begins to speak.

"I realize why I don't care for travelin'. Want to know why?" He doesn't wait for my reply. "Fine. I'll tell you. Limited supply of the liquor. And it doesn't matter how charmin' you are or how well you know the owners. Hell, I'm related to the owner, and she still won't relent and give me the key to the liquor cabinet."

I inch away from the door and wait for him to continue.

"Naturally, I offered to square accounts with Nat for any liquor used. She told me to shove off and informed me her mother-in-law had the key to the cabinet." He finally takes a deep breath long enough to shudder. "There's not enough charm in the world for that insufferable woman."

In spite of myself, I grin. "Sorry to disappoint you, but there is no liquor in my room," I say.

From where I stand, there's nowhere but the small stool in front of the vanity. As discreetly as possible, I sit down as though it's the most desired seat in the room. I tighten the belt on my robe three time before I look in Livingston's direction. He's still regarding me with eyes half-mast. Goose bumps break out across my skin, and my nipples poke through my nightgown.

He leans back in the chair. In the shadows, I watch him link his fingers behind his head. "What did you make of the staff?"

The question is abrupt but shouldn't be unexpected. Livingston and I can be speaking about one thing, and in the next breath, we've moved on to an entirely different matter. "That's no staff. That's an army."

Livingston crosses his legs at the ankle and tilts his head. "I wonder…would they go to battle with other staff?"

Perching my chin on my hand, I ponder his question. My imagination runs at full speed, and I let it. When an idea takes shape, I lean forward and smile mischievously. "Absolutely. All because a beloved gravy boat has been stolen."

"But of course," Livingston replies without missing a beat. "The Brignac servants have secretly been in conflict with another household for years. With the…with the Hiscock servants." He gives me a wink. I roll my eyes. He can't help himself with that last name. "They are consistently attemptin' to supersede one another in dinner parties."

"Dinner parties," I repeat.

Livingston holds a hand up. "You're cynical but have some faith and keep listenin'. All right?"

I nod.

"Dinner parties in Savannah are the same as they are in Charleston. For years and years, the Claiborne family has been known for their lavish parties, but the Hiscock family rose in the ranks, as if from nowhere and usurp them. Everybody begins to look forward to holdin' an invitation with the Hiscock family crest stamped on the back."

"How long does this rivalry continue?"

Livingston stands from his chair and sits on the Victorian bench at the foot of the bed. His elbows rests on his knees, and his hands dangle between his spread legs. His hazel eyes are intent and focused on the story at hand. "Years," he replies after a moment of thought. "Until the head butler of the Hiscock family decides to come forward and confesses that he saw another servant once use a gravy boat he believed to belong to the Claiborne family."

I gasp. "Do you think Claiborne knew about this gravy boat betrayal the whole time?"

"You think otherwise?"

With my eyes wide and shining, I lean forward, causing my hair to cascade around my shoulders and into my lap. "I don't know. The Hiscock family could have placed it there. It's families with old money you have to be careful around."

"You're directly implicatin' your family. Well…what could have been your family."

I shrug and give him a sly smile. "I'm sorry, but I believe in the right to expel gas."

As of late, our conversations have centered around the bachelors, looking through my family's ledgers, and now, consoling Nat as best as possible through her grief. This unexpected moment of humor and entertainment is well needed. Even something as trivial as a fictional who stole the gravy boat at the dinner party story.

However, now that our fictional adventure is over. The two of us look at one another and at how close we are to each other. I feel his gaze settle on my hair draped over my shoulder and then on my chest. In my excitement to hear the rest of his story, I abandoned modesty, and now my robe is gaping open, revealing what little cleavage I have. Doesn't appear to deter Livingston. His eyes are fire. His gaze is hungry. I clutch the edges of my robe to cover my chest, but it's too late.

I look at Livingston from beneath my lashes right as he perches himself on the edge of the bench. Our knees are inches apart. If he lunged forward, he could reach my lips with ease.

I've developed a taste for him, and now I want more. I want all of him, and that doesn't even feel like it'd be enough. Abruptly, I stand. He follows my lead.

Even though our bodies don't touch, I can feel the heat emanating from him. "Rainey, I can't leave," he whispers gruffly as though it pains him to make that admission.

My breathing slows, and I fight the urge to draw near to him.

His head slowly shakes from side to side. Those hazel eyes flicker between my lips and eyes as he slowly dips his head. "I can't."

I'm positive he didn't come to my room for this or to tell a peculiar tale. Livingston was merely doing what we've always done for as long as I can remember when we're hurting or have something to hide. He's leading his mind astray from the memories, but he will find a way back to the pain. The war continues to haunt him, and it probably always will.

He steps closer, and I let him. My palms land on the vanity behind me. I tilt my head back as he hovers above me. "I wasn't going to ask you to leave."

His gaze drifts from my eyes to my lips, over and over until I inadvertently lick my lips. Groaning, Livingston dips his head. My mouth meets his halfway. His hands remain at his sides. My hands remain on the vanity, but slowly, as he coaxes my mouth open with his tongue, my fingers curl around the material of his shirt, and I pull him closer.

I feel his lips curl into a grin as his knees knock against the stool. My feet slightly lift from the ground.

Livingston walks us to the bed. Only this time, he sits down first with me on top of him. I love this position and everything it brings. I love how Livingston gathers me in his arms, clutching at my clothes. He's fraught with desire and desperate to reach my skin. The frenzy from our kiss reaches our bodies until I'm feverishly moving against his cock.

Livingston pulls our bodies farther onto the bed. I protest at the absence of his lower body, but I gather some of my senses. He places me back on him while he lies in the middle of the bed, and I keep in mind what I want to do.

Do it. Be bold.

Excited at the possibilities, I lean down and kiss the side of his neck and smell the scent of him.

"I have one burnin' question to ask you," I say against his skin.

"Yes?"

"If I am the ward and you're my guardian, then why do you always speak with me?"

"Because I have to know what you're doin'."

"No, that's not what I was implyin', Livingston." I push back and look down. The material of my robe and nightgown became a twisted mess as we traveled up the bed. One shoulder is exposed. "You speak with me, and only me, when you need me."

With the truth laid bare, Livingston's shoulders straighten. And for the barest of seconds, his eyes fill with something close to fear. He grins at me and attempts to bring my face down to his. I evade at the last second. "Please, enlighten me. Name one time."

"You've needed me every year of your life." My voice is casual and light. I toy with the buttons of his vest and undo them as though they're my own clothing. Livingston lets me. "Of course, you never realized. Kings never do."

His brows furrow in deep concentration. I'm inching close to the truth, and we both know it.

His hands grip my bottom. My legs spread farther, and he presses me against his cock. Closing my eyes, I moan.

What would he do if I took control? I think of every time I've touched him, and his response.

With me, you do what you want.

With my mind made up, I press my palms against his chest. A questioning gaze meets mine as his hands fall to his side. That half-smirk appears as he waits for what I'll do next.

My heart races because I'm not entirely sure where to start or what I'm doing. But I love this position of power. I know very few women who can say they've had the opportunity to take charge of Livingston Lacroix. He never stays with one long enough.

That will not happen with me. "Take off your shirt," I demand.

Both brows lift, but Livingston obliges. And while I straddle him with my nightgown hiked to my thighs, I watch him take off his clothes. His fingers move fast down his shirt, and when I see all that bare olive skin, my blood tingles in anticipation. Livingston sits up—his face is momentarily close to mine—to slide his hands out of his sleeves. Muscles bunch and flex as he throws the shirt to the ground and lies back on the bed. I stop myself from touching him.

"Your turn," he says.

My eyes reluctantly look away from his body and meet his hot gaze. "Not yet."

I untie my robe. Livingston's eyes are hungry at the chance to see exposed skin that he doesn't notice my belt gliding out of the loops around my waist.

It's only when I'm holding the silk in my hands that he arches a brow at me. I return the gesture and lean down. "Trust me?"

If he was a smart man, he would say no because I don't even trust myself around him. With Livingston, I feel as though I can do anything, and that's a dangerous emotion.

One corner of his mouth lifts. "Who else would I trust?"

"Then hold your arms above your head." He obeys my request, giving a short laugh filled with confusion and uncertainty. He tries to lift his head and look at what I'm doing, but can't.

I'm in the process of tying his hands together and lift my eyes to his. "Trust me, right?"

His head slowly lowers to the pillow, and his eyes become half-mast. My stomach dips at the sight of those light eyes. "Continue."

I do just that. My heart pounds so hard and fast it feels as though my chest is rattling, but I manage to tie him with impressive knots. He won't be getting away anytime soon.

"Fool," I whisper against his lips. With my palms against his bare chest, I lift my upper body and stare down at him.

Livingston appears nonplussed. He's in bed with a woman. This is his natural habitat. Besides, he thinks he'll be able to slip free. "You truly believe you've tied me up?"

"You truly believe I didn't?" My eyes veer to the knots around his wrists. "Go ahead. Pull."

The tug is light, but when he realizes the knot isn't going to budge, Livingston pulls harder against the bonds, this time with both hands.

He tilts his head back, the veins in his neck straining against his skin as he tries to look at my handiwork. The whole time, he moves his wrists left and right. He can move them every way he pleases, but he isn't going anywhere. I smile down at him.

As though he can sense my satisfaction, his gaze zeroes in on me. "Untie me. Now."

"I'm afraid I cannot do that. Of course, a lady would. But as you've said before, I'm no lady."

His eyes gleam with the promise of revenge, but also desire. He wants to be furious, but he's also incredibly aroused.

My fingers move to the top button of my nightgown. Livingston watches the action with a hungry expression as it comes free.

"This is not the first time you've intruded into my room," I say.

"Not true," he replies, sounding winded. "This is a guest room."

"Still my private quarters," I point out and let another button free. "Even if it's for a short time. Nonetheless, you're quite the teacher, and I've learned a great deal from you."

Again and again, Livingston's eyes bounce between my face and my hands. Never lingering in one place for long.

"When the king of seduction is also your instructor on all things sensual, how do you repay him?"

Livingston's face is cautious, his chest rapidly rising and falling.

"You let him free?" he croaks, watching the third button slip free. My hands brush against my breasts that are beginning to feel heavy.

"You show him what you've learned."

Groaning, he closes his eyes and tilts his head back against the mattress. I smirk.

When the last button is free the material parts, exposing most of my breasts but still covering my nipples. A muscle along his jaw jumps as he watches me, and then his mouth parts. I feel emboldened by his reaction and him being tied. I can go as slow as I please.

Reaching up, I cup my breasts. My eyes stay fixed on Livingston's as I pluck my nipples. My back arches from my own actions.

"Raina," he groans.

Very few people call me by my Christian name. Even fewer say it in such a throaty whisper. My core becomes wet, and my skin burns. Keeping him tied up is just as much torture for me as it is for him. My nightgown gapes open as I lean down and kiss Livingston. His head lifts from the bed. He attempts to take control with nibbles and sucks and bites, but I evade each time. His arms jerk against the silk, veins taut against his damp skin. He tries time and time again until there's a fine sheen of sweat on his body.

With my hands on his biceps, I begin to kiss my way down his body. The tips of my breasts brush against his stomach, and when I reach the buttons of his pants, I move between his legs.

Breathing through his nose, he watches me. Leaning in, I begin to unbutton his pants. Every button of his that comes loose makes him shake.

I can see the outline of him through his pants, but when his cock springs free, it's still a surprise to see how hard and ready he is.

My hand moves up and down his cock several times before I lower my head. And with my eyes on his, I wrap my lips around the crown of him, keeping a small grip around the base.

Curse words slip from his mouth as I go deeper, using my tongue to explore the smooth, long length of him.

I lift my gaze to his and see that with every rapid breath he takes, his abs contract.

With every suck and pull I make, Livingston's hips impatiently buck, and when I try to take all of him in my mouth, he nearly roars.

The sound shoots a delicious heat through my body.

"Fuck," he bites out. I go deeper, and he chokes on my name and tries again. "Raina, I swear I'll come in your mouth."

I pull my lips away and see the way his body is shaking. He's past the point of losing all control, and I want him to.

I rub him against me before I slowly lower myself onto him. My eyes fall shut, but I hear the harsh groan from Livingston. He stretches and fills every part of me, and I can barely take a breath. But the longer he's in me, the more my body adjusts to him. The pain isn't near as bad as it was the first time. There's pressure but only from the size of him. No, it feels…good.

Placing my hands briefly on his stomach, I weakly open my eyes, and I see Livingston staring at me with his chest rapidly rising and falling.

With my legs remaining on the mattress, I raise my hips an inch. The action causes him to push farther inside me. As delicious heat spreads through my bloodstream, Livingston hisses in a sharp breath. That wasn't a hiss of pain, but pleasure.

Of that, I'm sure.

Leisurely, I lift my hips again. The friction the move created was nearly unbearable, but I couldn't stop. I don't think anything could stop me. Not even the ache in my legs or the sweat that's causing my nightgown to cling to my skin.

Breathlessly, I grab the material and pull it up and over my head.

Livingston groans. "Christ."

Feeling bold and confident, I resume riding him. Tingles spread throughout me as I slide up and down. The way he fills me is just right. Even our bodies align perfectly. I move faster, eagerly chasing for that perfect, blissful moment where I slide down, and he fills me.

My eyes open, and meet Livingston's gaze. A muscle along his jaw jumps as though I've struck him. I move down his length once more, and I see the twitch in his body, and his arms jerk.

"I don't need you," he grunts.

I stop moving and place my palms on his chest. My fingers splay across his warm skin and travel down the length of his arms. His body shakes beneath me. "Oh, Livingston. Of course you do." I bend lower to whisper in his ear. "You can't function without me."

With ease, I pull on the ties, and he's free. In a flash, he sits up. Our positions change, and his hands wrap around my waist. His kiss is assertive and demanding. Everything he couldn't do while tied up, he gives with his hands and lips.

I wrap my legs around his waist, and when he thrusts into me, so fast and deep, my hands grip his back.

There's no teasing strokes or pauses for kisses. Livingston has no semblance of control. He's like a wild animal that's been set free.

With his hands on my hips, he moves faster, his body relentless. Just when I think he's going to end all the prolonged anticipation I've built for the two of us, he pulls back.

"On your stomach."

Panting and on the verge of falling apart, I stare at him

with wide eyes. "What?"

"On your stomach," he repeats, this time more sharply.

I comply, unsure of what he's going to do. When my stomach touches the sheets, I lie still and wait, heart racing. Livingston takes my hands and guides them to my side. He doesn't tie me up like I did to him, but I won't move.

I feel the prod of his cock against my legs, but only for a moment before it's taken away and replaced by the brush of his finger. Gently, he pushes my legs apart while his finger slips inside me. I'm so sensitive right now that I know I won't last much longer.

I moan and try to move my hips, but Livingston places a hand on the small of my back and stops me.

I realize this is his form of retaliation. I tortured him, and now he needs to do the same. I'd expect nothing less. My body shakes with anticipation.

His finger slips away, taking away his expert touch. I nearly cry out in protest, but then his chest touches my back. His skin is so hot I'm positive I've been branded by him. He pushes my hair so it's off my neck and falling across one arm.

"Je vais te baiser si fort que tout le monde saura que tu es à moi," he growls before he bends down to kiss the back of my neck.

And without another word, he slides in me. From this angle, I feel him so deep, I moan so loudly I turn my face into the pillow. This feels almost too good.

He pushes in and out. Every time he drives forward and his body is brought back to me, I gasp. My lower body arches, trying to keep him in this position for as long as possible.

Deeply embedded in me, he extends his hands so our fingers are linked. "Raina, why do you torture me when you know I'll do the same?"

"Livingston, please," I pant.

"Say please again." He pulls out of me until only the crown of him is in me.

Desperate for release, I close my eyes. "Please."

His head touches my shoulder, and he whispers into my ear, "Since you asked nicely."

Every movement of his hips is different. There's no teasing. No torment. He's not stopping for anything. Not even if someone bursts into the room right this second. Besides, he can't stop. Everything has been building in my core driving me into a state of frenzy. If he doesn't end the torture, I will.

Squeezing my eyes shut, I grip his hands tighter and moan into the pillow. I don't wait for him. My body shudders as I cry out, chanting Livingston's name while I spasm around him.

He squeezes my hands so tightly I think they might break.

When the thrusts slow, he falls on top of me, touching my hair and kissing my skin. *"S'il vous plaît. Ne me quitte pas,"* he whispers against my hair.

Opening my eyes, I weakly squeeze his hands back, and my body convulses.

I love this broken man so much. I love him so much there's no possible way I can leave him.

CHAPTER THIRTY

LIVINGSTON

There's a certain protocol I've perfected after the act of sex.

Throughout the years not a single woman has walked away unsatisfied, and that's because I always make sure that no time is spent lingering in bed. Nothing good can come out of dawdling around.

No, it's best if everyone goes their separate ways because too much time can lead to long embraces that every woman seems to want after sex.

Apparently, every woman but Rainey. When she's finished, she's like a cat stretching after a long nap. Her arms above her head, her toes pointed at the footboard, and the sheets still drawn around her feet. Even though she's content, if I reached out and interrupted her, she just might hiss at me.

I smirk at the image she makes. Her hair is in a disarray and scattered about her. Her skin is flushed and damp. She's panting just as bad as me, but instead of thinking how I should let her rest, I'm thinking of how I can take her again.

Get up. It's time for you to leave.

Rainey chooses that precise moment to turn and smile at me.

Leave? How can I leave when she gave me a smile like that? So trusting, and sincere and almost innocent. I think I'd give anything to have her smile at me like that again.

"Do you make a habit of residin' with your conquest after

you've been intimate with them?" she finishes her question with a long yawn.

I can't help but smile. I hear the thread of jealousy in her voice when she said conquest. She wouldn't be envious if she didn't care. God help me for being pleased, but I can't help myself. Recently, I've been driving myself mad when she's with the bachelors.

I lie on my back, staring up at the ceiling, and lace my fingers behind my head. I'm undecided on whether I should be flattered or insulted that she was close to falling asleep after sex. Rainey sits up, holding the sheet in front of her body. Her dark hair trails down her back. It's so long the ends brush against the dimple above the crease of her butt.

Let the sheet slip, my mind thinks wickedly.

Tu est parfait.

I know what's beneath all the many layers of her clothes. I know it's what a man wants, and better yet, I know her reaction goes beyond every man's wildest imagination.

She will make one of the bachelors happy.

The thought should soothe me. So why are my hands balled into fists?

"Livingston?"

The sound of Rainey's voice guides me back to the present, and I look at her. "I'm sorry. I didn't hear you."

Did I accidentally speak my thoughts aloud? Rolling onto my side, I tug on the corner of the sheet. She bats my hand away, and I grin at her. "No, I don't stay with my conquest. And you're not a conquest."

Just as I suspect, my remark gets a reaction out of her. She turns in my direction so quickly the tips of her long hair brush against my arm. Her brows nearly reach her hairline. "Oh."

Hardly any room is between us, but she's too far away. I want my arms around her. Breasts to chest, and legs intertwined. "Come here," I drawl.

Wrapping my hand around her wrist, I pull her toward me. Rainey freely falls. Her body becomes half draped over mine, and her palms settle on my chest.

The two of us are silent for a moment. I could've fallen asleep within minutes if there weren't fingertips tracing languid circles across my chest.

"May I ask you a question?" Rainey quietly asks.

"You may."

Rainey shifts so she can look me in the eye. "Why didn't you attend Miles's memorial? I searched for you," she admits quietly.

I tilt my head in her direction. I can only stare at her. It was only a matter of time until this was asked, but hearing Miles's name still feels like a punch to the gut.

"Why are you silent?"

I take a deep breath. "Because I knew you would ask this question. Didn't think it'd be tonight."

Rainey pauses. "I've thought about it since his memorial," she confesses.

"I'm shocked you didn't say anythin' sooner. I appreciate your ability to be forthright. It's the one thing I can count on in this world."

"Well, I would have said somethin', but the discovery that my family is penniless was a big distraction."

"As it would be for most."

"Why weren't you there?" she persists.

Taking a deep breath, I look at the ceiling. It's far easier to look away from someone when you're telling the truth than in the eye.

"I didn't want to believe it." Rainey's so still, it's like I'm holding onto stone. "I drank the day away, tryin' to convince myself that if I didn't show, then he wasn't gone."

"I wish that was so. Then I wouldn't have attended," Rainey remarks. "None of us would have."

My hold on her tightens before I continue. "Do you know Miles fought the Battle of St. Quentin Canal in France? He was on the Hindenburg Line while I engaged in the Second Battle of the Somme. We were both in France but towns apart from each other. Out of all his family and friends, I was the closest to him."

I swallow and continue talking because if I stop I know for certain I won't say another word. "When I was comin' home, I asked about him. So many soldiers were missing in action on both sides. There was another man in the 30th infantry division with the last name Pleasant. For a moment, they mistook Miles for him and said he was accounted for. I felt relief. He was all right. But that was momentary when they realized their blunder. I knew somethin' was wrong. I just knew it, and when I arrived home and saw you at the train station, I wanted to tell you, but I couldn't. You looked so beautiful and hopeful. I just couldn't."

I take a deep breath.

Continue!

Rainey is the only person who will understand.

She didn't see what I saw or experienced, but my gut tells me there's no better person to be forthright with.

"Every now and then, I wonder if I had got to him if I could have helped him. Even if I was too late, I wouldn't have let him stay out there." An anguished breath escapes me. "I wouldn't."

"I know that," Rainey urgently whispers. "Everybody knows that."

"Sometimes, I tell myself he died of natural causes. Perhaps he had a stroke, or a virus got the best of him. I envision him walking through the forest, sitting down with his back against a tree. He falls asleep and just never wakes up. It's just him, the trees, and the animals," I confess, ignoring the crack in my voice.

"That's a good story."

"The illusion doesn't last long. But it's always soothin' while it lasts."

"I agree. Keep that fantasy for as long as you can."

Rainey pauses. "How terrible was it?"

This is dangerous ground. Dangerous ground!

I don't speak about this with anyone. It's far too sobering. There's no glib quip I can say to transition into a different topic.

Briefly I close my eyes, we both know what "it" refers to. I try to answer her question without thinking about the dark memories, but it's nearly impossible. "What I saw over there...I can never forget it. You can't prepare yourself for what you'll do. You think you know, but it pales in comparison to the truth. When I left, I thought my decision was noble, and now that's it over, I question whether all the nightmares and recollections were worth it."

"It was noble," Rainey says fiercely.

"Perhaps at first. In war, there are battle lines, but in the end, all men bleed the same."

Rainey is silent as she soaks in my words. "That may be true," she starts out slowly. "But you cannot dwell on this, Livingston. It will destroy you. You are not the sum of your decisions, or the worth of your words. But the contents of your soul."

I take a deep breath. "Rainey, I've seen some depraved things."

"You are a wonderful person, though." Suddenly, she pulls away and sits up straight. "Don't look so doubtful, Livingston Lacroix. I mean it."

If only we believe in ourselves the way we do in others. Perhaps that blind sacrifice is the definition of love. To place all your hope and trust in someone else because they need it more than you do.

I don't know. The closest I'll ever come to love is Rainey. But it's not enough to be a connoisseur of the emotion.

Rainey reaches out and sweeps her fingertips across my cheek. "You wanted so badly to save the people around you that you forgot to save yourself," she says softly.

Her words shoot a chill down my spine because a part of me is desperate for Rainey to ignore my stubbornness and the barriers I have and try to save me. Sometimes I feel that helpless.

Clearing my throat, I sit up, causing Rainey's hand to fall away from my face. "I appreciate your kindness."

"Have I ever been known to be kind? I prefer to say what

I mean and mean what I say."

"Fair enough." I become silent and rest my head against the headboard. Carefully, I look at her from the corner of my eye. She resumes her spot next to me. Once again, making small circles across my chest.

"What do you think you'll do now? Go back to the shippin' company?"

I've thought about this very question many, many times. "No. I don't believe I will. Workin' at the shippin' company was never satisfyin' for me."

"There has to be somethin'," she says, gently prodding. "Somethin' that will bring you joy."

You bring me joy.

"No, nothin'."

"This isn't a question you'll immediately have an answer to. You have to think it through," Rainey replies.

"I've thought about this many times. The dilemma is, I don't know who I am."

"Not at all?"

I hesitate to answer as I think of every pleasurable past time of mine that didn't include sex or liquor. Finally, I think of one hobby.

"When I was younger, I wanted to be an architect," I announce into the silence.

Beside me, Rainey tenses for a moment before she continues her soothing strokes.

"It's foolish, though," I quickly say.

Rainey stops her ministrations. I feel the absence of her touch almost immediately. She sits up halfway, resting her weight on her elbow. "It's not foolish."

"That's kind of you to say. But no need to be patronizin'."

"I'm not. I see no issue with bein' an architect."

"There is when you're a Lacroix, and your family has a successful business."

She nods in understanding. "You've been workin' for the shippin' company since your parents passed away. How much joy has it brought you?"

"Should a job bring you joy?"

Rainey sighs as she contemplates my questions. "I believe it should. Considerin' we have one chance to live our life. And as you said, your family has a successful business, so you have options. The privilege to choose somethin' different."

"Ah, but you're forgettin' that privilege is a prison."

I told Rainey the truth because I wanted her to know the truth. Because there's no one in the world I trusted more. I place my arm around her and bury my face in her hair because I was relieved to have the conversation over. But for Rainey, the conversation isn't over. She pulls back. I can feel her eyes roving over my face. "You should do what you want."

What would it be like to move about life pursuing something I truly enjoyed? The idea seemed so preposterous, thinking about it borders on cruel.

"We haven't argued in nearly twenty minutes. This might be a new record for us."

From Rainey's smirk, I can tell she knows I'm trying to change the direction of the conversation. I've told her more tonight than I've told anyone else. Her smirk transforms into a soft smile as she tucks her hair behind her ear. Something in my chest seizes at the action. Something unfamiliar and terrifying.

"I think it might be."

I kiss the crown of her head. "Good night, *le savauge*."

I waited several minutes until I heard her steady breathing. Even then, I was hesitant as I whispered the words into her hair, "*Vous êtes la seule chose pure à laquelle je puisse m'accrocher*."

And I closed my eyes and fell asleep because I was so, so tired, and Rainey gave me peace. In life, it's not our place to question the pain someone else experiences. We only need to recognize it.

And that's what Rainey does. Peacefully acknowledges my torment. That's why no one can have her, and no one will take her from me.

CHAPTER THIRTY-ONE

RAINEY

The next morning, I wake up with a smile on my face and the space next to me empty. The only sign of Livingston's presence is the rustled sheets. Brushing my fingertips across the mattress, I think of what happened last night.

I don't care for regrets.

Nothing in life is done in vain. We learn from our choices one way or another. And last night, I learned I love Livingston Lacroix with every fiber of my being.

The thought causes my toes to curl and me to bury my face in my pillow, but it's true. I knew I loved that stubborn bastard before, but now I realized the extent and what I would do to have him.

But first I had to tell Livingston the truth of how I felt about him. The mere idea of expressing my feelings and being vulnerable makes my stomach churn. I know Livingston cares for me. I know he does. I don't know the depth, though, and that's what makes love so impossibly chaotic. You can move as deep in your own heart as you please, but you will have to be brave long enough to learn whether your heart can be loved back.

With a shaky sigh, I sit up and get dressed. Breakfast is certainly finished, but Livingston is as familiar with Brignac House as I am, so he has to be close by.

I finish dressing, tucking my blouse into my skirt. When

I glance at the floor, I catch something from the corner of my eye. It's the belt from my robe, curled around one leg of the bench in front of the bed. My cheeks turn red as I think of everything we did. Or better yet, what I did. I would do it again.

Walking down the stairs, I begin to search for Livingston, but I don't have to look very far. I hear his voice coming from the parlor. There's a second voice. It's muffled, but clearly, it's female. As I approach the door, I relax because I recognize the voice as Nathalie's. I should give them privacy. It's been quite a while since they've seen one another. But I don't draw back. The pocket doors aren't fully closed, giving me a small look-see into the room. Nat stands on one side of the room, holding a paper in her hands, and Livingston stands on the other. I smile at the sight of him.

I love you. I love you. I love you.

"You have a telegram from Étienne," Nat says emotionlessly. "I read it."

Livingston reaches for the telegram, but Nat holds it away, her body rigid. "Why are you lookin' through the Pleasonton finances? Are they penniless?"

My fingertips rest against the doors. The racing of my heart causes a hitch in my breath. The blunt way Nat directs her question is not like her and causes me to flinch. It's difficult to see her so detached. I would love to tell her the truth of my family's finances. I'd love nothing more. But I can't.

"If Rainey wants you to know her personal business, she'll let you know," Livingston smoothly answers.

Nat walks away from the window and sits down. "From the telegram, it sounds bleak."

"How would you know?"

"Because I can read between your words."

Livingston's silent then snorts. "It's a telegram, and it's from Étienne. Of course it sounds bleak. He can make a rainbow sound bleak."

At his reply, my lips curve into a smile.

"He would only send you a telegram if it was urgent."

"Then I suppose you have your answer then, now don't you?" There's an edge to Livingston's voice. He's reaching his threshold with this conversation and isn't about to go much further.

"Marry her," Nat says.

I can't help but lean in. Very gently, I place my fingertips on the door and wait with bated breath for Livingston's answer. The seconds that pass by are agonizingly slow.

"Pardon?"

"Marry her," Nat repeats. "Offer your hand and put an end to the financial burden her family has. God knows our family has more money than we know what to do with."

All I can see is the rigid way Livingston holds himself. "I don't believe marryin' her is the correct way to go about things."

"Why not? You love her, don't you?"

There's a long pause from Livingston.

Answer her. Please answer her.

"No. I would never love someone like Rainey."

I think it would have hurt less if he drove a sword straight through my heart.

My eyes close and with a shaky breath, I push away from the door. I can't listen to another word. My skin feels sticky, and my heart is racing in my chest. I can't decide whether I'm going to spontaneously burst into tears or become sick. I feel dreadful.

I can hear Momma's voice in my head, lightly chiding me, "This is why a lady never eavesdrops."

My hands curl into fists as I feel tears building behind my eyes. My nails dig into my flesh as I fight to control my emotions and take deep breaths. This is Livingston "King of the South" Lacroix, why did I ever expect something different?

You have your answers now, I tell myself, trying to find a break in the clouds in this stormy situation. *You had a pleasant time with Livingston. It's time to focus on saving your family's home.*

"Ma'am?" a servant says from behind me, breaking through my thoughts. Turning around, I find a confused servant looking at the envelope in their hands and back at me. "Yes?"

"Are you Miss Rainey Pleasonton?"

At that, I frown and stand straighter. "I am."

The man holds the envelope out for me to take. "This is for you."

Sure enough, I see my name written in elegant script. Who is this from? I smile at the servant. "Thank you."

He dips his head and walks away. I don't waste a moment and tear open the envelope with one of my nails. I don't have the faintest idea who it's from, but I gladly welcome the distraction.

Dear Miss Pleasonton,

Under the circumstances of which we met it feels boorish to say I enjoyed meeting you, but I enjoyed meeting you. My sisters and I are having a gathering tonight at Rosemound Manor, and I thought of you. I hope it's not presumptuous of me to extend an invitation to you so soon after the memorial.

We would love to see you there.

Sincerely,
Loras Breymas

Slowly, I lift my head. Instinctively, my gaze drifts toward the closed doors where Nathalie and Livingston remain.

They couldn't still be talking about Livingston's lack of love for me, could they? I had no desire to stand with my ear pressed against the door one more time and be rejected again. Once is enough.

To think, I was going to tell Livingston the truth about how I felt. To think, I was going to stop seeing the bachelors for someone who could never love someone like me.

Like me.

Tears of humiliation build behind my eyes, and I blink furiously.

I will not cry. I will not cry.

Who was I? Was I that repulsive? Was Livingston that bored with his life that he was merely entertaining himself, waiting until a lady of his stature and refinement made her way into his life, with someone like me?

Why do you think he calls you, le savauge? Anger reminds me. *He will never, ever love you. Don't love him back.*

I'd rather feel anger than pain and sadness. I've become so intimately familiar with anger's warm embrace that I nearly sigh with content when I feel its dark grasp.

With anger, I know what to do, and it doesn't involve love in the slightest. Folding Loras' invite in half, I jut my chin out and walk upstairs. I make a point of looking forward and not at the doors behind me.

Yesterday, there was a man who looked at me with interest. He didn't seem bored with me.

Tonight, I will pay him a visit.

And that man is not Livingston.

CHAPTER THIRTY-TWO

LIVINGSTON

Why not? You love her, don't you?"

My heart races from my sister's simple question because everything between Rainey and me has become an intricate mess. There are no words to explain what Rainey is to me and our relationship. And I don't want to explain it. I feel defensive of what we have. Even with someone as trustworthy as Nathalie, I trust no one to understand that between good and bad, black and white, and love and hate is Rainey and me.

No one can understand, but the two of us.

"No," I finally reply, because it's the simplest reply. For good measure I add, "I would never love someone like Rainey."

I regret the words as soon as they leave my mouth. I went too far. I wanted to appease Nat with my answer, but all I've done is given my sister an opening for more questions. She looks at me with something close to disappointment. I don't attempt to explain my words. I'll only bury myself further.

Sighing heavily, Nat looks me over with blank eyes. *"Vous pouvez vous mentir, mais vous ne pouvez pas me mentir."*

"C'est la vérité."

Nat looks unconvinced. *"Les gens peuvent mentir avec des mots, mais pas avec leurs yeux."*

The way her eyes bore deep into mine makes me shudder. Nat knows the truth, and she's waiting for me to confess. She can stand here all day because it's not going to happen. I stand my ground, looking her right in the eye. Nat doesn't know what she speaks of. If I'm lying it's to save Rainey.

At last, she gives in. Nat takes a step back and shakes her head. "Liv, I may be your little sister, but I've made my own mistakes in life. I believe I can offer advice."

Never in my life did I think I'd live to see the day where Nathalie would be giving me guidance on life. That's when you know your life has shattered into millions of bits. "Oh, and what's that?" I ask, trying to keep my voice light.

"Only a fool allows fear and pride to get in the way of love." She regards me with the gaze of someone who knows my future because she's lived it.

A chill drifts down my spine. "Nat—"

"Did you ever think your life would turn out the way it has?" she asks, cutting me off abruptly.

Her question gives me pause for a moment. "Never."

Nat nods. "I only envisioned love and family for me. Never this." She stares out the window. Her eyes remain blank. "I don't know what to do now."

"You do exactly what you did after our parents passed."

"Liv, there's no closet beneath the staircase to hide in," she says with a straight face.

I smile and gently elbow her arm. "The closet remains at Belgrave."

Nat's shaking her head before I can finish my sentence. "I need to stay here for now."

That's not the answer I want to hear. I think both Rainey and I envisioned Nat coming back to Charleston with us. Brignac House is not where she belongs. This place has stolen part of her spirit.

"What is here?"

"Nothin'. But things must be put to rights."

At that, I nod. I understand the need to finish what you've started. Even now, I have the urge to find Rainey and tell her what Étienne's said in the telegram

"Whenever you decide to come home, we will be waitin' with open arms."

Nat tilts her head, and for a moment, she stares at me with hopefulness that I don't anticipate. "Everyone?"

I find myself nodding before she can finish her question. "Of course."

Because I don't know how to make this better. Because there's no time to build a closet beneath the staircase for her to hide in, I offer my arms to her.

For the first time since I've arrived, Nat's eyes well up with tears. She rests her cheek against my chest. My arms securely wrap around her. She doesn't sob, but her small body gently shakes.

I don't know how long we stand there. But I would've stood there for as long as she needed me to. Nathalie was my little sister and one of my best friends.

Soon, her cries turn to sniffles. She takes a step back, searching for something to wipe her eyes. I grab a handkerchief from my pocket and hand it to her.

"Thank you," she says as red slowly stains her cheeks.

"It's quite all right."

She blows her nose and gives me a weak smile, but I can already see the walls she's built around herself coming back up. "Excuse me. I need to gather myself."

I step to the side to let her pass. "Of course."

She brushes past me, tightly clutching my handkerchief. Once she's at the door, she stops and looks at me. "Liv?"

I lift a brow. "Yes, Nat?"

"Love her or let her free."

Nathalie walks out of the room, softly closing the door behind her. As I walk back to the table to pick up Étienne's telegram, my sister's words linger around me while Rainey's scent clings to my skin.

Heavily, I fall back onto the settee behind me and drop my head into my hands.

I don't know how to love a person with Rainey's strength and will. But I can't let her free.

CHAPTER THIRTY-THREE

LIVINGSTON

I've had my fair share of uncomfortable dinners. But I firmly believe those dinners have been preparing me for the time spent at Brignac House because no dinner can compare to the agonizing silence surrounding this table.

I want to believe it's because of Oliver's death but my sister and the servants appear undaunted by the quiet. In fact, I've never seen a staff serve food around a dinner table so quickly and silently.

My eyes keep lifting, expecting to see Rainey sitting across from me. She would be just as amused by this spectacle. But she's nowhere to be found. She was noticeably absent for lunch and I haven't seen her all day.

After enduring two courses with no one saying a word, I decide to speak. "Where is Rainey?"

Nat's gaze veers toward Matilda, almost as though she's judging her reaction. Matilda stares at her plate with intense focus. Is she in a trance? Then, abruptly, she lifts her gaze and looks around the dinner table as if a conversation has been taking place the minute we all sat down, and she's ready to participate.

My God, this woman is strange. I'm counting down the seconds until our train leaves for Charleston.

Leonore wipes the corners of her mouth before she speaks. "I believe she's in her room. She isn't feelin' well." Very swiftly, Leonore looks away, and takes a drink. A red stain creeps onto her cheeks.

I arch a brow. Leonore is lying for her daughter. I shift in my seat, and look at my plate, thinking on how to best answer her. "How unfortunate. Please give her my regards."

She dips her head and gives me a strained smile. "I certainly will. I think it's the travelin'. It can be awfully taxin' on the body."

I'm willing to bet my entire trust fund that if I went upstairs and walked into Rainey's room, I wouldn't find her ill and lying in her bed.

"That's interestin'," Nat cuts in.

All eyes turn to her. My sister points toward the doorway. "Before dinner, I saw her in the hallway upstairs and briefly spoke to her. She said Loras sent her an invite to have dinner at their house." Nat stops speaking and thinks over her words. "Or perhaps it was Rea?"

"Why in God's name would you allow your good friend to go there?" Matilda asks.

My emotionless sister looks her mother-in-law in the eye. "Because she's a grown woman, and your petty feud with the Breymas family has nothin' to do with her."

Death extracts many emotions out of us. For my sister, it brings nothing out. I do believe the part of her that once cared what people thought of her is pushed to the back of her mind or died with Oliver. Typically, I'd celebrate my sister's bold words, but all that echoes in my mind is that Rainey is at the Breymas home...near Loras.

Sitting up straight in my chair, I look at my sister. "When?"

"Before dinner. I presumed she accepted when I saw her getting into the car."

"And you let her leave?"

"Was I supposed to stop her? I didn't have orders. Mrs. Pleasonton, should I have stopped her?"

Leonore lowers her spoon back to the soup bowl. "Stopped who, dear?"

"Rainey from goin' to the Breymas home," Nat patiently explains.

"Rainey's sick," Leonore says without batting an eye. "I spoke with her in her room, and she had a terrible fever. Are you sure you saw Rainey?"

It's clear to see Leonore is willing to continue with the 'sick charade' the entire night and clear onto tomorrow if she has to. I have to stop myself from groaning in frustration.

Nat lifts her gaze to the ceiling as though she's deep in thought. "I swear it was Rainey. The woman was wearin' a deep blue dress. Very darin'. She will turn heads. If she doesn't find a man willing to marry her by the end of tonight, I'll be shocked." My sister gives me a meaningful expression that I can read all too well. *She can and will find someone else you fool.*

My hands curl into fists, and my body vibrates with anger at the picture my sister paints. I don't know if I've been this angry before. I know I should gather myself and take a deep breath, but I can seem to think of only one thing, and that's Rainey.

The day I kissed her, I was doomed. I understand that now. My life is a disaster, though. I can barely take care of myself let alone somebody else. Especially someone like Rainey. I am not meant for her.

"Oh, that's not necessary, sweet boy. She needs her rest."

Looking over my shoulder, I smile at Leonore. "No, no. I insist. Excuse me, ladies. I will be right back."

I leave the dining room with the image of worry on Leonore's face. Striding across the foyer, I take the stairs two at a time. I know she isn't in her room. I just need to see for myself.

I rap my knuckles against the door and wait. After a few seconds I repeat the process.

"Rainey," I say with a dangerous edge to my tone. "You missed dinner."

I let the seconds pass before I turn the knob. The door is unlocked. Of course, it is. This is Rainey. She won't sneak out of the room like anybody else and ban entrance to her room. Rather, she'll welcome everyone in to announce her absence. She would show her escape like a trophy.

Making a small circle, I take in the spotless room. "Raina, Raina, Raina...*je te trouverai.*"

CHAPTER THIRTY-FOUR

RAINEY

I arrived at Rosemound Manor a quarter after dinner started on purpose. I didn't want to run the risk of seeing anyone. Especially Livingston. I stayed in my room for the whole day, deviating between anger and misery. When I didn't come down for lunch, Momma came to see me. She took one look at me, and her eyes narrowed, then she rushed toward my bed. "What's wrong? What happened?"

I told her about my feelings for Livingston, and the conversation I overheard between Nat and Livingston. I had to relieve the pressure in my chest. I thought if I did, it would take away the pain, and it did, to an extent. Momma quietly listened, nodding every so often. Her eyes filled with sympathy as though she understood my plight.

When I was finished, she reached out and covered my hand with hers, and said, "Oh, Rainey."

I told her of the invitation I received from Loras. She asked if I was considering attending, and I told her yes.

"I can't see him right now, Momma," I said, my voice breaking. "I can't."

She nodded, and much to my surprise, she told me she would tell everyone I was ill and would be in my room for the night.

With her, I found myself making an effortless exit out of Brignac House and ended up here.

Thanking the driver, I close the car door behind me and

look toward Rosemound Manor. At once, it becomes apparent why Matilda has a distaste for the Breymas family. Their home is built on a hill, looking directly upon Brignac House.

Like most plantations in the South, Rosemound suffered throughout the years. The two-story, wood-frame home was painted yellow but chipping in some areas. The gable roof needs repair, but two dormer windows flanked a pediment with a fanlight in the middle. However, it wouldn't matter to Matilda that Rosemound Manor wasn't as grand as Brignac. All that mattered is the Breymas family could look down upon the Claibornes.

I could see movement coming from the first floor. For the first time, I question the hastiness of my decision. I only know Loras and Rea, and that's being generous. Everyone else would be a stranger. But the alternative would be sitting across from Livingston in the Claiborne's dining room, and concealing my heartache, which seems far worse.

Thunder rumbles in the distance. I jump at the sound before I walk toward the steps leading to the porch. The front door opened before I had a chance to knock. There was no butler to greet me, but instead, Rea Breymas.

She has a smile waiting and ready on her face. "You came!" she says happily before she leans in for a hug. Almost as though we've known each other our whole lives.

I have a feeling it's the half-empty champagne glass in her hand that's responsible for her over-exuberance.

Grabbing my hand, she pulls me inside and kicks the door closed behind me with the heel of her foot. "I told Loras it was fruitless to send you an invitation, but he wouldn't be convinced otherwise." She looks at me and smirks before she takes a long drink. "Looks as though I'm wrong."

Her disposition is a stark contrast from how she was at the funeral. I didn't like her before, but this Rea, I did. In a way, she had a manner about her that reminds me of Nat. What set them apart was that Rea moves almost like a cat and smiles at the people around her as though she knew what they were thinking of her. Nathalie was trusting, bordering on naïve, and unworldly. But that was before Oliver passed away.

Now I didn't know what to think.

Rea leads the two of us deeper into her family's home, and my confidence falters when I see the number of people around me. Nothing but strangers. Anger and adrenaline fueled my actions up until now. Surrounded by strangers, I'm beginning to doubt my decision. I don't have to stay all night. I can make pleasant conversation and then slip away without anyone noticing.

Rea and I walk into what I believe is the sitting parlor, although it's impossible to tell with so many people. I think I spot a settee and chairs pushed against the wall. The green curtains are pulled back with ecru tiebacks.

My eyes widen when I see a man stumble and narrowly avoid spilling his drink all over the silk material. Damask wallpaper the color of almond and gold clings to the walls. With the exception of the pictures on the walls, anything of significant value is noticeably absent. Judging from the man I just saw, that was a wise decision on the Breymas' part.

I lean toward Rea. "Do your parents live here?"

"Hmm?" She finishes taking another drink before she nods. "Oh yes. Well, Loras lives in Savannah. But I live with them. Right now, they're travelin'." She squints real hard. "I can't remember where they said they were goin'. Loras will, though. Where is my brother?"

Before I can tell her that her parents' whereabouts truly aren't that important, she stands on her tiptoes and looks around the room. Somehow, she spots him clear across the room.

"Brey? Loras Breymas! Look who's arrived!" Rea hollers across the room. If that isn't enough, she gesticulates wildly.

At once, he catches his sister's gaze and then looks at me. His eyes widen with surprise. He waves and begins to walk toward us.

"Loras and I don't get the chance to socialize as much as we wish to," she confesses with a small slur. "When the opportunity arises, we must take it."

I don't know what to make of her words because I don't know her well enough, so I nod and give her an amicable smile.

When he reaches us, he also brings along friends of his. My momma and daddy raised me with manners, so I say hello and introduce myself. But I don't have it in me to stand there and endure any stiff and polite conversation. My motivation for coming here tonight was purely driven by anger, and to prove to Livingston that even though he may not love me, someone out there might.

And I know my thinking might be childlike and foolish, but when your heart has been cracked in half, you will do anything in order to save it from breaking any further.

After some time, his friends break apart. Rea leaves to get another drink, leaving me with Loras. Chewing on my lower lip, I think of what to say. I'd rather have the floor open and swallow me whole than endure a long, painful stretch of silence.

"What would you prefer I called you, Loras or Brey?"

"My friends call me Brey, but if you want, you can call me Loras."

I nod. "I'm glad I asked. Loras it is."

"And what about you? Is Rainey short for anythin'?"

"My name is, in fact, Raina." The second my name slips from my lips, I picture Livingston above me, driving his cock in and out of me. Seconds later, he groaned and repeated my name over and over.

After that, it felt as though he forever staked claim to my name.

"You can call me what you wish," I rush out, noticing it's been several seconds since I've said a word.

His gray eyes glint as he looks at me. He smiles, revealing straight, white teeth. "Rainey it is."

Why do I feel a sense of relief? I push the nagging question aside and keep my focus on Loras. "There are you and Rea. Any other siblings?"

"Yes, one younger sister."

"I don't think I saw her at the funeral. Is she here now?" I begin to look around the crowded room.

"No, she's unfortunately away at the moment. Her name is Juliet."

I mull over the name for some time. "What happened there?"

Loras tilts his head to the side. "Pardon?"

I realize how blunt my question came out, but there's no stopping now. "Well, you and your sister have unique names. When your momma got to Juliet, was she simply too exhausted to come up with anythin' creative?"

While I prattle on, Loras's smile widens. And when I finish, he shakes his head ever so slightly. "As much as I would love to give you an entertainin' and detailed story for her name, the truth is she's named after my maternal aunt. If you'd like, the next time I see my momma, I can ask her if there were any uncommon names she had in mind for Juliet."

"Please do."

A guest from the party walks up behind Loras and pats his back, saying hello. He gives them his attention, and a courteous smile before he immediately turns to me. "Although, I'm beginnin' to wonder if our nanny Toy's name was never up for consideration."

There's only one person I know named Toy, and she's an elderly woman with more fire in her blood than me. She's quite possibly the only lady I was afraid of as a child. To be honest, I still am. "Wait…are you speakin' of Toy Waring?"

Loras's eyes widen. He looks as shocked as I am. "You know her?"

"Of course. She caught me in her garden when I was a little girl and was fit to be tied."

"What led you to be in her garden?"

I lift a shoulder and look away evasively. I'm used to people being au fait with my history. It's nice being able to distribute pieces of information about my life at my discretion. "Let's say I had a…colorful childhood that was rich with adventure."

He lets out a loud laugh. "And those adventures never led to trouble?"

I shake my head. "Never. Except the time when your

nanny Toy caught me in her garden and nearly walloped me with her cane."

Loras shudders. "You must be fast. Rea and I could never seem to dodge that dreaded cane."

Rea walks toward us, carrying a champagne glass in her hand. Her eyes have a look of disinterest as she searches the room. "What are you discussin'?"

"Juliet's lackluster name," Loras provides.

"Juliet. Juliet," she repeats, taking great care to pronounce each syllable. Finally, she scrunches up her nose. "Yes, very lackluster."

It's hard to ignore the note of bitterness that sinks into Rea's words.

"I believe I haven't met your sister, but Loras said she isn't here."

"Yes, unfortunately she is away at the moment," Rea replies.

Brother and sister gave me the same answer. Why?

"I believe you might have seen Juliet in Charleston several times. Her fiancé lives there."

"Who's her fiancé?"

Loras begins to answer me, but he looks at Rea and closes his mouth. He rubs the back of his neck. "Ah. You know, his name has slipped my mind."

Furtively, I look between the two of them. He's lying. What are they hiding?

Loras clears his throat and dips his head, his eyes focused on something behind me. "I believe someone is here for you."

Looking over my shoulder, I find Livingston. My heart becomes lodged in my throat. My lungs become restricted, and his light eyes are fixed on mine. His strides are long and confident. The women around him stopped and stared. Even though I was hurt, I still felt possessive of him.

They can't have him!

What can I do, though, when Livingston won't have me?

Livingston doesn't notice the attention the women are giving him. As he advances on me, I see the furious glint in his eyes. He looks ready to tear someone apart.

Swallowing, I look for a way out, but Livingston is coming from that direction.

I'm trapped.

I knew Livingston would discover I wasn't at dinner, but I depended on Momma giving me some time. When it came to the three M's — me, men and marriage — there's nothing she wouldn't do. If she had to lie to Livingston and our hosts, then so be it.

Livingston reaches me. I can feel the anger radiating off him in waves. There are no preambles or friendly smiles. "Come with me. Right now," he says through clenched teeth.

Charmingly, I smile at him. "I didn't know you were invited to this party."

"Rainey, now."

Already, people are beginning to stop and look in our direction. They may be strangers, but I don't want them listening. I smile at Loras and Rea. "If you'll excuse us for one moment?"

Eyes wide, Rea nods and steps back. "Of course."

I take the first step into the crowd. Livingston isn't taking any chances of me slipping away as he presses his chest against my back. The second his body makes contact with mine, I gasp. I can't help myself. My reaction is instinctive.

The moment we reach the hall, I shove him away. I breathe deep through my nose and try my best to ignore Livingston's presence behind me. My footsteps are fast down the corridor. I don't stop until it's dimly lit and private.

I lean against the wall, cross my arms, and wait for Livingston to speak.

With his hands on his narrow waist, he stands in front of me. "For someone who's supposedly sick in their room, you look remarkably well," he says.

I grab the material of my dress, creating an elegant waterfall of blue around me. "We all have our vices of self-care. Lookin' nice and goin' to a party is mine."

He follows the action. His eyes hot. "Since you feel better, can we leave?"

"You can," I say pointedly.

With his head tilted to the side, he angles his body closer. "You're upset with me."

"Now why would I be upset with you?" I say, ending my question with a sickly sweet smile.

Livingston narrows his eyes. "I have one good calf left. I would like to keep it that way. Now tell me, why are you so heated?"

I mirror his movements until we're a hair's breadth away. "I'm not heated," I enunciate slowly. I pull back quickly because even when I'm hurt and angry with him, there's the undeniable attraction between us.

Livingston groans and drags his hands through his hair. "Rainey, just tell me what's botherin' you."

"Nothin'. But what did the telegram—"

"Telegram? What tele—" His voice fades as he begins to understand. "Are you speakin' of the telegram Étienne sent? Why would a telegram make y—"

I watch as the realization that I was there to hear his conversation with Nat sinks in. Eyes marginally widen, lips part. But at once, his face becomes a mask of cool indifference. "Rainey, I don't know what—"

"There you are," a man's voice says, interrupting what Livingston was about to say.

Livingston and I turn at the same time and see Loras standing in the hall. If Loras found us a minute earlier, I would've been relieved, but then Livingston spoke. But now, the smallest part of me wanted to know what Livingston had to say.

Livingston straightens, his body subtly blocking mine. "Yes, we needed some privacy to speak on a matter of great importance."

Loras is silent, then says, "I hope everythin' is all right."

"Unfortunately, we need to be on our way."

"Rainey?" Loras asks, waiting for my confirmation.

I could stay here all night, but so would Livingston. He's

not leaving until I do. Regretfully, I nod at Loras. "Yes. I'm sorry. But I'm afraid we must be gettin' back."

Before Loras can reply, Livingston places a hand on my lower back. "You were a gracious host, and your home is lovely. Have a pleasant evenin'."

In a matter of seconds, Livingston took every polite farewell and thrusted them into one clipped good-bye. We brush past him, and I attempt to give Loras an apologetic smile.

As we walk down the hall and out the front door, I'm aware of footsteps behind us the whole time.

"I think you should let her go," Loras says quietly.

At once, Livingston's posture straightens. His shoulders stiffen. Those words, as calmly as they're spoken, cause Livingston's chest to begin to rise and fall rapidly.

Slowly, Livingston turns to Loras. "What?" His voice is deadly calm.

My gut told me this wasn't good. I place a hand on his arm, as though my touch can convey the danger of this situation.

We need to leave. Now.

"I said I think you should let her go," Loras repeats.

Livingston walks back to the house, breaking away from my hold.

What I was attempting to avoid all along has begun to happen. Guests from the party begin to find their way onto the porch to find out what the noise is all about.

Shaking my head, I can't help but groan. This is quickly turning into a disaster.

"She doesn't need you."

I can't see Livingston's face, but I see the outline of his body. The set of his shoulders. They drop for a moment. Maybe he realizes how foolish this is and will walk away. But then, without warning, he charges Loras like a bull. His head meets Loras's stomach, taking the wind out of Loras. The two of them fall to the ground with a giant thud.

In a flurry, they become a tangle of limbs. Their boots scuff against the gravel, and grunts sound from them. Some guests on the porch appear horrified but most are fascinated and can't look away.

I rush forward and then stop, unsure of how to intervene. "Livingston, stop! Stop it!"

His eyes are wild as he fights for top position and to get as many hits in as possible. I dig my feet firmly into the ground, wrap my arms around his waist, and pull him back. On the opposite side, I can hear Rea shouting at her brother to stop it and go inside. A crowd has gathered, and over Livingston's panting, I can hear their whispers.

As hurt as I am by him, the need to protect him is stronger. I don't want these strangers to see him this way. I don't want his actions to be the talk of Savannah. They don't understand him.

I shove him once more and hurry forward, holding his face between my hands so he's forced to look at me and only me. "Stop it."

He breaks eye contact with Loras, and I'm finally able to make eye contact with him. Some of the fight goes out of him. His chest moves up and down rapidly as he sucks in air. But his eyes continue to swing between Loras and me.

"Let's go," I urge and begin to guide us away from the house and the crowd that's gathered around us. I need to get him away from here.

Before I get into the car, I look back at Rosemound Manor and see Rea on the porch. It's too dark for her to see the regret in my eyes, so I lift both shoulders. In return, she waves and walks back inside.

I slide into the back seat, next to a furious Livingston, and slam the door behind me.

"Brignac House. Please," Livingston says to the driver, his voice brusque.

For several minutes, all that can be heard is the sound of the car motor. I'm still hurt and slightly confused by what happened at the Breymas's home.

Livingston shifts back in the seat, and faces me. I pointedly stare out the window. "Rainey, I know you're upset, but you have to understand—"

"Not here," I say out of the corner of my mouth.

"Then when?"

"I don't know," I reply, wishing the driver would go faster. I shouldn't be in close quarters with Livingston. I don't know whether I'm capable of slapping him or kissing him. Perhaps both. After everything, I'm emotionally bereft. I want to pack my belongings and leave Savannah immediately, and then lick my wounds in Charleston.

Thankfully, the driver pulls into the Brignac driveway. I nearly sigh with relief and place my hand on the door handle, waiting until I can make my getaway.

As though he can read my mind, Livingston leans in. "We will talk."

Finally, I look directly at Livingston right as the car comes to a stop. "No, we will not." At once, I open my door. I'm so anxious to get away from him that I nearly stumble but then quickly right myself. Droplets of rain begin to hit the crown of my head and shoulders.

Growling, he surges out of the car and hurries after me. If I was home, you could place a blindfold on me, and I'd find my way inside. But here, my steps aren't quite as fast, and Livingston's quickly catching up to me.

"Rainey, stop. Rainey. I said stop!"

I begin to walk up the steps when his hand curls around my arm. I whirl around right as his feet land on the first step. Our bodies are inches apart.

"I'm tired," I announce somberly with my shoulders held high. "I believe it's time for me to retire."

"Perhaps this is why Pleas created your dowry. You are far too inexperienced for this world. Look at you now. I found you at the home of someone you just met and now you are refusin' to explain what could make you so bothered with me!"

His words are meant to light my anger. He wants to get a reaction out of me, and I want to give him one. Desperately. But I also want to show him that I have many weaknesses, but with each year I discover my strengths and tell myself, *"Look at you now. Look at how you've grown."*

"Go about your business, Livingston. What I do doesn't pertain to you."

"You are my business, Raina!"

He gazes at me the same way he did all those years ago in the dimly lit hallway at Belgrave. And although he might not remember what he said, I do...

CHAPTER THIRTY-FIVE

RAINEY
1914

"Checkmate." I smile victoriously, and lean in. "Inquirin' minds want to know. Did you intend to lose two games in a row?"

Sitting back in his chair, Livingston nearly growls in frustration. He's always been terrible at losing. "Let's play again."

I sigh and glance at the clock on the mantel. "I can't. I need to be goin'. We played almost eight games."

"And now we're preparin' to play the ninth." He begins to line his pieces back into their correct positions.

My neck is stiff, and my buttocks have gone numb from sitting in this chair for so long. Do I have the energy in me to play another game? No. I could fall asleep right here if I close my eyes for too long.

But will I play another game? Yes.

On the lounge is my brother. He sits forward and closes the ledger in his lap. He's been there for as long as we've been playing chess, calmly going through the family accounts, a weekly routine of his. He's so quiet the only times I remembered he was in the room was when he took a break to stretch or get a drink.

Miles pulls out his pocket watch, takes one look at the time and shakes his head. "It's half past one." Twisting around, he looks at me. "I take it we're stayin' here for the night?"

"Yes," I reply my eyes already on my pieces, considering what my first move will be.

Sighing, he stands and grabs the ledgers. "Then I believe it's time for me to turn in," Miles announces.

Livingston and I watch him take his jacket that's draped over the back of a chair. At the beginning, my brother's visits to Belgrave were several times a week. But when I began to stay overnight at Belgrave, so did Miles. I think Momma made him stay for propriety. She didn't say it, but I knew her far too well and knew she thought it was too unseemly for me to stay at Belgrave unchaperoned.

However, this was Livingston. And even if Livingston couldn't remember, we all knew he was Miles's best friend since childhood. He's been in my life since the day I was born. I recognized Livingston was handsome, but I had no intention of being forward. The man had been in a terrible accident. All I wanted was to see him get better.

"Good night, Miles," Livingston says, his voice cordial.

My brother stops midway to the door and shakes his head ever so slightly. It's still jarring for him to hear Livingston not call him Pleas. "Good night."

Miles walks out of the room and up the stairs. Lately, the guest rooms have become our rooms. In the last month, I've lost track of the number of times we've stayed here overnight. I knew Livingston was in good hands. He had his twin and his doctor on call. Not to mention a slew of servants who could help.

But I felt responsible for him, and I didn't trust anyone else for that matter. He almost died. I almost lost another person. Someone I didn't know the world without. I wanted to protect him from any harm and shield him from the curious eyes of society until he regained his memory.

Everyone in Charleston couldn't help themselves but speak on the attack of Livingston Lacroix. Who was his assailant and why? How long would it be until he showed his face in public? People visited Belgrave, but Nat was just as vigilant over Livingston as I was and would only allow close family and friends to see him.

Her protectiveness was valid. She was his sister.

What was my link to him?

Exhaustion suddenly gets the best of me. I sit up straight, bring my arms over my head, and yawn. When I lower my arms, I'm tired but prepared to play one last game with Livingston. But across the table, I find him regarding me with curiosity. His eyes linger on my throat and drift across my chest. As though he can sense me watching him, he meets my gaze. His curiosity has turned to interest.

Immediately, I look away. My heart's racing far too fast. I need to get away from his probing gaze. Suddenly, I push my chair back from the table. "I'm very tired. I can't play another game."

Livingston sits back in his seat and crosses his arms over his chest. "You're quittin' on me?"

"Afraid so," I reply and stand. "I think I will follow Miles's lead and turn in for the night."

"Very well then."

I stand there, look down at his coal black hair. I'm not going to leave him by himself. Left to his own devices, he'd roam the halls of Belgrave all night if he could.

I place my hand on his shoulder. "You need sleep."

Beneath my palm, his muscles bunch. "No, I don't."

"Everybody does, Livingston," I say gently.

He lifts his head. Those hazel eyes may not have years of memories behind them, but he can still feel emotions, and his frustration is palpable from the set of his shoulders to the rigid set of his jaw. "Why sleep when I can aimlessly walk through the halls of a home that is unfamiliar to me?"

My heart lurches at his words. "Someday, they won't be unfamiliar, and everybody and everythin' will become clear."

Resting his elbows on the table, he leans forward. His head drops as he rubs the back of his neck. "When will someday come?"

"Soon."

At my reply, he looks at me from the corner of his eye and

smirks. "You sound so sure of yourself."

"Because I'm positive it will happen."

"Why?"

"Because you were born to survive this," I say without hesitation.

There's no immediate recognition in his eyes. It would be naïve to expect him to remember those words. However, it doesn't stop me from saying them because he needs the reminder. And so do I.

You can be the most buoyant person alive, but you will inevitably find yourself overcome by life. It happens to everyone.

"Come on," I urge. "I'll walk you to your room."

"I don't need an escort," he grumbles as he stands.

"Oh, my apologies. I meant walk me to my room," I reply smoothly and slip my arm through his. "This house is so enormous that every time I stay here, I want to request a map for each wing."

"I could use that map," he says agreeably as we step into the foyer. It's dimly lit with a servant standing beside the front door. Typically, Ben holds that position, but since the attack, a servant has been stationed directly beside the front door at all hours. Livingston knew it was for him. Of course, he did. He might grumble remarks under his breath here and there, but I think he relied on the knowledge that if he ever lost his way, someone could lead him back.

"When I walk the halls at night, I almost feel as though I'm walkin' through a forest. The steps I take out of my room are not guaranteed to be the same ones I take back," he says.

"Then don't take the walks," I reply, my tone quiet. As we walk up the stairs, it feels as though the silence of the home becomes more pronounced. Our voices are defined, and our words echo to the high ceilings, only to fall slowly around us like snowflakes.

"I want to."

"But you need to sleep more."

He shrugs as we step onto the second floor and head

toward the family quarters. "I don't need sleep. I'll sleep when I remember."

"Livingston, you can't mean that. You don't know how long that will be."

He's nodding before I can finish my words. "I certainly do."

"What makes you say that?"

In the middle of the hall, he stops. I come to a halt beside him and watch as he takes a deep breath. "If I stay awake and keep active, then perhaps I can come close enough to my memories to capture them."

My God. I wasn't expecting him to say that. My heart tugs at his admission. "I can understand that," I nearly whisper.

My words are the truth. Livingston and I clash so frequently because we're too much alike. I know he's headstrong and tenacious. He's not staying up all night out of pleasure, but necessity. Nonetheless, his confession is a strike to the gut, and I have to stop myself from stepping forward and giving him a hug.

We stand there in the hallway, silently staring at one another, waiting for the other to speak. I don't know what else I can say to make this situation better. I look around the hallway and note my room is far closer than I realized.

Clearing my throat, I gesture to the closed door on the left. "My room is here."

Tucking his hands into his pockets, Livingston looks behind him with a brief nod. "Very well then. Good night, Florence Nightingale."

I'm not deceived by the nickname. He started saying it after I accidentally spilled a bowl of clam chowder on his bed and nearly scalded his arm. Livingston never missed an opportunity to say it. I almost missed *le savauge*. But I would take Florence Nightingale because it showed there was still a piece of the old Livingston I knew.

I dip my head in his direction and sigh. "Good night."

I walk past him, taking notice that he still hasn't moved. I open my door when he asks, "Why are you always here?"

I think his question over. "Because I'm a close friend of the family's, and I want to see you get better."

He nods, seeming to accept my answer. "We argue far too much."

"Always have."

"We argue, yet we are close friends?"

"I'm a close friend of the *family's*," I repeat, placing heavy emphasis on the word family.

He nods but doesn't look convinced. "Are you anxious to leave my presence because your husband is waitin' for you?"

I'm so surprised by his question that it takes me several seconds to answer. "If I had a husband, chances are I wouldn't be sleeping here right now." That's not true. If I was married, and Livingston truly needed my help, I'd tell my husband to shove off. My friend needed me. "But there is no husband. And I'm not anxious. It's late."

Livingston doesn't appear the least bit put off by the time. "Why are you not married?"

I'm sure people have asked themselves that in private conversation. *"Whatever was wrong with that Pleasonton girl? Why couldn't she find a husband?"*

No one had the courage to ask me.

"I could ask you the same thing," I reply.

"I don't know why I'm not married."

When I realize how insensitive my retort was, I cringe. He asked because he truly didn't know. He wasn't goading me.

Say you're sorry, you brat!

Livingston merely smirks, though. "Care to enlighten me why I have no wife?"

"Because you're a shameless seducer," I offer with a smile.

Livingston's nods, his eyes twinkling. "Ah. I sound charmin'."

"You have a slew of admirers and an abundance of hostile lovers." There's no awareness in his eyes. The blankness staring back at me is still jolting to see. I pointedly look away, and pick at invisible lint from my skirt.

"And I am unmarried because I've yet to meet someone

who can handle…"

"Hostile humor?" he suggests.

I snap my finger and smile. "That's precisely it."

He smiles back, and his eyes crinkle at the corners. Seeing him relaxed pulls at me, making my stomach continuously flip until I feel dizzy.

I lean against the wall for support and hold a hand to my heart. "That truly hurts."

He crosses his arms and slowly approaches. "I met you at the same time like everybody else, but I see you differently…" His brows furrow as he continues to look me over. "I could love you."

I can't tell whether that's a statement or an offer.

"Is that so?" I reply, trying to keep my reply light. My chest tightens at his words.

He's not himself. He doesn't know what he's saying.

Livingston lifts a shoulder, but he boldly keeps his eyes on mine. "You drive me mad. And you don't behave how a woman should."

"You flatter me," I cut in.

He's closer than before. So close I can smell him. Has he always smelled so good? Yes, he has. When I was a young adolescent with stars in my eyes, I discovered the opposite sex and decided they weren't pests after all. Anytime Livingston would visit and he would walk past me, I would inhale the crisp, clean scent of him, and I felt as though a thousand butterflies were set free in my chest. I never told a soul. But I finally understood what every girl my age was speaking of when they talked of infatuations they had for boys our age.

I forgot all about that until now.

"You didn't let me finish," he says. "I think that's different and original."

"Different and original," I repeat. "Those are two words no one has ever used to describe me."

"Think you could love me?"

He's not himself, he's not himself, he's not himself.

But I was. I had my memories in order and my mind in

place. There was no explanation for how I was reacting, which was flustered and almost delighted by his words. We've always had an intense repartee between one another that never gave us time to consider one another as anything else but word-sparring partners.

Right then, the light on Livingston shifts. I see past the teasing, his womanizing ways and the charm I've watched him reserve for the world. I know he's not giving me that charm now.

He stares at me with a naked vulnerability, and a hunger that takes my breath away.

He leans in so our faces are inches apart. "Could you love me?"

CHAPTER THIRTY-SIX

RAINEY

My fingers tightly curl around the railing as I shake away the memory. I was foolish then to ever give weight to his words. He didn't know what he was saying. Shortly after our conversation in the hallway, Livingston's memory came back. No one knew why, or what brought about his memory. Maybe time is what his brain needed to heal.

His entire family was elated, and even more so to realize that Livingston could answer a burning question for them: who attacked him. Which in a surprising twist was one of Nat's good friends, Scarlett Gould. It was a case of mistaken identity. She was after Étienne the entire time.

In the midst of all this celebration, I smiled. I was truly happy. But my heart twisted and tugged as though it was being tormented. I was going to lose my time with Livingston, and I didn't want that. Perhaps I cared for him more than I realized. I knew it was unfair of me to hold hurt against Livingston when he didn't know he caused it. So I pushed the time out of my head as best as possible. If it didn't exist for Livingston, it wouldn't for me. That was easier said than done.

I want to ask why he doesn't love me, but I don't. It's easy to admit your love for someone. Far harder to ask why someone doesn't love you back. No one can do that and walk away with their pride intact.

Tears fall down my face. In a hurry, I brush them away but

they seem to keep coming one after the other.

You played a dangerous game, and you lost.

"Rainey. Please, stop!" Livingston reaches me and grabs my arm, turning me around. He opens his mouth but stops when he sees my glassy eyes. He reads into my tears as something else entirely. "What happened? Did that fella make an advance toward you?"

With the backs of my hands, I wipe the tears and shake my head. "No. Loras was a perfect gentleman."

"Then tell me what's wrong. Tell me how to make you happy!" Livingston drags his hands through his hair and turns to walk away from me, then comes right back. It's like there's an invisible rope tied between us. We can only walk so far before we're yanked back to one another. "Rainey, I can't..." His words fade as he stares at me with agony in his eyes. "You overheard me speakin' with Nat. Does this have to do with the telegram? Because I'll let you read it. I'll tell you what Étienne said."

He doesn't wait for my reply before he reaches into his back pocket and produces a folded piece of paper. I take it from him and read through it.

```
TRIED CALLING STOP
EXAMINED FINAL LEDGER STOP
TODAY THE TEMPERATURE WAS HIGH STOP
CLOSE TO ONE HUNDRED AND FIFTEEN STOP
GIVE EVERYONE MY LOVE STOP
E.
```

Confusion doesn't begin to describe how I feel. "What is this? What is Étienne talkin' about?"

"When we have to pass important information on, this is our subtle yet creative way of communicatin' to each other. He was informin' me that he finished lookin' through your family's accounts. There's no money, and it was worse than we thought. The accountant wasn't attentive with the bookkeepin'. It will take a lot more than your dowry to pay off your family's debts."

"How much?"

Livingston hesitates for a moment. A flash of pain enters his eyes. "One hundred and fifteen thousand dollars."

A shallow breath escapes me. All this time, I've been hoping we owed far less or that the accountant was wrong in his estimation, but this was worse than I could ever imagine.

"I wanted to wait until after we were back in Charleston to tell you. Not here. But I don't want you to think I'm hidin' somethin' from you."

Right then I realize that Livingston truly doesn't know that I heard what he said to his sister.

"Dammit! I don't know want to do."

I stare back and take a deep breath, trying my best to gather the courage for my next words. "Tell me why you can't love someone like me," I blurt.

His head rears back as though I've struck him. "What?" he says, his voice ragged.

It's out, and now there's no going back. I need to keep going. I need answers. "I heard you tell Nat you couldn't love someone like me. Why? Why did you say that?"

The rain beats against my body. The material of my dress is heavy and itchy. My hair has fallen and hangs around my face. Livingston's hair clings to his forehead with the ends curling out. Droplets of water gather to the edges of his perfectly molded face before they fall away.

I cross my arms and forge ahead. "Was I merely like every woman you've been with?"

A look of horror crosses his face. "Absolutely not. You're more than that. I—"

"Because I love you," I say in a rush. My heart is beating so fast my entire body shakes. I'm surprised I can get the words out. "I don't know how I let this happen. But it did, and I do. And I thought you should know the truth. I love you, and I believe these strong feelin's won't go away anytime soon."

I exhale and wait for Livingston to reply. But he just stares at me with his mouth partly open, and his brows furrowed. I hate this silence. It's maddening.

"Livingston, say somethin'."

He shakes his head ever so slightly. The bewilderment fades from his eyes. "If I was to ever want to hear those words, I'd want them to be from you. But Rainey—"

I lift my hand, cutting him off. I take a step closer to him. "Please don't say you love me as Miles's little sister or Nat's best friend. Do you love me?" I repeat, emphasizing every word by tapping his chest, where I know his heart still beats.

I want him to speak, whether good or bad because Livingston is so remarkably skilled at responding with his body. There's never any need for words. But my question is worthy of an answer.

I am worthy of an answer.

Livingston captures my hand, linking our fingers together, and takes a deep, shuddering breath. The longer he remains silent, the further my heart breaks. It's an interesting thing. The breaking of a heart is never heard by another soul, except for the person it belongs to and the one doing the breaking.

"Rainey, we both know how temporary life is no matter how permanent it may seem."

He delivers his words with a conciliatory tone that, at first, I don't sense the rejection weaved throughout them. I rather he was blunt and to the point.

Inaudibly, I swallow and remind myself not to cry. "So you will spend your life alone, keepin' the company of people who have zero substance and no love to give rather than findin' people who want to love you and believe in you?" I say, my voice croaking at the last words.

Livingston flinches as though I've struck him. "Not fearful. Aware."

I want to fix this beautiful broken man so, so much. If I had the option to choose between making Livingston's life pain free or having mine financially secure, I would select a pain-free life for Livingston.

"It's fear," I press. "You are your own worst enemy."

What I'm saying is the truth, and we both realize it. Livingston stands on the doorstep of the past, and I can't pull him back to the present.

But Livingston sees I'm getting far too close to the truth. His shoulders stiffen as though he's preparing for what I may hurl his way next. "You don't know what I've gone through, Rainey. It's my decision how I choose to live."

For several seconds, I can only stare at him. "You're right. And it's my decision to find someone in this world who will love me the way I deserve to be loved."

His eyes briefly close. "I know you do," he says, his voice breaking.

Livingston knows, yet it still isn't enough. All the time we spent together I was slowly falling in love with him, believing that maybe, just maybe, he was falling in love with me too. But for him, I was simply a warm body for his arms to wrap around. I was someone who made it easy for him to forget his nightmares.

"You were right to warn me not to fall in love with you, and I was wrong not to believe you." I don't wait for Livingston's reply. I leave him standing there with his hand outstretched, preparing to grab my arm.

After several seconds, he shouts, "You're gonna leave?"

I don't reply, but my heart wants me to. So badly.

"Fine. I don't need you! I never did!" he shouts.

Don't respond. Don't respond. I pause on the first step. My eyes briefly close. If Livingston's intentions are to take a knife and drive it as deep into my chest as possible, then he's succeeded.

Don't respond.

Abruptly, I turn around. Because I'm headstrong and impetuous. The need to find the last word and capture it as my own is far greater than my rationale.

I rush toward him in a fury and don't stop until we're a hair's breadth away. "Of course you need me, you foolish man. I was born for you. What is a king without his queen?"

Livingston stands there with his mouth slightly parted. I've stunned him into silence, and he's devastated me into pain.

I take a step back, my voice calm and even. Inside, though, I'm slowly crumbling. "Don't ever speak to me again."

He calls my name. I continue to walk up the steps; what

is there to say? We've already said our truths. There's nothing left of me he can possibly break.

When I enter Brignac House, I walk up to my room. A part of me desperately hopes Livingston is trailing me. Maybe he didn't mean what he said just now. I don't look behind me because I don't want to further break my heart or let him see me cry. But as I step onto the second floor, I realize how foolish my hopes are. Why would he follow me?

When I reach my room, I don't go inside. I rest my back against the door, close my eyes, and allow my tears to fall. I should've never let any of this begin. But I can't very well blame Livingston for everything. When he attended my dates, I engaged in conversation without fail. I let him into my room time and time again. I simply don't know where to go from this.

"I hope you don't mind, but I told him where you were."

Quickly, I sniffle and wipe away my tears before I lift my head and see Nat standing at the end of the hallway. She blends in remarkably well with the shadows with only her nightgown and robe standing out. Does Nat make it a custom of walking the halls of Brignac late at night, or is this new?

I push away from the wall, trying to regain my composure even though she most certainly saw me begin to fall apart outside my room. "I didn't know you were up."

Nat takes a step forward, crossing her arms. "I didn't know my brother could run after a woman. Seems we're both surprised tonight."

I fight the urge to drop my head into my hands. "You heard us outside?"

"Of course. I was in the sittin' room, and listenin' to the two of you."

"Oh."

"Brignac House is the darkest and loneliest home I've ever had the misfortune of livin' in. Havin' you, your momma, and Livingston here has brought life and joy to this suffocatin' place," Nat confesses in a flat tone.

"Nat." I take a step forward, intent on comforting her, but

she lifts a hand, stopping me in my tracks.

"I've been consoled and hugged so much these past few days. I can't bear one more." She leans forward and gives me a bleak smile. She's trying so hard. "Let's pretend we're back at Belgrave. Let's pretend I never met Oliver, and the war never happened."

Her words send a chill down my spine because they can reach out and touch nearly everyone in the world. We've all been affected by the war. If we all had the chance, I think we would wish away the damages and heartache that came with war. Miles would still be here. So would Oliver. And Livingston wouldn't be the shell of the person he once was.

I nod and give Nat a shaky smile. "Okay. Let's do that."

Sitting back, Nat smooths the material of her nightgown across her knees. "You love my brother, don't you?"

It seems extraordinarily wrong to place my burdens on someone whose pain is greater than mine. That's why me, Momma and Livingston are here to begin with. To let Nathalie know we love her.

"Who Étienne?" I ask, feigning indifference. "I love him as a brother. He's a stern man but has always been kind to me." I finish my words with a smile.

Nat doesn't smile back. "You know which brother."

My smile fades, and my heart begins to pick up speed. Averting my gaze, I look at the floor. "I've loved Livingston before I knew what the word meant."

"My brother is a fool. But most men are."

Sadly, I nod. I don't have much experience with men. Just Livingston. But what he's shown me has hurt so badly.

There's a silence between us that neither of us try to fill.

"My family is penniless," I say aloud.

"Is the telegram Étienne sent about you?"

Closing my eyes, I nod. I'd forgot about what Livingston said. What waited for me at home felt impossible to face. I didn't know what to do now. Everything felt utterly hopeless.

Nat turns toward me. "The invitation I received for a bachelor ball isn't connected to your family's financial problems, is it?"

My brows lift; I'm surprised no one informed Nat about the dowry, Livingston's involvement, or the bachelor scheme. Then again, I didn't tell her either. When she moved to Savannah, Georgia, I rarely saw or spoke to her. It seemed as though she carved a new space next to Oliver and enjoyed being Mrs. Claiborne. "Serene conceived the idea about the bachelors."

Her eyes widen as though that's explanation enough. "That sounds like somethin' like she would suggest." Nat pauses. "But why a bachelor ball?"

I proceed to explain my situation from start to finish, making sure to leave no stone untouched. I tell Nat about each bachelor and the outings I've been on with them. I tell her about the dire situation my family is in, and how Livingston and Étienne had been pouring through the accounts to see if anything could be salvaged.

Speaking privately with Nat in such a manner makes me feel as though everything is back to normal. The one thing that's missing is Nat's cheerful demeanor. I don't know if that will ever return because when you lose someone you love, you lose a piece of yourself.

"If Livingston was reluctant to be your executor, did he offer his assistance in a different form?"

"Yes."

"Money," Nat says flatly.

"You know your brother quite well."

"But you declined."

"I did," I confirm.

"Because you're far too set in your ways and refuse to accept what you consider charity. Especially when the benefactor is my brother."

"It's not that simple." Abruptly, I stop talking. "Well, it is," I finally concede. Resting my head against the wall, I think of my next words carefully. "Have you ever loved someone so much, you would do anythin' not to endanger that love? I just know he offered me money out of obligation to Miles, and I don't know when or if I'd ever be able to pay him back. Sooner than later, Livingston would resent me. And contrary to what everyone may think, I'm fond of the...disagreein' we do. Well, used to do. I think I destroyed what relationship I had with your brother."

"I understand more than you know," Nat says quietly.

When I look at her from the corner of my eye, I see her staring at her hands. At that moment, I know without a doubt, she's thinking of Asa Calhoun. I was made privy of how she felt about him early on. For the longest time, I was the only person Nat confided her feelings to, and although I couldn't fathom what she saw in Asa, I didn't tell a soul.

The day Nat told me Oliver proposed and she said yes, I told her to be certain and not to make any rash decisions because I saw how she and Asa looked at one another. And in the summer of 1913, the two of them spent a lot of time together. But then everything abruptly changed, and then Oliver appeared.

Nat assured me that Oliver loved her, and that was all she needed. But sitting here now, I knew it wasn't. For Nat, it always came back to Asa. I understood that now. I never thought it'd take me having a broken heart to come to that realization.

I exhale loudly before I speak. "Then you know why I couldn't take his money."

"I do."

It feels good to be understood.

Sighing, I briefly close my eyes. I need to be getting to my room. Livingston will be coming upstairs soon, but I don't want this time with Nat to end. It's quite remarkable really. I came to Savannah under the impression that my best friend needed me, and I would do the consoling. But in this hallway tonight I needed my best friend far more than I realized.

I look at her, watching as she looks straight ahead with a faraway look in her eyes. "Will you be okay after we leave?"

She glances at me. "Will you be okay after you leave?" Nat asks, skillfully turning my question back onto me.

The very thought of traveling back to Charleston and going about my life makes my heart drop to my stomach. "No, but I don't have a choice."

Nat nodded, her face showing no emotion. Seeing her so detached and removed from reality is still hard for me to accept. I can't decide if the Nathalie sitting beside me is a grieving widow or a woman grieving for the life that she could've had. I believe it's both. I believe it's going to take a long time for her to heal, and she can't do that here. Just a few days at Brignac House and I'm anxious to leave.

"Come home," I say instinctively. I would hate myself if I didn't ask. "Everyone would love to see you, and you can meet your nephew, and shake your head at everythin' Serene says."

The smallest of smirks graces Nat's lips. There's a brief flash of the Nat I know and love, but it's gone before I can take a breath. I lean in and lower my voice. "You can't grieve here." Urgency coats my words. "You just can't."

As if to prove my point, there's a loud wail that comes from the private quarters of the house, toward Matilda's rooms. I jump and stare with wide eyes down the hall.

Nat shakes her head and looks at me. Her eyes are sad. "No, I can't. I need to stay here." There's a louder scream, this one followed by the sound of an object shattering against the wall. A bleary-eyed servant rushes upstairs.

"Nathalie," I say with urgency.

"I'll be back. I think I always knew I'd come back. Perhaps not in this way." If Nat's careful with her words and even more so with her eye contact. She knows as well as I do that if I'm able take one good look, I'll be able to see the truth.

"Were things so bad between you and Oliver?" A chill sweeps through me as I say his name. It feels decidedly wrong to be asking such a question the day after his funeral, and in his own home. But this is a question that has weighed on my mind. It needs to be asked.

"Not...bad. Just wrong," Nat confesses, all the while she manages to keep her gaze fixed on the floor. "Wrong because we were wrong for each other. People make wrong decisions when they're hurt or angry."

In an unforeseen show of affection and gentleness Nat grabs my hands between hers and cradles them. She looks at me with eyes that have seen too much. "Don't let that be you. Don't make a wrong decision."

CHAPTER THIRTY-SEVEN

LIVINGSTON

I am the first one up the next morning.

Probably because I didn't sleep a wink. I spent the entire night agonizing whether I should go to Rainey's room and tell her how I truly feel, but the truth is, I don't know how I feel. The mere thought of her going back to Charleston and proceeding with this bachelor façade makes me see red and builds a fury in my chest that's almost impossible to contain. However, I know it'd be selfish of me to keep her to myself when I know she wants a family someday.

I'm not surprised to see that Rainey doesn't arrive for breakfast. No one makes mention of it. I certainly don't plan on it. Nat claims Matilda is feeling under the weather and is laying down. I don't know if that's the truth, or not. But this is the most comfortable meal I've had at Brignac House.

It's only when our luggage is being taken to the car and Lenore and I are saying our good-byes that Rainey comes downstairs. I thoroughly look her over, trying to see if there's anything that might show she had a restless night. But she looks beautiful as always.

Before I went to bed I passed by her room and stopped. I wanted to go inside and be with her. It was a need that went beyond myself. My fingers twitched and my arm lifted toward the doorknob before it stopped midair. I didn't deserve to be in the same room with her.

"Nathalie, I wish I could stay longer," Rainey says as she

goes in for a hug.

"I'm grateful you came for the time that you did."

Rainey pulls away, looking my sister in the eyes. "If you need anythin'. Anythin' let me know, all right?"

Numbly, Nat agrees and walks us out the front door. I, for one, am ready to leave Savannah. I don't want to say good-bye to my sister but this has been the most peculiar trip with eccentric people, and unexpected behavior. My own being the most unpredictable. I don't know what possessed me to charge Loras. When I stepped into the Breymas home I searched for one face: Rainey and found her next to Loras. He regarded her with more than open curiosity or friendliness. He was attracted to her, and it seemed as though with every word she spoke he leaned in closer to her.

Let her go.

When Loras said those three words, all I envisioned was letting Rainey go and watching her leave me, only for her to never come back. The idea felt as though my heart was being ripped out of my chest. I was going to lose something vital to my existence and this pompous bastard would be the reasoning for it. And like an angry brute, I allowed my Lacroix temper to get the best of me and charged him. I didn't have regrets immediately following. In fact, I'd never felt more alive. I wanted everyone to see Rainey didn't belong to them.

But all too quickly I would make a mess of things and destroyed any hopes of her belonging to me.

The car door slams behind me. I place my head against the headrest, and sigh. On our way to Savannah, I felt the heavy weight of Rainey's gaze but as we begin our journey back to Charleston it's almost as if I don't exist. She converses with her momma. They discuss the weather, a brunch Leonore has the following week, and a charitable auction their church is hosting in two weeks.

The two of them remain very polite, however the tension radiating from Rainey causes me to shift uncomfortably in my seat.

I've never been happier to see a train station in my life.

But as we collect our tickets and head toward the platform, I realize the small enclosed space and tension isn't done.

It's only begun.

We take our seats. I'm not surprised to see that when Rainey sits down, she pointedly drops her handbag and hat onto the seat beside her, and solemnly looks out the window. Sighing, I take the aisle seat beside Leonore.

I stretch my legs out in front of me, preparing for what will be a very, very tense and quiet ride. I'm right about one thing. It's tense. But sitting beside Leonore, it's not quiet. Rainey's momma can discuss shards of grass and make them one of the world's greatest wonders.

Leonore taps her throat, and winces. Immediately, Rainey takes notice. Her black brows furrow as she leans close. Her and her momma may bicker but her concern is evident. "Is everythin' okay?"

"I do believe all that talkin' I did with Matilda caused my voice to become sore."

"Do you want me to order you some hot tea?"

"Would you, dear?" Leonore asks, her voice becoming more strained by the second.

Rainey stands and goes in search for one of the waiters. Leonore tips her head toward the aisle, and then looks directly at me. "That was an…interestin' trip," she says in a clear voice.

I arch a brow. What sore voice?

"It certainly was."

Leonore continues to stare at me with her solemn eyes. "I don't care much for travelin' but I think of Nathalie as a daughter. I would do anythin' for that sweet girl."

"I'm glad to hear that. She's always thought fondly of you, and I know she will need all the support possible as time goes on."

Almost instantly, Leonore's eyes tear up. "Losin' a spouse is certainly difficult."

Nervously, I look around. I didn't mean for my words to make her cry. I've seen enough tears these past few days to fill the Ashley River, and I don't want to see more. Leonore gathers her composure, and smiles. If it wasn't for her glassy eyes, you'd never know she'd been tearful.

"You intend to spend eternity with one another but life has other ideas."

I nod as though I understand when in reality I don't. Perhaps, I never will. For as long as I can remember I've wanted it that way, and now I'm not so sure...

Leonore tilts her head and looks at me. "Tell me, Livingston do you intend to marry?"

I sit back in my seat and cross my arms. I can't help but arch a single brow; there's a reason for her question, and I want to know the direction of this conversation. I'm far too tired and not alert enough for Leonore or her daughter. I lift a shoulder and fix the sleeve of my jacket. "Oh, Mrs. Pleasonton I don't believe marriage is in my future."

"That's what I believed about my Rainey before she began these..." She pauses, trying to formulate her words. "Before these men began courtin' her."

I sit a bit straighter in my seat. "That so?"

She nods. For a woman with a sore throat she's remarkably talkative.

"People have always said you and Raina have a brother and sister bond, but I never agreed." She stares straight ahead, a faraway look in her eyes. "When she was born you were not impressed with her." She smiles softly. "Of course you weren't. You were only a child yourself. But when Miles left the room you reached out and wrapped your hand around her small one. I don't think either of you have let go ever since, have you?"

Her words cause a shiver to rock through me. I hold Leonore's gaze, reminding myself to appear indifferent. I smile at her. "I suppose one might consider us close when we're not bringin' one another agony."

"That may be true, but I think we show the best and worst parts of ourselves to the people who love us the most."

"Here you go, Momma," Rainey interrupts, holding a teacup with steam rising from the top.

At once, Leonore places a hand against her throat and

winces as though every swallow since Rainey's been gone has been agony. "Thank you, dear. I don't know what I would do without you."

"Oh, I believe you would manage," Rainey mutters beneath her breath.

"Maybe for a day here of there, but I would notice your absence; you're all I know." Leonore smiles at her daughter and takes a sip of tea, as she lowers the teacup she gives me a pointed look.

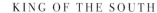

CHAPTER THIRTY-EIGHT

LIVINGSTON

Where is love born from?

Does it take a second of direct eye contact? Or is it an accumulation of innocuous moments that start the fire?

I've looked at this question from all angles, and I still don't have a definite answer. There's a possibility I'll spend the rest of my life searching for the answer.

But I need an explanation now because I don't know if I can take being in this purgatory for much longer.

My footsteps feel as heavy as my heart as I walk toward the front door of Belgrave.

There's no headache to mock me over the previous night's actions. I'm clearheaded. Didn't have a drop to drink. I knew alcohol would only incite me to make my way out of my house, toward Rainey's. I cannot be trusted around her.

Right now, she's hurt. She made that abundantly clear at Brignac House. It's only been a day since we came back from Savannah, but the urge to see her is overpowering. However, when she's hurt, she needs time to herself. But I need to explain my feelings before it's too late. Yet this situation is beyond me. I've spent nearly my entire adult life escaping the clutches of love, only to fall right into its possession and now I don't know what to do.

I hesitate at the threshold of Belgrave. I grew up here, and I'm questioning whether I should enter or knock. At the last second, I decide to knock. Rainey might be here and as badly as I want to see her, I don't want to see any more pain in her eyes.

Surprisingly, the person who greets me on the other side is Serene. Her eyes widen momentarily before they narrow. She stares at me as though I'm the bane of her existence.

"Oh, it's you," Serene states with no emotion.

"Yes."

With my nephew held tightly in her arms, I swear he's grown since I've seen him last. They've even begun to call him by his middle name, too. It suits him.

Serene peeks around me as though she's searching for someone. "You're by yourself."

"Yes," I repeat.

Serene pats my nephew's back in repeated, motherly gestures, while maintaining the blaze of fury in her eyes. "A smarter man would have showed up with support. You know… witnesses."

"Well, I never claimed to be smart."

At that, Serene snorts, and looks me up and down. "What did you do to Rainey?"

The color drains from my face. One day. Just one day is all it took for Serene to get the truth from Rainey. But how much of the truth was she able to get? As angry and hurt as Rainey might be with me, I can't see her telling Serene everything because if she did, I wouldn't be alive and Serene would be feasting on my insides for betraying her friend.

I feign indifference and brush past my sister-in-law. "I was a gentleman, and escorted Mrs. Pleasonton and Rainey, so I'm baffled as to why you're askin' if I did anythin'."

Serene snorts and follows me. "Yeah right. And I'm a wilting wallflower."

Her sarcasm isn't lost on me. "Has it ever occurred to you that Rainey's the dangerous one?" I ask without bothering to look at Serene.

She scoffs at my question. "Impossible. You did something, and you need to fess up."

I lift a brow and look over my shoulder. "What did Rainey tell you?"

"That the two of you had a difficult conversation in Savannah. But it's obvious you upset her."

My eyes briefly close. If Serene wanted to drive the knife deeper into my chest, she succeeded. It's agony not speaking with Rainey. Even when I was in France I wrote to her, and she always wrote back. Without fail.

Rainey was loyal, fearless, and beautiful. To have something so firm and solid ripped out of my life so abruptly makes me feel as if I'm drowning.

"Now talk to me, or I'll make you change Trace's next diaper," Serene continues, pulling me out of my thoughts.

I once changed Alex's diaper and nearly passed out from the smell. The fear of encountering something like that ever again makes me speak. "Rainey told me she loved me while we were in Savannah. I didn't say it back."

"You said nothing?"

"Well, she might have overheard me tell Nat that I could never love someone like her, and that was a lie. I didn't mean it! But I didn't tell Rainey that."

Serene is ominously silent, staring at me as though I've spoken a different language. Then, she springs into action and whacks me upside the head. "You idiot!"

"I realize that! That's why I'm here!"

Sighing, Serene steps back and shakes her head. The frustration drains from her features, but I'd prefer if it didn't. This means she's running out of hope. "Oh, Livingston."

"What do I do to make this better?"

"Oh, no, no, no, no." Serene laughs and shakes her head. "This is something you need to figure out yourself. And didn't you once tell me to remind you to never listen to my ideas?"

"I was a fool. Now, help me."

Serene's smile fades. "Livingston, I can't," she says gently. "And neither can Étienne. Listen, contrary to what you exhibit to the world, and your party boy ways, you're a pretty smart guy, and I believe if you thought over this carefully, you'd figure it out." Serene bites down on her lower lip and looks away, as though she's knows something.

Apprehension fills me. "What?"

"I know I shouldn't tell you this, but you should know the bachelors have been relentless since she came back from Savannah."

"When have they not been relentless?"

"True," she slowly concedes. "But this time it's different. It's as if they know you and Rainey aren't spending time together anymore." My heart quickens with alarm for what she's about to say. "And there's one bachelor Rainey's expressed interest in since your return."

"Who?"

"I cannot tell you."

"Why not?" I demand.

"Because it's none of your business. Because you hurt her and maybe this man can make her happy."

Perhaps truer words have never been spoken but they're lost on me because the thought of Rainey with another man sends me into a blind rage. Things are in utter shambles there's no denying that. But Rainey is connected to me.

With my hands on my hips I begin to pace. All the faces of the men I saw the first day Rainey brought them to Belgrave flash through my head. "No, no, no. It's none of my concern. I don't care," I say aloud.

Abruptly, I turn to Serene and snap my fingers. "It's Beau Legare isn't it?"

Serene quirks a brow. "He's not one of the final men."

Dammit, I should know this. I saw them at the blasted picnic. But I wasn't speaking to them, I was staring at Rainey, and playing a war of words with her. "Hiscock!" I blurt.

Serene tilts her head. "Who?"

"Taylor," I amend.

"The dude who doesn't want his wife farting? We crossed him off the list."

I rub my fingers against my lower lip and remain in deep concentration. For the next several minutes, I deliver a barrage of names Serene's way. Serene shakes her head, chuckling at a number of the names.

Soon, I give up the fight and throw my hands in the air. "I don't care," I repeat not for the first time.

"Clearly," Serene murmurs. And then she leans in with an excited smile, and whispers, "I think we may have a love match."

I rear back as though I've been punched in the stomach. "Like hell," I mutter.

Turning on my heels I walk out of Belgrave. I realize then that this obsession will never fade. She could dance with every eligible bachelor she desires and have dinner with them all until she could eat no more. She could even decide to marry one of the many men at her disposal. But I would destroy this Earth looking for her. I would rip every house from The Battery to Ashley River inside out trying to find a way to be with her.

Just to have a moment with her.

She is the phantom echo of the heart I once had before everything changed.

The amount of love she has for me is irrelevant because every part of me beats for her.

CHAPTER THIRTY-NINE

RAINEY

O f all the things I thought that would interest you, I
didn't think this would be it."

I look at Conrad from the corner of my eye before
I continue to stare at the endless blue water in front of me. "I
am a woman with many unique interests."

"I could not agree more."

I was prepared for Conrad to take me to lunch or to the
park. Instead, he parked alongside The Battery. He guided us
onto one of the main docks toward a smaller boat and asked if I
wanted to go fishing. It sounded refreshing and impulsive and
the very thing I needed in my life. I took his hand and stepped
onto the boat.

I was hesitant of how the time would pass, but surprisingly,
I get to know Conrad a bit more away from the constraints of
Charleston society. He's far less suave and more human than
I thought.

"I didn't know you had a boat," I blurt.

"I don't. This boat belongs to a friend of the family. They
like to go crab fishin' on occasion."

The boat moves in rhythm to the waves, and the scent of
pluff mud greets my nose for a millisecond before it disappears.
It's been like that since we stepped onto the boat. High tide was
two hours ago, but the wind has picked up. There's a probable
rainstorm on the horizon. If you're not prepared, the scent of
pluff mud can be rather pungent and knock you off your feet.

I'm immune to it. The dark-brown miasma is a Lowcountry essential that brings character to all my memories. However, it isn't precisely what you want to smell during an outing with someone you're attempting to get to know better.

I could picture Livingston shaking his head and leaning into me so he could whisper into my ear.

"Why would he go crab fishin' at such an hour? You know how to pick 'em, le savauge."

I find myself looking to my left as though he's there. I'm going mad.

"My brother and I fancied ourselves fisherman," I blurt.

I stare at the fishing pole held between my hands feeling the weight of Conrad's eyes. I'm sure he's shocked by my confession. He has spent most of the time talking about himself, which I've enjoyed. I've told him very little about myself, so I continue and ignore the pain I feel in my heart as best as possible.

"Although, when we didn't have fishin' rods, we would use a fishin' net and repeatedly circle it through the water in hopes a fish would swim right into the net."

"And did you ever catch one with the net?" Conrad asks in a jovial tone.

I fix my gaze onto the water and smile softly. "Every so often, yes."

I'm being selective with the story. Telling him bits and pieces, because the truth is, Livingston and Étienne are part of that memory. And Livingston was the one to teach me how to use the fishing net. He told me patience was the key. "You're in the fish's terrain. Give yourself some time before you pull away. The fish will come to you."

Livingston was right. With that fishing net, I caught many fish. Each time Livingston would grab the fish, he would cup them between his hands and ask if we should let them go. I always said yes and would never have anything to show for my efforts, but Livingston and I knew. Perhaps that's why the memory hurts. Because not only is my brother there, but so is Livingston.

An angry heart beats the hardest. It will cause words to pour from your lips. Words you never knew you were harboring. Strength grows inside you until your hands shake and your breath becomes choppy.

An angry heart is remarkably dangerous.

But now? Now I feel a numbness throughout me. I've lost enough people in my life to recognize I'm still in shock.

When I returned to Charleston three days ago, I began to nurse my broken heart like a bird tending to a broken wing. I haven't seen or spoken to Livingston once. I have no disillusions in his absence. I made my desires of what I want out of life clear for him, and in turn, Livingston made it clear he didn't want the same. What more was there to say?

Naturally, Serene has taken over everything pertaining to the bachelors and the impending ball. Her wisecracks never ceased to put a smile on my face. More than once, I had to stop myself from asking about Livingston. As hurt as I was, I still wanted to know his whereabouts and if he missed my presence as much as I missed his. But Serene and I cautiously avoid the subject of Livingston. I got the sense Serene wanted to touch on the topic, but she didn't know how. I almost wanted her to bring him up because then I could ask her if she could help me try to understand where everything went wrong. Was it Livingston that changed, or did I?

You foolish girl, you already know the answer. Not once did Livingston ever change. You did.

I'm the one who fell in love and expected him to embrace the change. I wanted him to accept my love.

There are moments I regret what I said. I lost so much. We would look at one another, and there was no need for words. We already knew what the other was thinking.

I missed that so much. I missed him so much.

But I couldn't regret saying how I felt. It was akin to a secret, and secrets will suffocate you.

"Have you made your choice?" Conrad asks after a beat of silence.

"I'm in the process."

Conrad becomes silent. "Will you make a choice?"

I appreciate honesty and try to give the same in turn as much as possible. "Absolutely."

I picked up the fragments of my heart as best as possible, but I knew I left pieces behind. I have no other choice. If life has taught me anything, it's that time runs and never walks, goes up but not down. I have to make the best out of this situation because I have no other choice.

Knowing the amount of debt was much higher than originally thought was still shocking. But I had spoken with Étienne. In his stoic voice, he explained what he discovered. He was careful with his words, but it was apparent, even to me, that Miles purposely mishandled the funds. It didn't make sense. It wasn't like him to be underhanded and secretive. It pained me to think he lived with the knowledge that our last name was on so many creditors' lists and he felt he couldn't tell me. But like most older brothers, he was protective. Likely, Miles thought he was shielding Momma and me from any burden or embarrassment. He never thought he would die.

Calmly and rationally, Étienne said, "Perhaps, you should truly consider the bachelors with a shred of earnestness. Even with your dowry, you would have a deficit of fifty-five thousand, but don't let that number be defeatin'. Creditors will be far more lenient when they see a debt steadily bein' paid."

He continued to go on in great detail about each amount that was logged into the ledger incorrectly, as though I would question his findings. But I listened with one ear open because all I could do was interpret his prior words and repeat them in my head: the bachelor plan is your only plan. You're out of options.

When I attended each date, I had more determination than ever that I would see this through. I would choose a bachelor, and I would find a way to pay each and every debt.

"There's somethin' I need you to know."

Conrad looks at me expectantly. His dark eyes are searching.

"Whoever I pick...I can't promise I will love my husband

at once. It will take time."

"I understand."

I nod and look down at my laced fingers on my lap. He understands now, but will he understand after what I'm about to tell him?

As though he can sense the bleakness of my thoughts, Conrad places a hand over mine. "Tell me."

"My family is penniless. And we have been for quite some time. There are creditors who expect to be paid, and I intend to use my dowry," I say in one giant rush. Once I'm done, I take a deep breath.

Conrad's silent. I watch him, attempting to determine what he's thinking. Is he furious with me? Embarrassed to be in the same company with someone like me? Loudly, he clears his throat. "I wasn't prepared for you to say that."

"Does it change your role in the bachelor competition?"

"Absolutely not." He leans in, lifts both brows, and smiles. "In all honesty, my family's closest friends are swimming in a mountain of debt. Most of the Charleston elite are close friends with local creditors."

I smile back at him. I believe there's much more to Conrad. Much more than I ever realized.

His smile fades as he scans my face. "If you choose me, I'll give you everything you want."

To understand me means to realize I want love. Can Conrad give that? I want to ask, but I have no desire to be turned down by another man.

"I appreciate that," I say softly.

When I arrive home, I find Momma in the sitting room having tea and reading a copy of *LIFE*. The moment she sees me walk through the doorway, she nearly hurls the magazine behind the settee and stands. She makes no attempt to hide the anxiousness in her eyes.

"How was your afternoon, dear?"

"Enjoyable."

"And who did you see?"

"Conrad. You know that, Momma."

I'm convinced Momma has each bachelor memorized by name, age, job and social stature. She's no better than Serene. I think if she was to sit in a room with Serene longer than ten minutes, she might come to realize she has more in common with her. She might, dare I say, find Serene pleasant.

"Ah, Conrad. Strappin' man. He's one of Livingston's friends, is he not?"

My face remains neutral at the mention of Livingston's name. Inside, my heart soars at the sound of his name. When will that reaction fade? "I believe he is."

"I'm astonished this man isn't inclined to remain a bachelor for the rest of his life like Livingston."

I wince. It can't be helped. Momma is being humorous, but I know all too well that Livingston belongs to nothing and no one, and he prefers it that way.

"The ball is in five days. Are you prepared?"

I'm so grateful for the subject change I don't mind we're right back to the bachelors. "Do you mean to ask have I chosen a bachelor?"

Momma regards me for a heartbeat longer than normal. "I believe I have."

"Oh, Raina, that's wonderful. I'm—"

"I told Conrad we're penniless," I blurt.

Momma's happiness dwindles. "What? Why?"

"He has a right to know."

"And you trust him not to say a word?"

"Momma, I'm far too tired to care. If all of Charleston knows, let them know."

She rears back as though I've visibly slapped her. I might as well have told her life isn't worth living. To Momma, you may seem to have nothing, but you always have your pride and status. And I was willing to give that up just for a moment of tranquility and peace.

Standing in front of me, Momma grips my forearms tightly. "No, no, no. You're not thinkin' this through properly." Her eyes widen imploringly. "This must stay private for now. Once you've chosen a bachelor and feel you can trust them, then you tell them the truth."

Frowning, I step back, out of Momma's grasp. "All I've done since the minute you've told me about our financial situation is think everythin' through."

"This is why you must continue to listen to me."

Wary, I observe Momma. Seems as though the minute I began listening to her, things began to go awry. She maintained her innocence about having no knowledge of Miles's will and the contents, but I've continued to have my doubts.

"Be truthful with me, Momma. Did you have anythin' to do with this dowry?"

"Are you still goin' on about that?"

"Can you blame me?"

With a tilt of her chin, Momma stares down at me as though she's the queen and I'm one of her loyal subjects. "Fine. If you must know, I might have mentioned to Miles that your daddy's will stipulated you had a dowry."

Slowly, I tilt my head to the side. I knew Momma was involved, but I didn't know in what capacity. "So you planted the seed."

Momma narrows her eyes. "No."

"Yes," I persist. "You had Miles do your biddin' so you can say you had no involvement."

With each word I say, Momma's face becomes a patchy red. "That is enough!" she yells. Pausing, she breathes deep through her nose and stares intently at me. "I'm your momma. I want what's best for you even when you don't believe it's the best. If I have to be underhanded in my ways, then so be it. I'd do it again if I had to."

"Has Livingston always been the executor?"

"When you were a child? Don't be ridiculous, Raina. Livingston was just a young man. Your executor was one of your uncles."

"So why Livingston?"

"Because sometimes you don't see what is in front of you."

I stare at her with disbelief. "You want me with him?" I holler.

"Well, who else?" Momma hollers back. "You're goin' on with the bachelor scheme. I thought this would end when you came to your senses, but that hasn't happened!"

Momma's telling me so much right now. I can only shake my head and stare at her in shock. "Don't you remember? I told him I loved him, and he didn't say it back. I put my heart out there for him to hold, and he let it fall and watched it shatter."

"Raina." Momma opens her arms to me. She pats my back before she pulls away, holding me at arm's length. "I know you're heartbroken, but I don't think you should act in haste. I believe Livingston cares for you."

I make a slow circle around the room. "Interestin'. I haven't seen him once since we came back. If he cares, he does a remarkable job of hidin' it."

"You are a complicated person to love, and so is he. I might be upset with him right now for hurtin' you, but I've watched him grow up. I love him too. I've seen you both lose so much. I've seen the two of you hold onto one another when you could have pulled apart. I think that's important to remember."

I didn't want to remember anything that would give me hope. Hope would light a candle of faith that maybe Livingston might love me. And how long will that be?

"He loves you, too," Momma insists. "Why the stubborn boy didn't say it, I don't know. But he does."

My heart was thumping wildly in my chest. This was all too much. Placing my hand over hers, I give her a weak smile. "I appreciate everythin' you're sayin'. But I don't think we're meant to be."

"Rainey, you need to go to him."

I shake my head. "I can't."

"Why not?"

"All my life, I've watched women cave. Cave to society, cave for families, and cave for love. I thought I would never be like that but look at me." I spread my arms. "Look at me. All I do is cave. I've had more dates over the past sixty days than I've had in six years just to protect my family from public ridicule." I take a deep breath. "If I seem stubborn, it's because I am. If I appear hurt, it's because I am because I know my worth, and it's more than this."

Momma's mouth opens and closes. I've stunned her to silence. After a few seconds, she dips her head. "Very well. Just promise me that before the ball, you truly think this through. I can try to lead you in life, but I can never lead your heart."

"I promise."

"I believe I'll go retire to my private quarters for the rest of the afternoon. I trust I'll see you for dinner?"

I nod and watch Momma mold back into the calm and composed Southern lady I've always known her to be. If I didn't feel her arms around me minutes ago, I would have questioned whether the moment happened, and I saw the brief display of emotion.

Once Momma leaves the room, I promptly sag against the wall and close my eyes. I want to go to Livingston right this instant. I want to tell him about my day, and when I'm finished, I want to feel his arms around me.

I want to, but I can't.

CHAPTER FORTY

LIVINGSTON

A clear mind, one that's not muddled by alcohol, is far more unnerving than I ever anticipated.

If I'm being honest, I haven't faced my thoughts and emotional upheaval since my brother and parents died. There was so much to do, and when I grew restless, there was always a willing woman and liquor cabinet that could be opened. It became a comfort, a way to alleviate all my pain. But I knew something was wrong with me. The war just brought it out of me.

I don't want to live in fear of the past, but I don't know anything else. Reminders are everywhere. A specific scent can immediately bring back moments from the trenches. Once, there was a large crash directly outside my office window. The next thing I knew, I was crouching behind my desk for cover. After several deep breaths, I stood. Sweat made my shirt cling to my back. I'm beginning to believe the shadow of my nightmares will always follow me.

Over and over again, I would remind myself that I wasn't there. I was safe. I was still alive. And then I would occupy my time by doing something that was rarely expected of me: I begin to plan for the future.

My steps are sure and oddly confident as I walk down the street. It certainly isn't derived from my sleepless nights. Just last night alone I reached for Rainey over three times only for my hand to meet empty space. She really wasn't beside me.

No, my confidence is born from my recent decision. When I walk through the door of my brother's company, EAL Corporation, my grip on the folder tightens as though the papers are going to fly out of my hand.

The receptionist, Myrtle, looks at me dubiously. She was hired shortly after the war broke out, and it looks as if she could be my mother's age. Every time I come in here, she frowns at me as though I'm up to no good and will only distract Étienne and his employees. In the past, she might've been justified, but today I came for a reason.

"I'm here to visit with the man who refuses to smile," I say to Myrtle before I walk past her and head directly to Étienne's office.

"Good mornin'," I greet as I shut the door behind me.

Étienne lifts his head and then immediately glances at the clock on his desk. "Mornin'," he says, surprise coating his words.

"Yes, I am aware of what time it is," I say as I sit across from him. "And no, I'm not sufferin' from the effects of alcohol."

"I wasn't goin' to say that. You look remarkably clearheaded. Which is interestin' considerin' Rainey has to choose a bachelor in…" Étienne clucks his tongue as he tallies the days. "Six days?"

"Three," I immediately reply. I have the deadline memorized.

"Three days," Étienne repeats.

I drum my fingers on the leather-bound folder on my lap. I didn't come here to discuss Rainey. All I seem to do is think about her. She needs space, and that's precisely what I've given her. The days haven't become easier though. Even before I claimed her bed as my own, her place in my life felt like the ground beneath my feet. Always there, unwavering and strong. Without our sparring, I felt lost, wildly reaching for anything to break my fall.

Had I felt this way before? No. I didn't stay long enough with a woman to find out. I entertained the idea of bringing home a woman, but the desire wasn't there as it typically is.

But it will be. The second I'm able to disregard what it is I feel for Rainey.

My brother whistles, pulling me from my thoughts. "That's certainly a short period of time to find a husband."

I lift a shoulder, attempting to appear indifferent. "It's her choice."

"I think we both know it's not, though." He looks at me carefully. "The most interestin' thing has occurred since you came back from Savannah. Suddenly, Rainey has turned to me as though I'm the executor of her will and askin' me about her family's accounts. Any reason for that?"

Twins are connected in such a way that they know when the other is hurting or hiding the truth. Between the two of us, Étienne was more adept at recognizing when something was wrong. He can regard me for a matter of seconds and just know.

"What happened?" he asks, his voice flat.

"Nothin'."

Étienne narrows his eyes. "Lies."

"There are no lies," I lie.

Étienne shakes his head before I finish my sentence and goes about organizing papers on his desk. "You can be deceitful if you wish, but I think you're forgettin' who my wife is. Serene tells me everythin'."

I rub both hands down my face. "Why inquire when you already know the answer?"

Étienne lifts a shoulder. "I wanted to hear if you might have anythin' else to say."

"I don't." I sit a bit straighter in my chair. Prepared to endure the weight of my brother's stare. At the last moment, I decide to speak. "I made several missteps with Rainey. I won't deny that. She's upset with me and told me to never speak with her, but in time, she'll realize this is all for the best. Right?"

Étienne continues to regard me.

"Yes, it's better this way…you helpin' her with the finances and givin' advice. I offered her a loan, and she declined. I tried to give her another option."

"I think we both now realize she and Mrs. Pleasonton are in deeper than we imagined."

Closing my eyes, I roll my neck. "I know."

"It's bad, Livingston."

Étienne proceeds to pull out the Pleasonton ledgers in his possession. "There are legitimate miscalculations that could have been caught if their accountant went over the books again. But then…" Frowning, Étienne pours through the pages before he points at an entry toward the bottom of the page. "You have this and this." He points at one last invoice. "This service was to pay for new drapes in the sittin' room. Instead of deductin' from the already inaccurate total amount, the same amount from the line above was used. There are mistakes like that on nearly every page."

"So transactions were bein' undisclosed."

Étienne nods. "And not very well."

"I miss Pleas dearly, but for the life of me I can't figure out why he allowed this."

"I don't think we'll ever know."

"Have you explained this to Rainey?"

"To the full extent? No. Besides, she and Serene have been runnin' about the house speakin' of nothin' but the ball."

I tilt my head to the side. "That so?"

Étienne nods. "If I hear about Rainey's gown for this ball one more time, I might lock myself in my office and not come out until all of this is over."

I've never cared much for women's clothing. Just what was underneath. But it was torture not knowing what she'd be wearing simply because I knew whatever it was it'd be to entice and put all eyes on her. And any color on her would be flattering. Red would accentuate her cheeks when she inevitably becomes miffed by one of the bachelor's opinions. If she would be bold enough—and I wouldn't put it past her—to wear black, it would blend with her dark hair and highlight her creamy skin. The color blue merely brings attention to her beautiful eyes. Dear Lord, am I truly losing my mind over the color of her gown?

"If I was a bettin' man," my brother continues, "I'd say they're at Belgrave havin' another fittin' or Serene is helpin' Rainey prepare for her next date with one of her bachelors."

Inaudibly, I swallow. "Pardon?

"The bachelors," my brother repeats with zero enthusiasm. His eyes flick in my direction. "Surely, you didn't think Rainey would cease seein' the bachelors because you're not speakin' to her? If anythin', the men have been circlin' her even more." Étienne is watching my every move. I need to appear indifferent, but his words are making that remarkably difficult.

Breathing deep through my nose, I look in the direction of the window and count to ten.

"In fact, last night Serene said she had a pleasant time with one of the bachelors. Somethin' about a love match." He suppresses a sigh and shakes his head.

All I hear is love match. Serene said nearly the same thing when I was visiting with her. "Who is the bachelor?"

Étienne's gaze veers toward the corner of the ceiling as he thinks of the name. For being such a smart man, he's taking a remarkably long time to answer. "I don't recall. Aidan, Beau, or Conrad, perhaps? The name started with one of the beginnin' letters of the alphabet." My brother shrugs. It's of no importance to him.

Sixty days ago, my response would've been vastly different. Relief is the first word that comes to mind. Being Rainey's executor wouldn't be looming over my head. That would be cause to celebrate.

Right now, the sixty days seemed to have gone far too quickly. A part of me expected for it to never get this far. Either Étienne or I would find an inconsistency in her family's ledgers and discover money hidden somewhere. All we discovered was they were deeper in debt. And when I try to think which bachelor it could possibly be that is a love match, none of them have a perfect place beside Rainey.

"Everythin' all right?"

"Absolutely," I bite out.

"Because you look furious."

"I'm not," I lie.

"Well, you should be."

I arch a brow. "If my family could tell me how to appropriately respond with anythin' pertainin' to Rainey, I would greatly appreciate it. When the bachelors first came about, I wasn't open enough to the idea, and now I'm not furious enough?"

Étienne gives me a sardonic smirk. "Which, I might add, you came to Serene for help. She didn't embed herself into what this bachelor debacle has become."

He had a valid point. "Do I regret includin' Serene? Yes. Do I wish I had a more effective plan for Rainey? Absolutely. But the truth is, I didn't."

"Don't ask yourself easy questions you already know the answers to." Étienne sighs before he continues. "It's unmistakable to anyone with a pair of eyes that you care for Rainey."

"Of course, I care for her." My pulse thrums beneath my skin because I know we're getting far too close to the truth.

"But what's preventin' you from bein' with her?"

Dragging a hand down my face, I sigh. War has woven its way into my soul, but so has this woman. The two can't inhabit the same space. It just isn't possible. They both are too demanding. All for different reasons. And the very idea of Rainey encountering that side makes me shudder. I've opened up to her about a select amount of stories, but those were only just the beginning.

Tired of the constant internal push and pull, I slap my palms on my knees. "I love her. That's the truth!" Worn down, I sag against the chair. "Are you pleased with yourself? I love her."

To my brother's credit, he doesn't look satisfied with my misery. Just continues to solemnly watch me. "Have you told her this?"

"No."

"Why not?"

"Because it seems as though everyone I love, I lose!"

Spoken out into the world, my fears don't seem so big. They're small and inadequate and are impossible to get back. Between the two of them, this one is my biggest fear. The way I see it, when it comes to people I love, I'm simply not unlucky, just born without luck. Slowly, but surely, people passed. Always unexpected and no less devastating. It seemed short-lived to love her with everything inside me when she was bound to be ripped away from me.

I know my fears are foolish, but my confession has been told to the right person. No one knows better how I feel than my brother.

Étienne becomes quiet. He leans back in his chair, thoughtfully rubbing his stubble on his jaw.

"You're right. I'm not goin' to say you're wrong. You're right. But can I be honest with you?"

I hold my hands out in front of me. "Please do. That's why I'm here."

"Maybe our loss allows us to love with more intention. The truth is, the most dangerous love is the one that causes you to be vulnerable. And that's all love. In the end, it's the most profound. I promise you. If you refuse to believe me and be stubborn like most Lacroix men, that's all right. Live in the purgatory you've created for yourself or accept the love this woman has and wants to give to you." Étienne takes a breath and lifts his shoulders. His somber expression never wavers. "And besides, this is Rainey. She's awfully similar to my own wife. I don't picture her comin' back and professin' her love to you once again."

He leans in and holds his index finger up. "You have one opportunity."

I straighten in my seat and feel the hairs on the back of my neck stand. Because that opportunity came and went in Savannah in the pouring rain.

Swallowing, I look away. "I know that."

"Good. Now, what's in the folder?"

It was only a matter of time before Étienne noticed the folder. I'm simply surprised it took this long. I wave the folder in the air before I place it on the desk. "I'm here for two things. The first is that I've come to a decision, and it requires your help."

Étienne is wary as he slides the folder across the desk. "You haven't found yourself the executor of another dowry, have you?" he asks dryly.

"God, no." Impatiently, I fling a hand to the folder. "Just take a look."

Once again, his curiosity gets the best of him, and he opens the folder. It only takes a minute at best for Étienne to understand what my intent is. By the time he turns to the second page, his lips are drawn into a thin line, and one thick brow is arched.

His eyes veer between the papers in his hands and back to me. Ever so slightly, he shakes his head. "You're sellin' your shares of AT&T?"

"Absolutely."

Étienne looks at me with disbelief. "This isn't somethin' you can nullify. Once the papers are signed, they're signed."

"I'm quite aware of how documents work."

"I'm beginnin' to think you don't," Étienne mutters under his breath.

"I'm beginnin' to think you underestimate me far too often." From there, I tell my brother my intentions. My plans are broad, and by all accounts, I'm taking a tremendous risk. But I have a plan. One I've thought over carefully. The longer I talk, the broader Étienne's smile becomes. And by the time I finish, something close to respect fills his eyes.

"I have to admit I was skeptical at first. But I believe you've thought this through. I'll help you."

My shoulders sag with relief.

"You're right, though. This is a tremendous risk but quite possibly the best one you can take. Now go to Rainey and tell her you're sorry for everythin'."

A headache starts to build near my temples. I could explain how I feel a hundred times over, but Étienne wouldn't understand. He's happily married to his soulmate.

I look out the window. "I'm loving her the best way I know how." I take a deep breath. "From afar."

"I thought Serene and I were bound to love from afar, and I almost lost her."

I turn around. "Yes, but—"

Étienne holds up a hand. "I know. It's different. But is it really? You're about to lose the love of your life out of sheer stubbornness."

"I will talk to her. Not today but soon, all right?"

Étienne nods, pleased with my reply. He drums his fingertips on his desk, his attention moving back to the leather-bound folder. "What is the second thing you wished to speak with me about?"

Clearing my throat, I say, "I think we both know that my occupation at the family shipping company was not workin' out."

My brother dips his head. "Fair enough."

"I went to college and received the same degree as you, but I was merely the spare to the heir."

At that, Étienne winces. "I wish you wouldn't say that. Mere minutes separate us. I just happened to arrive first."

"Thank God for that. I couldn't handle the pressures you face. I'm not equipped to run a business."

"What are you made for?"

"To find you clients for your business," I reply.

Étienne leans back in his chair and lifts a brow. "Why do I need your help to find clients?"

"Because you have the charm of a hedgehog mixed with a cactus."

"You flatter me," Étienne says dryly.

"But I can speak to anyone about anythin'. You find the task of conversin' painful and tedious, do you not?"

With his fingers steepled together, Étienne watches me carefully. He's intrigued to say the least. "I can't argue with that."

I go in for the kill. "Your primary concerns are businesses you can invest in with capital and returns. With me, my responsibility would be to keep consistent communication with your clients and findin' new leads."

I have the pleasure of seeing the complete surprise on my brother's face. Just because I didn't want to manage a business didn't mean I wasn't aware of the inner workings.

"Asa helps me find new leads."

"Asa is consumed with AT&T," I counter.

For several minutes, Étienne is quiet. I can see the wheels in his head working, processing what I've told him. There's a high probability he will decline. Étienne prefers to handle every aspect of the business on his own, and every person who was hired had remarkable resumes and glowing references. I would be not be an exception because I was his brother.

"All right." Étienne leans forward and extends his hand out between us. "I'm interested to see what you will bring to the company. You'll be treated like everybody else."

I shake his hand and smile at his words. "I would expect nothin' less."

I stand because even I know to quit while I'm ahead. Étienne hands me my folder, and I gladly take it. This is a victory I didn't know if I would win, and at the moment, I bask in my accomplishment. Only for a moment, because my next thought is, "Tell Rainey!"

It's second nature to share every part of my life with her.

Not yet, I remind myself. *Soon, but not yet.*

"I wish you the best of luck," Étienne says.

"Thank you," I reply and walk out of his office. Once I'm out of the front door and on the street, I mutter under my breath, "I will be needin' every bit of it."

CHAPTER FORTY-ONE

RAINEY

"Evening gowns have certainly changed since 1912," Serene remarks.

As the maid bends down to fix the hem of my dress, I fuss with the bodice. "Are you sure?"

Serene swats my hand away. "Trust me. I know what I'm doing. This is perfect."

Typically, I trust Serene. We are one and the same in a lot of ways. She simply says what I'm thinking in a less articulate way. It certainly drives the point home, though.

Today I'm questioning everything. I didn't get any sleep last night, and when it was time to wake up, my body decided it was time to sleep. I only woke when my maid was shaking me, telling me it was almost time to leave for Belgrave.

When I arrived, Serene unknowingly had me dress in the same room I stayed in after Livingston's attack. Very little in its appearance has changed. The bed still faces the fireplace; it simply has a different quilt across the mattress. Fresh flowers are on the nightstand.

Serene was already dressed in her evening gown when I arrived. The maroon chiffon evening gown was trimmed with beads, and her sleeves elegantly fell to her wrist. After recently having a baby, she looks comfortable in the relaxed fit of the dropped-waist.

The entire time I got ready, she kept my mind preoccupied by talking about her kids, and Étienne, and how she missed

Nat. We spoke of everything but the bachelors and Livingston.

When the maid was done with every button, Serene takes a step back and looks at me. "This dress is so beautiful on you."

Nervously, I toy with one of the straps of my dress and look at myself in the full-length mirror. The dropped-waist evening gown is sage green. There's an iridescent gold overlay with sequins. Every time I move, they sparkle in the light. The back dips to a V, exposing more skin of my back than I'm used to. My favorite part is the train that dramatically flares away from the dress, reminding me of a gold waterfall. And when it's time to dance, I can slip the convenient ribbon loop around my wrist to keep it off the floor.

"Are you sure?"

"Positive," Serene says before she turns her attention to the maid. "That will be all. Thank you."

Once the maid is out of the room, Serene turns to me. I busy myself by grabbing my gloves from the vanity.

"There's still time to change your mind," Serene says gently.

Repeatedly, I stroke the silky material. "There's time for no such thing."

"Of course there is. Say the word, and Étienne will gladly tell everyone to leave. Believe me, he lives for that kind of shit."

"It's very kind of you, but no."

Serene takes one of the gloves and begins to gather the material together. Patiently, I hold my hand out and wait.

"Are you certain about my hair?" I blurt.

Serene momentarily stops bunching the material into her hands and lifts a single brow. "This question again? For the umpteenth time, it looks fantastic."

She stretches the opening of the glove, and I slide my right hand in. "It's just…I'm not accustomed to wearin' it down in public." Serene slides the material up my arm until it stops at my elbow. I begin to adjust the glove to fit my hand while she works on the other glove.

Serene had suggested I wear my hair down in loose waves with one side pinned directly above the ear, and it sounded good at the time. But the more time that went by, the stronger my nerves became. I was so close to using the magazine on the dresser to fan myself. It was far too hot in here.

Compose yourself, Rainey. You are fine. You knew all along it would lead to this.

Serene holds the glove open for me, and we repeat the same process as before. With our heads bent in concentration, I ask a question I've been thinking about all day. "Do you think he will be here tonight?"

At my question, Serene stops adjusting the glove before she continues. "I don't know. He hasn't told Étienne or me otherwise." When she's finished, she steps back. "Do you want him to be there?"

Of course, I do. It's probably for the best if he isn't, but I miss him so much.

Serene knowingly nods. My silence is the only answer she needs. "This is your bachelor ball. Your night to show him and everyone how beautiful savage can be."

Her emphatic speech brings a faint smile to my face. I want that more than I realize. "Thank you."

Serene steps beside me and turns me to face the mirror once again. "I'm married to a Lacroix. Listen to me when I say they go wild for wild women." She points at me and swipes her finger up and down. "This will capture Livingston's attention and make him realize what a fool he is." She meets my gaze in the mirror. "That's what you want, don't you?"

Before I can answer her, there's a knock on the door. "Come in," Serene says.

I expect to see a maid, but instead, it's Momma. She smiles at the two of us, and when she sees my dress, her eyes widen. "Oh, how beautiful."

My brows furrow. It's not what she said; it's the hurried, dismissive way she spoke. She wanted the conversation to come to a close so she could say what's on her mind.

Serene looks between the two of us and walks to the door. "I'll leave the two of you."

Momma doesn't wait for the door to close before she advances toward me. Her eyes are wide, furtively moving around the room as though she doesn't know where to sit. She's starting to worry me.

"Momma?" I say although it comes out as a question.

"The debts are paid," she blurts.

Slowly, I lower my arms to my side. "Pardon?"

Momma stares at me with watery eyes. Her bottom lip quivers ever so slightly. "The collectors informed me before I left for Belgrave that they were paid in full days ago." She steps forward and clutches my hands. "We can keep the house. You don't have to do this."

Surely, I'm dreaming. At any moment, I'm going to wake up and discover none of this is real. Blinking rapidly, I wait for Momma to disappear right before my very eyes. When that doesn't happen, I pinch my arm.

Momma slightly shakes me by my arms and laughs breathlessly. I haven't seen her this happy in such a long time. "Don't you see, sugar? We're saved!"

This is great news. Wonderful even. But I have so many questions that I don't know where to begin. I shake my head, trying to get a grasp on the situation. "I don't understand. How? When?"

"I don't know when. Just that they're paid." Letting go of me, Momma clutches her hands to her chest and looks toward the ceiling. "This is a miracle."

"Yes, it is," I numbly say because it's a miracle that doesn't make sense.

But here is my chance. I could call Serene back to my room. I could tell her that I've changed my mind, and I don't need the dowry. For the time being, my problems are over. But that's not entirely true. I still have one problem. One deep, painful problem that refuses to heal, and when I'm alone, it hurts the most. It dwells in every conversation, laugh, argument, kiss, and embrace Livingston and I have had. Another man will never be Livingston, but at least I won't be alone.

"Who paid the debts?" I ask.

Momma regards me carefully. She is starting to become more composed. "Are you askin' me if I know if Livingston paid?"

Rapidly, I nod and wait for her answer.

She shakes her head. "Sugar, I truly don't know."

I don't know whether I feel relief or disappointment. He once offered to give me a loan so I wouldn't have to go through with the bachelor plan. But I knew the offer was based upon his friendship with Miles. My pride had a life of its own and dictated that I decline the offer.

"All I know is that the debts were paid in full, and it was done anonymously."

I was inclined to believe it was Livingston. Very few people knew of our financial situation, but I couldn't prove it.

I needed more time to think this through. More time to talk this out. I need more time.

There's another knock on a door. Serene peeks her head inside. "Rainey? It's time."

The ballroom at Belgrave is breathtaking.

The heavy curtains are pulled back from the windows. The French doors are open, allowing in fresh air. The marble floor is spotless, allowing light from the chandeliers to reflect in every direction. A quartet is set up in the far corner of the ballroom. The sound of their instruments fills me with peace, and I'm tempted to close my eyes.

It's a black-tie affair, and everyone is dressed in their best attire. I admire the guests before I step into the room. Once I do, I know I'm going to be enclosed by the bachelors and the guests.

"Ready to go in?" Serene asks quietly.

I turn to her, and see her regarding me with concern. I smile at her. "Yes. Of course." For good measure, I step forward, knowing that after this, I can't go back.

At once, Conrad is in front of me as though he's been waiting for me the entire time. "Rainey, there you are. You look beautiful."

"Thank you."

"Shall we dance?"

"Of course." I accept his hand and allow him to escort me into the throng of dancers.

For the next hour, I dance until my heels ache, and even then, I continue to dance. I feel dizzy from all the spinning, my throat is raw from speaking, and my left palm is sweaty from being held in so many hands.

While I'm dancing with Duncan, I spot Taylor Hiscock's sister. I could picture Livingston leaning into me. *"Made a wise choice there. No one wants the name Hiscock."*

I can't help but smile. My heart aches at the thought of Livingston. I've continuously searched for him, and he's nowhere to be found. It's foolish to expect him to come.

The dance comes to a close, and when we stop moving, my feet sigh in relief. Duncan walks me to the edge of the ballroom, and when another male guest asks me to dance, I politely refuse. I need a small break.

I stand by myself and bask in the silence. It's a brief reprieve from all the activity around me.

And then, out of the corner of my eye, I spot Livingston. My heart stutters and stops at the sight of him. Like most of the men here, he's wearing a tuxedo. His is tailored to his body. His dinner suit nearly matches the color of his hair. He recently shaved, and his sharp planes and angles of his gorgeous face are on display.

My God, I've missed him so much.

His eyes prowl through the crowd as though he's in search of something. His gaze drifts past me, and then immediately veers back to me. His eyes widen a fraction before he starts to walk through the crowd.

My breathing becomes shallow. What is he going to say? What am I going to say? I gave up hope that he would come, but now that he's here, my tongue suddenly feels far too big for my mouth.

I link my hands together and try to take deep breaths as I see he's quickly approaching. He breaks from the crowd and stands directly in front of me, the very picture of perfection.

His eyes sweep me from head to toe. "Hello, Rainey."

The deep timbre of his voice causes goose bumps to break out across my skin. I dip my head. "Livingston."

He leans forward, from the waist up, and says with his eyes on mine, "Would you care to dance?"

I could go the rest of my life without another dance. I don't tell Livingston that, though. "Sounds lovely."

When he holds my hand in his, it's akin to a jolt of electricity going through my body. I remain impassive and allow Livingston to escort us. In the crowd, Serene and Étienne stand by my Momma and watch us.

"Did you get the chance to dance with each bachelor?"

"Yes, I did. It was lovely," I say politely.

Can he feel how badly I'm shaking?

Livingston nods and doesn't make one of his signature retorts. For all his womanizing ways, Livingston is a practiced dancer. We glide across the marble floor so effortlessly my feet barely touch the floor.

With his eyes fixed on something behind me, he indifferently asks, "Do you know which bachelor you'll pick as your husband?"

"Stop," I plead.

Livingston innocently blinks and looks at me. "Stop what?"

"You know what," I whisper.

"I'm strikin' a friendly conversation."

"But we haven't spoken to one another since Savannah."

Livingston somberly looks me in the eye. "If I reached out to you, would you have listened?"

I keep my gaze fixed on his Adam's apple as I think of my reply. I lost count the number of times I wanted to speak with him and know how he was.

"That's what I figured," he said sadly.

He didn't realize how hard it was to stay away from him and how difficult it is to express how much I missed him.

Only a small moment of silence passes between us before Livingston speaks. "How are you?" he asks.

I lift my gaze and find him staring at me. "I'm fine."

Carefully, I look him over. I notice the bags under his eyes. However, there's a clarity in his hazel eyes. I'm desperate to know what's led to that clearness. Is there someone new in his life?

"How are you?" I ask, my voice uncharacteristically squeaky.

He looks at me with a tinge of sadness. "I've been all right."

I don't want to hear all right. I want to hear every aspect of his life, starting from the moment his feet stepped onto the train platform in Charleston and went on his way. I told him to never speak to me again, but I didn't mean it. Can't he see that?

I didn't mean it.

We follow the couples dancing across the ballroom floor. To spectators, we look as though we're having a polite conversation. They don't see that my heart is being torn to shreds.

"I've begun workin' with Étienne," he blurts.

My eyes widen with shock. I wasn't expecting to hear that. "When?"

"Days ago. I'll be workin' with his clients and attemptin' to find new leads for his company."

I smile at him. Even though Livingston tries to remain nonchalant about his new role at EAL Corporation, it's evident he's excited about it. This is good news. This is what he needs. "That's wonderful," I say.

"And recently, I sold my shares of AT&T."

At once, my mind starts to race. He sold his shares. I don't know the value, but I know they have to be worth a great deal. Here it is. Here's the intro for him to tell me he paid off my family's debts.

"Why?"

"I don't want to stay at the Lacroix house. I need to create a fresh start."

My heart nearly sinks to my stomach over his words. I swallow before I speak. "In Charleston, right?"

"Of course," he says softly. "The land across from the

Belgrave plantation?"

I nod uncertainly and wait for him to continue. "It was once part of Lacroix-Livingston land, but my father sold it. For several years, the fields were planted and tended to, but crops became bad, and they went neglected. Soon, I plan to have it tilled."

I knew the land he was describing. Every time I arrived or left Belgrave, I saw the wide expanse of acreage. Overgrown weeds sprouted from the ditch. Grass would make feeble attempts to grow in the untended soil but always failed. And during the fall and winter, you could see the lines from past years where seeds have been planted.

Next to Belgrave that was always well-maintained, the land was nothing but a blight. But this is another step toward a future. A future I hope he could see he deserved. "I'm happy for you, Livingston."

I meant that. No matter how I felt about Livingston, that's all I wanted. For him to stop being tortured by the past and have peace. He deserved that more than anyone.

There's a second where the two of us are quiet, gliding across the ballroom floor. I try to keep the news Momma broke to me upstairs, but I just can't. "Someone paid off the debts. All one hundred and fifteen thousand dollars."

Carefully, I watch Livingston for any tell that might give him away. His brows furrow as though this is news to him. "Truly?"

"Yes. Momma just told me."

His eyes widen, and his mouth opens and closes several times before he says, "That's great."

Reluctantly, I nod. "It is."

He wasn't giving the impression he knew anything about the debts being paid, which confuses me even more. I was so certain he did it.

We turn, following the sound of the music. "And now you can do as you will."

My eyes widen. Throughout this entire process, Livingston has put up a fight. I don't know what to say.

"No, I can't."

He looks down at me, his hazel eyes searching. "Why not?" he quietly demands.

I stare back at him, imploringly. "Because I have to make a decision."

I miss him more than I ever anticipated. But the lust was temporary. I still wanted love. I still wanted a future and a family.

The hand on my waist tightens as though he can sense the direction of my thoughts.

"Livingston, please be honest with me. Did you do this?"

Slowly, he shakes his head. "I didn't."

"But—"

"Rainey," he cuts in, his voice quiet. "I didn't pay the debts."

If he didn't pay the debts, then who did? There's no time to wonder about that. The song begins to draw to a close. While other dancers begin to smile at their partners, and slow their steps. Livingston and I draw closer. His grip on me is so tight there is no way I can break free. He leans in until his cheek is pressed against my temple. He can't leave. There's so much I need to say to him.

"I've missed you," I whisper for only him to hear.

"I'm so sorry for hurting you," he says against my ear. "I love you, Raina. I've loved you for years. Admired you for your quick aim as a girl with your bow and arrow. Applauded your strength when your daddy died. Recognized your beauty when I came home from France. I loved you all along. I've loved you when I didn't know anything else. If you pick a bachelor today, that's fine. I can love you from afar again."

He finishes, and I don't breathe. I only repeat his words over and over in my head. I didn't imagine them. In the middle of the ballroom, I briefly rest of my forehead against his chest. I close my eyes and breathe deep.

"Rainey?" Serene says from beside me.

My eyes flash open. I lift my head from his chest. With wide eyes, I stare at him, breaking the hold Livingston has over me.

Before I can say anything, she grabs my hand and pulls me away from him. I feel a sense of panic and stop myself from reaching out to him. Will this be my last time alone with him?

Serene and I weave our way through the heavy crowd, forcing me to face forward. We stop beside the double doors where Étienne stands.

"You look lovely, Rainey," he says in way of greeting.

"Thank you," I say hurriedly.

I look around Étienne, in the direction where I left Livingston, but he's gone. Did he leave? He can't leave.

"There's an impressive number of people here," he mentions casually.

"Mmmhmm," I reply. Where did Livingston go?

"I saw my brother dance with you."

At that, I stop searching and stare at the hulking man beside me. Everyone in Charleston is afraid of Étienne. From his no-nonsense approach to business, to the fierce scowl on his face. He isn't as imposing and fierce as everyone thinks. Growing up, I watched how he protected Nat and, at times, even me. And when he married Serene, you could tell there was nothing he wouldn't do for her.

"Yes, it was kind of him," I say cordially.

"Nothin' kind about it. He loves you," he blurts. "And you love him. And you've loved one another for years. That's irrelevant right now. What you need to ask yourself is, if time took him away from you, what would you do?"

"Time?"

He nods, his eyes sharp and focused as he waits for my answer. It's a weird question. One that I've never considered because it's impossible. But for the sake of answering, I imagine Livingston being here and gone the next. It would kill me. It would be as painful as losing Miles. But if time took him, and I knew he was out there somewhere, I'd wait for him because there will never be another Livingston Lacroix.

Étienne nods and smiles. "Yes, he'd wait for you, too."

For several seconds, I stare at Étienne. That's the most I've ever heard him talk.

Serene walks back to us, lightly clapping her hands. "Are you ready?"

There's no more delaying. Time to decide. "Yes. I'm ready."

Before she has a chance to get everyone's attention, I grab her arm and pull her back to me. Urgently, I whisper my decision into her ear.

Serene nods her head in understanding, and when I'm done, she squeezes my arm. "Very well."

I can feel Étienne's sharp eyes on me.

Serene nudges Étienne, so he looks around and loudly clears his throat. Immediately, people begin to quiet down. There are shushes and whispers and silence across the ballroom as all eyes turn in our direction.

My heart is beating so fast I think I may faint. My God, please let this end.

Serene smiles at all the guests. "When my lovely friend Miss Rainey Pleasonton expressed interest in finding a suitable husband I was more than happy to help her find the perfect husband. But we had a dilemma because she deserved the very best. However, I think we can all agree that it's going to take a strong Southern man to stand next to Miss Pleasonton."

A small ripple of laughter moves across the room. I smile at everyone, and then I spot him in the corner watching.

Livingston.

He didn't leave after all. With his arms crossed, he watches me with something close to sadness.

Serene looks at me from the corner of her eye before she says, "I'm beyond thrilled to announce that after all the men she spoke and courted with, Miss Pleasonton has chosen Livingston Lacroix."

There's a pregnant pause in the room. Everyone in the room looks around.

I hear a guest say, "He was one of the bachelors?" I notice Conrad and Duncan throw up their hands in frustration.

Murmurs grow louder as people talk amongst themselves and search for the man of the hour.

Finally, everybody spots Livingston, and in unison, they part so there's a small path for him. I take a deep breath and stop myself from walking to him.

Livingston pushes away from the wall. His arms are at his side. I could have hit him with another arrow and stunned him less.

Between Étienne and Serene, I wait to see what his response will be. Livingston can say no. I'm making a bold declaration by choosing someone who was never in the running.

Slowly, he begins to walk toward me. His eyes never leave mine the entire time. I ignore the voices around us and my own fear for what his answer will be.

When he reaches me, he doesn't wait for me to explain myself. He doesn't wait for anything. He frames my face between his large hands, and in front of everyone, he kisses me soundly on the lips.

I hear the gasp, and then claps echo in the room.

I don't care. I don't care about anything except for this.

Livingston loves me.

I place my hands over his to keep him in place.

Livingston loves me.

He pulls away. "You are forever my queen. The only woman I need. I love you, *le savauge.*"

I nod, afraid to even speak. "I love you too."

"I'm still stubborn, and I'll drive you mad."

At that, Étienne snorts.

"I know that. I'll continue to drive you mad."

"God, I hope so."

He kisses me for a second time. And while Serene tells Étienne she knew the whole time we would be together, we kiss. While Étienne talks about how quickly the guests can begin to leave his home, we kiss.

And when the guests consider whether Livingston was a bachelor the entire time, we kiss.

Throughout the years, we have found ourselves at war with one another, but with love, we found peace.

CHAPTER FORTY-TWO

RAINEY

T hat's it. I'm finished."

I barely spare Livingston a glance. "You've said that several times. Keep goin'."

My fiancé spreads his fingers and then loosely shakes his hand before he reluctantly picks up his pen and continues to write out an address on a cream-colored envelope.

Fiancé.

I have a fiancé. It's been almost two months since the bachelor ball. I keep expecting all this to be a dream. That I'll wake up at any moment with Livingston ripped from me, and the two of us bickering at one another. He hasn't left my side once, but we bicker frequently. And I prefer it that way. If it was any different, I'd be concerned.

"The invitations need to be mailed by tomorrow mornin'. We've postponed this for as long as possible."

Livingston grunts. "We wouldn't want that, now would we?"

"No, we wouldn't because we have to answer to not only Serene but also Momma."

Livingston's eyes marginally widen before he hastily finishes writing the address and then moves to the next name on the guest list. If I knew those two ladies would've been the best motivation, I would've started with that at the beginning.

He's making significant progress when he stops and inspects the list. "Who's all invited?"

"My momma is Leonore Pleasonton, so everyone."

"Of course."

"And because Leonore Pleasonton's daughter is marryin' a Lacroix, she will treat this as a royal weddin'."

Livingston lifts a brow. "A royal weddin' she has only three months to plan?"

"Momma could plan it in three weeks if she had to."

"I don't lack faith in her."

I continue to address the invites but stop when I get to Nathalie's name. I hold the envelope between both hands and sigh "But did I tell you I've spoken to Nat recently?

"At least one of us has," Livingston mutters under his breath.

I give him a pointed look and shift in my seat toward him. "She will be here for the weddin'."

Livingston lifts his head and points his pen at me. "Ah, but how long will she stay afterward?"

"That I can't answer."

"For the life of me, I can't fathom why she doesn't come back to Belgrave for good." Livingston's frustration is palpable, but I understand. Time has passed since Oliver's passing, and Nat continues to evade the discussion of coming home. I know she isn't happy at Brignac House. I saw with my own two eyes, and I'm certain it hasn't gotten better for her.

"I question why she remains there, too. But I think what's keepin' her there is a someone from her past."

Livingston slowly blinks at me. He doesn't have the slightest idea who I'm talking about.

"Asa," I supply. "She doesn't want to come back to Charleston and see Asa."

It takes Livingston several seconds before his eyes light up with understanding. "Oh, yes. Asa." He shakes his head. "Christ. She still has that childhood crush on him?"

"Is it considered a childhood crush when you're no longer a child and very much an adult?"

"She's a widow now," he mutters.

"And so now her heart is black and passion is dead?"

At my sarcasm, Livingston lifts a brow and smirks. "Maybe. Maybe not. Either way, if she came home, she'd discover that things have changed."

"Not everythin'," I say quietly.

Many things I'm certain of, and one of them is Nathalie's love for Asa Calhoun.

"You're right," Livingston says as he stands. He walks over to his desk and moves aside papers to reveal the plans for our home.

"More progress?"

"More progress," he confirms and moves back to me. He lays the prints out in front of me and, in-rapid fire, begins to describe how he envisioned the structure of the home, windows here, columns there, a spiral staircase in the foyer. I nod with a small smile. He's so excited that his mouth can't keep up with his imagination.

I gave him my input here and there, and he makes the proper changes, but my one request I refused to budge on was a library. Give me a library, and I will be content for life. A builder has been chosen, and progress would soon be made on the land Livingston purchased months ago across from Belgrave.

As for the Lacroix home, it was in a trust for Étienne, Livingston, and Nathalie and had been that way since the death of their parents. The three of them could rent the home out, use it for storage, and place every terrifying picture of their ancestors against the walls. Options were endless. One thing was not: the home could never leave the Lacroix family.

The same couldn't be said for my childhood home.

Debts may have been paid, but that didn't mean Momma and I were free from debt forever. Between the two of us, there was no income, and the upkeep of our family home was too great. Momma didn't put up a great fight. The one thing she tried to resist was my dowry going anywhere outside the family. Her argument was I didn't get married in sixty days, but I found a suitable husband in sixty days. And now she was in legal proceedings, fighting tooth and nail to keep the money.

She had no energy left in her to fight to keep the house. Honestly, I think she knew it was time to let go of it, and I think she also wanted a new beginning. Although there were good memories in my childhood home, there was no possible way of escaping the past when it was all around you.

The money from the sale of the house (and furniture) would go toward her next home. Although finding one that met her standards would be interesting.

By that time, Livingston and I would be married, and if all went well, our house would be partially built, and Livingston could see some of his dreams come true. He still struggles with nightmares from the war, but it isn't quite as acute as before. I know his job at Étienne's company helps tremendously. It pulls him out of the dark shelter he had slowly built for himself. He was never going to be the old Livingston. He saw too much in France. But he was making progress, and there were moments when he would mention what he experienced almost as though it was a fleeting thought. I never prodded too much. It was his choice to tell me what he wanted to.

Out of all the positive changes in my life, there is one thing I still can't figure out. Who paid off my family's debts? To this day, Livingston asserts it wasn't him, and he had zero involvement. I've tried to find out, but whoever it was took great care in making sure their identity was kept a secret. They don't want to be found. At some point, I had to ask myself what was more important to me, finding them or holding onto this new life I have. Because, in essence, that's what I have with these debts paid.

I have to accept the fresh start and never let go of what Livingston and I have.

"All this is wonderful," I say. I shake my head, unable to comprehend that his mind could create something like this.

Livingston looks at me, his hazel eyes cautious with hope. "Truly?"

"Absolutely. I love it."

Unexpectedly, he leans forward and captures my face between his hands and kisses me soundly on the lips. This will never become old. The way my heart speeds up will never be too overwhelming. My fingers curl around his wrist, holding him in place.

When he pulls away, his thumb brushes against my cheek. "I love you."

I smile. "Forever?"

"Of course." He presses his forehead against mine. "For what is a king without his queen?"

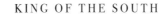

EPILOGUE

NATHALIE
TWO MONTHS LATER

I step off the train and shield my eyes from the sun. As people hustle to their next destination, conversations, laughter, and hugs occur all around me. The grip on my valise tightens as I make my way through the crowd and out of the train station. The smell of coal wafts from the steam dome. It mixes with the humidity, creating an acrid scent that is anything but pleasing.

Even though it's December, that stands for nothing in Charleston. As I wait in search of a cab, the hairs on the nape of my neck stick to my skin. I make no effort to brush them away.

It's been nearly a year since I've visited Charleston.

It's been four months since the passing of my husband Oliver. By my mother-in-law's standards, I should still be in mourning, clutching a handkerchief to my chest as I aimlessly walk through the empty halls of Brignac House, mumbling about what could have been and what once was. But I can't remain there forever, surrounded by grief. When I told Rainey I would return home, I meant it.

The time had to be right. The grief in my heart spent. When I left Brignac House, it would be for the last time. Matilda said as much when I was packing my valise. Her eyes were red-rimmed and exhausted from no sleep as she leaned into me, her breath foul, "You were never meant to be a Claiborne. You never gave him a child or knew how to love him. You're just a shameless strumpet."

She was wrong. We shared the same space for several years, but we knew nothing about one another. However, her words lingered in my mind, emphasizing my last argument with Oliver. "You don't love the person you married; you love the vows that you said."

As much as I wanted to, I couldn't refute those claims. I realized my husband was right. I never loved Oliver. Not like a wife should. But as much as he claimed to love me, his actions never matched his words.

It was a marriage of convenience that turned into a marriage of doom, and neither of us could find a way out.

I made mistakes, but I still deserved happy moments in my life. I was only going to find those moments away from Brignac House and back with my real family. I'd yet to meet my first nephew, Trace. On top of that, Livingston and Rainey were to be married. That was an event that I wouldn't dare dream of missing.

I like to think I was somewhat responsible for the two of them becoming engaged. What money I did have to my name was gone. Everything I had saved was given to pay the Pleasonton debts. Only Étienne and I knew, and I intended for it to stay that way.

I believed everyone deserves a chance at true love even when they believe they're unworthy of it. My brother didn't think he could heal from the war, and Rainey was resigned to live a life married to a man she hoped she could learn to love.

I was the result of that pointless hope. I didn't want my best friend to have the same miserable ending as I had.

My brother and Rainey needed each other, and I wanted to help. I couldn't be there in person, so I supported them the best way I knew how.

"Where to, ma'am?"

Numbly, I smile at the driver and immediately give him directions. I knew Charleston like the back of my hand. If there's a shortcut or backroad that leads to Belgrave, I know it. But I'm not going there. Not yet, anyway.

The car abruptly lurches forward and onto the road. I take a deep breath and remind myself I need to remain composed. I'm almost there.

The driver briefly looks over his shoulder at me and at my suitcase. "Are you stayin' a short while?"

"No. I'm here to stay."

I draw my valise closer to me and remind myself that what I have in my suitcase is all I need. I've spent several years in a loveless marriage. I stood by Oliver through a massive betrayal.

You betrayed him too, remember?

I close my eyes and when they open, we stop in front of a white building. My heart furiously pumps in my chest.

"What brings you to the church, ma'am?" he asks

"Oh, I'm just here to break up the weddin'." Leaning forward, I hand him the cab fare and open my door. "Now you have a good day, okay?"

I slam the door on a visibly stunned driver and face the church. Sweat freely falls from my temples as the sun beats down on me.

Today, Asa Calhoun is getting married. Today, another woman is trying to take what is rightfully mine.

I don't know what I will say when I finally see him. But I do know that what happens next will change everything...

ACKNOWLEDGEMENTS

HUGE thanks to my beta readers- Talon Smith, Kim Svetlin, Alyssa Cole, Allie Siebers, Melissa Jones and Beth Suit. Thank you for always dropping everything you're doing, reading through the rough draft, and always having faith in me.

To my proofreaders: Rea Loftis, Michelle Clay and Kim Svetlin! Thank you for everything! I don't know what I'd do without you ladies.

Annette Brignac and Michelle Clay from Book Nerd Services. You ladies are beyond amazing. Your hard work never goes unnoticed. I can't thank you enough.

Talon, my perfect baby angel, for the AMAZING edits.

Thank you to Juliana Cabrera from Jersey Girl Design for formatting *King of the South* in the most unique way. ;) Now get back here and love me!!

MAC PACK- You two are my forever tribe. The friends every person deserves. You pull me away from my self-induced panic and reminded me to breathe. I'm lost without you two.

And to my husband, Joshua. Thank you. Thank you is never enough. You are a quiet support. You always help with the kiddos. Consistently believe in me. You are my surviving trace.

I love you.

ABOUT THE AUTHOR

College seemed like too much stress for me. Traveling across the world, getting married, and having five kids seemed much more relaxing. Yeah, I'm still waiting for the relaxing part to kick in...I change addresses every other year. It's not by choice but it is my reality. While the crazies of life kept me busy, the stories in my head decided to bubble to the surface. They were dying to be told and I was dying to tell them. I hope you enjoy escaping to the crazy world of these characters with me!!

For more information on Calia Read

www.caliaread.com

Visit her Author Page on Facebook
www.facebook.com/CaliaRead

Follow Calia on Twitter @ailacread

Printed in Great Britain
by Amazon